BLACKSKYY

THE LADY IN BLACK SERIES

BOOK ONE

JANET STEVENS COOK

SBI

STREBOR BOOKS

NEW YORK LONDON TORONTO SYDNEY

Strebor Books
P.O. Box 6505
Largo, MD 20792
http://www.streborbooks.com

ISBN-13 978-1-59309-113-2
ISBN-10   1-59309-113-3
LCCN 2007923509

First Strebor Books trade paperback edition July 2007

Cover design: www.mariondesigns.com

10 9 8 7 6 5 4 3 2

Manufactured in the United States of America

For information regarding special discounts for bulk purchases,
please contact Simon & Schuster Special Sales at 1-800-456-6798
or business@simonandschuster.com

DEDICATION

I would like to dedicate this book to my father, James Stevens. It is because of his stern hand, loving heart and wise words that I am the woman I am today. He would be proud of the character *Skyy*, because, all my life he has preached about being strong and independent and Skyy is the epitome of a strong Black Woman. I miss you, Daddy.

I also dedicate this book to my family. One night, my beautiful daughter Kelsey stated matter of factly that she never met a writer that did not write. After a bit of a writer's block, she got my butt moving and writing again. Thanks, Kels! You are truly the sunshine of my life. I am grateful for your free spirit and creativity.

Quinn, I look to you for strength, discipline and determination. Your passion for basketball has helped me to nourish my passion for writing. I feed off your successes on and off the court. I thank you for your love, support and allowing me to witness your relentless pursuit of The Game.

To the Big Dawg. What can I say? Thirty years. You are always there for me and the fam. Thanks for your generosity, friendship and honesty.

To my Mom, thank you for everything, you have always been my biggest fan. You instilled a self confidence that is unparalleled.

To my sorors of Delta Sigma Theta Sorority Inc. Allison, who re-read my book after three years and made me realize that I should brush off the dust and begin to diligently seek a publisher. Jan, thanks for your vision, editing and counsel.

Dwayne, when I met you in the bank, you told me that you could help me get my book published. Your follow-up is awesome. Thanks for introducing me to Zane.

LaRee, Jackie, Briana, Hailey, Lynn, Michelle, Dominique, Pat, Rashelle, Cindy, Ibonee, Betty, Big D, Terry, Rod, Marcel, The Beautiful Judge Tanya, Jeff-Jeff-Jeffy, Mia, Annette, Tina, Emmet and all of the family and friends who are always there through the good and the bad... I find such comfort in the unconditional love that we share.

Zane, thank you for making my dream come to fruition.

I also dedicate this book to all of the people who have been hurt, pained, brutalized, persecuted and neglected, yet survived! Thank you for showing the world that being a victim is a state of mind.

INTRODUCTION

My name is Sandora "Sandy" Knight. My people call me *Skyy*, but the people who don't know me call me...the *Lady in Black*. But with all of these aliases, who am I really? I don't know, I guess you can call me...a *ghetto cosmopolitan*, a *hip-hop sophisticate*; and a *sensitive assassin*. I am an oxymoron, an enigma, but most times I don't know who I really am. But, what I do know is that I have a purpose in life—a destiny that I cannot run or hide from. I am a vigilante. I fight for those who cannot fight for themselves. I help the helpless. I am a tight-ass, fine-ass, phat-ass vigilante and these are my stories. An urban fairy tale, if you will, and this is how it all started.

CHAPTER 1
New York, 1977

Damn, I can't believe this shit! These heroin dealers are gonna come up in here and try to play Zee like this. *No tellin' what the fuck Zee's done now*, thought Sandy.

"Where's the fuckin' money, Zee?" screamed Six, who at six feet six inches, towered over his intended target. His thick gold rope chains rattled as he shook with rage.

Like a true addict, Zee trembled, either from fright or from her addiction. She even couldn't tell the difference. Zelda was the poster child for heroin addiction, waxy skin, ashy complexion, dark circles under the eyes, sunken cheeks, excessively thin, hollow expression, scratched up skin, matted hair. It was as if she and smack were "old friends"; there was nothing that Zee hadn't done with her beloved drug. She had done it all, injected it, smoked it, sniffed it.

"I never got nothing," said Zee. "He gave me an empty bag! I keep t…, t…, tellin' y'all that," Zee lied through her rotting teeth.

Zee prayed that she could convince her accusers that she really didn't have the money. Zee glanced over at the cookie jar where they had already found some of the money that she had hid. She glanced past the thugs into the bedroom. She prayed they did go into the room and into the dresser drawers. What if they found the gold key to the locker at Penn Station? She closed her eyes and thought, I don't care if they rape, torture, or kill me, my babies are never gonna want for nothin', they are gonna have the life that *I* should have had. That was the least that *Lord Bless* could do for me. Got me hooked on this SHIT!

For a moment, Zelda closed her eyes, as she remembered playing the piano, a beautiful black baby grand. Her two long black pigtails swinging as she playfully bobbed her head as she went from "This Little Light of Mine" to "The Sting" to "Beethoven's Fifth Symphony." She was a child prodigy and could play any song by ear or read the most complex concerto. At fifteen, her gift from God had led her from a small town in North Carolina all the way to the Big City of Dreams, where she met the man who would change her life, forever.

ℳ ℳ ℳ

I held my breath so that no one could hear me, and pinched my baby brother as tears rolled down his terrified cheeks. Malcolm was scared. Shit, so was I! But I would not let Malcolm know it. I had to protect him from these crazed fools.

As Malcolm and I hid in our tiny one-bedroom flat, no air conditioning, the closet felt like a sauna. I closed my eyes and allowed myself to drift for a bit and tried to play like I was on a tropical island like Hawaii, or some exotic fuckin' place. Right now this sauna was the safest place on earth as me and Malcolm hid from a gun-crazed giant who called himself Six and Low Down, a psychotic, wannabe drug dealer. I was snapped back to reality when I heard the voice of a TV newscaster say that it was the hottest summer on record.

Summers in New York were always so hot, that the kids in the 'hood would have to open the fire hydrants just for relief. Before the cops could get to shuttin' off the next hydrant, the youngins would turn them back on again. Of course, some folks were so poor that once in a while they would actually take baths in the hydrant water.

A *wannabe drug dealer* is the worst kind of brother, because he is too stupid to be a real drug dealer, but *loco* enough to try to prove that he *should* be in charge. His whole game is about trying to prove something. Well tonight, Low Down, with Six's help, was sure trying to prove something. The outcome tonight would make a point to the entire 'hood whether

Low Down was *the Man* or not. It was simple, he either had to get the money and kick Zee's ass, or he had to kill her to make an example out of her. Either way, tomorrow, motherfuckers would be at his feet or trying to punk him for his position.

Malcolm and I had been in that closet for what seemed like an eternity. I was proud that Malcolm was able to contain his emotions. Most four-year-old boys would not have been so cool. Malcolm had seen a lot in his four young years, but unfortunately for me, I had seen more. He had seen his mother sexually violated by a countless number of strangers. From time to time, he also had been propositioned by men so vile that he would respond by regurgitating. Malcolm was always hungry. He had a longing and hunger not only for food, but also for his mother's love and protection. Malcolm never felt clean, or safe. He just closed his eyes, rocked himself, and quietly cried silent tears of both pain and terror.

My blouse was so wet with sweat and tears, that it clung to my caramel-colored skin. My mother, "Zee," named me Sandora, but all the kids called me Sandy because my skin was the color of sand. I smiled, as I remembered myself jumping rope. Life was good, before Zee was introduced to the "heh' ron."

I was so hot and tired, that I thought I would pass out at any moment. However, I clung to Malcolm like he was the only person on earth. It's a shame that Zee had to put us through this shit. All of the rehabs that the church referred her to, she couldn't seem to stay in any of them. Zee was so high, half the damned time she didn't know *what* I had to do to pay the fuckin' bills. Most times, I felt that it was a mistake that I was born. No one should have to live like this. Malcolm is the ONLY reason why I didn't slit my wrist a long time ago. He was the ONLY reason worth living.

I smiled, looked at Malcolm, and whispered, "my pride and joy." Malcolm was an innocent bystander in a cruel, cruel game. He was the only thing in my life that was "good" and "pure." I vowed that when he was born, that I would always be his protector. I would protect him with my own life if necessary. It was pure instinct that made me grab him and push him into the closet within seconds of the drug boys' invasion of our apartment. I began to rock Malcolm, trying to keep us both from losing it. They had no idea that we were there.

I closed my eyes and said a silent prayer: "God, please keep my mother safe." As triflin' as Zee was, she was still my mother. I prayed that God would miraculously give her some kind of wisdom to shut the fuck up, or tell the truth, so that we could all get out of this alive. While at the same time I prayed for my mother, under my breath I whispered, "I hate you, Zee." I hated that she could put us in this kind of danger, over and over again.

Right now, though, as I gaze upon this poor excuse for a woman, I felt a weird kind of, I guess the word would be, *love*, sprinkled with a generous helping of hate. And then again, I always wondered, *What kind of pain drove her to drugs in the first place*? Why did she always choose drugs, over her children?

Suddenly, we were startled by the sound of LD and Six ransacking our crib, as they went from the kitchen to the living room. Zee panicked, as her attackers started toward the bedroom. "I said I don't have no money!" said Zee, barring the entrance to the tiny bedroom.

"Oh, I see what you wanna do. You want som'a dis." LD snickered, while grabbing his dick. "Go 'head, take off your clothes, bitch." LD looked at Six, winked his eye, and licked his lips. Pulling out a shiny switchblade, LD licked the length of the knife like a child would lick a lollipop.

"Where is that *fine* daughter of yours? What's her name, Sandy?" LD questioned Zee and looked at Six to help bolster his manhood. LD was in the zone now. He could have his cake and eat it too. LD would have both Zee *and* Sandy, and then kill the cheating heroin addict, as an example.

"Sandy ain't here. She took her brother over to the park," said Zee while she took off her clothes. "Just kill me and get it done with," she whimpered.

As I carefully pushed the closet door open to peek through, my eyes widened as LD took the knife and traced the various private parts of my mother's naked and shivering body.

"Zee, I'm gonna try and be nice." LD smirked and smacked his lips.

But then without warning, he screamed, "Look, bitch, where is the money?!"

"Baby, let me just help you relax. Let me make you feel like a real man," Zee said as she knelt down before LD, unzipped his pants, and began to blow that scum.

As LD got lost in the moment, Six stepped in, grabbed Zee by the hair and put his massive hands around her throat. "You either give us the money now, or I will kill you and come back to kill your two kids later."

Zee looked into the bedroom, then up at the ceiling, smiled, and said, "Do what you gotta do."

Angered by her defiance, Six retaliated by closing his hands even tighter around her throat. Zee's ninety-eight-pound, smack-drained frame shook as she resigned herself to death. In a way, it was as if she had made peace with herself, and preferred death to the life that she had lived. Rather than her life, or her children passing before her eyes, Zee felt her last "high" before passing out in Six's hands.

After having to put his semi-aroused manhood back in his pants, LD angrily grabbed Six by the shoulders trying to pull him off of Zee.

"What the fuck are you doing? You gonna kill her before I get some pussy?" growled LD. He wanted to fuck Zee, call in his crew to run a train, get the money, and then kill Zee on the street in front of her crib. How would he be able to make a name for himself now if she were already dead?

In a fit of rage, LD dragged Zee's lifeless body out of our rundown apartment. A bunch of the 23rd Street Crew hovered in a corner underneath the stoop playing dice. Like radar, a crowd began to form and everyone came in front of 1249 Amsterdam Avenue to see what was up. I ran to the window, telling Malcolm to stay put until I said he could come out. Through the torn window shade, I watched the spectacle below.

"If you fuck with my money, or you fuck with my shit, *this* is what happens!" shouted LD. By this time mothers and their "illegit" kids had come on the scene. Old women and even a couple of workin' stiffs wondered what this fool was doing with a lifeless, drug-filled, naked body.

"If you fuck with Low Down, then you plan to go *Down Low*," and with that, LD took his knife and gutted Zee like a wild animal, starting from her neck going straight down to her stomach and stopped past her navel. It was the most horrible thing that most folks had ever seen yet no one did or said anything. Everyone started to disperse, running for dear life into their apartments and shutting their doors. The young dudes began slapping each other high-five and an occasional, "Oh, shit!" could be heard.

All in all, at the expense of my mother's life, LD had in fact established himself as THE MAN that night.

Back in the apartment, I finally let Malcolm come out of the closet. I looked around the place and everyone was gone. For good, I hoped. Again, I peered outside to see Zee lying lifeless and alone on the sidewalk, with her body torn apart. Although I was stunned, I shed no tears. Somehow, a long time ago, I resigned myself to the fact that eventually there would be a night something like this. Zee had done too much shit to too many people. I told him that Zee probably went to the store, and quickly closed the window so that Malcolm could not see what I had witnessed. He knew I was lying but did not tell me so.

In the distance I heard faint cries. I snuck to the front door and hastily peeked out into the hall and saw three old ladies holding hands and praying. Unfortunately, as the women prayed, the only thing that I can remember was how a sense of anger washed over my entire body. Anger, not sadness.

Then there was nothing but silence. A sound that so permeated that rundown joint, that it was a sound and a night that I would never forget. I vowed to make LD, Six, and Lord Bless wish they had never been born. As I said my own silent, but deadly prayer, I closed my eyes tight and began to create Skyy.

CHAPTER 2
Washington, D.C., 2006

I blinked my eyes hard and looked around, realizing that I was sitting at my desk in my office, and not in our tiny flat in Harlem. My face felt flushed and my heart was beating wildly as I took a long deep breath. *Get a grip on yourself, girl*, I thought. For a minute, it seemed like it all just happened yesterday. A single tear rolled down my face, as Deena James and her little flunky Karen Anderson slithered by my office.

"Hey Sandy." They snickered in unison. Those two bitches were as jealous as they came. The young girls call women like that "haters" and that's just what they were.

I started working at Bledsoe Communications, Inc. (BCI) when I was nineteen after a brief stint as a covert spy. I had been recruited by my life mentor to join him in a special forces military unit. However, I quickly realized that while my martial arts training and youth proved me an invaluable asset to the American covert troop, I had to make my way back to the states to be close to Malcolm.

So, at nineteen, I traded my secret life for one more normal and mundane. I gladly took a position as mail clerk/general gopher at the prestigious BCI. As a loner and almost a recluse, I graduated high school with honors, so it was easy to receive a full academic scholarship into Howard University. I always enrolled in early classes and was usually finished by noon or one p.m. I would then work at BCI from one p.m. to sometimes nine or ten p.m., then go home and try to study. Upon graduation, I took a full-time position as a production assistant and have spent the last fifteen years working twelve-hour days at BCI, and they act like someone just handed me the VP spot. People sometimes hate the fact that smart women don't need to sleep their way to the top of the corporate ladder. On the other hand, dumb women think that letting men take advantage of you will get them much higher than they already were. The sad thing was that even though they slept with half the company, Deena was just an Executive Assistant and Karen was a Departmental Secretary. How pitiful! If they stopped and did some real work for a change, stayed out of other people's business, and went back to school, they would probably surprise themselves and get some justified promotions. But then again, what did I care about girls who not only hated other women, but also hated themselves.

Deena and Karen took it upon themselves to enter my office without being invited. *Damn, that's what I get for not keeping my door shut*, I thought.

Let me just shed some light on these two sisters. Karen is a dark-skinned sister, with the worst blonde weave I have ever seen. Every time I see her I wonder if Beyonce does charity work because somebody needs to hook a sista up. The bad thing is that she thinks her shit looks good. The girl is just confused. Although she is a legit size sixteen, she *insists* that she is a size ten, therein lies the confusion. She also never met a piece of "cheap" jewelry that she didn't like because I swear she must wear every piece that she owns every day. Also, Karen claimed that she is a college graduate, but when she was up for a promotion, I peeped her resume and found out that she did a few semesters here and there at Prince George's Community College. I ain't mad at Karen, she's done pretty well for herself, considering her background, but she needs to keep it real.

If you can believe it, her girl Deena is worse. Deena is one of those light-skinned women who calls herself Creole. She was born in Mississippi, spent two years in New Orleans, and swears she's the original Voodoo Priestess. The only thing about her that's Creole is that tired Gumbo she brings to every office potluck. Unlike her girl Karen, Deena spends every dime of her paycheck on clothing. Her clothes are tight and cheap. She lives at home with her momma, and doesn't even own a vehicle. I always ask myself why a woman would want to put everything she has on her back only to lay on it! She thinks all men in BCI want her because of her beauty. Ironically, it is the same old story: Boy meets Girl. Boy bangs Girl. Boy tells his boys. Girl gets reputation. Easy *come*, easy go.

"Hello, ladies. How are you both today?"

"Sandy, I was just gonna ask you that question," Karen sneered. "But by the looks of that suit, I would say not so good." Karen looked at Deena who backed her up.

"Yeah, Sandy, you know you my girl, but I think my momma just gave a suit like that to Goodwill, and I don't even think they took it!" Deena laughed.

"I thank you ladies for your fashion tips but I have a meeting to chair in New York this evening," I said in my most patronizing voice. "Karen, did you get my draft regarding the New York deal?"

"Yes," Karen timidly replied.

"Well, have the finished document on my desk by close of business. Thank you, ladies, for your couture commentary. Have a productive day." With that, I strutted out of my office, leaving the two office flunkies speechless.

As I walked to the elevator, I thought, *No, this suit would not make the cover of Vogue or Essence, but this is just a cover, baby. One day you two heifers will meet the real Sandy, or shall I say Skyy?*

My personal assistant handed me a message that the limo would be fifteen minutes late. Good! It was eleven fifteen a.m. and I had a few moments to spare. I went into the women's bathroom instead of the executive washroom. I looked in the mirror. *Those wenches were right. My look is pretty lame.*

I had to admit that I was a sad sight, highlighted by my sandy brown Naomi Sims wig, which sat on my head made me look ten years older. Shit, I paid $500 for this human hair wig. Please, with the hours I work, I don't have time to sit in a hair salon all day long, like Deena and Karen. Which reminds me, *I need to get another one while I'm in New York*, I thought, looking around to see if there was anyone else in the bathroom.

I was alone, so I took off the wig and smiled a devilish smile as I admired the beautiful bob haircut that bounced as I shook my head. There were glistening strands of blonde that flowed through my hair. I gave the term "short and sassy" a new meaning. "You are a bad bitch," I said admiring myself, and I was.

I was five feet eight inches and a perfect size eight. I had legs for days and always wore at least four-inch heels. My towering frame was both powerful and intoxicating. My measurements of 36-26-38 fit perfectly into any ensemble and always made me stand out. That is why I always had to downplay my beauty and sex appeal.

My eyes were almond shaped, yet deadly. I rarely showed emotion, good or bad. The years had taken most joy away from me and I was cynical beyond belief. Though my eyes were breathtaking they were usually very empty. My lips were hands down my most sensual feature. The fullness of them made most people stare because of the combination of the perfect shape and their exotic sensuality. I'm not trying to be funny but I am probably the most stunning-looking woman that most people would ever meet, not beautiful, not drop-dead gorgeous; just SUPER HOT!

Looking down at my Movado, I noticed that it was eleven twenty-five a.m.

I'd better go, I thought, placing my wig back on my head, adjusting my plain, wool crepe, brown Jones New York suit, and checked my immaculately polished brown Joan and David pumps.

What a polished, conservative brown mouse I am, I thought. But that's all right. You can't win the game, if you don't wear the uniform. Although the thought of my outfit made me wince, I strolled outside and slid into the limo that was waiting for me on the corner of Twelfth and G Streets with the vanity DC tags that said "BLESD 3."

I had not slept peacefully in over a week. The picture of the beautiful girl with the big black eye stayed present in my mind all the time. The look in her eyes had pierced my soul, so I decided that tonight would be Ashley's night. "Skyy" would make it right and "Sandy" would finally be able to sleep.

As the limo pulled away, I unfolded the day's *Washington Post*. Reading always calmed me down. The front page headline read, "Another Young Girl Found Butchered in a Local School Yard."

CHAPTER 3
New York, 1950

James Bledsoe, the "respectable" founder and CEO of BCI, was not always so decent and revered. Back in the day, he was the drug lord and kingpin who had my mother killed. Back then, they called him *Lord Bless*. His father, Pastor Jeremiah Lord Bledsoe, was one of the most prominent and charismatic preachers in Harlem. At six feet five inches, he had a presence that was captivating. In the '50s, the First Baptist Church of the Rock was often visited by the likes of Miles Davis, Zora Neale Hurston, and even once by James Baldwin. In 1960, Pastor Bledsoe had become one of the most outspoken civil rights leaders in New York, opening his church doors for speakers and strategic planning meetings. Rumor has it that the first conversations about the March on Washington were held between A. Philip Randolph, Martin Luther King, and Pastor Bledsoe at the First Baptist Church of the Rock.

Jeremiah Lord Bledsoe II was born on October 16, 1950. It was like the Lord delivered this child himself because Pastor Bledsoe was the happiest man on this earth. Ophelia, the Pastor's wife, had a hard pregnancy. She was a tiny, unattractive woman who at her heaviest probably weighed about one hundred pounds, stood at about five feet one inch and was very fragile. People often wondered what Pastor Bledsoe saw in her, because they were as different as night and day. Ophelia almost died during the birth of her first child, which prompted her doctor to later tie her tubes.

While Jeremiah and Ophelia were initially heartbroken by the news, they simply poured every ounce of love they had into their son. Having a "Jeremiah, Sr." and a "Jeremiah, Jr." in the house was confusing, so Ophelia began to call Jeremiah, Jr. "James." When asked why, she always said, "Don't ask me why I chose the name James. I do know that it's a strong Christian name and it is easy to remember."

Well, if that was the case, why didn't she name her son James to begin with? Anyway, she and Jeremiah doted on James something terrible. This kid wasn't just born with a silver spoon in his mouth; he was born with an entire silver table setting. James only wore the finest clothes, went to all-white private schools, and had his first car at fifteen. If you couldn't figure it out, he was spoiled rotten, by not only his parents, but also by the congregation. Lord Bless, James could *do no wrong*.

James was the spitting image of his father and learned early in life that he had the capacity to charm just about every woman he met. His first experience came from his mousy mother, who would give in to her son's every demand. See, that is the problem with many African American men. Mothers act like they are damned near married to their sons. In some households, they treat their sons better than they treat their husbands. Maybe it's because, unlike their husbands, in their sons, they always have a "captive audience." You women need to check yourselves. Sorry, I digress.

James lived as a royal in his own house, the crown Prince of Harlem! You had the Pastor just adoring him and showing him off as his heir to the throne, his mother who obeyed his every word, and his "subjects" who were ambassadors of this, presidents of that, club owners, and so on, showering him with gifts. It is no wonder why he started to feel entitled to certain things that other mere mortals were not.

Reared like many pastors' children, James rarely saw his father. This fact would later cause him to live by a separate set of "life rules."

Pastor Bledsoe spoke at many churches around the country and had other pastoral duties that often kept him out late or all night long. "A pastor's work is never done," his father would always say. On rare occasions, the Pastor would take his little prince with him while he performed his "pastoral work." James felt proud that in house after house, his father was able to make so many of these married and unmarried ladies of the church shout out the Lord's name, over and over, just like in church. "Sister Jones needs a private moment with the Lord," Jeremiah would tell his son. "You let me know if you hear Deacon Jones at the door, alright?"

Although Pastor Bledsoe ruled his church with an iron fist and was well respected all over the country, it was Jeremiah Lord, II that ran the Bledsoe household. He had a smile that could charm the devil and used his quick wit and looks to get him over in every situation. James didn't know what "spare the rod, spoil the child" meant, because he never got a spanking. And this was back in the day when parents would spank their kids with a belt buckle, shoe, ironing cord, or whatever they could get their hands on.

Even with all the attention and material things that any young child could ever want, James was not satisfied. He didn't want to share in his father's notoriety or fortune. James wanted his own fame and adoration. Although he liked being respected like his father, the problem was that James did not really *know* the Lord and was not really interested in developing a relationship with Him. Sure, James was at church every Sunday and even had a solo once a month in the Youth Choir. Unfortunately for Jeremiah, the only thing that James saw was the adulation that was directed toward *his* father, Jeremiah; he didn't understand that *the* Father that the church was referring to was GOD. James thought his father was "The God" that everyone was praising. With all of his comings and goings, speeches and vigils, prayer meetings and revivals, the Pastor neglected to ensure that his own son knew and loved God. The one person that needed a little private pastoring, who truly needed to know *the* LORD didn't really know God or his father very well.

A little knowledge can be very dangerous, especially in the hands of an intelligent person. Therefore, if you have a man who is knowledgeable about a subject but doesn't necessarily subscribe to it himself, that man has no problem manipulating the truth to fit his own personal agenda. That is just what James did. Because the Pastor and the congregation wanted so hard to believe that the fruit didn't fall far from the tree, James was able to fool the entire congregation, everyone *except* for William Denver

Williams. Although, Harlem's most notorious drug dealer in his day, was better known as "Billy D."

Billy D was what I call a "cussin' Christian." He went to church every Sunday and was probably one of the largest financial contributors. A cross between Nat King Cole and Ike Turner, Billy D wore the biggest hats, the loudest suits, and sang with the smoothest baritone voice imaginable. In the 'hood, he was known to beat a prostitute to a pulp, then bring her to church the next morning. All the members of the First Baptist Church of the Rock knew that Billy D ran hoes, numbers, and drugs. But because he was always so generous, folks simply turned their heads, hoping that Billy D would eventually give up his secular ways. Meanwhile, the church was happy that when the choir needed new robes or the youth group wanted to go on a trip and the church couldn't raise enough money, Billy D was always there to save the day.

Pastor Bledsoe had a love/hate relationship with Billy. Quiet as it's kept, while Jeremiah despised all of the flaws that Billy D so flagrantly represented, he never closed the door on him because he always felt that one day he would save Billy's soul. Although Billy D admired his hustle, he really thought that the Pastor was a sucker who should be living larger and getting more money from his congregation. However, after all was said and done, Billy D asked God to forgive him for his sins and help him to live like a strong Christian man. Little did Billy D know that every night, the Pastor prayed for the exact same thing.

As James began to get older, Billy D began to see James for who he really was becoming, rather than through the rose-colored glasses that the Pastor, his mother, and the entire congregation shared. Only Billy D could see that even at a young age, young James had mad game. Billy D would watch James dazzle women, young and old; to secure anything and everything he wanted. James was both slick and sincere at the same time and had such a genuine flair, that Billy D forgot about his relationship with God (and the Pastor) and began to plot how to get James to join forces with him. James was not only smart, handsome, and articulate, but also had connections that could help to expand Billy D's drug business.

James was so charismatic, that Billy D could see him establishing con-nections with those civil rights leaders and white boys in Washington that could even land him near or in the White House. The possibilities were endless! Billy D's gold teeth glistened as he smiled at the thought of sitting in the Oval Office wearing a bright red suit and shoes to match, as he began to concoct a plot to trap young James.

CHAPTER 4
New York, 2006

Bledsoe Communications, Inc. (BCI) is an African-American-owned, multi-billion-dollar-generating, diversified conglomerate, Fortune 500, international communications firm that can comfortably rival companies such as Disney, CNN and BET. BCI offices are located in D.C., New York, Chicago, Los Angeles, Atlanta, London, and Tokyo. It owns newspapers and radio stations in New York and Atlanta, newspapers in Chicago and D.C., and television stations in L.A. and London. In fact, James Bledsoe is so *bad*, that he single-handedly negotiated a cutting-edge, digital, and all-music-format television station comparable to MTV in Tokyo. That is quite a coup considering that Tokyo is one of the largest global markets and essentially, anyone wanting to record and promote music in Japan, would have to go through BCI. Moreover, the Japanese cannot get enough American music, especially hip-hop.

All in all, James Bledsoe has come a long way from New York drug kingpin to respected, international businessman. He has won countless awards, from local boards of trade to the NAACP Image Award. Now there's a joke! Imagine a man who had beat, killed, and abused Black people winning an NAACP *Image* Award, only in America!

As Vice President of Marketing for BCI, I have the herculean task of managing 150 people and a $250 million advertising budget. My job is tough because I constantly commute between the Washington, D.C. and New York offices, in addition to making my rounds to all of BCI U. S. and other global offices. You are probably saying to yourself, "All right!

Sista's got it goin' on, jet-setting all over the world! She probably graduated from Harvard University with an MBA or something." As a proud graduate of Howard, I do mix and mingle professionally with Wharton MBA's as well as Rhodes Scholars. I am one of those people who *worked* my way to the top, without having to touch a single button on my blouse.

Although Mr. Bledsoe may be a little scandalous with some of his staff members, he does reward hard work and hustle. Zee always said a little hard work never hurt anybody! That's why folks be hatin' me so bad. Don't sleep, though. I am sharp! I am the sister who would get to work at 6:30 a.m. and not leave some nights until nine p.m. I always know the names of all the night security guards and janitorial personnel because they make sure that I get to my car safely. Back in the day, the BCI cleaning woman's Honda Civic was nicer than my broke-down Chevy Chevette—now I'm rollin' in a limo.

Wow, it's four p.m., and I slept through the entire trip to New York. I was surprised that I was able to sleep so hard, because I keep picturing some madman butchering children. *That serial murderer has to be stopped*! And oh yeah...those two D.C. hoochies got on my last nerve in the office today. All I know is if that memo is not on my desk upon my return, I *will* fire Karen's ass. I smirked at the thought of firing Deena's girl Karen, and smiled when I saw the beautiful New York skyline, as the limo crossed the George Washington Bridge. I had two hours before the meeting started, which meant I had just enough time to grab a bite to eat and freshen up.

As if on cue, Mike, the limo driver, pulls up to the corner of Fifty-Seventh and Broadway. I immediately jump out of the limo and run into my favorite spot in the world, Tony's Pizzeria.

"Ahhhh...who is this gorgeous lady?" yelled Tony.

"*Bon giorno*, Antonio," I said as we embraced and Tony kissed me on each side of my face.

"Sandy, beautiful as always! What brings you to New York this afternoon?" asked Tony.

"BCI business, what else?!" I said. "May I have the usual?"

"Of course, *mi amore*," said Tony, motioning to an aproned man behind the counter.

"How is Tony, Jr.? He's going into his senior year of NYU, isn't he?"

"Yes, and he has managed to get straight A's! At the rate he's going, he said he will graduate magnet, magna, mag-something or other, and should get a full scholarship to law school. Not bad for a man whose dad has a sixth-grade education!" Tony beamed.

"Not bad at all, Tony. Let me know if he wants to go to Yale. Don't forget I have contacts there. Malcolm is on the Alumni Committee."

I was a disciplined martial artist who very rarely ingested junk food. I did not drink, smoke, eat beef, or pork. My only indulgence is pizza. Pizza has always been a food that I could find comfort in. I remember that there were many days that Malcolm and I would have nothing to eat, but Tony would always have a slice or two of pizza for us. Tony never realized just how often he saved our lives. That is why I have no problem writing an anonymous check to NYU every year to pay for Tony, Jr.'s "scholarship." He wants to be a lawyer just like Malcolm!

As I sat and savored every bit of the delicacy made with delectable mozzarella cheese, homemade tomato sauce, and fresh risen dough, I realized that it was five p.m.! I rushed to finish my food, gulped down the Coke, and kissed Tony goodbye. I knew that traffic would be a bear, so I jumped out of the limo and went right up to the executive washroom on the fifty-second floor. Luckily, we pulled up to the Bledsoe building at 5:30 p.m. on the nose, so I had time to splash some water on my face and reapply my make-up. After locking the bathroom door, I glanced at my watch, 5:40 p.m.

I entered the lounge area and sat in a Yoga position on the expensively carpeted floor and began a five-minute Yoga exercise. After the exercise, I inhaled, then exhaled, and thought of my most recent visits to Tokyo, Osaka, and Sendai. I also remembered the long and exhausting nights of training in the hills of Fujiyama. It seemed like so long ago. Feeling empowered to negotiate a deal that would put BCI on the map in Japan I pranced around the conference room. As I glanced around, I noticed all of the appropriate marketing materials were placed just so. I glimpsed the back of the room and saw a fully stocked bar with assorted snacks. I grabbed an Evian and sat at the head of the table.

At 5:55 p.m., Mr. Currothers and Ms. Sneed of Burrell Advertising entered, followed by other BCI personnel and the meeting started at precisely six p.m.

Tonight Burrell Advertising was pitching me to secure a $10 million advertising campaign for our new television station in Tokyo. Japan is a country with 126 million people and 100 million television sets. With those numbers steadily growing, obtaining the right firm to launch us into this market was important. Although I was one of the highest paid VP's of Marketing, I had set my sights on becoming the first African American female CEO of a Fortune 500 company. Mr. Bledsoe was close to retirement age, and at least once a month, he talked about purchasing a yacht and sailing around the world.

James and his wife were not blessed with any children, so there were no legal heirs to the empire. His right-hand man, Roosevelt Guidry, although brilliant, was nothing more than a "yes" man, in no way could he be considered a leader. He barely had the balls that God gave him and was a notorious turncoat. He had the concepts of international trade down cold, but gossiped more than most women. Rosie, as I call him, knew every nuance as far as foreign trade was concerned, was fluent in three languages, but had the nastiest, most bourgeois attitude that I had ever seen. Don't get me wrong, I am not judging but Rosie had issues. He showed up at the corporate offices with PMS at least twice a month and there was no getting around his mood swings. Rosie was as unstable as a three-legged chair. Like it or not, I was their heir apparent and everyone knew it. If I could make this Tokyo deal work and create opportunities for us in other Asian countries, the BCI "kingdom" was mine.

The Burrell presentation was flawless but I still had to hear from Bozell, another nationally acclaimed ad firm, next week. Since Burrell was one of the largest African American advertising agencies in the country, I would probably go with them.

Now that the presentation was over, Burrell and BCI staff members began to help themselves to the open bar. I shook my head with contempt because the only thing worse than a public drunk, is a public drunk in a work environment. However, the good thing for me is I could usually get pertinent information about folks after they have had two or three drinks. That is why I always ordered a fully stocked, premium call brand bar with very light snacks for most of my meetings. Shit, it ain't my fault if my competitors are stupid enough to overindulge. Some of my best negotiating came as a result of information gathering at those "informal receptions." I pride myself at being able to deny myself luxuries that most people find so appealing.

At eight p.m., I motioned for the catering company to begin the clean-up and usher the guests out. Everyone finally left by 8:30 p.m. I had a big night ahead of me so I had to get a move-on. I picked up my Louis Vuitton duffel bag and went into my office. Another perk of my job is having a plush office at all of the BCI locations. The New York office was by far the most luxurious; for example, in my office I had a small closet full of clothes, a bathroom with a Jacuzzi and steam room, a stereo system, and a wet bar.

I closed the door to my office and began to prepare myself for the night's events. My evening ritual always began with a little Miles Davis, "Goodnight My Love." The irony of that song always put me in the mood for battle. I slowly began to take off my clothes, fold them, and gently place them in the Louis Vuitton duffel. I looked at my long, sleek honey-colored frame in the mirror. At five feet eight inches, I weighed 135 pounds and had curves in all the right places. I worked out daily and it showed. My matching black thong and bra set fit perfectly. As I gazed at myself, I thought of a Black Panther getting ready to attack, which is why I love wearing the color black; it made me feel like I was the descendent of both Queen Cleopatra and Cleopatra Jones. I took off the Naomi Sims wig and marveled at my sleek, sexy short haircut. Standing there in the mirror at that exact second made me feel a type of exhilaration that I just can't put into words. I truly was an AFRICAN WARRIOR.

After Miles, I decided to put in a little Maxwell. I began my warm-up with a little Tai Chi, and then moved on to a series of karate moves. Both in work and at play, I must always be mentally and physically prepared for any attack. But I did know that for this attack, if executed correctly, would result in a young girl's freedom. However, if this mission failed, I could be killed, imprisoned, or both.

The *Lady in Black* had been getting a lot of headlines lately. The nation was trying to guess who the one-woman vigilante force was. However, there were a lot of people who wanted this crime fighting to stop. But I would never stop. I had to fight for those who could not fight for themselves. I also had to make *Lord Bless* pay for what he did to my mother.

I slid on my Issey Miyaki black pant suit, my four-inch black Jimmy Choo boots, accessorized with black Dior sunglasses and a black French beret. I knew that I was a *bad* sister. I made John Shaft look like a punk and am just ready to KILL that fuckin' BILL. Now I was focused and ready. But I needed a little something to loosen me up, so I popped in my Beyonce CD and played the song, "Deja Vu" and started to kill that beat "baby I swear it's deja vu," but then in mid song, I knew that it was time.

Let the games begin.

CHAPTER 5

New York, 2006 (Friday night)

I met Ashley Stewart Petrone in early December. She was such a pretty girl and had the bluest, yet the most melancholy, eyes that I have ever seen. I was in Midtown New York and had just left my office and was on my way to the New York Center of Martial Arts, which was located in the Bronx.

The New York Center of Martial Arts was one of the premier martial arts schools in the country. They trained their students in various forms of Kung Fu, Judo, Karate, and Tae Kwon Do. Most of Hollywood came to Master Kwan to either use his teachers or seek his expert advice on technique and authenticity. There was a time when you would see Larry, I mean Laurence, sneaking in and out of the Center. Keanu did not have the balls to come to the Bronx.

As a fourth-degree black belt in Karate, I had won twenty-five tournaments and had given the school every one of my trophies. Part of the responsibility of having a black belt is to come to a facility and teach. Although I chose the center for many reasons, the primary reason was because not only did Master Kwan introduce martial arts to me, he also saved my life.

Before I continue, I must make a profound statement. I know that God has put me on this earth for a reason. That reason is to help fight for the rights of people who are helpless. And it's not just about me, I do believe that everyone on this earth has a purpose and that it is incumbent upon each of us to find out what our purpose is. Therefore, I do not find it amazing that so many people have helped me, nor am I amazed at how I risk my life to help strangers. I simply do what I was put on this earth to do. I have been very fortunate in that although I have had many, many challenges in life, I have had many angels surrounding me.

Okay, back to Ashley. One dark, crisp, evening, I was crossing Gun Hill Road when I saw a little girl crying in front of a dilapidated house. Not only was it 8 p.m. and pitch black, it was about thirty degrees, and the little girl did not have a coat on. I walked up to the shivering child and asked her what was wrong. "Nothing," she mumbled. I looked at the girl, knowing that she was lying, trying to figure out just how old she was. She appeared to be about nine, but had on a little black tight dress and what looked like smeared red lipstick.

"Where is your coat, honey?" I asked.

"I don't have a coat," Ashley said. "My father sold it."

I looked in my gym bag and pulled out a sweatshirt and sweat pants.

"Here, put this on."

"Thank you, miss," Ashley stated very politely.

"Are you hungry?"

"Yes, ma'am. I have not eaten in two days," she replied, looking down at her feet.

"Two days! Damn," I said under my breath. "You're coming with me to dinner. I was dreading eating by myself," I lied.

So much for my workout.

"Do you have to ask your folks for permission?" I asked.

Ashley glanced toward the tenement in which she lived and looked like she was deep in thought. Her mother had always taught her not to talk to strangers, but nowadays, she had no one to trust. "No, my dad will be busy for a while," she said, slightly tenuous.

"Where should we go?" I asked and Ashley's attitude began to brighten slightly. "By the way, my name is Skyy Knight. What's yours?"

"My name is Ashley Stewart Petrone. It is a pleasure to make your acquaintance." Ashley smiled and extended her hand.

"Okay, Miss Ashley Stewart Petrone, where shall we dine?" I asked, as I showed off my deepest curtsey.

"Let's go to that Chinese restaurant across the street," she said. "The owners are very nice."

We walked into the House of Hunan after eight p.m.; the restaurant was nearly empty.

"Hi, Ashley, how's school?" asked the Asian female owner.

"I don't know, ma'am. I haven't been in two weeks," Ashley replied.

"What do you mean two weeks?!" I asked.

"I've been helping my dad," said Ashley.

"How have you been helping your dad?" At that point I just was not going to beat around the bush anymore. "Let's order, Ashley. Then I want you to tell me what has been going on in your life."

We started our meals with egg drop soup, followed by sesame chicken and broccoli, fried rice, and egg rolls. I told Ashley she could have ice cream if she ate all of her food.

The young Cantonese woman wrote down the order and disappeared into the back. It was at that point that I looked into the saddest face I have ever seen and started listening to one of the saddest stories that I have ever heard.

Ashley began with her biological father, Timothy Stewart, who had died of a heart attack when she was just four. Her family lived in a modest home in Queens in a typical suburban neighborhood. Ashley's dad earned enough so that Ashley's mom did not have to work. Her mom's main responsibility was to care for Ashley and her older sister, Phoebe. After her father's death, her mother was left to raise the two sisters alone. The problem was that, being a typical housewife, Mary Stewart had no marketable employment skills and had no concept of financial planning, and with the family living paycheck to paycheck, Tim had died leaving the family in debt. Mary Stewart and the girls eventually had to resort to living on welfare. Like many people trapped in a cycle of poverty, Mary drank so that she could cope with her circumstances, and it wasn't long before the Stewart family lost their meager home.

Fortunately for Mary, she was pretty attractive for her age. At thirty-nine she looked as though she was still in her very late twenties. Her long blonde hair, vibrant blue eyes, and gymnast's build still kept men's heads turning, so it was only a matter of time before a man came on the scene to rescue the damsel in distress. Unfortunately for Mary, three months after Mary lost her home, she married a local hood rat named John Petrone, a con man who was all talk and no action. Mary, Phoebe, and young Ashley moved in with John's mother in the Bronx, which should have been Mary's first clue that it wasn't going to work out for them.

Mary and Jay (John's nickname) argued constantly about Jay's employment status or lack thereof. Mary shared tales of her life with her previous husband, even if her stories were a little bit romanticized and fictionalized. Jay assured her that it was only a matter of time that he would get his big break.

"Yeah, right," retorted Mary on the regular. Mary knew deep in her heart that she had fallen for the oldest trick in the book and that Jay was a straight loser.

Meanwhile, the entire family lived on Mary's welfare check and sparse baby-sitting jobs. Jay lay around the house drinking beer, waiting for his "big break" to find him. Realizing that she had jumped out of the frying pan smack dab into the fire, Mary began to threaten to leave Jay. She knew she had sunk to the lowest level ever and had to get her kids out of this horrendous situation. Mary also had seen Jay look at Phoebe through drunken and lustful eyes, more than once.

In Jay's head, Mary's leaving meant that the welfare check would be gone too, so Jay began to think of ways to keep them from leaving. Getting a job was definitely out of the question, so Jay decided that it would be easier for him to make Mary psychologically, and then physically, unable to leave.

Even though he spent most of his time with a beer bottle in his hand, Jay had been around the block a few times. He had seen how the addicts in his streets seemed to stick to the neighborhood, never venturing too far. So, one night, while he invited his friends over to watch the Jets vs. Redskins game, Jay introduced Mary to heroin.

"You have been under a lot of stress, Mary. Try this. It will calm you down," Jay lied.

Mary should have been suspicious of his sudden "sweetness." After polishing off a bottle of gin, Mary slurred, "Jay, I have always taught my children that drugs are bad. So I cannot and will not do this."

Jay motioned to his "friends." "Grab her arms, guys." Vinny and Sal each grabbed one of Mary's arms and held her down. As Mary screamed and tried to struggle, Jay put a towel in her mouth to muffle the sounds. Taking off his belt, Jay tightened the buckle, exposing the blue-green vein in Mary's forearm. Mary struggled to restrain her arm and her eyes bulged with fear as he took a hypodermic needle, filled with a clear liquid, off the coffee table. As Jay thrust the needle and the liquid into Mary's vein, within seconds he watched as Mary's face turned flush. The fear in her eyes was replaced by euphoria, and then finally into a lifeless, drowsy state.

"What do you say, boys? She's still a sweet piece of ass, even drugged up?" Jay smirked.

"Yeah, man. Can I do her?" asked Vinny, as he eagerly unzipped his pants.

"Yeah, man," said Jay. "That's the least I can do. Sal, you can go next."

For the next two hours, the three men took turns having sex with a smack-filled mother. As the heroin coursed through her veins, Mary could only see cloudy figures and shadows, while her body felt like it weighed a thousand pounds. Although she felt a lot of poking and prodding going on around her, the only thing that kept going through her heroin-filled mind was how for the first time in a long time, she felt relaxed.

After the smack had run its course, Mary awoke and found herself half-clothed, sore, and bruised in places she never could imagine. Without thinking, or perhaps still a little high from the heroin, Mary went into the kitchen, picked up a knife from the counter, and ran the blade across both of her wrists. Unfortunately, it was Ashley that found her mother lying in a pool of her own blood. Instinctively, Ashley called 9-1-1, hoping that her mother was still alive. However, it was too late and Mary was pronounced *DOA*, dead on arrival.

Although Mary had a sister who lived in upstate New York, the juvenile authorities did not send Ashley and Phoebe to live with her. A cruel twist of fate named their legal guardian and left Jay with full custody of Mary's young girls, which suited him, just fine. Seeing the handwriting on the wall, sixteen-year-old Phoebe knew that she would soon be Jay's next victim, so she ran away from home the day after Mary's funeral. Before she left, Phoebe took Ashley aside and told her to be strong, and that Ashley was safe because she was still young. Phoebe promised that she would come and get Ashley as soon as she found a job and a suitable place to live. Ashley knew her sister would be back so they hugged good-bye and Ashley had a sense of hope.

With Mary and Phoebe gone, the check that Jay received for being Ashley's guardian just wasn't enough. Jay began to bring men to the house and asked Ashley to do "little favors" for them in exchange for money. It started with Ashley just sitting on these snakes' laps, to giving them hand jobs, to oral sex. Just before she turned ten years old, Ashley was having sex with at least one man every night. Not only could he watch the degradation of this innocent young child, of course, Jay would help himself whenever he got good and ready.

The night that I met Ashley, she had been kicked out of the house because one of Jay's clients could not get it up, and had demanded that Ashley be punished by forcing her to stand in the cold for two hours without a coat.

"This sick motherfucker was going to pay!"

While trying to hold back tears, I told Ashley that God loved her and would always protect her. I told her that I was one of his helpers and would put an end to the abuse once and for all. Although I hated to leave her in that sick situation, before I could act, I needed to do my homework. I asked her to meet me on Friday at the same restaurant. She agreed. We hugged and I told her that she must keep this secret to herself. I gave her my number and told her to feel free to call me if things became more critical than they already were. It was important that Ashley act as if everything were normal.

"On Monday, I am coming back to the Bronx. Have everything packed and ready to go. Do not tell anyone, Ashley. You must act as if everything is normal. Follow my lead and my instructions to the letter. Remember, Monday night is the night. Meet me at the House of Hunan at eight p.m. If you need me before that, call me."

"Thanks, Skyy."

As much as it hurt my heart, I said good-bye to probably the sweetest girl in the world. No child should ever have to endure that kind of pain. I should not have had to deal with that type of pain. I will protect Ashley and all of the little girls and boys like her. That is my mission.

So let it be written. So let the shit be done.

After I walked Ashley home, I immediately called Mike the limo driver and asked for him to meet me at the restaurant and pulled out my laptop. The familiar young woman came over to my table and gave me a look that said, "Are you back again?"

"The kitchen will be closing soon," she said. "Would you like to order anything?"

"Tea, please," I said.

"Yes, ma'am. Coming right up," she replied.

As I hooked my laptop up to my cell phone, plugged in my earplugs and logged into the special screen with my personal identification code, BIRD, I waited to hear Charlie Parker's voice.

"Whazzup, Skyy?" asked Charlie.

"Hey Bird," I replied.

"Where are you?"

"New York. Just got a real pitiful case, Bird, and as usual, I need your help."

"Give me a sec to grab a pad. Fire away, Skyy."

"Name: Juliano 'John' Petrone. Address is 541 Olinville Avenue, Bronx, New York. Sidekicks are Vinny and Sal. I have no more info than that but I know within a few days you will have all the goods."

"You give me too much credit, Skyy."

"Later, Bird."

"Three days, Skyy."

I unplugged my laptop from my cell, took off the earplugs, and placed all of the electronic gear into my gym bag, as Yang Lee, the owner, approached my table with the tea. As I sat there sipping tea, I thought about Ashley. I wanted to do this as swiftly and efficiently as possible. I didn't want Ashley there for another moment, let alone three whole days.

Three days was *a lifetime* of pure hell. I sure hoped that Bird didn't have any trouble tracing those scumbags, but then again, he never did.

Mike pulled up in front of the House of Hunan and phoned me. I slid a ten-dollar bill on the table and left the Bronx and the restaurant behind. After an hour in the car, Mike pulled up in front of my loft in SoHo. In the exclusive uptown buildings of the Village, the tenants act like they run your household, trying to tell what type of parties you can have, what type of guests are allowed. There is even a committee that does a background check before they offer a lease, to determine if you are "their" kind of people. When I am in New York, I prefer to stay in SoHo because everyone is into their own thing, and once you make the cut, no one asks any questions.

CHAPTER 6

New York, 2006, three days later

I conducted business as usual at BCI that week. This time, Bozell made their presentation for the Tokyo deal, and I hosted a large meeting for all of the regional sales managers.

Like clockwork, three days later, I heard "Bird of Paradise" on my ringtone. I picked up my cell phone and listened as I heard, "The bird is in flight," and then the caller hung up. I smiled.

It was five p.m., and I was going to leave the office early for a change. I pulled out my cell to call my boy, Mike, to bring the limo around to the front of the BCI building but then decided against it. I quickly changed into my signature black outfit and decided to hop on my bike. As I rode through the city I felt a certain thrill that is indescribable. As I approached a light on the East Side, I took my helmet off, so my beautiful hair could breathe and so I could really think.

I hopped onto the black leather seat of the rawest Yamaha imaginable. My motorcycle literally purred as I drove through the city. I was at one with my baby. I headed down Broadway toward Thirty-Fourth Street and pulled up in front of Madison Square Garden. I jumped off and went down into Penn Station, heading straight for the lockers; 003, 004, 005, 006, 007, using the key, I opened the box, removed the package inside, ran back outside, hopped on my bike and headed to the crib.

On Mondays the traffic is always heavy, so I leaned back and visualized myself on a tropical island to relax myself. I started doing this visualization thing when I was a kid. I didn't know that it was some real psychological technique-like shit. It was just that, like most kids like me, I wished that I lived someplace else. It wasn't until years later, when I watching *Oprah* she had this shrink on who was talking to these lame white women how visualizing saved the lives of these men in the bush in Cambodia. The shrink was making a connection between these POW's and these bored housewives. At the time, I didn't pick up on the connection, however, I did manage to learn and expand on the visualization piece. Whenever Zee would have company, or I would have to fuck some man because the rent was due, I would pretend I was in St. Maarten or Brazil or Tahiti. It would put me in a different place, a different mental zone where I did not have to concentrate on a motherfucker banging me, wanting me to call him "Big Daddy." I could see how these POW's needed to picture themselves somewhere else, so that they could get through the craziness that was going on around them.

I opened the package, and took a deep breath, and read through the dossier that Bird had prepared for me. Juliano "John" Petrone was born on May 28, 1965 in Camden, New Jersey. Petrone's rap sheet was as heinous as the day is long, with charges ranging from rape, sodomy, child pornography, kidnapping, breaking and entering, to grand theft auto, just to name a few. He had been in and out of jail or some kind of detention center since he was thirteen years old. It is amazing how many hardened criminals are allowed to walk the street, let alone have custody of children. I wondered why he wasn't under the jail. Vinny's and Sal's rap sheets looked pretty much the same. The hairs on the back of my neck stood up, as I thought about how much I would enjoy bringing them down.

As I sat patiently while Mike waded through rush-hour traffic, I am in Paris, where I am sharing lattés in a café overlooking the Seine with this deep, dark African prince. Some may call this crazy, I call it stress management.

Whizzing through the city on my bike is also calming. I figured that riding would better prepare me for the battle that lay ahead. The next thing I knew I was in my *Lady in Black* stealth fashion and pulled up to the House of Hunan. As I literally paraded into the restaurant, I saw what looked like a pile of blonde curls on a table near the back of the restaurant. I walked around the table and saw Ashley crying with a black eye.

Instinctively, I held this broken child in my arms, gently rocking her back and forth. We said nothing, because nothing needed to be said. Moments later, I ordered food for Ashley, knowing that she for the time being would be protected and safe, while I was handling business. Little did Ashley know, she would be with her aunt in Rochester, well before Christmas.

After the food came, I brushed back Ashley's hair, kissed her on the top of her head, and told her that I would be right back.

By that time, Mike had pulled up in the limo, as if on cue. "Ready, boss lady. Are you?" he said.

"I was born ready," I replied. As I slid into the limo, I began to prepare myself mentally. I had to be ready to take down three grown men. According to the dossier, they should've been good and drunk by nine p.m. Sloppy drunk, probably. However, just to be on the safe side, I grabbed my Glock. I instinctually reached into the secret compartment of the limo and felt around for my knife. This knife was like a security blanket in that we were such old friends. *Sting* had a three-and-one-half-inch pearl handle and a beautiful steel four-inch blade. She had helped me out of many "uncomfortable" situations and I never, ever left home without her. I pulled *Sting* out of her case to make sure she was cold, sharp and ready for use, and then placed her back in my leather coat. My adrenaline was pumping as we approached the house. "We are here, Skyy. Remember, I got your back," said Mike.

"You just keep your fine ass in the car," I replied. "I do not want you involved in this."

"You mean any more than I already am," said Mike.

"Aren't you the quick one?" I said as I got out of the car. Mike was holding the door and as I passed him, I brushed a quick kiss across his cheek as he whispered, "Be careful, *mi amore*. I love you," he said under his breath. I squeezed his forearm real tight.

As I approached the front door, I heard loud laughter. *I guess there is a party going on*, I thought. *Well, I'm gonna have to turn this party out.* I banged loudly on the door until a drunken Vinny came to the door. The sight of fresh meat made him salivate, smile, and rub his dick.

"What can I do for you, little lady? Would you like to join the party?" he said.

"Yeah, as a matter of fact, I would," I said. "Do you have any money?"

"Naw, but I got something better," said Vinny. "Hey Sal, looky here. It's our lucky day! I got some fine Black pussy for us."

"Let me see what you have first," I said. Vinny went to the kitchen and pulled out a big bag of weed and a smaller bag of white powder.

"Hook it up," I said as I sashayed over to Sal and slowly, methodically straddled his legs.

"Damn, you're a fine muthafucker," I purred as my stomach turned. Meanwhile Vinny was excitedly lining up the powder. I quickly perused the room to see what weapons may be laying around. These guys were low budget. I was sure they didn't even have a switchblade. I heard muffled noise in the back room.

"Who is that?" I asked the stupid one.

They both answered, "Jay is spending a little quality time with his daughter," and they both busted out laughing.

At that very moment my mind snapped and I angrily grabbed Sal's scrawny little neck and began to twist it like a fuckin' chicken. He was out like a two-bit whore who just got paid. *Dumb is out, Dumber to go*, I thought. While busy filling his nostrils with coke, Vinny had not even realized what had happened.

"Come here, lover," I cooed. "Don't walk though, baby, I want you to crawl."

"Cunt, what did you just say?" asked Vinny surprised yet a bit nervous.

"Crawl, bitch!" I growled, almost scaring myself. This whole scene had taken me to an incredible level of rage and at that moment I whipped out my Glock. Staring down the barrel at punk-ass Vinny, I saw that my trigger finger was literally twitching. "Crawl to me now, bitch, did you not hear me or do you need some help?" and I cocked my gun. Reluctantly, Vinny got on all fours and began to crawl at the same time as pitiful tears rolled down his pathetic, miserable face. When he got within striking distance, I put the barrel of the gun on his sweaty forehead and said, "So you like to fuck little girls, huh?"

"What are you talking about?" whimpered Vinny, as sweat continued to pour down his face.

Wham! I hit him right across the face with my gun.

"I said you like to fuck little girls, don't you?" Vinny began to sob. "You like fucking little girls, but now you're acting like one," I whispered. "Get up off the floor, you piece of shit."

Vinny slowly stood up, never taking his eye off the barrel of the Glock.

"Now turn around, face the door, and bend over," I said.

Vinny lunged and tried to swing on me. Instinctively, I moved to the right, causing Vinny to fall to the floor with a huge thud.

"Oh, baby, you got to come stronger than that." I cold cocked him again with the butt of my gun and placed the stiletto heel of my Prada boots on his Adam's apple. I whipped out my nylon rope, and tied his hands and feet real tight. I had done this a hundred times before and could do so with my eyes closed. I taped his mouth and expertly put my two forefingers at the sides of his temples and applied just the right amount of pressure in just the right spots. Mr. Macho Man went straight to sleep, like a baby.

I heard Sal start to move around so I stepped to him and hit him on the side of the head with the gun and began to tie "Dumb" up like I had tied up "Dumber." I took out the manila envelope that Bird had left for me in the locker and pulled out the two rap sheets for Vincent Perillo and Salvatore Nunez. I taped each rap sheet, nice and neatly, to the prisoners so the police would have no trouble finding out what priors Dumb and Dumber had.

I knocked on the bedroom door.

"Go away, we're busy," said Jay.

"Oh please, open the door," I said mockingly. "I want to join in."

Silence. Then the door slowly opened, and a young girl opened the door.

It was Ashley's sister, Phoebe, who had come back to check on her sister. Her face was bruised and she was practically nude. I looked directly at her and without a word from me she on cue went directly into the bedroom and slowly began to gather her things. She thankfully went into the living room and lay under a big blanket she found on the couch. She hoped that she would never see that living room again. Thank God she knew not to shower, because the police would want to do a rape kit, and the DNA they would gather from Phoebe would be enough to nail him.

"Who the fuck are you?"

"I am your worst nightmare, a Black bitch with an attitude, a gun and a reason." I slapped him hard in the face with my Glock. A huge gash materialized and blood spewed out all over the place as he hit the floor. Overcome with hatred of how he had hurt those poor girls, I stood over him and began to pummel him, harder and harder, until his face was mush. "Sick motherfucker!" I wanted to kill him. But I knew I didn't want for his blood to be on my hands. So, I took the rope and tape and hooked ol' boy up.

As I looked around at the destruction, it was almost as if *Sting* called out to me. "Please, Skyy, let me at him," I heard *Sting* whisper. Clearly I was going crazy. I started to laugh. Nothing could be as bad as what he had done to Phoebe, Ashley, Mary, and countless others. I slowly turned around, cocked my head to the side and just stared at Jay. With a stroke of brilliance, I walked back over to Jay, unzipped his pants, grabbed his super small penis and, with one fell swoop, cut the mutherfucker cleanly off.

I smiled for a minute realizing that that human waste would never abuse another person. Then a wave of incredible guilt came over me. Like a zombie, I went to the fridge and retrieved some ice, packed the organ in the ice, and placed it in a plastic bag. I picked up a crayon and wrote DICK on a sheet of construction paper and taped it to the bag. Then I retrieved more ice, placed a towel over the entire area, and packed his groin with ice. *You will never molest another child again, but you'll probably be someone's ho in prison*, I thought, as I emptied the bottle of Jack onto his wound.

I grabbed Phoebe, picked up Ashley and we got into the limo. I had Mike escort Ashley and Phoebe into the fourth district police precinct. Ashley had written in her diary, accounts of everything that had led up to this evening. There were pictures, provided by my boy Bird, and copies of the perpetrators' rap sheets.

I also had taken the liberty to forward copies of this information to the Bronx Assistant District Attorney, who was my brother Malcolm's best friend, and former Yale classmate. I didn't want to involve Malcolm directly in my drama, but I knew that after the ADA received this information, Malcolm would undoubtedly place himself in a position to be the DA on the Petrone case.

Before Ashley and her sister Phoebe went into the precinct, I told them I had contacted their Aunt Lana, and that she would be waiting to take them home with her. I also told them that they couldn't tell anyone about me and that the only thing I wanted for them to do was to keep me in their prayers. Although Ashley would never see me again, she would never forget me. She and her sister would be starting a new life. A life of love and peace. Ashley would finally be able to do something I never had a chance to do, play with dolls, jump rope, and do other girly things. But, as they say, it's all good. Everything happens for a reason.

And that...ladies and gentlemen...is just a little something that the *Lady in Black* does on a regular...a typical day at the office.

CHAPTER 7
Washington, D.C., 2006

Mike had the ride hooked up with all of my favorite goodies for a post-battle reception.

I mentioned earlier that I do not drink. Let me rephrase that: I do not drink often nor do I get drunk. I only allow myself *a drink* after I have successfully captured a criminal and have eluded the police. My ritual is one shot of brandy, a slice of cheese pizza, and a bottle of Evian. Then I cap it off with the second shot of brandy and fire up a Cohiba cigar.

After my first coup, to my surprise, Mike had secured the services of another limo driver, a recent Chilean dissident who didn't speak a word of English. This was a special treat because, Mike had joined me in the back, and he was on his third shot.

"Easy Boy, we have all night," I said. "By the way, how are your classes going?"

"Great. I had a final today. Sometimes it's hard trying to find time to study when I am driving you all over the world. That's why I am looking forward to tying one on with you. Where are we going, Boss Lady?"

"Don't forget, darlin', in six months you will be the proud recipient of an MBA and our plan will nearly be complete. I can finally see the light at the end of the tunnel! I'm going to call Puma and see if he wants to head over to that new club, Brasil. I feel like dancing. We have a lot to celebrate."

"I thought you may feel like hanging out, look what I bought you." Mike held up a long black Vera Wang dress, complete with plunging neckline. He then handed me a pair of Manolo Blahnik sandals.

"You really spoil me, *Miguel*," I said. "You think of everything."

"After all that you have done for me, this is the least that I can do, *mi amore*."

Mike kissed me with those soft pillow-like lips of his. One of these days, I am going to have a heart-to-heart with Miguel. But for now I'd have to put that conversation on ice. Nothing too deep right now, not after what I had just been through.

"Skyy, have you heard about those school murders?" asked Mike.

"Yeah, I read about them in the paper on the ride up. They sound pretty gruesome, another crazy motherfucker on the loose," I said.

This sounded like something that I might need to look into, but enough drama for one day. I'd have to deal with this later. But for now, I needed to clear my head, so I took out my cell phone and hit number four.

"Puma, are you busy?" I asked.

"Hey baby, where are you?" he asked.

"I'm in New York, with Mike and we wanted to know if you felt like partying. We are heading up to the new club, Brasil. I feel like a little salsa and a little tango."

"Give me half an hour. I am just leaving the Bronx," I said. "We'll pick you up at your place."

"I'll be waiting, beautiful," he said and hung up.

My boy "Puma Todd" is about forty-nine years old but looks like he's thirty-five. Puma put the "F" in fine! He has a mane of beautiful locks, that hang just below his shoulders. Puma does 200 push-ups, 300 sit-ups, and runs five miles daily. He is a vegan vegetarian and does not touch alcohol or any other non-organic substances. Puma is a man's man and has a heart of gold. He was awarded a Purple Heart for his service in Vietnam after his arm was nearly ripped off by a grenade. After many hours of therapy and a lot of hard work, the damage to his arm is hardly noticeable. The boy is just plain *BAD*.

Although Puma was drafted shortly out of high school and after our lit-tle "encounter," his martial arts background and tough-as-nails demeanor helped him land a spot as a Navy Seal in the U.S. Navy. These special forces is an elite division of military men who are taught a variety of survival skills, hand-to-hand combat, etc. They are the upper echelon, the crème of the crop of soldiers who were extremely disciplined and fearless.

Puma received many accolades from his commanders, which was unusual for a Black, non-commissioned soldier in the late 1960s. His soldier buddies nicknamed him "Puma" because like the mountain lion itself, Todd was a secretive cat who typically avoided people. And again, like a real puma, on those rare occasions when he was forced to attack, it was swift and vicious. For example, he single-handedly saved an entire unit of fifty men, who were surrounded by the Viet Cong. Puma earned a Medal of Honor, and caught the eye of a very prominent congressman, who recommended Puma to the elite CIA-Special Ops Unit that was forming to handle the Pinochet situation in Chile. Puma traveled around the world with the military, and spent a lot of time in South America.

Like me, Puma had never been married, and I didn't recall him dating anyone seriously. See, I know y'all thinkin' that the boy is sweet, but trust me; brother is as straight as an arrow. As a matter of fact, he had always had a major thing for me. Every once in a while, Puma jokes about us settling down, getting married, and having kids. I always play if off, because I know that I will *never* marry, it's just not in the cards for me. You see, I have *major trust issues*. I was so abused as a child, that I know that I could never fully trust a man romantically or otherwise. I've always had to look out for myself, so I have no idea how to let a man do it. I would never let my guard down long enough for any relationship to fully develop. It's one thing to have friendships like I have with Puma, Mike, and Bird, but it is quite another to love someone so hard that it aches. I do have to admit though; sometimes I do try to visualize myself being married and baking brownies and shit. I would have on a little yellow sundress and would be sipping lemonade by my pool. There would be two little girls in the back playing basketball, while my son would be sitting at the table in his football jersey, working on a science experiment or something.

But I know that that will never happen for me. Too much baggage, I am damaged goods; my mother made sure of that. Oh, I know that she did not do it intentionally, but she really didn't do anything to stop it either. So, what's done is done, and there is no use crying about it now. The good thing is that I have Malcolm and his family to love. They are my pride and joy in life.

We arrived at Puma's studio in lower Manhattan. As luck would have it, we made it back up town to Spanish Harlem in record time. *Party time! Brasil* is supposed to be off the hook! The good thing about this club is that there were not a lot of young hoochies hanging out, half naked. The crowd was mature and fun, and the dancing didn't stop until the last person left. It was like partyin' ole school. You won't see a bunch of sisters standing around hoping and praying that some sorry sucker in a tired suit with a business card asks them to dance.

Now let me talk about brothers who go to clubs in suits. It's one thing to go to a Happy Hour directly from your office and still have on your work clothes. But what I don't understand is why a brother would want to go into a hot club and wear a suit. A man wearing a suit in a club doesn't make any sense to me, unless he is perpetrating. He probably collects trash during the day, goes home, showers and puts on a suit so that he can look like a baller. Another thing, if I dance with you, please do not feel obligated to buy me a drink, and please do not expect me to hold a fifteen-minute conversation with you. Also, PLEASE, whatever you do, don't give me your business card unsolicited. Phew, the craziness never ends. See, that's why I usually keep my Black ass at home or I bring my own arm jewelry, so that I can deflect these tired men.

We walked in the joint and it was live. As soon as we got in the door, Mike grabbed me and dragged me onto the dance floor and just started a situation which created a dance scene. Miguel is a great dancer, but I remember when Miguel Jesus Maria Perez could *not* dance. I also remember a time when he would not even utter a single word. You see, Miguel was one of my early *Lady in Black* rescues. Basically, I helped to give him a new life.

CHAPTER 8
Santiago, Chile, 1980

M iguel Jesus Maria Perez was born to Juan and Gabriela Perez in
1965. In 1975, Juan Perez was hand-picked by General Augusto
Pinochet, the notorious Chilean dictator, to be an attaché to the
United States Government. As a graduate of the Universidad de Santiago
de Chile majoring in International Diplomacy, Juan was a military genius,
and as Pinochet and his cronies well knew, Juan Perez was a notorious
sick fuck.

Although Juan was married, with children, the regime knew of his side
interest in little boys. There was a great deal of poverty during that time
and there was an especially large homeless population among the children
in Chile, a factor that Juan openly exploited. During his reign of power,
he had lieutenants in the Chilean military build a special underground
dungeon, where he would hold the young boys captive.

After the bloody coup of 1973, the Marxist Chilean government was
extremely tumultuous. The U.S. government was sending special covert
forces in and out of many South American countries, like Chile. There
was a great deal of covert CIA activity going on while President Salvadore
Allende was still in office. After Pinochet, his Marxist regime, and armed
forces took over, U.S. officials became very uneasy and did not trust him
or his hand-picked administration in office. There were about $961 million
corporate American dollars in Chile that had to be protected, therefore,
the covert CIA Special Forces were to be involved. Puma Todd was one
of the soldiers sent to Chile to protect the "American interests."

By 1975, the Pinochet regime and Juan Perez were buck wild, openly breaking old laws and creating new ones, because they did not have to worry about any repercussions. If you were in with Pinochet, your shit was gold. So, suffice it to say that Juan was the man in Santiago. The world was his oyster, and he wasn't afraid to crack a few shells to get his pearls.

Unfortunately, Juan's son Miguel had a personality like his mom, humble and caring. Juan hated how weak and soft his son Miguel had turned out to be, and hated his wife for the effect she had on him. Miguel was a quiet, reserved young man, and did not participate in any traditional sports like futbol. He excelled in academics, and would rather read than play sports or hang out with his friends. Miguel was not your typical Chilean boy; he was very soft-spoken and to others seemed a little feminine, which was due to the fact that he lived in constant fear of his father. Juan was concerned about his son's masculinity, as rumors circulated about Miguel being gay. Ironically, one day Juan summoned Miguel to discuss Miguel's sexuality.

"Miguel, word has come to me that you are interested in men. Are you having sex?" asked Juan.

Miguel blushed and looked down at the floor in response to his father's question. "*Papi*, I have not had sex, and do not plan to until I fall in love," replied Miguel.

"You are fifteen and you have not had sex yet?" asked Juan.

"No, *Papi*, I have not," replied Miguel, still uncomfortable with his father's questions.

"If you have not had sex with a woman, then I would be inclined to believe that you're gay. So, I will ask you a direct question, are you gay?" demanded Juan.

"No, *Papi*, but I heard that you are," replied Miguel, as he began to be annoyed with his father's inquisition. "I've heard that you torture and abuse *los niños pobres*. I also heard that once a month, different American and Chilean businessmen come to play in your Chamber of Horrors. Last month after one of your all-night parties, I saw your henchmen carrying out three plastic bags. I wonder what was in those bags, *Papi*?"

Ironically, the Chamber of Horrors was located in Barrio Bella Vista, and near the historic Mint Palace, La Palacio de Moneda. Juan and one of his comrades accidentally discovered it while walking through some of the ruins left by the aerial bombings of President Pinochet's military regime. The Chamber must have been one of the filthy little secrets left "undiscovered" after Allende's suicide in the presidential quarters of La Palacio de Moneda.

"Your insolence will not be tolerated," said Juan, slapping Miguel across the face. "How dare you address your father in this manner! You will pay for these accusations. I don't know who you think you are talking to, I am Juan Perez, Special Consultant to General Pinochet. I will not allow you to stay in this house and disgrace the Perez name any longer."

At that moment, Captain Diaz, the head of the Chilean underground *policía*, came in and grabbed Miguel. "Take him away," said Juan and Miguel was gone.

The next morning, the school was notified that Miguel had been shipped off to a Swiss boarding academy, and Juan told Gabriela that Miguel had run away. Gabriela knew better, but had neither the capacity nor the inclination to challenge Juan's authority. She had tried it once before and ended up in the hospital. "*Vaya con Dios*, wherever you are, *mi hijo*," Gabriela prayed.

Little did she or Miguel know, but Juan had sentenced his own son to the underground Chamber, which was worse than Miguel ever could have imagined. It was cold and dark and had the biggest rats that he had ever seen. Captain Diaz searched Miguel for weapons and then stripped Miguel of his clothing, like a common criminal. Miguel felt lightheaded and queasy as Captain Diaz' search seemed very inappropriate as he lingered a little too long around his private parts.

I guess they are all pedophiles; I've got to get out of here, and soon. When the word gets out that I am Juan Perez' son, I am sure that all of Father's secret enemies, and I know he has many, will be down here to literally fuck me up, maybe even kill me, Miguel thought.

Miguel was thrown naked into a cell with a boy who appeared to be sixteen or seventeen.

"You get clothing later. Adios," said Captain Diaz.

Ten minutes later, a guard came to the cell, opened it, and threw Miguel a T-shirt, some shorts, and a pair of sandals. Miguel tried to pinch himself because at that point he really hoped that he was dreaming.

"What is your name?" the boy in the cell whispered.

"Pedro," Miguel lied. "What is yours?"

"Camillo," he said, and then there was silence, as though Camillo knew that the walls had ears.

"How long have you been down here?" Miguel asked.

"I think I have been here for sixty days, but I have lost count. Since there are not windows, it is hard to keep track. I have been here the longest and I think I am the oldest."

"Where are the others?"

"There are about twenty others ranging in age from about ten to eighteen. They are too scared to speak because they have seen first-hand what happened when you open your mouth."

"What happens?" Miguel asked, afraid of what the answer would be.

Miguel had to strain to hear, as Camillo whispered to him in fear. "One boy was caught telling another new boy about what to expect down here and some of what had been going on. A guard overheard him," he said, pausing to look and listen for the footsteps of a guard. "That night, a special meeting was called where approximately ten guards and Juan Perez himself attended. Juan had brutally sexed and sodomized the boy, and then cut out his tongue." Miguel could feel the boy shiver, as he continued to whisper his story. "As we all watched in horror, he told all the boys that the same would happen to anyone else who is caught talking," Camillo whispered. He could barely finish his story when he immediately went into the corner of the cell to throw up.

Although Miguel had often been the recipient of his father's temper, he could not believe that his father was capable of such a brutal act. Miguel had to get out of there as soon as possible, and Camillo would have to help him.

"Okay, we gotta get out of here," Miguel said desperately. "How can we do it?"

"I have been thinking of a plan for about a month now," said Camillo. "I started developing my plan to escape the minute after Pepe's tongue was removed. The best time that we can escape is during one of 'the parties.' It will be risky because there are so many people there. But it's the best time to do it, because the guards always let us out so that we can change," continued Camillo. "They are so excited about getting ready for the party that they are not as careful about our whereabouts."

"They actually make you change clothes for the party?" asked Miguel.

"Yes," said Camillo. "They make all the boys dress like girls. They allow us about two hours time to put on an expensive dress, heels, a wig, perfume, and make-up," whispered Camillo, looking around to see if anyone was listening. "I figure that during that time we can disappear."

"Has anybody ever tried to escape before?" asked Miguel.

"No, not that I am aware of," replied Camillo. "Everyone else is too scared, but not me. I would rather die than have to participate in another one of those rape fests," said Camillo.

"When is the next party?" asked Miguel.

"I overheard one of the guards talking about Friday night," responded Camillo.

"Well, today is Monday, so that means we have four days to prepare," said Miguel. "Are you sure you can trust me?"

"*Mi hermano*, I have no choice, besides I have a feeling that God has sent you." Camillo sighed.

The two young men huddled in the corner, and continued to devise a plan.

Juan sat in his study deep in thought. Had he been too hard on Miguel? He wanted the best for his son. But he could not tolerate the embarrassment of having a gay son. Earlier, Miguel had denied that he was gay. Juan was *not* gay, which is why he demanded that the boys always dress as women. Juan was a "ladies man," and he loved women, *didn't he*? It was just that Juan wished that he could control these internal urges, and that the sight of a naked young boy's anatomy didn't send his blood rushing through his veins. That didn't make him sick, did it? Not at all, reasoned

Juan. He was *un fuertisimo hombre*, and it was okay that he liked a little diversion here and there. What really repulsed Juan was *weak men*. He detested weakness, and Miguel appeared to be turning into what was his worst nightmare. Keeping Miguel in the Chamber for about a week would toughen him up; make a man out of him. For Juan, this week of torture would have to cure him from having any desires for young boys and at the same time, make a MAN out of Miguel. Juan was sure of it.

Tough love, he thought. All the Americans were talking about that concept. Juan would use tough love on Miguel.

✗ ✗ ✗

"There is a young guard who I often see praying. His name is Jose Martinez," revealed Camillo. "I also hear the other guards make fun of him because he never participates during the parties," Camillo explained.

"Well, it sounds like Jose is our man. I will try to speak to him today," said Miguel. "When does he usually come around?"

"He is the guard that they send to deliver our one meal a day, which I think is usually around lunchtime," said Camillo.

"We only get one meal a day?" Miguel asked.

"They want to keep us weak so that if we try to run away, we won't get very far," said Camillo.

"I guess they think of everything," replied Miguel.

"That they do but we'll outsmart them, won't we, Pedro?" said Camillo, extending his hand to shake.

For a half-second, Miguel forgot that his new name was "Pedro," but instinctively extended his hand and said, "With God's help we will."

Camillo nodded, and smiled, which was something he had not done in a while.

That afternoon, Miguel saw Jose carrying food trays to the prisoners, and immediately fell to the floor pretending to be sick. Jose rushed to the cell and asked, "Is everything all right?"

Miguel grabbed Jose's hand and looked him straight in the eyes and said, "Friday, Camillo and I will escape and you will help us. Won't you?"

"I cannot," said Jose.

"God knows your heart, Jose," said Miguel. "He knows that you do not like these parties and do not want to see these boys being tortured and killed. With this simple act of kindness, you can help to set things straight and you can begin to atone for some of your sins. And I know that you know that, *the wage of sins is death in a fiery furnace.*"

Jose closed his eyes. "Yes, you are right. I can no longer continue to hide my shame. I cannot do this alone," said Jose. "I know someone who can help you. They call her *La Senorita De Negra*. She will be at the party on Friday and she is going to be the make-up artist that puts the makeup on the boys. No one knows who she is, but me."

"*Bueno*," said Miguel. "We will need a bit more food so that we can gain some strength, and you will also need to sneak us two knives and a handgun. Can you handle that?"

"*Si*," said Jose.

"*Muchas gracias*, Jose," Miguel said, as he extended his hand in friendship. And in a gesture of friendship, Jose shook Miguel's hand.

During the next few days, Miguel and Camillo prepared for their escape. Very quietly, they did push-ups and sit-ups, ran in place and practiced breathing exercises. One of the many perks of being Juan Perez's son was that Miguel had the opportunity to take fencing lessons. His instructor also thought Juan was a little soft and thought that the other boys may pick on him, so he had taken the liberty to also show Miguel a little bit about knife warfare. Although at the time, Miguel felt that the lessons were a little unnecessary, he now thanked God for knowing how to use a knife for purposes other than eating food. When he knew that no one was listening, Miguel shared some of the secrets of self-defense with Camillo.

On Thursday, the two received more than just the usual rice and water. They were given rice and beans, biscuits, plantains, and juice. On Friday, Jose provided Miguel and Camillo with the same diverse menu. As Jose placed their tray on the floor in their cell, he uttered, "I am coming with you," and left. Jose had taped two knives to the bottom of the food trays.

Early Friday evening, as the girl's clothing was being delivered, the boys could smell the aroma of food being prepared for the huge banquet-sized table. They heard footsteps going up and down as servants artistically displayed a variety of delicacies and libations for the anxious guests. Miguel could hear several of the boys quietly sobbing, because they knew what was in store for them.

After the boys were dressed, *La Senorita De Negra* began to apply make-up one by one. "*Que Linda*!" whispered Miguel. "Do you think that is her?"

"*Sí*, that is her," responded Camillo.

"She barely looks eighteen," said Miguel in amazement.

"According to Jose, she is actually younger than that," said Camillo.

"I can't believe this *shit!*" thought Skyy. "Grown-assed men, trying to pretend that they aren't sick and twisted. No matter how much make-up and clothes they put on them, after they undress these boys, they will still have penises. Sick motherfuckers! Look at these boys! Half of them are scared shitless! Wondering 'why me?' How did they end up here? What did they do to deserve this? I want to shake them and say, 'NOTHING!' They are the sick motherfuckers, not you. These boys were just 'unlucky' enough to be born poor. Little do they know, these nasty little men are about to become the 'unlucky' ones! LA NEGRA is about to turn this sick little party out!"

As I was plotting my strategy in my head, it was Miguel's turn for make-up. After I finished expertly applying the make-up, I took his wig off the mannequin and placed it on his head and whispered, "I am *La Negra*. A knife is in your wig. Good luck and Godspeed."

Precisely at eight p.m., the first guests began to arrive and the band started to play loudly as the *Man of the Hour* entered the room. Juan wondered where his son was, he wanted Miguel front and center so he could have a good seat when he witnessed the barbaric festivities. Juan asked one of the guards to direct him to his son. He winced as he gazed upon his son dressed to the nines, complete with sequin dress and stiletto pumps.

He approached Miguel and asked, "Son, are you okay?"

Silence, as Miguel's eyes glared at his father through the heavy mascara on his eyelashes and dark eye shadow.

"Miguel, I asked you, how are you?" demanded Juan, grabbing him and shoving him into his cell.

Camillo stood frozen in his tracks as the architect of his nightmare approached his cell mate. "Son?!?" he wondered.

"How do you think I am doing, Dad?" said Miguel. "You made my life a living hell and now you will spend the rest of eternity there." As he looked directly into his father's eyes, Miguel gently thrust a knife into his father's rib cage. His instructor was right, the element of surprise is the best offense. Look your enemy directly in the eyes and go for the kill.

As his father's body slumped to the ground, Miguel quickly searched Juan's body for any weapons and found a small .22-caliber gun, Miguel stuffed the gun into his underwear, under his gown. Since the cell door was still open and unguarded, Miguel and Camillo were able to slip out. As they were walking down the hall, they noticed a guard approaching. Camillo and Miguel froze in their steps. As he got closer, they realized that it was Jose, who immediately took Miguel by the arm. Just then, a big burly guard approached the threesome and asked, "Where are you taking them?"

"*Señor* Juan asked for these two personally," said Jose.

The burly guard approached Camillo, licked his lips, and grabbed Camillo by the balls. Miguel could see Camillo's eyes darken and body tense up.

"I've had my eye on you for a while," said the guard. "I will see you after *Señor* Perez has his way, if there is anything left." With that, the gigantic guard released Camillo's testicles, laughed, and walked away.

They were three feet from the back door when suddenly, Captain Diaz stood in front of them blocking the doorway and questioned, "Where do you think you're going?" The three would-be escapees froze in their tracks, each trying to figure out how to get by the Captain without making too much of a scene. It was then that they heard the sultry voice of a *real* woman.

"I've been looking for you all night, *querido*," said Skyy, trying not to throw up. "Let's go someplace where I can show you how much I have missed you," said Skyy, as she distracted him with the caresses of her deadly hands.

"Not now, Sandy," said Diaz, as he tried to shake off Skyy's grip. "I think I have a situation here. It looks like these three are trying to escape," yelled the Captain.

While I gently massaged his back with my left hand, I retrieved my knife by its pearl handle, that I had holstered in my bra with my right hand, maneuvering it so that I had the knife properly positioned and ready. Just as Captain Diaz recognized Miguel, I lunged, and reached for the gun in his holster. Instinctively and quickly, Miguel grabbed the gun from the cleavage in his dress and capped Diaz, twice in the stomach. His belly was so fat that it acted as a silencer.

As I checked to make sure that scumbag was dead, Miguel checked to make sure that the coast was clear. As they exited the Chamber, we hugged and I handed Miguel a pocket full of money. At that instant Miguel looked deeply into my eyes for about three seconds. He then turned and ran and kept running for the next few hours. I stayed behind, to make sure that Miguel and his friends had enough of a lead to escape.

It would be several hours before Perez' and Diaz' bodies would be found, because the party-goers assumed that Juan and the Captain had their own "private" party going on with the new boy and Camillo.

CHAPTER 9
South America, 1980

Jose was able to stash three pairs of pants, T-shirts, sweatshirts, coats, and shoes in a backpack that he had hidden in the brush about a mile from the Chamber. The escapees did not, however, stop to change until they were about two miles away from the secret prison. Since it was so late in the evening, they stopped in a bar and went into the bathrooms to change. When the initial two women came out as boys, no one noticed because most of the patrons were too drunk to care. As easily as it was for them to slip into the bar as "girls," it was easy for the three to leave as men.

They were all so tired that they were tempted to stop and rent a room for the rest of the night, but quickly decided against it. They pressed forward for fear that by this time, their escape plot had been discovered. Before the group took off, Miguel was able to talk the cook into packing them same empanadas and water. He knew that they needed to get out of the city, before they were recognized. From the southwest side of the city, Miguel and his newfound friends followed the banks of Mapocho River, northward out of the city.

After a few hours, the three young men were getting hungry and Jose encouraged them to stop at the next farm. Knowing his colleagues, he argued that at this late hour, if there were any manhunts underway, they had probably ceased and that everyone was probably asleep by now. Jose knew how lazy the bullies at the Chamber were, and that they probably looked for escapees for an hour, maximum.

"I am sure that initially a manhunt ensued but after an hour's time, they decided not to let all that food and drink go to waste," said Jose.

"The Commander probably made a toast to honor the slain Juan Perez and Captain Diaz." Camillo laughed.

As they opened the door to the barn, they were relieved to find that there was no one there. They collapsed in a secluded area of the barn, on a soft bale of hay and began to devour the empanadas given to them at the bar in the city. As Camillo reached for one last empanada, he turned to look at his partners who were fast asleep. Shortly thereafter Camillo fell asleep too.

At about noon, the threesome awoke to the sound of the cocking of a sawed-off shotgun.

"Who are you?" she questioned.

Miguel and the others tried to focus, but the haze of light behind the woman's head made it difficult to see her face. The only reason that they knew that she was a woman was because they could see the outline of her figure and her skirt.

"Who are you?" she asked again, annoyed by their silence.

"We just escaped from a prison called the Chamber in Santiago, where I was tortured and held captive for a long time," said Camillo. "Here, look at my scars," continued Camillo as he took off his shirt and showed his scars and bruises. The woman started to cry, and told the story of her grandson, Emilio Cheyre Bachelet, who had been missing for three months. She told Miguel that he reminded her of her grandson.

Señora Cheyre formally introduced herself and offered them lunch, maps, and some money. She told them that they must be going because she heard some women in the village speaking of a manhunt that was sweeping across the outskirts of Santiago. The military and *el policía* were looking for the killers of Juan Perez and a high-ranking captain in the militia. Señora Cheyre gave them enough food and water to sustain them for a day or two. As she watched them run, she bowed her head while tracing the sign of the cross on her chest, *in nome de padre, hijo, y espiritu santo, vaya con Dios.* Kissing her index and middle fingers she looked toward the heavens and blew a kiss into the air.

While the trio of friends moved eastward, toward the Andes Mountains…

I, *La* Senorita De Negra, on the other hand, was not so lucky. After the guard had uncovered the two murdered men, the Chilean military officials were immediately called in to search every nook and cranny of the Chamber. As they interviewed each of the party-goers who were in attendance at the heinous soiree, I tried the best that I could to quietly slip away unnoticed, however, my connection to the plot was detected.

"Senorita, *donde va? W*here are you going?" asked a military police officer. "We have not as yet inspected your person. Would you be so kind as to hand over your evening bag and your cosmetic bag?"

This was the most polite official that I had ever met in Chile thus far. I grinned and told myself that this was going to be a breeze. The Chilean official searched my bag and found the usual contents. I continued to smile, and was relieved that he did not check my person. Or at least I thought so, until it happened.

"Please step forward so that I may check you, or shall I say, um, excuse me, I need for you to, um, please allow me to," the guard stammered, embarrassed by the whole scene. Then a big, burly guard grabbed me and said, "I do not know what his problem is," and he grabbed my dress and tore it.

The gun that was strapped to my leg was made visible at that point and then the burly motherfucker exclaimed, "I got her."

At this point, every guest came to see what the commotion was about. That's when big burly motherfucker, who I'm gonna call "BBMF" from here on out, proceeded to kick my ass and throw me in the cell.

I don't know how long I was out, when I was suddenly awakened from a beautiful dream by the cold water that was thrown on my face. I opened my eyes to see three angry men glaring at me, with BBMF in the middle of this threesome. I had to dig down deep to find the strength that I would need to get through this. But *trust*, as grim as it looked, I had no doubt that God had my back, and I could get through whatever was in store for me. I said a little prayer, and took a deep breath, to prepare myself for what was next.

The Andes Mountains
Somewhere between Chile and Argentina, 1980

Meanwhile, back at the proverbial ranch, Miguel and his entourage knew that they would have to cross the Andes Mountains, into Argentina if they wanted to escape. Luckily for the group, Jose was *mestizo*, and had learned a little of the *Aymaran* language of the Andes people from his grandmother. Jose was able to get great advice about the best routes to take, where it would be safe to stop and rest, and how they could find food within mountain range.

The terrain was treacherous and the mountains were so high that they spent most of the trip lightheaded. For weeks, the three escapees traversed from the temperate tropical rainforests, to the snowy mountain peaks of Cotopaxi. Because they weren't really prepared to be exiles of their beloved country of Chile, the threesome did not have the appropriate gear for the wide range of climates that they would face in their journey, but they persevered. They had good and bad days as they traveled further into the mountains, sleeping in the ancient Incan acqueducts at night and traveling on the ancient Incan roadways during the day. A few times, Miguel and his companions were so weary that they almost slid off of the cliffs.

After a week of being in the mountains, an overwhelming sense of exhaustion set in. Camillo had suffered from two months of extreme malnutrition in the Chamber, and his legs felt like rubber. The mountains were more than he had bargained for, and he wasn't sure if he would be able to endure. The exposure to the elements was insufferable; at times, winds whipped around them at fifty miles an hour, causing temporary blindness. Camillo felt that he was too weak and delirious, and would not be able to continue the journey, and begged the other two to stop and return to Santiago. Jose and Miguel insisted that they press ahead, and that whatever was in front of them was better than what would happen to them if they returned home to Santiago. They were wanted men, and would face a fate worse than they had experienced in the Chamber.

Camillo knew that Miguel and Jose would not leave him, but he also didn't want to hold them back. So, while Miguel and Jose were taking a nap, after an hour of reflection and prayer, Camillo decided to put himself out of his misery and throw himself over a cliff. Disillusioned and saddened by his act, yet committed to the future, Miguel and Jose made a pact that they would honor Camillo's bravery and experience by continuing on.

Grieving for Camillo's suicide and delirious from the entire ordeal, Jose and Miguel continued their journey. After nearly a month of wandering through the range, despite the treacherous conditions, there was finally hope in that they could see lights up ahead. It looked as if it would take them another day to get to the foot of the mountain, to what looked like a little resort village that Miguel and his family used to ski at when he was a child.

The most wonderful aspect of this town was that they were not only out of Santiago and Chile, but they were now in Argentina. Mendoza, a small year-round ski resort town, was located at the foot of the Aconcagua Mountain, one of the highest peaks in the world.

When Miguel and Jose finally reached their destination, they were overwhelmed with joy. It had taken them almost a month to cross the Andes into Argentina, and they were exhausted, hungry, and suffering from low-grade hypothermia. As they approached the hotel, they realized that they looked very worn and haggard, as they inquired about lodging for the night.

Before Miguel and Jose could get to the front desk, they were approached by a young, clean-shaven Black gentleman, who ushered them away from the reception area.

"Do you know that half of Chile is looking for you?" said Todd.

"Who are you?" asked Miguel.

"They call me Puma Todd," said Puma. "United States Central Intelligence Agency."

Miguel and Jose looked at each other and smiled, as if they had just met Santa Claus in person.

They followed Puma to his car and hopped in. Miguel and Jose were asleep before they left the driveway of the chalet. Puma drove about an hour and a half east of Mendoza, and stopped at a dilapidated shack. Miguel and Jose got out of the vehicle and followed Puma into the rundown house. The interior looked nothing like the outside because it was smartly furnished and had what appeared to be a million dollars of high-tech surveillance equipment.

"This is a safe house for a CIA Special Forces Team," said Puma.

"How did you know who we were?" Miguel asked.

"Your friend, *La Negra*, got a message to us before she was captured," said Puma. "That is why I was on the lookout for you three. The team had a hunch that you would show up in Mendoza. We knew that Miguel had to leave Chile. According to our extensive files, this place was a favorite vacation spot of the Perez family."

"Was *La Negra* captured?" Miguel groaned. "Is she all right?"

"As far as we know, she is still alive," said Puma. "But I haven't heard from her since our last contact. I am hopeful that she hasn't been or will be tortured or killed. Which is part of the reason I brought you here, we need your help to rescue Sandy."

"Sandy?" Jose asked.

"Yes, Sandy is *La Negra's* real name. She has been operating as a mole within the Perez clan."

"What do you mean by a 'mole'?" Jose asked nervously.

"She is a spy with the CIA, am I right, Puma?" Miguel retorted.

"She is indeed," said Puma. "And since she saved your lives, now you boys have to help me rescue her."

"Certainly, but we must also rescue the other prisoners, and put an end to the Chamber once and for all," Miguel said. Jose nodded in agreement.

Puma Todd called in two other agents, Tim Mathers and Shane O'Neil and introduced them. The five men then devised a rescue scheme and discussed how they would sneak back into Chile. Because Miguel and Jose were wanted men, Puma had insisted that the two provide them information about the Chamber, and then CIA agents would take it from there. However, Miguel and Jose insisted that they wanted to go back to help. After many minutes of arguing, Puma conceded and agreed that

Miguel and Jose could definitely help expedite the mission. Puma gave the two young men five hours of rest and replenishment, while the CIA team finalized the plot to rescue Skyy and the rest of the Chamber prisoners. At approximately midnight, the band of five bordered a chopper that took them across the Chilean border in four hours. They left at midnight because Jose knew that there would be only a hand full of guards in the Chamber in the early morning hours. The U.S. military was poised and ready for back-up, with soldiers, and had seven hundred and twenty-seven waiting at the Arturo Merino Benítez International Airport.

At 0400, the five commandoes arrived at the Chamber, and since the guards were fast asleep, they took the guards at the Chamber by surprise. Armed with Glocks and silencers, Tim and Shane swiftly took out the four guards before any of them could wake and warn the others. Puma removed the keys from one of the dead guards and handed Jose the keys to open all of the cells. The boys in the cells awoke to the sound of the cell doors opening, many of them began to cry, thinking that it was "party" night. Even with the cell door wide open, they didn't know what to do. Puma and Miguel had to go from cell to cell to lead the boys out, assuring them that they were free to leave and go home to their families. Puma left Tim and Jose behind to help the boys find their way out.

Puma, Miguel, and Shane were on a mission to find Skyy. Though the time that he had spent with Miguel, Puma could sense that Miguel was indeed different than most boys his age. Miguel was not only smart, but he was also courageous; Puma felt a special bond with Miguel. Since Sandy hadn't been in the Perez regime long enough to get enough reconnaissance information, Puma was lucky that the son of Perez was on his team. Miguel could certainly provide them with the information that they would need to get in and out and save Sandy.

Miguel, Puma, and Shane snuck into the Perez estate to find Gabriela Perez bedridden. She was extremely ill and was knocking on death's door. She faintly smiled at the sight her son, because she had feared that like her husband, her son was also dead.

"Mama, I am back," said Miguel.

"Oh, I am so happy to see you," said Gabriela. "I thought you were dead. But you must quickly go, *mi hijo*, for they will surely kill you."

"Mama, we are looking for a young woman named *La Negra*," said Miguel.

"*La Negra*?" exclaimed Gabriela. "That bitch was involved in this whole Chamber business. She killed your father! She is being held captive, which is what she deserves," Gabriela said with tears in her eyes.

"No, Mama, *La Negra*, I mean Sandy, saved my life. Now we must save hers. Can you please help us?"

Gabriela told the three men to hide in her bathroom, while she summoned the head guard at the estate. The guard reluctantly told the sick woman that the American woman was being held at the local police precinct and that she was being guarded by Pinochet's own special henchman. The guard reassured Gabriela that there was no way that *La* Negra would be able to escape.

N N N

Days had passed and they were torturing me slowly. At first they were nice, with Juan's death, and the local police were working with American officials. These last couple of days had been rough though. I decided if I got out of this one alive, I would go back to the States. This shit was insane.

"Who are you, and what is your name, *puta de madre*?" BBMF screamed.

I wish this motherfucker would cool out, thought Skyy. *What this boy needs… is a good fuck.*

"For the last time, my name is Sandy Gonzales. I was born in the United States. I came to Chile to locate my mother Isabella Sanfuentes Gonzalez. All I know is that her last known whereabouts were in either *La Dehesa* or *Lo Barnechea* barrios. I have not been successful and I ran out of money. I met Captain Diaz one night, he asked me a lot of questions and when he found out that I was from New York, he asked me if that was where all the movie stars lived. Since I lived in *La Manzana*, he thought that I could be a make-up artist for his 'show.' I knew a little something about make-up application so I jumped at the chance to make some money. I figured that he could also help me find *mi madre*."

"Why did you have the gun?" asked the polite official.

"I'm from the streets of New York," I said. "I always have protection because a girl never knows who will not take no for an answer."

The polite officer smiled but BBMF did not.

"I do not believe you, Sandy Gonzalez, or whatever your name really is," BBMF said. "I think you are one of those Americans that cannot keep their nose out of my country's business. I think that you helped those two boys escape. I also think that you killed Perez and Diaz."

"Why would I cut off my major sponsor?" I asked. "That doesn't make any sense." *You stupid idiot*, I thought.

"It really does not matter to me about the murders. I hated Perez and his perverted parties," said the polite official. "However, I do feel that the more pressing matter is the involvement of the United States government. I cannot work with the dirty Americans any longer. We must get to the bottom of this, Ms. Gonzalez, and I do hope that you can provide us with the assistance that we are requesting. Is that a deal?" His eyes widened, hoping that his "good cop" approach would make Skyy confess her involvement. "If you cannot provide us with the truth in a timely manner, I will have no choice but to let Sergeant Vasquez question you alone."

"Why don't you believe me?" I asked. "I swear that I am telling the truth."

"Good day, Ms. Gonzalez, and good luck," and with that, Mr. Polite Police Official and the Sergeant Nondescript were gone.

"I guess it's just you and me, sweetheart," said BBMF, unzipping his pants as he approached Skyy.

With my hands tied above my head, and my feet tied to the bottom of the cell bed, I closed my eyes and began to think about both physical and mental ways to escape. And just as BBMF was about to lie on top of me, I felt the weight of his entire body. I opened my eyes and realized that BBMF was passed out cold. I adjusted my body and let his body fall to the ground. I looked up to the ceiling, closed my eyes and said, "Thank you, God."

"Just in the nick of time, as usual," said the finest man on the planet. "I've been called many things, but I think that being called 'God' outside of the bedroom is a first!" He smiled and winked at me.

I smiled when I saw that this fine man was my boy Puma and said, "What took you so long?" I laughed. "I almost became a memory, not to mention poked to death with a human pencil. Did you see the size of his dick?"

Luckily for me, Puma had shot the BBMF in the rolls of fat in his neck with a dart filled with poison. He had expertly hit the intended target, as hard as it was to find.

Puma began to hack off the handcuffs when the gorgeous young man rushed up, gushed, and asked, "Are you okay?"

"Yes, I am fine, baby," I replied.

"You sure are." Puma flirted.

"We need to get me out of here and quickly," I said. "I'm sure they expect BBMF to be a 'minute man,' so the others should be back shortly."

"Who?" said Puma.

"Never mind." I smiled. "It's a long story, let's go."

CHAPTER 10
New York, 2006

After Mike and I finished dancing, we sat down for a drink.

"Are you having fun tonight?" asked Mike. I nodded as I eased myself into the private VIP section.

"Yes, I am," I responded. "Tonight I saved the lives of two young girls and now I am with two of New York's most eligible bachelors. It doesn't get any better than this."

Just then Puma walked up. He had been dancing with some salsa diva that kept him in her clutches and on the floor for at least a half an hour. And just as sleek and sultry as he had been on the dance floor, like a puma cat, the salsa diva turned around and Puma had disappeared into the crowd.

"Whew, I just can't party like I used to," Puma said as he breathed heavily. "I think I will call it a night."

"Yeah, I guess it is getting late and Mike and I need to be heading back to D.C.," I said.

"You're going back tonight?" asked Puma. "I thought that maybe we could have lunch or see a movie tomorrow."

"I wish I could, but I have to close this Japanese deal and I need to tie up some loose ends in D.C. before I come back for the big presentation next week," I responded.

"So it's a date then, next week?" asked Puma. "Don't stand me up, girl. I know you have a few minutes for an old friend."

"Old friend is right," I said. "Did I see you doing the Robot?" We all laughed and finished off our drinks.

After we dropped Puma off, Mike and I headed back to my loft in SoHo, quickly changed our clothes, hopped in the limo and headed back to D.C. We pulled into D.C. at approximately five a.m., and I had a nine a.m. meeting. I was restless and knew I would never be able to sleep, so I threw on my Seven jeans, T-shirt, Timbs, bandanna, leather jacket and damn near ran to the garage. Riding was such a release for me. The Knight was for ridin' into the Black Skyy.

⚡ ⚡ ⚡

"The presentation didn't go as well as I expected, I don't know why the data on those handouts were so off. Luckily for me, I knew the figures by heart," I thought.

I went to the bathroom that was the closest to the conference room to freshen up and prepare for the next part of the meeting. "Boy, I guess I really can't hang like I used to. These last thirty-six hours have been a bear," I thought.

In the bathroom I noticed that had a run in my stockings, so I rushed to my office to get another pair and brought them back to the bathroom to change. You pay $50 for stockings and they should never run. They should damn near walk for you and they should repair themselves. Anyway, I started changing when I heard the door to the bathroom open.

"Girl, I am so tired of this job," Deena said.

"I am so tired of these people and taking all those damned notes at those boring-ass meetings. I am especially tired of Ms. Sandy," cackled Karen. "Yeah she gets on my last nerve with all that kissing up to Mr. Bledsoe."

"It didn't look like Mr. Bledsoe was kissing up to her," said Deena. "Although, you have to admit that her presentation was like that, she was definitely on point."

"Well, all I have to say is that she better leave my man alone," Karen replied.

"Wait a minute, baby, your man Mr. Bledsoe is *married*," said Deena.

"Only for a minute," said Karen. "I told you that he is divorcing Tanya."

"I'll believe it when I see it," said Deena. "You know what they say; 'it's cheaper to keep her.'"

"Tanya does seem like the type that would try to take a man for everything he has," said Karen. "But he doesn't love her; she needs to just leave him alone."

"What are you talking about?" Deena asked. "Tanya helped him build this company."

"Says who?!" Karen scoffed. "Tanya is always going to some Delta luncheon and is forever on some shopping spree, and spends all of their money."

"Sounds like you 'straight hatin','" said Deena. "And I think her 'shopping sprees' are about buying clothing for the women she helps through her nonprofit organization. You're just jealous." Deena laughed.

"I'll show you whose hatin'," said Karen. "One day Mr. Bledsoe will be mine, mine, all mine and Miss Tanya and Miss Sandy will be the ones who are shit out of luck."

"Yes, but don't forget, Karen," said Deena, "What goes around, comes around."

"Well," Karen said, "then it is time, that I got mine. I almost made sure that Ms. Sandy got hers. Did you see that look on her face when she discovered that two pages from her report were missing? I could hardly contain myself."

"Did you do that, Karen?" asked Deena.

"But of course. I would do anything to sabotage that bitch, and that was only the beginning," said Karen. "I have been dropping little hints to Mr. Bledsoe on how he should fire Sandy. He does stick up for her a lot, telling me how invaluable she is. He needs to remember how *invaluable* this pussy is."

"No comment," Deena replied.

Just then Karen and Deena heard a toilet flush. I strutted as hard as I could to the sink to wash my hands, reapply my lipstick, and fluff my wig. As I smoothed the hem of my St. John suit, I looked toward the two witches, who were standing there with their mouths hanging open and eyes bulging. Smoothly, I walked up to Karen and looked her up and down with disdain and pity and said, "Guess what, Karen, you are so *fired*."

"I'm what?!" said an exasperated Karen. "You can't fire me. I'll tell Mr. Bledsoe."

"No, no sweetie. *I'll* tell Mr. Bledsoe," I said. "I'm going out to dinner with him and his wife tonight."

"I'll get you if it's the last thing I do!" Karen snarled.

"Let me tell you something, Miss Wannabe Homewrecker," I said. "You have *no* idea who you are fucking with. I have had little skeezers like you for lunch and spit them out. You don't know anything about me. So I would advise you to go to your office, pack your shit, and go. You have about an hour to pack your raggedy shit, leave your corporate trinkets behind, and be escorted out by security." As I turned to walk away, I stopped in my tracks, turned on my heels and said, "Oh, and by the way, enjoy the rest of your day, Deena," and walked out of the ladies room.

CHAPTER 11
New York, 1978

It has been a year since Momma's death. The images of her last moments are still so vivid in my mind. Sometimes it all seems like a dream. There were happy times for us in the beginning. Before heroin there was laughter and joy. There were sounds of Momma playing the piano. The one frame that is forever stamped in my brain is of one Sunday afternoon after church. We came home and had a huge lunch; Malcolm had spread out three coloring books, and began to color. Mom played the piano—I can still hear that bright song, "The Candy Man." Then I start to sing and dance like I was Sammy Davis, Jr. "Who can take the sunshine, wrap it in a dream? The Candy Man, the Candy Man can, the Candy Man can 'cause he mixes it with love and makes the world taste good."

The world sure doesn't taste good now. The world is mean and cruel and ugly, and it doesn't matter that you're only fifteen. I have to take care of Malcolm all by myself and it's been real hard. I almost had to drop out of school and I had always been an "A" student. I could barely make ends meet financially while regularly attending class. For the most part, Malcolm had blocked out Zee's murder. He bopped around the house like nothing had happened. Well, I guess that was best. Let little man enjoy his youth. He was also an "A" student and I was working toward getting him into a private school in upstate New York. It was an all-white school but every year they gave a full scholarship, including room and board, to some ghetto kid.

When a reporter from *The New York Daily News* had come nosing around after an informer told him about Zee's untimely and barbaric demise, he decided it best to not do the story. He did, however, tell me that he would do everything possible to help me so I could effectively elude the authorities. Unfortunately, his wife didn't want a fifteen-year-old girl and her baby brother to live with them. The reporter, Van Green, kept in touch and suggested that St. Mary's Episcopal Prep School in the Catskills would be a good place for Malcolm to excel. It would allow him to get away from these dangerous streets that could only harm him. Somehow, Mr. Green already knew that I was a lost cause.

So I put all of my energy into finding us food, paying the rent, and gathering the necessary paperwork for Malcolm's application. The hardest job of all was not letting anyone think that we were living alone. I knew that any minute Social Services could come into our apartment and take Malcolm and me away. That would mean that I would be separated from my lifeline, which I could not let happen. I told all the tenants in the building that my grandmother had come to live with us. She never came outside, I explained, because she had real bad arthritis and a heart condition. No one ever asked any questions because the bottom line was that no one cared. Most neighbors felt that Zee got what she deserved and if her kids had to pay the price, oh well. So be it.

I turned tricks to pay the rent and buy food. Hell, I had to handle all this stuff when Zee was alive. So it was easy. A couple of brothers recruited me to sell drugs, but I just could not do it. I do not know which of the two evils was less, but at least while I was prostituting, I felt like I had more control. More importantly, I knew that I was only hurting myself and no one else. In my opinion, people who sell drugs hurt themselves, the people who buy it, their families, and the whole damn community. Naw, I'd sell a little pussy any day.

I had it all figured out. In order for Malcolm and I to survive, I would have sex with one man a day. Just banging one man a day, gave me the time that I needed to finish high school at an accelerated speed and take care of my brother at the same time. I only charged $25, because I gave no head and did no anal. That bargain basement price was golden to most men, which meant I never had any hassles. So, I earned about $750 a month.

Since our Section 8 rent was only $150 and with expenses for food, clothes, electricity, and miscellaneous, I was able to put aside about $250 a month. Since I was too young to open a bank account without parental consent, I hid my stash in a cookie jar. So far, we'd been doing okay, and as crazy as our dysfunctional life was, Malcolm and I were doing a lot better now that Momma was gone. There was virtually no stress and not a lot of unnecessary bullshit. When it comes down to it, Zee's life was one big mess. Now at least Malcolm could do his homework in peace and we prayed every day before we ate and when we went to bed.

Everything was going well, until one day, out of the blue, the shit hit the fan. It was broad daylight and I was going to meet a previous client at his place for a private party. Malcolm was going to going to the eighth-grade dance, and he needed a suit. The man told me that he would pay me $250 to dance for a group of businessmen. At first, I thought that it was too good to be true, but I wanted the money, and didn't want to dip into our stash. The party was in the Bronx, so I took two trains and walked about three blocks. The address was 347 Gun Hill Road, which was odd, because it was an apartment located over a martial arts studio. Before I went up to the flat, I looked at those men and women kicking their feet and chopping their hands; they seemed so graceful, yet powerful. I was so mesmerized by their movement that I watched for about five minutes before I hurried upstairs.

When I arrived, there were about six men and a lot of empty beer cans. I looked for Mr. Thompson who staggered toward me and said, "Okay, baby, let's go."

"May I have my money, please?"

He handed me $100, and I counted it on the spot.

"I thought you said two hundred-fifty dollars? I took two trains and walked a mile to dance for six old drunks and you gonna give me a hundred dollars?" I turned around to leave.

SLAP. I felt the sharp sting of his fat stubby hand, as I fell to the floor.

"Bitch, you got six men here who are waiting to see you dance. If you keep talking, they will want more than just a dance," Mr. Thompson threatened.

At this point, I did not know what to do. I was caught between a rock and a hard place. I knew that I was outnumbered, and as soon as I took off my clothes, I was fair game for a train or anything. Then I thought about trying to outrun them; shit, they were all drunk anyway.

"Go ahead and sit down and let me change into my costume."

"You don't need no costume. Just take your fucking clothes off NOW."

I had no choice so I began to take my clothes off, all the while looking for an open window.

"Isn't that bitch gonna dance?" drunk number three screamed.

"I ain't paying for this shit," drunk number five slurred. Then he pushed up on me and pinned me down.

"I'll pay for this, though," and he began to unzip his pants.

I managed to push him off and grabbed a heavy ceramic lamp. I hauled it over his head and it came crashing on the floor. One down, five to go.

The next drunk grabbed me and slapped me down to the ground. I started screaming as loud as I could until drunk number two placed his hand over my mouth. I bit his hand and was able to work my way out from under him. I headed straight for the front door when Mr. Thompson grabbed my hair. He slapped me again to the floor and turned me over on my stomach. I screamed at the top of my lungs, as Mr. Thompson ripped my panties off. Suddenly the door busted open and a middle-aged Japanese gentleman walked in. It was the guy that I had seen teaching downstairs.

"Get off of her," Master Kwan said.

"Get the fuck out of here, old man, or you're next," slurred one of the old drunks.

"I said, get off of her," Master Kwan repeated. "Can't you see that she is only a child?"

"She's old enough to suck my dick," Mr. Thompson shouted.

He should never have said that because that old Japanese guy commenced to kicking his ass something terrible. It was like I was watching a Saturday afternoon Kung Fu movie. Every time one of the drunks tried to jump into the fight, Master Kwan would kick or hit them, and they would fall down in pain. After a while they all stopped trying to jump in. After that, the ass kicking was official and the martial artist helped me up, and covered me with his jacket.

"Come with me downstairs and I will call the hospital," said Kwan.

"No, sir, please don't do that," I said. "May I please just come downstairs and rest a while before I go home."

"As you wish," he said.

We took the fire escape so that I would not be seen coming into the front of the studio. Master Kwan gave me some clothing that one of his female students had left behind and patched up my cuts and bruises. I glanced in the mirror; unfortunately, I looked like Rocky's stepsister. Kwan instructed me to lie down on the cot that was folded in the corner. My fist was still clenched with the $100 that I had received. Thankfully, I would still be able to buy Malcolm's suit and shoes. I smiled to myself and then fell asleep.

Two hours later my own sneezing awakened me. I looked around the room. The man was nice but his place was a wreck. There was a strong mildew smell that permeated the entire studio and there was dust and cobwebs everywhere. I shuddered at the thought of a spider crawling on me. I looked at the clock. Shoot, Malcolm was home and there was no one there to greet him and help him with his homework. I peered in the mirror and fixed myself up as best I could. I glanced into the studio and saw the Master showing this series of moves to the class and then the class followed. *Man, I would really love to do that shit*, I said to myself. Maybe one day.

Master Kwan caught my eye and ran to the back. "Thank you for everything, Mister," I said. "I'm sorry, but I didn't catch your name?"

"You may call me Master Kwan," he said.

"Thank you, Master Kwan," I said. "You saved my life. If there is anything I can do, just ask."

"There is an old parable about the man who saves another man's life."

"What happens?"

"The man in repayment saves another life and it goes on and on and on," he said.

"How can I repay YOU, sir?"

"By living an honorable and clean life, young lady," he said. "That's all anyone can ask."

"May I come visit again, Master Kwan?" I asked.

"Anytime, Ms."

"Skyy, Skyy Knight." I extended my hand to shake his.

Rather than shaking my hand, he grabbed my hand and pulled me close to him and hugged me. *Now, that was the best medicine on earth*, I thought.

I ran all the way to the station only to realize that I had just missed my train. I sat on the bench and recalled what had just happened. I called myself Skyy. Everyone knows my name is Sandy. I grinned. I liked that name, Skyy. At that moment, I experienced an epiphany. I will use *Skyy* as my alias, whenever I am in a dangerous situation. And just like that, I had joined the ranks of Superman, Wonder Woman, Pam Grier and all the other bad-assed crime fighters. Master Kwan said that I had to save someone's life, and that would make us even. *We shall see*, I thought.

I dozed most of the way home on the train ride. When I exited the train, I broke into a full trot trying to make it home as quickly as I could. I missed Malcolm and needed to see his face full of sunshine. I walked into the crib and it had been ransacked. Malcolm was huddled in the corner.

"Malcolm, what happened?"

"When I came into the apartment, there were three dudes in here looking for something. They kept saying something about a key. Anyway, they started breaking things and throwing things. Then they found the cash in the cookie jar and took off."

"Are you all right?"

"Yes, but now we don't have any money," Malcolm said, his eyes welling up with tears. I held Malcolm for about an hour. Or I should say we held each other. Just when you thought it could get no worse, it did. It always seemed to get worse and worse. Just then I remembered a saying that I heard the minister say a long time ago: "God don't give you no more than you can handle."

I tried to hold on to that for a minute. Then I thought, *God must think I'm Hercules because he has sure given me a lot of grief, pain, and misery.*

CHAPTER 12
New York, 1977

The next day after the break-in, I walked Malcolm to school. I had to turn a few tricks that day because the rent was due. Let me just say something right here and now; if you ever have any money that you are trying to stash, never, I say never put it in a cookie jar. Zee used to do that stupid shit and I just followed suit. Well, they say the acorn don't fall far from the tree. That dumb move set us back about two months.

I had just finished my work for the day and was feeling good. My last john had given me a $100 tip. He had asked me how old I was, and I said eighteen. He told me to stay in school and made me promise that I would never prostitute again. Meanwhile, as he was banging my lights out, he kept referring to my body being a temple and talking to me about having a future and blah, blah, blah. What a hypocrite. I think he just felt guilty for doing it with someone that was probably his daughter's age. I wasn't gonna argue. I took the money because I sure needed it. I had about three hours before Malcolm came home, so I decided to take Master Kwan a little gift.

I scooped up a bouquet of flowers. I thought that they might help to brighten up the place. When I arrived at his studio, he was sitting in an office chair in the back.

"Master Kwan," I said. "I brought you these as a token of my appreciation."

"You did not have to, Ms. Skyy, but thank you," he replied.

"No, seriously, thank you for everything," I said.

Skyy looked around the room. "Master Kwan, may I sweep up a little? You know, sort of tidy things up for you?"

"That would be nice. This place does need a woman's touch."

I grabbed a broom and proceeded to sweep. After that, I went to the store and purchased a mop, bucket, rags, Lemon Pledge, and room deodorizer. An hour later, the room looked good as new.

"Wow. I have never seen the place look so neat," said Master Kwan.

"Thank you but it didn't take much. I can clean whenever you want," I offered.

"Well, I would like to make you an offer, Ms. Skyy. Can you keep this place clean and run errands for me every day?"

"Are you offering me a job?" I asked.

"Yes, and more," he continued. "I would also like for you and your brother to stay in the apartment upstairs. I kicked Mr. Thompson out. Bad habits, you know. Anyway, I have done some snooping. It appears that you and your brother have lost your mom and have no guardian. I can act in the capacity of a guardian."

I was shocked that Master Kwan, who appeared to be so disinterested, knew so much about me. How does the saying go, when one door closes, a window definitely opens. I ran over to Master Kwan and gave him the biggest hug imaginable.

"I would love to move upstairs. Heroin addicts keep breaking into our apartment anyway. It's just not safe. There are also a lot of bad memories that I would just as soon forget. My brother Malcolm will be starting a fancy prep school in the fall. This arrangement will be perfect. But there is just one more thing."

"What is it?" Kwan inquired. "Ask away."

"May I learn karate, sir?"

"I was waiting for you to ask me," he said. "From the minute I laid eyes on you peering in the window I knew what you would be a martial artist. You strike me as a warrior, a little lady that has been through a lot. But, more importantly, one who has survived. You have the heart and brains of a true warrior."

"I love the grace and the beauty of the karate moves," I said. "You know, I always wanted to be a dancer. To me, karate looks like a different type of dance with precision, skill, and strength."

"Come. Let me give you your first lesson," said Master Kwan.

We practiced for about two hours, and I was both elated and exhausted from the workout. Drenched from perspiration, I went upstairs into our new apartment and took a shower. I looked around our new home and imagined how it was going to look after we moved in, and tidied up a bit. By then, it was time to go home and get Malcolm.

When Malcolm arrived home, I told him about the big move. I thought that he would be sad about leaving his friends but he was happy. He said he was tired of not feeling safe, and that he always felt that he had to watch his back. He admitted that he was always hesitant about going to school, and leaving me alone in the apartment. Now that we were moving, he would feel better about going to school. Just then someone started to bang on the door. I wondered who that could be? I told Malcolm to stay still. When I heard someone say "It's LD, let me in!" I grabbed Malcolm and went through the window onto the fire escape. This scene was surreal because it had happened before, before Zee was murdered. The two thugs came bustin' in the door. They started searching for something. *What in the world was everyone looking for?* I thought. Then I heard them saying that there was some key that went to a locker that had a lot of money.

They searched the crib for about an hour and then they left. I immediately started packing and told Malcolm that we were leaving tonight. We took the train to the Martial Arts Center and told Master Kwan that we wanted to move in at once. Malcolm only had one more week of school so I would let him miss those days. The arrangements for him to start private school were already set, and he would leave in a month to participate in a summer program that would help him become acclimated to his new environment before the school year started. We had only one more month together. My eyes started to water at the thought of not seeing Malcolm every day. I knew, though, that this was the best move for him. He would undoubtedly get excellent grades and be exposed to the type of people that we only read about and see in the movies. Malcolm deserved the best in life and that I could give him. I knew that one day Malcolm would be somebody.

><< ><< ><<

On the train ride uptown, I kept thinking about what I may have left in the apartment. Why was everyone breaking in? I guess that they knew something that I didn't. I remember that on the night Zee died, those dudes kept asking her about some cash. I thought Momma looked kinda funny before she died. It was almost as if she was trying to tell me something. I had to dash back to the crib right away.

"Malcolm, I'll be right back. I have to go to the store."

"All right, Sandy, I'm going to help Master Kwan move some furniture."

"Remember, Malcolm, stay in the studio. If you are hungry, there are sandwiches upstairs. Do not leave. Don't even go to the store without me or Master Kwan. Got that?" I hugged my brother tightly.

"Got it, sis," Malcolm hugged me back. It was almost as if he didn't want to let me go. That is one hug that I will always remember.

While sitting on the Number Two train, I started thinking. What had Zee left in the apartment? Had that been why she was killed? Somehow, it all began to make sense. Those thugs LD and Six kept talking about some money. It had to be a large sum or they would not keep coming back to find it. Also, word must have got out on the street because everyone was trying to find out what was up.

I took out my key. I wondered if that asshole super had changed the locks already. Knowing him he hadn't, because he was as lazy as they come. All those times our rent was late, all those times I had to get on top and do all the work. I cringed. I remember one time he made me get on top while he ate a tuna sandwich. Shit, hopefully now, those days were long gone. I vowed to NEVER fuck another guy unless I wanted to.

Perfect, my key still worked. I turned the knob and let myself in. I knew that I had to get in and out quickly because I did not know who might show up. I started in the kitchen. I knew Momma had spent a lot of time in the kitchen. Most mothers spend time in the kitchen cooking nutritious meals for their children. Zee spent a lot of time in the kitchen cooking her drugs.

Shit, I found nothing in the kitchen. Slowly I searched the living room/dining room. Nothing. Damn. I entered the bedroom that all three of us had shared. I looked through the closet. There was still some of her clothing that I had not gotten rid of. I fumbled through old suits, coats, and dresses. Zee hadn't worn those clothes in a long time. Toward the end, Zee had barely changed her clothes. The sad thing is before heroin, she was an immaculate dresser.

I went to the chest of drawers. I looked in the top drawer where she kept her knickknacks and memorabilia. My report card from the third grade. *All "A's."* I smiled. I gazed upon several ceramic arts and crafts projects that Malcolm and I had done in grade school. Then I came to a Mother's Day card. The card was dated 1972. Malcolm and I had made the card in an after-school program. I opened it and a gold key sat right in the middle of the card. The words "WE LOVE YOU" were in red crayon and we had signed our names in blue. There were three brown stick figures, one larger than the others. They were hugging under the bright yellow sun. My tears began to stain the card so I closed it. Before I closed the card, I noticed a slip of white paper. It had the numbers "007" scrawled on it and an address. I recognized the address as Penn Station at 34th and Broadway!

I picked up the card and a couple other items and put them in my backpack. I put the key in my shoe and I was on my way. I decided to go through the fire escape instead of the front door so that I would not be spotted. Word travels fast in the 'hood and I knew fools had already found out that Malcolm and I had split.

I took the D train to the Thirty-Fourth Street station and went inside and looked for a locker with number 007. It seemed like there were a million lockers. Fifteen minutes later I came upon locker 007. I took out the key and it fit! I turned the handle, opened the door, and stared at a big brown paper bag. I snatched the bag and ran into the women's bathroom. I looked around and went into the stall and opened the bag. To my surprise, there were wads of $100 bills tied together in bundles. There was about fifty bundles altogether. There must be at least half a million dollars, maybe more! A letter on pink stationery was at the bottom of the bag. *I'll read this later,* I thought.

I took several wads of the money and placed them on different parts of my person: two in my shoes, one in my bra, and one in my panties. The remaining money I left in the bag and ran outside to hail a cab.

"Three forty-seven Gun Hill Road in the Bronx," I said. The cab driver turned around and looked me up and down. "You know that will cost about seventy dollars."

I peeled off a $100 bill and told him to get going.

"Yes, ma'am." The cab driver smiled.

When I arrived at the studio, a class was in full force. I motioned to Master Kwan to get his attention. He held up a finger and mouthed, "One minute."

A half-hour later he came upstairs. I opened the bag.

"Where did you get this from, Skyy?" Master Kwan asked with a tone of concern.

"My mother left this for me. She died because of it. I want to read this letter that I found at the bottom of the bag. I wanted you to be here when I did."

I began to read:

March 16, 1977

My Dearest Sandy,

Let me first start off by telling you how sorry I am that things turned out the way they did. You and Malcolm deserved to have been raised in a more nurturing environment. I remember the first time I saw your precious face, the day you were born. I thanked the Lord and made a promise to Him that I would love you and take good care of you. I hope that this money somehow makes up for all the mistakes I have made.

Do not be afraid, Sandy. I paid the debt for this money with my life. I knew that eventually Lord Bless would wonder if I had it. But at this point, since you have found it, I guess he still does not know so you are safe. I hope that this money will help with your college tuition and with the expenses needed to get you to that point.

Sandy, I know that I never spoke of your father but if for some reason you ever get in a jam, go to Lord Bless and he will not be able to refuse you. If you become curious enough, I know that you will find out the truth.

Sandy, I love you and trust that you will be fine. I have put you in God's hands and I am finally at peace. Give my love to your brother.

Mom

CHAPTER 13
Washington, D.C. 2006

James Bledsoe threw his head back in ecstasy, thinking to himself, *this bitch gave the best blow job EVER! She sure was ghetto but what did that matter?* He was married to the classiest woman in the world. James Bledsoe HAD IT ALL!

Karen grabbed the can of whipped cream. She loved chocolate sundaes, and so she sprayed the cream all over his penis. She leaned back to gaze upon her creation and then dove right in. Karen licked the shaft and each individual sac lovingly, knowing that she was pleasing her man. *That's right*, she thought. *James is my man and I'm going to do everything to make him remember why he needs to leave her.* She began to suck his dick as if it were her lifeline. *So who wants to be a millionaire? I do, damn it*, she thought. *After fucking James for the last five years, I deserve every penny I can get.*

Karen got up from her dick duty and expertly peeled the leopard print camisole off of her body. As she seductively squeezed her areolas, Karen started to tease him with her big Double D's. As he opened his mouth, she would place one in it, and then pull it out quickly before he could begin to suck. She placed her hands on them both and did a little shimmy, laughing out loud as his tongue literally hung out of his mouth. She grabbed herself and began to masturbate, because she knew how much James loved to watch her. She was pulling out all of the stops. Tanya couldn't come close to the skills that Karen had. She probably had no idea what James liked to do in bed. Today she would give him an ultimatum: either he leaves Tanya or he would never get any of this pussy again.

"Come on, baby. Get on top," James begged.

"I need to talk to you first," Karen taunted. She was not as dumb as she looked.

"Now come on, baby. I'll get on top," James connived as he commenced to climbing on top of Karen.

"No, I need to talk to you," said Karen in the sweetest voice possible. "I have been trying to tell you this for the past six weeks. It seems like we never have time to get together any more and when we do, all we do is screw."

"Now baby, you know it's not like that," said James, his dick so hard, he probably could have broken a cinderblock with it. "You know how much I love you and you know my situation. As a matter of fact, I'm taking a big chance just to meet you here today. Tanya could arrive any second."

"If you love me, you would not care if Tanya walked in," continued Karen. "James, you said that you were going to divorce her."

"I plan to. I just have to wait for the right time," said James. "It's very complex at my level. I stand to lose a lot of money if my timing is off, and Tanya could take me to the cleaners."

"Tanya isn't thinking about *your* money. You're the one that is always bragging about your wife who is the plastic surgeon and your wife who is that Chair of the Department and your wife is in charge of this Delta Committee and your wife with her old African money," mocked Karen. "Why would she care about *your* money?"

"You should know that women will take all a man's money if he leaves her just on GP," said James, looking down disappointedly at his flaccid penis. "How does that saying go? Hell hath no fury like a woman scorned."

"What do you mean?" Karen questioned.

Sometimes Karen is so stupid, James thought. He wondered why he messed with her at all. He could clearly have any woman he wanted, even at his age. *Just like fine wine, I get better with time. It looks like I'm going to have to get rid of her and soon*, he thought.

Karen continued babbling, "Well James, I've been thinking. You're having your cake *and* nibbling on Hostess Twinkies, too. You need to make a decision, her or ME."

Was she lunchin'? That was like asking Mercedes-Benz or Chevy Chevette; crème brûlée or ice cream; Dom Perignon or Riunite. Karen had to be crazy. Why couldn't she get it through her thick weave that it was just sex? Why did women always have to make more out of it? It was just sex, albeit great sex, but it was just sex. James loved, respected, and adored Tanya. There was no way that he would ever consider leaving her, no matter how many lies he told Karen.

James tried a little reverse psychology on Karen. "If you love me so much, you would not put this kind of pressure on me," said James. "I can't leave Tanya, not now. You have to give me a couple of years."

"A couple of years?!?" exclaimed Karen. "You expect me to wait *that* long? You must be crazy! I don't understand what will change in a couple of years. It's not like you have young children."

"That's not the point. You know how much I love you," said James, trying to distract Karen. "Come here and let me show you."

Karen softened a little bit, thinking to herself, *Let me put it on him again, and try this conversation later.* Just as Karen was about to mount James sixty-nine style, they both jumped as they heard a door open.

"Hey sweetie, are you home?" Tanya hummed.

"Oh, shit!" whispered James. "Karen, you gotta get your shit and go out on the balcony."

"It's cold outside and besides, I think that now would be a great time for all of us to talk," said Karen, refusing to budge from her position.

"Sweetie, is that you?" Tanya asked.

"You're crazy! Stay right here and don't move!" James grabbed a towel and tied it around his waist. He met his beautiful wife, Tanya, on the stairs and enticed her back down.

"Hey, babe, let's go skinny dipping. The pool is about eighty-five degrees. I missed you so much. How was your trip?"

"Slow down, lover," said Tanya. "I can't go swimming. I have to go back to the hospital. They called me on the way back from the airport. There is an emergency. They found another kid on the playground. They think it's the same serial child murderer but by a miracle this last one is still alive. She needs a lot of plastic surgery, though. I sure hope the police catch that animal and soon."

"Okay, darling." James quickly changed the subject. "Are we on for dinner tonight?"

"Of course honey," said Tanya. "B. Smith's at seven p.m., with Sandy, right?"

"Yes, as a matter of fact, she's coming to the house later this afternoon to pick up some papers and to strategize for tomorrow's meeting. Mike will probably drive us both to dinner tonight."

"Great. You know Sandy is my girl. Oh, by the way, I bought gifts from the Ivory Coast for the both of you. I'll surprise you tonight. Enjoy your afternoon. You sure do look sexy in that towel. Maybe I do have a few minutes," Tanya wished aloud.

"It'll be here for you tonight, Angel. Go handle your business and we can have dessert all night long." James then kissed her passionately. *Now that's a real woman*, James thought. *Karen must be crazy if she thinks that I could ever conceive of leaving a woman like Tanya.*

That motherfucker! thought Karen, peering through the door at the happy couple. *I can't believe he kissed his wife like that. He told me that he loves me. He told me that he would leave her. He ain't never gonna leave her at the rate he's going. It looks like I will have to help the process along.* Karen thought about it for about three seconds, stormed into the master bathroom and looked around. She took off the leopard thong and placed it on Tanya's vanity seat.

"James won't see it until Tanya does," Karen sneered. "This will make James realize once and for all that he cannot underestimate me." Karen smiled as she went to the window and viewed the grounds of the estate. "If you play your cards right, Karen, you could be Queen of the World, too! One day this could be mine."

James ran upstairs.

"Are you still here? Why haven't you put your clothes on?" asked James. "Do you realize the magnitude of what just took place?"

"Yeah, your Little Miss Perfect wife almost got a lesson on how to satisfy her man," snarled Karen.

"Damn, why must you be so ghetto all the time?" asked James. "Now get your things and go. Sandy is on her way and I don't think it would be a good idea for her to see you here."

"Sandy. That is the reason why I came here in the first place. She fired me, James," said Karen.

"She did? Why, what did you do?"

"What did *I* do? Why would you assume that *I* did something?" said Karen. "James, you're taking her side, and you don't even know my side yet! You *need* to fire Sandy and you *need* to fire Tanya."

"Okay, you know what, Karen?" said James. "I think that you need to go home before you piss me off any further. I'll call you next week," James said finally and ushered Karen outside the house and into her car.

Just as Karen got into her car, I pulled up in my Black Cadillac Escalade ESV.

"Now, you know you're just plain wrong, Karen," I said as I parked my truck. "But that's okay though because what goes around comes around. Today you just got a small taste of what is in store for you if you keep dipping in other people's stuff."

"Fuck you...you bi..." Before Karen could finish her sentence, James shoved her toward her car, trying to eliminate what he perceived to be a catfight in the making. He didn't want to have his dirty laundry to be aired in front of his bourgeoisie Mitchellville neighbors.

"Get in your car, Karen, and drive," said James. "Thank you for stopping by. I will take your complaint under consideration."

I went into the house and pulled out my laptop and my notes. I thought for a second and proceeded. "Mr. Bledsoe, I know that your relationship with Karen is none of my business. But I know that Karen is trouble, so I had to fire her today. She deliberately tried to sabotage my presentation. That type of insubordination cannot be tolerated."

"I agree, Sandy. You should have fired her long ago, because she has always had a problem with you," said James. "I have one hundred percent confidence in all of your business decisions, Sandy. You know that, don't you?" said James as he crept close to me.

Why is he always trying to holla? I thought to myself.

I took this as my cue. "Mr. Bledsoe, may I go upstairs to freshen up a bit and change for dinner?" I asked.

"Sure," he said. "You can use the bedroom closest to the master bedroom."

"Thanks," I said and made my exit.

James Bledsoe lived on a sprawling estate, on a lake and a golf course, in a gated community in Mitchellville, Maryland. Mitchellville was a suburb that was located about thirty minutes outside of Washington, D.C. The size and stature of the mansion would make any new-money millionaire proud, complete with indoor and outdoor pools, stable and ten bedrooms. As I climbed the mahogany wood staircase, I headed for the "pink room," a bedroom in the house that was entirely decorated in pink. *That was the happy room*, I thought. This room is the exact opposite of my personality and me. It is light, airy, relaxing, and serene. With my life as complex, angry, cruel, and dark as it was, I always enjoyed my time in Tanya's playfully pink room.

I undressed and then looked through my suitcase for my toiletries. Although it can be quite glamorous, traveling can be very grueling. Having two separate households was also becoming increasingly more difficult. I found myself needing to buy two of everything, so that I wouldn't have to leave things behind.

"Shit, I forgot my cologne," I said aloud. I put on my black Natori robe and grabbed my overnight bag. I went into the master bathroom to look for a fragrance of Tanya's I could borrow. I looked in the linen closet, or should I say, the linen room, for a towel and washcloth and pulled out the chair in Tanya's vanity, so I could sit down and decide which cologne I would use. Tanya had about twenty-five bottles from all over the world. As I pulled the chair out, I saw a pair of leopard print thong underwear.

"Ain't that a bitch? Karen is trying to start something. Well, as they say, don't start none, won't be none." I took the underwear and went into the master suite and put them in James' closet. "I guess your plan won't work this time, Karen. James will be livid when he finds these."

I took a luxurious bath to help me relax. I had been under such an extreme amount of pressure lately. The Ashley Stewart case still had me reeling.

Malcolm phoned me and affirmed that all three men were thrown in prison, and I had dreams about Petrone being gang raped in jail.

Besides constantly thinking about Ashley, I had been spending too much time in worrying about the *School Yard Murders*, which I knew that at some point I would have to get involved. So far, I had been able to elude the police and successfully assist New York's Finest with approximately thirty convictions. And I'd been lucky enough to not have suffered any serious injuries. Although, I guess I had a gut feeling that at some point, my luck would run out. The thought of not being able to fulfill my DESTINY sent shivers down my spine. For the first time in a long while, I had thoughts about ending the *Lady in Black* persona. Other than work, I had no life, romantically that is. Sure, I flirted with a few men here and there, but that was getting real old.

As I continued to celebrate my own personal pity party, a vision of Yvonne Savoy popped in my head. This time, as I focused I noticed what seemed strange when I last saw her, the black eyes under Versace sunglasses. Someone had to fight for people like her, fortunately for her; it had to be *The Lady in Black*.

As the warm water soothed my tired body, I threw my head back and closed my eyes. Rest, that was what I needed.

A half-hour later I was awakened by Mr. Bledsoe standing over me. He was such a pervert.

"What are you doing?!" I screamed.

"Oh, I..I..I'm sorry. I had been calling your for the past five minutes so I came up to see if you were okay. We have to go over the paperwork before it's time to leave for dinner."

"All right, just give me a few minutes. How much time do we have before Mike arrives?"

"One hour."

"Okay, give me ten minutes and I'll be downstairs."

I dressed in a conservative brown crepe Donna Karan pantsuit. I hated the color brown, it was so damned boring. I had to play the game a while longer, long enough to eliminate James. Oh, he would get what was coming to him and soon.

CHAPTER 14
Washington, D.C., 2006

When we arrived at B. Smith's, Tanya had already arrived, and was seated at the bar. She turned and motioned for us to join her as we waited for our table. You could sense the predators seated around Tanya, trying to build up enough confidence to introduce themselves to her. Out of the corner of my eye, I could see James' shoulders tighten as he approached, put his arm around her waist, and glared at her would-be suitors.

Dr. Tanya Owende Bledsoe was class personified. She was the product of a biracial marriage; her father was Senegalese and her mother was British. She was reared in the lap of luxury in Senegal. Her father was an African diplomat and had exposed Tanya to the finer things in life. Fluent in four languages, French, Wolof, English, and Portuguese, she was schooled in London, and went to college at Harvard. She had pledged the illustrious sorority of Delta Sigma Theta and she thoroughly immersed herself in spiritual growth and community involvement. Ironically she and James had met in church when they were undergrad coeds in Cambridge, Massachusetts.

Their eyes met one Sunday afternoon. Tanya quickly glanced away but James could not take his eyes of off her. After the service, he followed her into the parking lot and asked her out to lunch. She smiled, refused and told him she was flattered yet extremely busy.

James was not used to any woman refusing him, so he decided that he WOULD have her. He would follow her and make her go out with him, then dump her. However, with her continued refusals when he saw her on campus, he became more and more smitten and began to follow her like a puppy dog.

Eventually Tanya acquiesced and they began a beautiful courtship. James was enamored by Tanya's brilliance, commitment and spirituality and found himself being faithful for the first time in his life. He knew he would marry Tanya but had to first convince her.

Eventually, Tanya went to New York for medical school, while James followed and attended law school. As a medical intern Tanya got involved in a program called STOP (Stopping The Degradation and Violence Toward Women), a worldwide organization of medical professionals dedicated to helping the effort to stop the physical and sexual brutalization of millions of African women. One of the reasons that Tanya left Senegal for London was to escape the widely accepted culture of female mutilation that is commonplace in many African countries. STOP had allowed her the opportunity to go back and visit Senegal and many other African countries to see the victimization firsthand. STOP had always been a passion for Tanya, because she knew that so many of her family and friends had experienced the mutilation, firsthand. Every moment that she was not performing surgery, she was raising money for STOP or traveling to Africa to perform surgeries for the many women who were severely butchered and hacked away at with non-sterile and dull instruments. Like me, Tanya did not have time to raise a family of her own; she was on a mission to save the world. For Tanya, she felt that her work was like a divine calling, a preordination, as I did. Tanya and I had a lot in common.

It was Tanya's goal to build a series of clinics in various countries in Africa that could provide health and wellness resources for impoverished African women, as well as to provide the surgery that could also save their lives after female castration. Her clinics would also provide education on HIV and AIDS and dispense condoms. After all she had invested in BCI, Tanya wanted for Bledsoe Communications to fund these clinics, however, James did not agree.

When we arrived at the bar, Tanya embraced and kissed James on the lips. She was excited because she had just received great news.

"Honey, my administrative assistant just called and the Amerex Corporation is sending a check for $250,000 for STOP. Isn't that great news?!" she asked.

"Wow! Congratulations, Tanya! That's outstanding!" I said as I hugged her. "You really are an angel, you know. Working so hard for all those young women you don't even know."

"Sandy, I could have been one of those women but for the grace of God," she replied.

James interrupted, "That's wonderful, dear. I am going to see why it's taking so long for them to seat us. I guess they do not know who I am."

James strutted off, giving Sandy and Tanya a moment alone.

"I will never understand his arrogance," Tanya whispered. "How much longer do you think it will take?"

"Honestly, it will be a little while yet," I said. "How are things going on your end?"

"That hoochie Karen was at my house today," said Tanya. "Of course they didn't know that I knew. Does James think I'm stupid? Karen's the one with the double-digit IQ...not me. I have the Mensa card to prove it."

"That's so funny, because Karen planted one of her leopard get-ups on your vanity so that you would find it, march right up to James, and file for divorce. Stupid wench. You know I fired her ass today."

"Good," said Tanya. "But you know that we will still have to keep our eye on her. More importantly, has your contact provided any more info?"

Before I could respond, I saw James swaggering his way back to us.

"Our table is ready," he said.

We were seated at a table near the window in the front of Union Station. I ordered my usual, fried catfish, potato salad, and collard greens. Tanya ordered the spicy barbecued red snapper with roasted carrot puree, grilled potatoes, and asparagus tips. Boring-ass James ordered plain ole fried "yard bird," with mashed potatoes and gravy, and collard greens. I love B. Smith's with its elegant ambiance and delicious soul food.

After we placed our orders, Tanya presented us with our gifts from Senegal. She had purchased a Senofu hat for James. The inside joke was that she knew that he would not be caught dead in any type of African garb. Tanya presented a Grisgris necklace that she had blessed by a village juju priest for me. She had requested that the priest offer a blessing to ward off evil spirits and protect me. Tanya was such a good friend. As a matter of fact, she was the only female friend I ever had.

"Did you hear about Yvonne?" asked James.

"Yeah, I heard something about her having some kind of accident," Tanya offered.

"What type of accident?" I asked.

"She is at George Washington University Hospital. My assistant went to visit her and said she had a car accident," said James. "Phyllis said she had never seen anything like it. Her entire body was bandaged and she could hardly talk," he continued. "She started to cry while describing the scene to me. Tanya, I sent flowers from the two of us."

I thought to myself, *Car accident? I had just seen her Benz at American Service Center being detailed. She didn't have an accident, she married one and Calvin Savoy would have to pay.*

CHAPTER 15
Washington, D.C., 2006

I could not believe my eyes when I walked into the hospital room. Yvonne's exquisite dark-skinned face was black and blue. Both of her eyes were black and she had bandages on just about every body part imaginable. Outside her room, the doctor confided that Yvonne had a broken nose, separated shoulder, broken arm, broken ankle, and torn ligaments in her leg.

Yvonne Sanders Savoy was one of those women that lived in denial. She was raised in Baldwin, Long Island in New York. Her family was affluent. Growing up she spent summers in Martha's Vineyard and winters on Black ski trips. She was a third generation Hampton University alumna, and possessed a Wharton MBA. While writing her dissertation at U-Penn, she met what she thought was "the man of her dreams," Calvin, an All-American basketball player who played forward at Ole Miss.

Drafted in the very last round, Calvin had played for the Philadelphia 76ers for five years. However, he had spent more time on the bench, than on the court. That didn't stop Calvin from thinking that he wasn't just a man, but *the man*. The two had a brief courtship, and before she knew it, she was pregnant. Unfortunately for Yvonne, she and her mother pressured Calvin into marriage. Although he really liked Yvonne, he wasn't ready to settle down. Yvonne was so mesmerized by Calvin's charm, that she overlooked the fact that Calvin had a quick temper and had already hit her several times. Each time Calvin hit her, Yvonne rationalized his actions by chalking it up to his insecurities or his basketball injuries. Like far too many women, Yvonne wanted *desperately* to believe that Calvin could change.

And of course, like so many other men like him, Calvin didn't change. The beatings intensified and became more frequent. After her second child, Mia, was born, she confided to her mother about the abuse, and she suggested that Yvonne and Calvin try counseling. After the third session, Calvin tried to hit the therapist. Yvonne's mother was truly from the old "stand by your man" school. She told her daughter that she needed to find a way to hang in there. According to her mother, divorce was not an option, and that she would be a disgrace to the family if she proceeded in that direction. She then went on to further suggest that Yvonne needed to try to be a better wife to her husband.

Like they say, "De-Nile" is not only a river in Egypt; it also is often filled with many generations. Yvonne's mother would rather see her daughter married to a bench- warming, ex-pro basketball player and get her ass beat on a regular basis, than to be in a safe physical, emotional, and mental place.

However, despite the drama and adversity, Yvonne had earned an MBA in marketing, had three beautiful children, and had started her own advertising firm, the Savoy Group, which regularly handled all of BCI's local ad work. Yvonne had been spending a lot of time in our offices lately because she was planning to pitch for the New York and Atlanta office business.

I never heard Yvonne complain, nor had I ever seen her feeling down. She always had a kind word and a smile for everyone. From the outside, no one would have dreamed that she was experiencing any type of abuse.

"Honey, how are you doing?" I asked. "Is there anything that I can get for you?"

"Thanks for coming, Sandy," said Yvonne. "I'm a mess, aren't I?"

"You look great," I lied. "Are you sure I can't get you anything?"

"No, sweetie, I am fine," she said. "I think that I will need to reschedule my presentation. Can we push it back at least a week?"

"A week! Please, girl," I said. "You won't be back for at least a month; the doctor said that you will have to undergo extensive therapy." I paused for a second. "Yvonne, this is serious. Why don't you tell me what happened."

"I was leaving Saks after filming a promo piece, when I drove my car onto Wisconsin Avenue," she said, making it up as she went along. "Before I could get into the right-hand lane, a teenager in his momma's Jag ran right into me."

"Yvonne, my car is being serviced at the same place yours is," I said. "I saw your red Benz with Maryland SAVOY tags. Why don't you tell me the truth?"

Yvonne started to cry. "I'm too embarrassed to tell you the truth. My life is one big lie. I come across as this businesswoman that has it all together when really my life is falling apart."

"Baby, we all are going through one thing or another. This is not the time to be embarrassed. Let me help you!" I pleaded. "Honey, think of your kids. Do you want for them to see you like this? Are you ready to die? 'Cause I sure as hell would not like to attend your funeral," I said.

She sobbed deeply. "No. Sandy, you don't understand. He was so broken up about this that he actually cried. He told me that he loved me, and this was the last time."

"I do not mean to be condescending, but are you stupid?" I asked. "How many times has he told you that?! A batterer will always tell his partner that he is sorry and that it will never happen again," I said. "You need to pick your three children up and leave Calvin. If you don't, you will set a pattern for your children's future that will find them in a cycle of abuse as well. They are going to grow up thinking that this shit is normal. You are an educated woman, Yvonne, and you already know this."

Yvonne continued crying. "I do know this, Sandy, but it is so hard to leave. Calvin told me that if I left he would kill my daughters and me, and raise our son CJ alone," she continued. "I cannot take the chance of him making good on his promise. The look that he has in his eyes when he beats me is one of pure evil."

"All right, Yvonne," I said. "Do you really want Calvin out of your life?"

"Yes. I would be so grateful if he would just disappear," she said. "I know that it is wrong to think that way but I do; every time he goes out late or goes out of town, I pray that he has a fatal car accident. If Calvin died, everything would be perfect and although the kids would be sad, it would be a different kind of pain than a messy divorce or their momma dying at the hands of their father."

"Damn, girl, that's deep," I said. "You're in luck! I can take care of all of your problems."

"What do you mean, Sandy?" asked Yvonne.

"Can you give me all of Calvin's pertinent data?" I said. "Like his social security number, date of birth, etcetera."

"Why do you need that information?" asked Yvonne.

"Let me put it this way," I said. "I can take care of your problem, but you cannot utter a word to anyone. First, you must follow my instructions to the letter, and then by this time next week your problem will be over."

"How?" she asked.

"Just do what I say and don't ask any questions," I said. "I'm serious, Yvonne. If you want a good life for yourself and your kids, do not tell a soul about this conversation. Not NOW or EVER."

Yvonne gave me the details that I requested, we said a prayer together, and I hugged her.

"One week," I said.

"Thanks, Sandy. For some reason, Sandy, I trust you. I always have had a warm feeling when I was in your presence," she said. "There is definitely something special about you, and I thank God that you are in my life. I will follow your instructions implicitly."

After I left the hospital, I went home to my Dupont Circle townhouse. I quickly changed into my True Religion jeans, black leather chaps, fitted black long-sleeved Yamaha T-shirt, black leather rider boots and my black leather mesh Yamaha-embossed jacket. I opened the garage and started my Yamaha Midnight Warrior motorcycle. I hopped on and headed over to Connecticut Avenue and rode onto the Rock Creek Parkway and headed south toward the monuments.

I felt the wind in my face and it helped me clear my mind and center my spirit. As I sped past the Kennedy Center and around the Potomac

River, I felt a rush of excitement as I downshifted the 1800 cc engine and felt a euphoric purr between my thighs. As I passed the Jefferson Memorial and headed toward Hains Point, I took the sixteen-valve, air-cooled engine to the next level as I accelerated to ninety-five miles per hour.

Hains Point has always provided solace to me. I feel kin to the mammoth sculpture "The Awakening," the beautiful monster coming out of the earth at the tip of Hains Point. I took my helmet off and shook my hair as I gazed into the unbelievable dark horizon…the Black Skyy. I closed my eyes and said a prayer, *God give me the strength and wisdom that I will need to take down this bastard,* I thought. I was always so brutally honest with God, no sugarcoating, I just kept it real. God knew that I was about to save one of his children and destroy an enemy.

CHAPTER 16
New York, 2006

Before I left Hains Point, I called Mike on my cell. I told him that we would be going back to New York earlier than scheduled. Now I would be mixing business with pleasure. I already had my bags packed because I had business at our corporate headquarters. It would be a pleasure to kick Calvin's ass.

On the ride up, I contacted Bird and gave him the facts on Mr. Calvin Franklin Savoy.

"You know the drill, give me three days, Skyy," said Bird.

"That's great, Bird. I really want to nail this one."

"What's his M.O.?" asked Bird.

"Well, number one on my list is spousal abuse," I said. "However, rumor has it that his business, CFS Financial, Inc., is not doing too well. In fact, my sources tell me that Mr. Ex-NBA is close to being bankrupt and is looking for a way out."

"Well, if ole Calvin is up to something, I'll find out and get the evidence to prove it."

"I know that's right, Bird. You are the man."

ᴎ ᴎ ᴎ

I first met Charles Parker in 1980, after being recruited as a mole by the United States Central Intelligence Agency. Back then, covert activity was the name of the game, and I guess they figured that the combination of my prostitution and martial arts skills made for an awesome female spy. The fact that I was young, Black, and female further ensured that the enemy would never suspect me as being a serious threat. Shit, if they only knew!

Charlie was a cool-ass white boy who hailed from Philadelphia. Although he stood at nearly six feet, four inches, he was a social nerd/misfit and a communications whiz. While government and large corporations were beginning to fully utilize computer technology, Charlie discovered that he had a knack for hacking into systems and extracting certain types of information. The information Bird was able to obtain was often top secret and rarely disseminated. He felt comfort in tinkering with computers and quickly discovered the ins and outs of obtaining covert and very valuable information. He loved the classics, and ironically his favorite artist was Charlie Parker, so everyone called him "Bird."

One night, while we were in the field, the enemy took our camp by surprise and Bird, myself, and about three other men were captured by North Vietnamese troops. They thought that we may have had intelligence of other U.S. forces locations in Vietnam. They locked us up and bound us, while they tried to determine which one of us knew what. Because I was Black and female, they pretty much left me alone, because they assumed that I was simply the troop whore. Unfortunate for them, assuming made a fool out of them, not me, because I knew more about our field strategy than Bird or any of the other guys.

As the Viet Cong officers began to torture the four men, one of the guys, Billy Simpson from Iowa, caved in and told them that Bird was the one that they wanted. They thanked Billy for his information by slitting his throat. So much for saving his own ass. The Vietnamese Militia told us that anyone else who did not cooperate would get worse.

From then on out, the Asian soldiers focused their attention solely on Bird. They wanted to know the locations of our troops, but Bird was tough, and would not say a word. They even threatened to rape me and to kill the other two men. After four days in captivity, they killed Steve Young, from Las Vegas, and were becoming extremely frustrated because Bird still would not reveal any secrets. Finally, they decided to give him one more day to think about it, or face the consequences.

On the fifth day, a crazy-looking enforcer type came in wielding a machete. The soldiers questioned Bird for two hours, and still he would not give up any information. Suddenly, without warning, the Enforcer knocked Bird to the ground, grabbed his right leg, and lifted the machete over his head. The leader asked Bird the same series of questions. Again Bird didn't respond to any of his questions, he didn't even break a sweat. Consequently, the Enforcer chopped the leg off right above the knee. Blood spewed everywhere, and I have to admit, I was scared shitless. Bird didn't even scream, he just passed out cold. I lost it and begged the leader to release me so I could tend to his leg. Instead, they smacked me around and promised that the same would happen to me tomorrow if we did not provide the desired information. I used an old shirt to create a makeshift tourniquet and stop the bleeding and packed his leg with mud. There were only two of us remaining, so after we stopped his leg from bleeding, we prayed and talked with Bird, in order to help keep his spirits as high as possible. We told Bird that, at that point, we might have needed to give them what they wanted because it looked as though they were going to kill us all. Bird refused, because he was no snitch.

The soldiers and the Enforcer came in on the sixth day. The Enforcer flung the blood-stained machete around his head. The Leader stood before Bird and tried to question him again, and stressed the importance of his cooperation, as he leaned on Bird's right leg. Again, Bird didn't move an inch, although I could see in his eyes that the pain was excruciating. In a final attempt to persuade Bird to talk, the leader grabbed the fourth male, Darnell Davis, a brother from Cleveland, and threw him on the floor. Bird did not flinch, as the Leader appealed one last time to Bird. As the Enforcer approached him, Darnell sat up and looked directly into that devil's face and spat in his eyes.

"Rot in hell, motherfucker. My boy Bird ain't goin' out like that," he said. "Bird, handle your business! I'll be alright. I'm ready to be reunited with Momma anyways."

Darnell smiled as the Enforcer chopped his head off in one swift motion. It was all too much to handle, as I immediately passed out. So, the rest of the story is a little foggy in my mind, but Bird and I both made it out alive, despite the fact that Bird returned to the United States minus two legs. And now, you can understand why I trust Bird with my life.

Three days to the minute, my cell phone rang, or should I say vibrate. I was in the middle of a meeting so I excused myself to answer the call.

The caller said, "The bird is in flight," and hung up.

I ran into my office, shut the door, and logged onto my computer with my password, "yyks." Bird's smiling face appeared on the screen.

"Hey, Love, how are ya?" asked Bird.

"Great. I'm in the middle of a meeting so I don't have a lot of time," I said. "Whatcha got for me?"

"Your boy has been very busy," he said. "The Securities and Exchange Commission and the NASDAQ Surveillance department are both conducting investigations on CFS Financial for securities fraud."

"What?! Securities fraud?!" I said. "Do you mean to tell me that he is stealing money from his own clients?"

"Well, no," Bird said. "He is stealing for his clients. He is purchasing stocks on insider information received from his drug connection, who also happens to be an investment banker with Morgan Stanley. By the way, our boy also has a bad coke habit; he spends about a grand a day," he continued. "Anyway, he is making these stock purchases on specific companies that are about to be acquired by larger companies for the bulk of his five hundred clients, most of which are professional athletes, so we are talking millions of dollars. Calvin was a hero among his peers, not for his basketball prowess, but rather because he was making these guys millions of dollars. He would make calls to various financial newspapers and other media, making up rumors about the company. The stock would go up and then he would dump the stock."

"What is illegal about that?" I asked.

"Putting out false information to the public about a company and trading on insider information, or information that the public is not privy to, is illegal," said Bird. "It is a federal offense. Didn't you see the movie, *Wall Street*, Skyy?"

"Naw, I hate that Darryl girl, she creeps me out," I said.

"Anyway, I saved the best for last," said Bird. "SEC violations is not Mr. Savoy's guilty pleasure. Calvin Savoy is hot and heavy into child pornography and molestation. Pre-pubescent girls are his *thing*."

"Yuck. I've heard enough," I said. "Leave the pertinent details, his rap sheet, and any other data you have at the spot. I'll take care of Mr. Wife Beater. Thanks, babe."

"My pleasure. Have you sewn the 'S' on your chest yet?"

"Ha, ha, very funny," I said. "I have to admit, I've been feeling very weird about this whole vigilante thing lately, though. I'm beginning to second-guess my commitment. I feel as if there is no real purpose to what we are doing. Bird, for the first time in my life, I'm confused."

"You are the one who always says you are doing God's work. What or who has got you so down?" he asked.

"I am just so tired. For the first time in my life, I feel like I have no future."

"You have me. Isn't that enough?" asked Bird.

"I don't mean to sound so pathetic. I'm just a little nervous and anxious," I said. "Lately, all the press is talking about is the *Lady in Black*. I'm nervous that I will get caught or get caught up and killed. I'm not as strong as you think. There are so many times that I feel like that little girl hiding in the closet."

"Baby, rest assured, nothing will happen to you," said Bird. "You've been in the game too long. I believe, as you do, that this is your destiny, Skyy. Hold your head up and get tough. Think about all the lives that you have saved. Think about Yvonne's three kids. Get focused, Skyy. You have work to do."

"Thanks for your words of encouragement, Bird. I'll pick up the package this evening," I said.

"You're gonna love those pictures," mocked Bird.

"I'm sure. Love ya, babe."

"Back at ya," said Bird.

CHAPTER 17
New York, 2006

I telephoned Yvonne and let her know that our mission was just about accomplished and I asked her if she had any regrets about our plan. She assured me that she did not and that the reality was that she should have done this long ago. I guaranteed her that after all was said and done, she would have a better life for her and her children. I also let her know that we found three Swiss bank accounts that her husband was hiding money in, and that my investigator was trying to secure those funds.

Apparently, according to the Feds, Mr. Calvin Savoy had broken the Securities Exchange Act of 1933 and Securities Act of 1934. Bird said that the case against Calvin was airtight, and that the Feds were waiting for a few more pieces of evidence to arrest him. And then there was the icing on the cake, that nasty little business of cradle robbing. Calvin "Big Shot" Savoy was actually "dating" the best friend of his eldest daughter, Summer. Can you imagine that?! He started having sex with her when she was thirteen years old! Oh, Calvin Savoy is definitely going down! That will be the ultimate of mixing business with pleasure.

Satisfied that Yvonne wanted to go forth with our plan, I told her that there was no turning back and that everything would be wrapped up by tomorrow. I hit Mike on his cell, and told him to pick me up from my flat in SoHo at seven p.m. I knew that Calvin was due to meet an old friend at the Shark Bar at nine p.m. I was going to be there with bells on, and a bad black dress. *I got something for Mr. Calvin*, I thought.

Like clockwork, the limo pulled up to 307 Amsterdam Avenue. I slid out the car with my little black Vera Wang dress, that is just "low enough" in all the right places, my four-inch come-fuck-me-in-my-ass pumps and strutted into the Shark Bar. Tonight I am sporting my real hair, a short bob, parted down the middle, with crazy blond highlights. The icing on the cake is my signature, custom-made Jenisa Washington floor-length, black leather jacket. Jenisa Washington, and her trademark label Sold, was named Emerging Designer of the Year in 1999. Her designs are so *beast* and *off the hook*, that when I found out that she was "a sister" who was married to an up-and-coming Hollywood actor from Howard, I HAD to have one of her pieces. When I slip into my black leather Sold jacket, it feels and looks like, *butter.*

If all of this "black on black" wasn't enough, I always find a way to accentuate my look with a *pop* of the color RED. Whether it's with my signature red MAC Viva Glam lips, my red Chanel nails, a red scarf, or a *subtle* red push-up bra, like I was wearing tonight, *red* was as much of a part of the *Lady in Black*'s mystique, as the color black itself.

I strutted into the restaurant, giving much attitude, as I searched for my victim. Brothers were falling all over themselves as I glided past the hostess and headed for the bar. The suppleness of my caramel complexion was enhanced by my Viva Glam MAC-stained lips. As I passed by the bar, the signature scent of amber, vanilla, and sandalwood gently wafted behind me. Although I pretended not to notice, a few of the "brave" brothers tried to hook up with me, and as usual, I had no conversation for them. The *Lady in Black* was in the house!

I spotted Calvin at the end of the bar and made my way to him. He was sitting there scanning the room figuring out just who he could get with this evening. It was funny that sistas will buy the incredibly corny lines of men because they look a certain way and possess certain irrelevant credentials. My motto is that if you give too much unsolicited information, it usually is not true.

"Hello, handsome. Is anyone sitting here?" I asked.

"Yes, you are, gorgeous. May I buy you a drink?" said Calvin.

"Tonic with a twist of lime, please," I said in my most sultry voice.

Calvin caught the attention of the bartender and gave him my order, while he undressed me with his eyes. He told me that he was a single father because his wife had passed away two years ago, and that he was a salesman in town on a business trip. He told me that he was a little intimidated by New York women, being a Mississippi boy and all. Calvin told me he had not had a relationship since his wife died, because he just did not have time between traveling with his job and raising his kids. *What an asshole*, I thought.

After two hours of inane conversation about the good old days, when he was in the NBA, I was about to fall asleep. He went on and on about how he hadn't felt a woman in years. Boy was he good. He even made a crocodile tear fall down his cheek. So I played along and seductively suggested that I could help him through his fear and pain. I told him that I was into ménage à trois, and asked him if he knew of any other girls who may be interested. Calvin could hardly contain himself and told me that his girlfriend could join us. Just an hour ago, this motherfucker was telling me that he had not had a relationship since his wife died. Did the blood rushing to his penis make him think that I forgot his damned lies? What a typical stupid-ass mutherfucka. It would be pure joy to watch him go down.

We took a cab uptown to the Hilton and as we walked through the marbled lobby, I noticed a number of alleged undercover agents. I could always spot an undercover officer a mile away. I had been involved in too many sting operations. FBI and NYPD were scattered inconspicuously around the lobby. As we passed by, a young Latino agent held up a newspaper in front of his face and a headline read, "When Will the Lady in Black Strike Again?" *Wouldn't you like to know?* I thought.

When we got to the suite, I looked around and saw how large he was living, as he offered me a drink. After I refused, he poured himself a double shot of Remy Martin. As he lifted the crystal Tiffany glass of Remy to his lips, he picked up his cell and called his teenaged sweetheart.

After five solid minutes of sweet talk, Calvin coerced his girlfriend to sneak out of her parents' house and to meet him in the suite. Apparently, Sasha, his girlfriend of a year, was on punishment. However, the plan was for Mr. Savoy to pick Sasha up so that she could study with Summer for a midterm exam. If only Sasha's mother knew what a sick bastard Calvin was, she probably would castrate him herself.

Calvin told me that he would be right back and that I should make myself at home. But before he left, I made sure that I leaned into him and kissed him with a fervor that I had not known existed. I startled myself, because I felt a deep desire that had not been stirred in me for a long time. I slowly unbuttoned my dress and displayed my 38D's. I gently slipped my tongue into his open mouth and began my mission to quench this lustful thirst that was presently overpowering. The masculine scent of Versace clung in the air. *Damn, he's fine, but what am I doing?* I thought. It was as if I were outside of myself, unable to control my actions. I'd only had one sexual relationship that was related to romance and that was damn near twenty years ago. Usually, the sexual relationships I had were abusive and tortuous. However, right now, I was feeling very sexual, I was in control, and I liked it. I even contemplated having sex with Calvin, on my terms, before I took him down. For me, having sex on my terms is a goal that I secretly longed to obtain. Before we had arrived at the hotel, he had ordered champagne and lobster from room service. The room was filled with soft music, kisses, and caresses as I longed for a night where I would be pampered and adored. Although I loathed Calvin and everything he stood for, right now, I was totally turned on by the thought of him.

His kiss tasted sweet, almost like honey. I trembled as his tongue explored my neck and my ear, as he delicately sucked me into his spell. *Stop it, Sandy! Stop it now!* I thought. But I could not stop. I needed Calvin at that very moment like I needed air. I tried to envision Yvonne's bruised body in the hospital but his touch warmed me to my very soul and I became more excited. I could feel my lace panties getting moist, as my loins ached with longing as his fingers went straight for my femininity. What was I doing? I knew that I could not have sex with him because I would never be able to forgive myself.

I was lured into his web of deception, numb to all of my senses or sensibilities. Calvin had a presence that was intoxicating and enchanting and there was no denying that I hungered for what he represented. I wanted, and I needed, a man, a strong man who could take me away from all of my pain and misery. I was dizzy with desire and I reveled at the thought of the ecstasy that may have been in store for me, of my choice, my terms.

It took everything in me to come to my senses, as I got caught up in the moment and almost came all over his face. I pushed him away and playfully said, "Let's wait for your girlfriend, lover, but you can think about how sweet this pussy tastes while you're gone." I firmly placed his hand on my pussy, and kissed him simultaneously. "Hurry back," I purred, as he rushed out the door with a very hard penis. *Goodness*, I thought. *I hope he doesn't scare anybody with that tent in his pants.*

After Calvin left, I immediately took off my "little Black dress" and changed into my "kick-ass" black ensemble, which I knew would throw Calvin off completely. He had left a soft, alluring, lovesick puppy to return to the *Lady in Black.*

I instantly texted Miguel, to let him know that the coast was clear. Miguel was able to slip past the men downstairs and directed a photographer into the hotel suite. Mike introduced me to the photographer, a young rugged-looking man named Yan who had beautiful, piercing green eyes. I felt like a horny toad as I lusted after a man young enough to be my son. I instructed Yan to hide in the closet in the bedroom, while Mike hid in the closet that was positioned in the front part of the suite.

Earlier in the evening, I had picked up a package from Penn Station that had outlined Calvin's arrest record, and pictures with a variety of under-aged girls. It seemed that Calvin really enjoyed spending quality time with children, although not the kind of time Big Brothers and Sisters would envision.

There were pictures of Calvin with at least six different girls, all of which attended St. John's Prep School. I could just see Oprah eating this story up. Luckily, we had secured a new home for Yvonne and the kids in Scottsdale, Arizona. Yvonne and the kids could start a brand-new life, complete with a fabulous home, millions in the bank, and, more importantly, no knowledge of their father's horrendous past. The children would think that they were moving because their mother had just landed a huge contract and their father could not handle it. I am still trying to convince Yvonne that she needs to tell her babies that their daddy is dead. I know, I have a lot of nerve when a minute ago I was trying to screw him.

At any rate, the plan was to catch him in the act of doing coke, offering it to his girlfriend, and then having sex with his girlfriend, who was a minor. If all of the charges were combined, throwing a kidnapping allegation and the initial securities fraud, Mr. Savoy would be spending a very long time in jail. The trick, however, would be trying to secure those funds in those off-shore accounts. It would be tricky and would require Bird calling in a lot of favors but I knew that he could do it.

Calvin returned to the suite an half-hour later. I tried to contain myself as I looked at fourteen-year-old Sasha who was made up like a prostitute. I could only recall my own past and remember how many times I, too, had looked like that because I was trying to please some man. Thank God, Sasha's mom had the finances to get her daughter the counseling that I knew she would need after this ordeal is discovered.

Calvin seemed surprised when he saw me. "Why did you change?"

"I wanted to get more comfortable," I said. "Who is your friend?"

"I'm sorry," said Calvin. "I didn't catch your name earlier."

"My name is Skyy, baby," I said, directing my attention to his young companion. "Honey, what is your name?" I asked.

"Sasha," she told me.

"Shouldn't you be at home doing homework?" I asked.

"I finished it earlier," she retorted, as she cast her eyes down to the floor.

Calvin quickly interrupted the conversation by ordering Sasha to take off her clothes. Sasha pouted, and told Calvin that she did not want to do this again, not in front of another lady. Calvin reminded Sasha that as his girlfriend, it was her job to make him happy and take off her clothes in front of Skyy, which would make him *very* happy.

In an effort to distract him, I insisted that he share his nose candy with us. Calvin took out a small bag of white powder and poured it onto a mirror on the cocktail table. Sasha pulled out a razor blade and began to expertly divide the substance into five lines. Sasha snorted the first one herself through a tiny straw. In the background, I could faintly hear Yan snapping pictures, as this definitely was a Kodak moment. She offered me the straw and I politely declined her offer. Calvin quickly grabbed the straw from her hand and snorted the remaining four lines. *The only thing worse than a drug addict is a greedy drug addict*, I thought.

By now, Sasha had started taking her clothes off, while Calvin poured her, and himself, a drink of Remy on the rocks. Calvin took off his clothes and started to mount Sasha. I could faintly hear Yan feverishly snapping away pictures, so I turned on the radio and heard the Pussycat Dolls recite my anthem, "Don't You Wish Your Girlfriend was Raw like me." I glanced at the young nympho. A typical poor little rich girl that was looking for love in all the wrong places as a result of her father's absence. There was not enough of her daddy's money in the world that could make it all right to Sasha.

Calvin looked over at me and gave me a puzzled look.

"Why are you just sitting there, Skyy? Why don't you come on over and join us? You are the one who wanted ménage à trois."

"I'm letting you guys enjoy yourselves. I get turned on more when I watch," I said. "Let me pour you another drink, Calvin."

Realizing that this would be his sixth shot, along with all of the cocaine he had also consumed, I knew it was time to go in for the kill. I also figured that the guys downstairs could come in at any given moment. Our saving grace would be the fact that whenever two or more government agencies come together to bust a criminal, it takes forever for the bust to commence.

After I poured Calvin another double shot, I began my interrogation. I was getting tired of this whole scene. It was making me sick to my stomach. And just think, I almost gave him some.

"Calvin, let's play a little game. Do you like games?"

"I love games, baby, but why don't you take your clothes off first?"

Ignoring him, I continued. "If I ask you a question and you lie to me, I kick your ass. If you tell me the truth, I take a piece of clothing off. Is that fair?" I asked.

"Whatever, baby. First let me pour another drink." He did and I proceeded. *This will be easy*, I thought.

"Calvin, do you know how old that girl is?"

"Who, Sasha?" asked Calvin. "She's eighteen."

Wham, I kicked him dead in the face with the heel of my four-inch Prada boot. Blood dripped down the side of his face. He looked at me as if he wanted to retaliate but his arms would not cooperate. Calvin was so fucked up. Sasha ran to get him a napkin for his wound. I was in a zone now, and now there was no turning back.

"Is that right? I said. "Doesn't she go to school with your daughter, Summer?"

"No, she attends NYU," said Calvin. "Skyy, what the hell is this all about?"

I had taken out a short paddle, like the ones that the S&M folks like to use with their lovers, and I whacked him on the other side of the face.

Slurring his words, Calvin asked, "Bitch, what is this all about?"

I looked over at Sasha, and told her to go in the back and get dressed. I then walked over to Calvin and punched him three times in the jaw. Drunk and dumbfounded at this point, Calvin didn't know if he was coming or going. I enjoyed the fact that I could describe what was about to happen to him. I told him that he was going to be arrested and spend time in jail for the distribution of drugs, kidnapping a minor, having sex with a minor, securities fraud, and spousal abuse. I further explained that there were about ten agents downstairs from various local and federal agencies waiting to arrest him.

Too drunk and high to move, Calvin pleaded with me to help him escape. So, I asked him about his Swiss bank accounts. Calvin swore that there were no such accounts, so I kicked him dead in his stomach. After regaining what was left of his composure, Calvin said that if I helped him escape, he would give me a million dollars. *Now we're talking*, I thought. I told him to write down the bank account and PIN numbers. Calvin was so desperate, that he gave me all names, numbers, passwords and account balances.

Then I figured I would really fuck with him, when I asked, "So, where did you say that Yvonne was?"

"My wife?" he said. "I told you earlier, she's dead."

Damn, with all of the trouble he was in, why did he continue to lie? Now, I was beginning to lose my patience with him. I methodically grabbed *Sting* and gently placed it on his genitals, and asked him again plainly, "*Where* is your wife, Yvonne?"

Frightened by the threat of losing the only thing that really mattered to him, Calvin finally broke down and told me the truth. He sobbed as he told me that his wife was not dead, but in the hospital. He said that although he loved his wife, he could not control his urge to beat her. Calvin was so broken down that he confessed to all of his crimes, and then asked, through tears, if I would help him. I told him that he would have to pay for his sins by spending time in jail.

"Hopefully," I said, "jail will help you turn your life around and allow you to get the help you need." I also told Calvin that if he survived his jail sentence, that he would be better for it. He agreed and told me that the contact at the Swiss banks should transfer the money into Yvonne's account.

As I gazed upon a defeated man, blood dripped down both sides of his face and his naked six-foot-five-inch frame shook uncontrollably with sobs, as he contemplated his impending sentence. For a second, I almost felt sorry for him.

I told him to get dressed and then tied him up in the customary *Lady in Black* knot. I viewed the digital pictures that Yan had taken, as well as the others Bird had left for me and attached them to Calvin's chest. Calvin finally realized what had just gone down.

"Are you the *Lady in Black*?" he asked.

"What do you think," I asked, and left.

CHAPTER 18
New York, 2006

I put on my Sandy clothes, a wig, bland brown suit, nerdy glasses, and a big trench coat. As Mike, Yan, and I got onto the service elevator, about a half-dozen agents got off and ran in the direction of the Savoy suite. As always, Mike had thought of everything. He took the liberty of reserving two rooms downstairs on the tenth floor. Thank God, because I was exhausted.

As we exited the elevator onto the tenth floor, Mike handed Yan an envelope with $2,000 in cash. Yan was due to fly back to Cuba tonight. We occasionally used Yan because he was an excellent photographer and could easily slip in and out of the country. This was the first time, however, that I had actually met Yan. I was not happy that he had an opportunity to see my face close up, but I trusted Mike, since he had known Yan all his life, as Yan was Mike's cousin.

Mike and I walked arm in arm to our adjoining rooms. As we arrived at rooms 1003 and 1005, Mike handed me my room key and kissed me on both sides of my face.

"Sweet dreams, my love," Miguel whispered as he hugged me goodnight.

I gave him the biggest hug with all the strength I could muster. I told Mike that I was planning on sleeping in. In other words, *do not disturb*. Mike smiled, and said good night.

I went into the room, took my shoes off, stripped down to my underwear, and plopped down on the bed. For about ten minutes all I could do was stare at the ceiling. I was beyond exhausted. I was a physical and mental wreck. It was becoming increasingly more difficult to keep my composure. There was so much evil in the world. It seemed as if I could never ever help all of those that need it.

A picture of a sadistic butcher flashed before me in the form of a headline. "Another Child Found Murdered on the Playground." An overwhelming sense of depression hit me. Then sadness, as I began to cry and cry and cry. What kind of animal could kill innocent babies? Defenseless children who laugh and play and smile through rose-colored glasses. What kind of monster could slice and butcher a vulnerable soul whose main objective is to love and be loved. Thoughts of Ashley and Sasha kept flashing in my mind. I could not turn my brain off. The tears fell like a southern river, constant and flowing. The stream of tears washed through my body and provided me with the release I had needed for a long time. I knew that those tears represented years of pain and suffering that I had been holding inside for years.

I did not cry after Zee died, not even at the funeral. I did not cry after I was rescued from near death in Chile. I never shed a tear as I showered after all of the tricks that I fucked, while I scrubbed my skin until it almost bled. I had been living in a robotic, emotionless state.

There was only one person in the world that I knew could make me feel better; I reached for the phone and dialed my brother's number. After the second ring, I heard a familiar ten-year-old female voice say as politely as imaginable, "Salutations."

"Salutations yourself, Kenya," I said. "How are you, sweetie?"

"Aunt Sandy, is that you?" squealed Kenya.

"Yes, my love," I said. "You sound like such a little lady."

"I *am* a little lady," she retorted. "Where are you, Auntie Sandy?"

"I'm in New York," I said. "How have you been, baby?"

"Excellent," she said.

"By the way, congratulations," I said. "Your dad faxed me a copy of your grades."

"Thank you," she replied. "And that's right, you owe me one hundred dollars for all A's. Will I see you soon?"

"You will see me during the Christmas holidays. I'm spending a whole week with you," I said. "That is, if you can stand me for a week."

"Are you kidding?! You know how much I love you, Aunt Sandy," she said. "After all, you are my favorite aunt."

"I am your *only* aunt, silly," I said.

"You know what I mean. I miss you and can't wait until Christmas," said Kenya.

"Me either," I said. "Is your dad home?"

"Yes. Hold on, I'll go get him," said Kenya. "'Bye, Auntie Sandy."

"Bye bye, my love," I said.

"Whazzzuuppppp??!?!!" said Malcolm.

"Hey Malcolm. I am so glad you're home," I said.

"What's wrong, Sandy?" said Malcolm.

"Oh, nothing. I just wanted to hear your voice," I sighed. "Remember, baby, it's just me and you. I'm just a little lonely, that's all."

"I don't understand why such an eligible bachelorette is home alone," he said.

"Malcolm, you know I don't have time for men. I have big plans for my future. I want to be a millionaire before forty," I said.

"And I want a niece or nephew," said Malcolm. "Priorities, Sandy. What's the use in having a million dollars if you have no one to share it with?"

"I have you, Karen, Kyle, and Kenya," I responded.

"Sandy, you need to have a family of your own. You need to slow down long enough to meet a nice guy. You deserve all the happiness in the world, Sandy. You have worked hard all of your life. At some point, you will realize that at the end of the day, family is all that matters."

"You're right."

"I'm always right," Malcolm said laughing.

"When I'm down, you always make me feel better. I love you so much."

"Not as much as I love you. I gotta go, babe," he said. "Karen is preparing for a big trial and I have to help Kenya with a science project."

"'Bye, sweetie. Give my love to Kyle and Karen. I am sending two hundred dollars to Kyle and Kenya for getting all A's," I said.

"They are lucky to have you. I'll see you soon, babe."

"'Bye," I said.

The phone call did make me feel better. Malcolm's family was my family, and I needed them. I thought I was tough and I could handle the abuse that I had experienced. But sometimes I found it that tough to handle. As I started to cry again, I realized that this cry was long overdue. I also realized that it was okay for the *Lady in Black* to let her guard down and to feel some emotion. I cried myself to sleep.

I woke up to rays of bright sunlight streaming through the posh Manhattan window. I glanced at the clock. It was twelve noon! My uninterrupted sleep had lasted twelve hours. I noticed the red light blinking so I picked up the receiver and retrieved my messages. Mike had called three times. He had checked out and was eating breakfast in the hotel restaurant in the lower lobby. I jumped up and went into the bathroom. Reluctantly I looked in the mirror and saw that my face was bloated. All of that crying had left my face swollen and ugly. I looked like Quasimodo.

I turned on the shower and let the water run. The stream began to heat up and steam the bathroom. I went into the front room and retrieved my make-up bag. A little make-up could create the magic. I knew that today I would need more than just a little to do the trick.

I stepped in the shower and let the warm water cascade over my refreshed body. The liquid torrent flowed over my face. It felt so good. I always felt such a connection with water. When I retire, I will relocate to the Caribbean, somewhere on the beach. Water, to me, is like God's own elixir. My shower lasted for about fifteen minutes. As I got out, I draped a thick golden towel around me and walked over to the bed and sat down to contemplate my next move. I had not had the foresight to bring any extra clothes so I changed back into the ensemble that I had worn last night. It wasn't my objective to make a fashion statement, so I did not care what I had on. Mike would take me back to my flat in SoHo, and I would lay low for a while. I felt like I was slowly losing my grip, and needed a little time to regroup. The four-day weekend would be just enough time for me to unwind and get my chill on.

I went to the bathroom and decided to apply light make-up, just enough that my face would not scare any of the hotel guests. I spotted Mike in the lobby, impatiently tapping his foot and looking at his watch. I crept up behind him and wrapped my arms around him. He wasn't having it.

"It's about time, Skyy. Where have you been?" he asked. "Come on, let's get out of here."

"What's your problem? I decided to take advantage of the beautiful hotel room and sleep in. Is that a crime?" I asked.

Mike rolled his eyes and grabbed my arm.

"Let's just go," he said.

The limo was parked out front, so I told him that I wanted to go to the apartment in SoHo and then we would go back to D.C. Mike drove the car for about half an hour toward the Lincoln Tunnel. I thought that was strange but I figured that he needed to make a stop before dropping me off. After we hit the New Jersey Turnpike, he pulled over at the Joyce Kilmer rest stop, and got out into the back seat with me.

"Why are we in New Jersey?" I asked. "I told you that I wanted to stay in SoHo for a few days."

"I guess you didn't hear," he said. "Didn't you see the news this morning?"

My stomach and head started to ache simultaneously. Something told me that my wonderful morning was about to turn into a horrible afternoon.

"No, Miguel. What has happened?" I asked.

"After Calvin was arrested, he made his first phone call to a reporter at the *New York Daily News*. He has been singing like a canary."

"What do you mean, Mike? Please tell me that he has not told the press specifics about the *Lady in Black*." I sighed.

Mike began to give me all the details that he had read in the morning paper. Apparently, Mr. Savoy had decided that if he was going down, he was taking as many people as he could with him. He told the reporter that his contact at Morgan Stanley, Robert Epstein, had given him insider information. He named about twenty NFL and NBA players that he had purchased stock for knowing that the information was from a corporate insider. The snitch was trying to carve out a little deal. He was also trying to create a little celebrity for himself. Mike told me that the headline read, "Successful Stockbroker Seduced by the *Lady in Black*." I knew I should have killed that motherfucker. Calvin had given a vague description of me to the reporter. He had said I was a five-feet-ten-inch, light-brown-skinned sister who had a short sexy haircut and a black outfit. Thankfully that description fit half of the Black women in New York! Still I was pissed because now the public had a general idea of what the *Lady in Black* looked like. Damn. I started to wonder if he would pull the plug on the money in the Swiss accounts. I immediately took out my cell phone and pressed number three on my speed dial. I relayed all of the information that I had just obtained from Mike to Bird. He told me that he would call me back that afternoon.

I leaned back in the limo and closed my eyes. Mike suggested we go back to D.C. I wasn't so sure, now more than ever I felt that I needed to lay low. I had to play it smart. I told Mike to put the radio on the all-news station. Sure enough, the announcer was talking about the *Lady in Black*. He was interviewing some woman who said that she knew who the *Lady in Black* was. She said that she was positive that the crime fighter lived in a brownstone in Brooklyn. The announcer, Ray Love, talked to fan clubs that were forming all over the city. He said that he had purchased a T-shirt for his wife that read on the front, "Girls Kick Ass," and on the back read, "The Lady in Black Rules!" *Wow*, I thought. Although I was deeply flattered, I was more confused now than ever.

My cell phone vibrated. It was Bird. He said that the transfer from the Swiss account had been completed. "Great!" I thought. "At least Calvin didn't fuck that up. Time to make a move."

I was not sure who might have been watching me so I asked if I could crash with Mike over the long weekend, to which he eagerly obliged. We drove back into the city to Mike's apartment on the West side. On the way, we stopped and Mike purchased a red wig, long trench coat and a few toiletries and incidentals for me. I didn't want to risk going home right now to get my stuff.

I put the wig and coat on and walked into the apartment building. It was five p.m. and I realized I had not yet eaten. Mike suggested we call for Chinese to be delivered. I borrowed a big Yankees T-shirt from him, put it on, and sacked out in front of the TV. Mike said he had to study for a final so he went into the bedroom.

I grabbed the remote and turned on the TV. To my surprise, Sue Simmons, a veteran New York newscaster, was wearing a *Girls Kick Ass* T-shirt. The screen was split and Sue was talking to a younger newscaster who was interviewing a bunch of teenagers who had formed a *Lady in Black* fan club. The young woman was intently listening as a teenager depicted a story where this boy in school tried to attack her, and how she was able to turn the tables and kick his ass. She said she summoned the courage from the *Lady in Black* because she has become a role model for most of the girls in her school. According to the girl, she would never again be a victim. In the background, several young girls started chanting, "*Lady in Black, Lady in Black, Lady in Black.*"

God is so good. At that very second, I realized that I had to continue to fight. He had provided the affirmation I needed. I had to continue fighting for all the young girls who may be victimized. *Girls Kick Ass*. That phrase took *Girl Power* to the next level. Millions of young women needed the courage to fight back, in the classroom, in the boardroom, on the playground, and even in the bedroom. Shit, I was a bad bitch if I could empower and mobilize young girls like this. I smiled, and thought, *Girls Kick Ass*.

CHAPTER 19
New York, 2006

He held his breath as he watched the young girl climb the monkey bars. Beads of sweat dotted his brow, as he watched her braids bob from side to side and giggle with pure innocence. Keisha Williams was a free-spirited seven-year-old who was as spunky as she was smart. Her mom, Lashawn Williams, was proud that her daughter always brought home A's. It was hard to work twelve-hour shifts at the hospital and still find time to check homework. Lashawn dreamed of the day when she could work in an office as a receptionist, maybe even as an administrative assistant. A "9-5" office job would allow Lashawn to spend more time with Keisha, who in spite of her situation, was special.

The scent of Hanae Mori cologne lingered in the air and clung to his Everett Hall wool suit that hung on him like a cashmere glove. Nervously he placed a copy of the *Wall Street Journal* in front of his groin, as he ran his perfectly manicured hand through his dark, wavy curls. His mouth watered as he licked his lips with anticipation. He was so much smarter and smoother than all of *New York's Finest* combined. He was on a roll, and if things continued to go his way, Keisha Williams would be his tenth baby girl. No one in all of New York, or the country, had a clue as to who was responsible.

The combination of the sea urchin/uni and sashimi that he ate at the upscale sushi bar on the East Side made his stomach rumble. He regularly tipped the maître d' one hundred dollars, so that he could sit at the coveted table at this season's most popular restaurant. He was, after all, a gentleman. He wouldn't be caught dead at just *any* table, because he was, *The Man*.

While *The Sushi Set* was one of the trendiest spots in Manhattan, it always caused him to suffer from a little indigestion because his palate and digestive system were so delicate.

The sushi was the appetizer that would precede the catch of the day, because he was a gentleman who loved fresh, young meat. Today, Keisha tickled his fancy. He had been watching her for a month and was not sure if she was worthy of his attention. He purchased $5 worthy of candy from the corner store, because all but one of his victims loved candy. That one little girl told him that her mother did not allow her to eat candy, so he bought ice cream. Simple as that.

He had taken a little detour during his lunch hour and could not resist watching Keisha, and all of her youthful innocence, as he planned his strategy. He would take her this afternoon, during her after-school program. He already knew the routine; the teachers permitted the kids to play between on the playground between 4:30 and 5:30 p.m. He would offer her some candy and lure her to his bright red Mercedes convertible with the promise of a Barbie doll. Little girls loved his car, and then they grew up to be the big girls who loved his car, too! Females were so transparent and materialistic. That is why he was so repulsed by them. No, actually, he hated them.

Keisha had on little OshKosh B'Gosh overalls and a Baby Einstein turtleneck. *She is so beautiful yet so common*, he thought. Her mother obviously has no taste at all, because if he ever had a daughter, she would never wear that kind of clothing. His daughter would wear taffeta dresses and patent leather shoes. She would never, ever wear braids. Braids were so ethnic. As a matter of fact, if he ever had a daughter, he would never allow her to have friends who looked like Keisha. What a name, Keisha. That was so ghetto. Laquita, Lashawn, Tamika, those names were all so ghetto. There were millions of young girls walking around with the curse. White men would never take anyone seriously that had a name like Keisha, surely her mother knew that. Black women were so common, even the ones that he occasionally socialized with professionally. They always had attitudes and were often so *urban*. He had never met a woman, white or black, that was as civilized as he.

Truthfully, he really didn't feel comfortable around Black people, but he had met many white men who he felt comfortable with. He smiled as he thought about Ian, a man he found so attractive yet he did not have the balls to speak to. He was asexual, not really sure if he was gay, bisexual or what. His mother had ruined him for life. Ian schooled at Brown University and had traveled throughout the world. He was unemployed, because it was hard for an anthropology major to find a job. But he had more class than most. He loved Ian's lean, pale, sculptured body. Ian was the opposite of most of the Black women he dated. Their butts were so large, their breasts so abundant, their attitudes so over the top, and they were almost always so FAT. Although he tried to overlook these flaws in Black women, the thought of them just made his stomach turn.

As he went back to his car and got in, he thought, "Thankfully, none of these lowlifes has stolen it." He started the car and slowly pulled away from the curb, stopping for a brief minute to gaze at his prey one last time. The next time he saw her, she would be filled with fear. He would actually be doing her a favor. No one should go through life with a name like Keisha. *How absurd*, he thought.

Forty-five minutes later, he pulled into the parking lot that was housed underneath BCI headquarters. He took the elevator to the fifty-second floor and went to the executive washroom and splashed some water on his face to regain his composure. He was so excited about this afternoon's events that he could hardly contain himself.

He walked into the conference room and prayed that no one would notice how long he had been gone. There was a managers' meeting going on, and that bitch Sandy was running it. He hated her. She thought she was so smart and smooth. One day he would have to take care of her, too.

Sandy looked him dead in the face as he tried to slither into the meeting. "Glad you could join us," she said as smugly as she could. *What an asshole*, she thought. *How dare he come late to one of my meetings.*

Damn, he thought. *Now this is why I hate Black women, always trying to make me look bad. I will get her if it's the last thing I do.*

Two long hours later the meeting was adjourned. Three o'clock, only a half-hour to go. He wiped the perspiration off of his forehead. The anticipation was *a mother*. He went to his office and figured he could move a few papers around for the next half-hour.

Three thirty. *Finally*. He told his administrative assistant that he had to go see a client. He took the elevator to the garage and walked to his pride and joy. He gazed upon the car and saw pure perfection. A Mercedes-Benz was the only automobile a man of his means should drive. It was classy, dependable, and it exuded taste. Every businessman he knew sported a black 500 SEL. How droll and predictable. He was sophisticated and original, which is why a red Mercedes 500SL. *My, my, my. Sometimes I can't stand myself.* He sneered.

He slid into the car and put Ravel's *Bolero* into the CD player, which he thought was the appropriate selection because he was going to battle. As he merged onto the Hudson Parkway, the anticipation was beginning to overwhelm him as he cruised at about fifty miles per hour. As other cars whizzed by him, he sighed, as he savored every moment. Heads of pedestrians turned as he drove by. They were not used to seeing such a fine automobile. *Peasants*, he thought.

He passed the infamous Throgs Neck projects and drove around the corner to the elementary school. It was 4:30 p.m. on the nose, his timing was impeccable. He watched as Ms. Walker escorted the little rugrats outside to enjoy a breath of fresh air. Her biggest flaw was that she routinely would sneak around the corner to smoke some weed. Ms. Walker was as dedicated as they come but had a little drug habit. She rationalized it by thinking that she wasn't doing hard drugs like cocaine and heroine. Truthfully, as far as the law was concerned, it didn't matter how "hard" or "soft" they were, illegal drugs were illegal drugs. Most heroin addicts didn't start out as heroin addicts; they usually started with "gateway drugs" like weed or alcohol.

As Ms. Walker went around to the back of the building, he snuck out of his car and approached the schoolyard fence.

"Keisha Williams," he said.

Keisha turned and looked at the man and then ran to him.

"Did you call me, sir?" she asked.

"Yes, I did. Would you like some candy?" he asked.

As Keisha put her hands through the fence to take a handful of candy, she asked, "Do I know you?"

"Of course you know me. I am your Uncle Eddie," he said. "I used to baby-sit you when you were little. I've been in Hollywood, California for the last six years. I told your mom that we are looking for the next Rudy Huxtable for a new TV show. I want the producers to look at you for the part."

"Really?! I love the *Cosby Show*!"

"I know. Your mother told me. You have to come with me, because your audition is today."

"My mom didn't tell me about an audition. Why did she put these clothes on me then? Shouldn't I have on church clothes?"

"The producers want to see the natural look. They specifically did not want to see you dressed up."

"Okay," she said. "Let me tell Ms. Walker that I am leaving."

"Ms. Walker left and said she would be right back," he lied. "I already spoke with her and told her I was taking you. I even gave her a note from your mom."

"Okay, I'll be right there. I have to get my books."

"Just let me help you hop over this fence. If you take the time to get your books, we will surely be late for the audition."

As he gently lifted Keisha over the fence, he said, "We do not want to be late for the audition, now do we?"

"No sir, we don't," she replied as she eyed the car where he had de-activated the alarm. Her eyes widened and her mouth dropped, as she said under her breath, "Pretty car."

✴ ✴ ✴

The next morning I woke up and had to get my bearings. I had fallen asleep on Mike's couch and the TV was still on. There was a young male newscaster interviewing a woman who was crying. I grabbed the remote and turned up the volume. Lashawn Williams was holding a teddy bear that her daughter used to sleep with every night. When her daughter did not come home from school, she called the police, who immediately put Keisha on the Amber Alert list. Knowing how the police really reacted to crises in the projects, Lashawn gathered approximately twenty women who lived in her building and created a search party. The women combed the entire area and spent three hours looking for Keisha. By midnight, they finally went home. Lashawn received a phone call at six a.m. from the school principal; a janitor had found Keisha. Her lifeless body was on the playground wearing a pink taffeta dress and patent leather shoes.

The newscaster signed off from the crime scene and went live to the studio, where the Reverend Al Sharpton was ranting about there being a conspiracy to kill young Black girls. In his opinion, the killer had not yet been caught because the police did not care that young Black children were being butchered. That monster had struck again. This was the tenth child. Although he did kill Keisha, he had not butchered her. He had actually changed her clothing. What did that mean?

I had to face it. I would have to track down this madman and stop this madness. The *Lady in Black* had to capture the *School Yard Murderer*.

CHAPTER 20
Mitchellville, 2006

James looked over at his beautiful wife. Sometimes he could not believe how lucky he was. He had a wife that was both respected and admired. She was intelligent, elegant, and extremely sexy. The only thing that perplexed James was why she wouldn't give him none. From a purely sexual perspective, it did not matter because he had about three women that he was currently sexing. He was actually having trouble satisfying his three mistresses. All they wanted to do was have sex, but shit, he wasn't as young as he used to be and couldn't go like he used to.

He closed his eyes and thought for a minute. Damn! He and Tanya had not had sex in almost six months. It was that damned Third World organization she belonged to, she spent every waking second that she wasn't at work doing something for those damned African women. Why did she care so much about those people? She had a wonderful and fulfilling career, a handsome and successful husband. Why should she care about some Third World women who ran around with their titties flying? If they would just stop fucking everybody there wouldn't be such an AIDS epidemic. The thought of a continent full of women running around half naked made him horny. He put his hand under Tanya's silk robe, and cupped her breast.

Tanya moved her body, so that his hand would fall away from her breast. The very thought of him touching her made her ill. The thought of James repulsed her. She did not know how much more of him she could take. It took everything in her to even be able to talk to James. He thought he was so fucking superior. Although she did have to admit that James was smart. It was no easy feat to create a communications empire within such a racist society. But the man had such a HUGE ego. He was an asshole to the tenth power. He talked down to everyone, and felt he should always get special treatment. He walked around with his nose in the air like he was royalty. It was almost as if he had completely forgotten that he used to sell illegal drugs for a living. He also had completely forgotten that he was raised in Harlem, not Cambridge. To him, everything was Harvard this, Harvard that. Boy, did he get on her nerves. She closed her eyes and wondered how much longer it would take for her plans to be realized. Tanya's thoughts were interrupted by the sound of the phone ringing.

"Hello?" Tanya said.

The phone went dead. She knew it was that hoochie Karen. The phone rang again.

"Hello?" Tanya sang sweetly. The phone went dead again. It rang again. "Maybe you should answer it this time, honey. Whoever is calling doesn't want to talk to me."

James picked up the receiver. He knew it was Karen playing games. He would have Phyllis change his number Monday.

"Hello, James Bledsoe here."

"Hey baby, I need to see you."

"Roosevelt, I'm a little busy now. I'll call you back later."

"If you hang up, I'll come right over," said Karen.

"All right, Roosevelt, let me take this in my office. Tanya is sleeping."

"Two minutes, motherfucker," she said.

Karen was starting to take too many liberties. He had to end the relationship and he would do it right now. He got out of bed and put on his robe.

He grabbed the cordless phone and walked into his office. After James left the room, Tanya jumped up and ran into the master bathroom and picked up the receiver, putting her hand over the mouthpiece. It was the oldest trick in the book and James fell for it every time.

"I told you not to call me here," James said, trying not to lose his cool. She always made him lose his cool.

"I left you three messages and texted you twice. I need to talk to you."

"Can't it wait until Monday?"

"No, obviously it cannot. I need some money, James."

"Money? Why are you asking me for money?"

"Because Sandy fired me. I am unemployed."

"Most people who get fired file for unemployment."

"James, it takes a while before you can get your checks. Besides, a woman of my caliber cannot be seen in the unemployment office," she responded.

"Karen, this is not the appropriate time to have this conversation. Also, never call me on this line again," James said curtly.

"I won't call if you return my messages."

"Karen, I've wanted to tell you this for about a month now. It's over. Please don't try to call at home or work ever again."

"What do you mean it's over? You can't do this to me. I gave you five years of my life!" Karen screamed.

"Please, Karen. I love Tanya and I want to try and make my marriage work."

"James, you told me that you loved me. Was it all a lie?"

"Karen, I cannot talk to you right now. Tanya is in the next room."

"Meet me at your office in an hour."

"It's Sunday. I cannot just leave like that."

"You used to leave her when you wanted some pussy. Meet me at your office by noon. If you know what's good for you, you will be there. Good-bye," and she hung up.

James hit the off button on his cordless phone. He could not believe the gall that Karen had. He would meet her in two hours, give her $1,000 and end it for good. Billy D. had always told him never shit where you eat. *Damn, I wished I had listened to that advice*, thought James.

James walked back into the bedroom. When Tanya asked him who was on the phone, James lied and said it was Phyllis, his administrative assistant. There was an emergency that had to be resolved right away, so he would have to go into the office in D.C. He may even have to go to New York. As she continued to lay with her back toward James, Tanya smirked and thought, *I hope you have to go to New York, you lying motherfucker. I can't stand the sight of you. You don't realize it but you are about to get blackmailed, darling. Have a nice day!*

James jumped in the shower and tried to map out a plan of attack. He *knew* that he could not just stop seeing Karen. It was not that he did not want to, although her pussy was snapping. Anyway, James knew that Karen wouldn't just go away quietly, so he would have to get ugly with her and James had no problem with that. Twenty years ago, he would have just had her killed. However, that tactic, as lovely as it seemed, was too dangerous; he had too much to lose. He was a captain of industry now, and needed to play by the rules. He would feel Karen out, and then find a way to keep her on a short leash. She wasn't smart enough to be a *real* threat. Like always, all he needed to do was to tell her what she wanted to hear. *Shit*, he might even get lucky and get a little nooky today, especially since Tanya wasn't giving up anything.

One day soon, he would really have to talk to Tanya about her lack of interest in sex. Maybe they could see a shrink. He knew how much he excited her. Surely *he* wasn't the problem. He was determined to get his beautiful wife back. Hell, he would give Tanya an ultimatum. No, he would ask her to resign from the organization STOP. One thing at a time, though. First, he had to calm down Ms. Karen.

He hopped into his mint-condition 1998 black Maserati Diablo. Ordinarily he would have taken the limo, because it was rare that he would drive himself anywhere. Also, he did not want anyone to be in his business. An entrepreneurial limo driver would make a quick buck by selling a picture or two. He drove down Central Avenue, got onto the outer loop of the Beltway, and after he hit Route 50, he was at his office in twenty minutes. James parked on the street because all of the parking lots were closed on Sunday.

Ms. Ghetto Fabulous was waiting in the lobby, complete with her hands on hips. She had on a Lil' Kim-like zebra outfit that left little to the imagination. Her mammoth breasts were all over the place. James knew that the fact that he had quite a boner was quite evident. Why is it that such bad taste could get such a rise out of men, especially men with class? *Damn*, he thought. *I want to tap that ass, so BAD... Control, James. Control. You have a lot riding on this, no pun intended*, he laughed to himself.

James smoothly slid his hand around Karen's waist, told her how beautiful she looked, and how much he had missed her. He lied and begged her to understand because Tanya was onto them, and that they would have to cool out for a while. Luckily, Karen started to relax and let down her guard. The elevator opened and they got on. Before the doors shut completely, she walked over to James, unzipped his pants, stuck her hand into James' boxers, grabbed his penis, and slid her tongue into his mouth. Before they passed the second floor, Karen was already down on her knees. She quickly swept her weave into a loose ponytail, and was a little beside herself as she felt a surge of self-confidence. Karen felt like she was in control, once again and would use it to rock his world and get some money in the process.

Karen smiled at the thought of Sandy firing her. Hell, she secretly wished this had happened a long time ago. Why the fuck was she working anyway? A woman of her caliber should be chillin' and gettin' massages and pedicures. She should be meeting her girls for lunch at the Olive Garden and Applebee's. Shit, she was a class act, especially after she paid $200 for this outfit, and knew that she looked good. She would make James pay her the salary she made before she got fired. If he refused, she would simply threaten to tell Tanya. Karen smiled at her stroke of good fortune. *Shit, Sandy did me a favor by firing me.*

When they arrived at James' office suite, Karen began the conversation by telling James how broke she was, and that her rent and car note were due. Karen went on to tell James about a girlfriend of hers that was dating a married man, and how he paid her rent and other stuff. According to Karen, she would be even more valuable if she could "work from home," because that way, he could see her whenever he needed and that they wouldn't have to worry about nosy people in the office.

James masked his annoyance by not listening to her and by taking off Karen's clothes. Sex always put him in a good mood, and he was getting very tired of the games that Karen was playing. He knew that she was capable of anything. He had to play it cool and not show his hand. He would fuck her "one last good time," put her in a great mood, and then break it off with her again.

As James took off her clothes, Karen felt a surge of power and assurance. James could never refuse her, she thought. He loved her, and had told her that a thousand times. As he laid her on his custom Theodore's couch, she knew she had won the battle. She whispered that she loved him as they began having sex. As he slid into her waiting loins, Karen asked him if he would do anything for her, and James answered *yes*. As he began to climax, she asked James if he would continue to pay her weekly salary, and James responded, *"Yes, YES, YES!!!!!"* and immediately collapsed into Karen's clutches.

CHAPTER 21
New York, 1966

B illy D. had seen that James was growing bored in church and did not display the fire he once had as a younger fellow. He also knew that at sixteen, James was having sex with two girls in the choir, in addition to Deacon Jones' wife. Billy really liked the kid and knew that if he could persuade James to work for him that income would increase by at least tenfold. Billy D. decided that it was time to talk to James "man-to-man."

One night after a late-night revival, James' car would not start. Not knowing anything about cars, Billy had one of his low-level dealers disconnect the battery in James' car so that Billy D could conveniently be available to take him home. After five minutes of conversation with his young protégé, James agreed. Like everyone else, the kid knew that although Billy attended church, he was a dangerous criminal, which made him a little nervous. As he stepped into the immaculately polished Cadillac, he was immediately impressed. He was mesmerized at the style and grace of Billy's car. While en route to the Bledsoe home, Billy asked James if they could make a stop. James was fine with that because he felt like royalty, as many pedestrians stopped and waved as the infamous car drove by. Billy parked the Caddy in front of a late-night speakeasy called Foxy's.

It was already way past midnight, and since the Pastor had an early flight in the morning, he was way past sleep by now. Pastor was going to Atlanta to meet with members of the Southern Christian Leadership Conference. Since he was coming from a "church meeting," James would have no problems sneaking in tonight. But then again, he never did.

Foxy's was a cross between Madame Zenobia's in the movie *Five on the Black Hand Side* and the juke joint in *The Color Purple*. At 12:30 a.m., it was jumpin'! Everywhere you turned there were tight pencil skirts; short, blonde, bobbed hairstyles; torpedo-shaped breasts in tight mohair sweaters; and pointy-toed pumps. James had never seen so many Black "blonde-haired" women in his life. The brothers all sported suits with narrow-legged pants, sharp colored shirts, pencil-thin ties and Stacy Adams shoes. The setting was reminiscent of a cross between the dance scene in *West Side Story* and *Cooley High*.

At sixteen, and a true preacher's kid, James had never seen this type of lifestyle before. He was in awe at how much respect everyone paid Billy D. Realizing that young James was playing right into his hands, he introduced James to an eighteen-year-old "working girl," and asked her to hook young "Jimmy" up. The young lady named Mimi led the impressionable youth into the back room which contained a matching red velvet love seat and sofa. Mimi closed the door behind her, and offered James a drink. The young man had never had a drink of alcohol, so Mimi offered to make him one that tasted like fruit punch. James smiled and accepted.

Mimi told him to relax and that she would be right back. She went to the bartender and asked him to make her a Strawberry Daiquiri. She took the fruity concoction back into the room and handed it to him, who winced when after taking a big gulp of his drink. Trying to keep his cool and act mature in front of this caramel-colored honey, James realized that he needed to sip the potion. Mimi took off her hot pink polyester-blend outfit, and displayed her voluptuous yet toned and lean body in her Lucie Ann Peignoir Set and sheer Frederick's of Hollywood panties. James had never seen such a sexy get-up. The church girls that he boned always wore boring cotton drawers that, in most cases, did not fit. Mrs. Jones' underwear was always too tight. Mimi's panties fit her *just right*, and best of all, he could clearly see her pussy. James grinned and placed his hand on his lap, trying to hide his excitement. Mimi countered by moving James' hand and unzipping his pants. Before he knew it, he was standing up with his pants around his ankles, exposing his crisp white Fruit of the Loom briefs. She licked her lips in delight as she surveyed the length and extent of his apparent approval. For Mimi, who was accustomed to doing old guys that couldn't get it up, this definitely would be quite a treat.

Mimi straddled the boy and thrust her tongue into his mouth. He had never French kissed like this before. At that very moment, James prayed that Bill would adopt him, because he really could get used to living like this. The two kissed for what seemed like an eternity. He felt like a kid in a candy store, not knowing what to grab next. He tried to unfasten her bra. Like magic, it fell to the floor. *Wow, for her to be so skinny, her titties are so big,* he thought. Breasts were definitely a weakness for James. He sucked her breasts so hard that she pushed him away. Mimi revealed to him that ladies loved it when men sucked their breasts gently, so that's what James did. James didn't know it, but it really was what Mimi liked. As he sucked and kissed and sucked and kissed her, Mimi thought she had died and gone to heaven because all of her other clients didn't care if she liked it or not. Kissing was a "no no" in her profession, but since James was doing all the right things, she made an exception. Therefore, after an hour with Mimi's little instructions, James knew that he had died and gone to heaven.

James was a little anxious and tried to design a sexual strategy. He knew that Mimi was experienced and he did not want to disappoint her. She slid on a Japanese kimono that a client had lied and told her that he had brought back for her after a trip to China. Truth was that her client had bought it at a shop next to Nom Wah's Tea Parlor on Doyers Street in Chinatown. Mimi, however, didn't care where the kimono came from; all she knew was that wearing it made her feel exotic and powerful. Mimi left again to get another drink for her young, eager student; this time she told the bartender to include an extra shot of rum. After she handed James his second drink, she slid out of the robe while she allowed him to enjoy the liquid ambrosia. Either because he was already drunk, or because he was ready to finish what he had started, James found his drink to be less bitter. Five minutes later, James climbed on top of Mimi and for two solid hours they engaged in pure, erotic, animalistic sex. Raw, just like Mimi liked it, while James thought he was in love.

As he put on his clothes, he looked at his watch, 3:30 a.m. Oh well, who cared? He knew that his parents were asleep, and he had just experienced the night of life. Feeling like "a man" now, he gave Mimi a kiss on the cheek, and asked her for her telephone number. She responded by saying that Billy D. could get in touch with her.

James returned to the lounge where Billy D. was still holding court. The place was still packed and Billy was pleased with what he knew had just transpired. Billy threw James the keys to the Caddy and asked James to wait for him in the car. James obliged. Billy gave Mimi $200 and rewarded her with a small packet of white powder. She thought to herself that she hoped she could see the young man again. He was so tall, good looking, considerate, and best of all a willing lover. Her vagina got moist and her clitoris tingled, just thinking about the events of the evening. She wanted to definitely make sure that James became a regular client. Hell, she may even start giving it to him free; all she had to do was *please her* the way she did countless, nameless, faceless men. Before Billy left, he went into the room where the young couple had spent time and opened the closet door. Inside the closet was a decrepit old man named Jake. Old Jake held up a Polaroid camera in his right hand, and took the $50 bill that Billy handed him with his left. The old man handed him approximately ten pictures of James and the young prostitute. This was just the insurance that Billy would need to ensure that James would accept his offer of employment.

Ten minutes later, Billy D. got into the car and asked James if he had enjoyed himself. James confessed to Billy that he would love to see Mimi again. Billy told James that he would be happy to arrange visits with Mimi as often as he liked, but only if James would occasionally "run some errands" for him. James told him that his parents probably would not approve. Still trying to play the nice card, Billy told James that he would make it worth his while if he agreed. Billy finally conceded by asking James to think about it, and to meet him next Friday at Foxy's at ten p.m. with his decision.

During the next seven days, thoughts of Mimi consumed James. He longed to talk to her and wished he had gotten her number from Billy.

James was so caught up in Mimi that he refused to spend any time with his three girlfriends that week. He couldn't even concentrate in school, and as a result, failed two exams. James had it bad. He counted the days until Friday arrived, and he would see Mimi again. Every night before he went to bed he thanked the Lord for creating Mimi.

The week flew by as James anticipated sweet-assed Mimi. That evening, James dressed in his finest black trousers and a black silk shirt, splashed on a little too much Old Spice. As he dressed, he played his favorite song by Smokey Robinson and sang along, "Oooooooo, baby, baby." He held himself and danced slowly and imagined Mimi being in his arms. She was so different than the girls that went to church and were in his school.

James drove his father's Buick and parked in front of Foxy's at 10 p.m. sharp. As he walked up to the club, he noticed a brand-new bright shiny red Mustang convertible, and wondered what kind of a guy drove a car like that. *One day*, he thought, *it might be me*. He tried to play it cool, as he bopped into the place and asked the hostess if he could speak with Billy D. The hostess escorted him in and took his drink order. He described the drink that he'd had the last time he was there, and a waitress returned with what she called a "Strawberry Daiquiri." Considering what he and Mimi had done together, that sounded exactly right.

As he sipped his drink, for a brief moment, his heart stopped and he totally lost his composure when Mimi came into the lounge area and sat on his lap. James almost melted underneath her as she described to him how and why she missed him. Unable to contain himself, James escorted Mimi to the back room and spent an hour with her reenacting what they had done a week ago. Later, Mimi led James back into the lounge area where Billy was ready to talk to him.

"Are you ready to work for me?" Billy asked.

"What do you want me to do?" asked Billy, still intoxicated by Mimi.

"Like I said, run a few errands, make some deliveries, easy stuff."

"As much as I appreciate all that you have done for me and the church, I don't think I can work for you, sir. The rumor is that you are into illegal activity. I plan to go to college and be a businessman."

"Come with me, James. I want to show you something," said Billy D.

Billy led James outside and handed him a set of keys that had a running horse on the key chain. Billy told James to go over to the red Mustang and get in. When James went to open the door to the beautiful vehicle, to his surprise, Mimi was in the passenger side, wearing a red ribbon tied around her naked, succulent body. He gave the couple a $100 bill and told them to have a good time. They went to the local Holiday Inn and stayed for the entire night. The next morning, Mimi asked James what plans he had for the day. He said that he would go to school and then he had to go to work. Mimi asked him where he worked and James replied that he worked for Billy D. The rest reads like a classic novel.

Just as he had figured, James was a quick study and became one of Billy's star workers. James introduced Billy D to some of the white boys at his school. Initially, Billy simply wanted James to provide introductions so that no one knew that James was connected to the business. Meanwhile, James went to school and afterward spent every minute learning the "business" of the business. He had a special gift for numbers so he became Billy's accountant of sorts.

With so many legitimate contacts to tap into, James proved to be an invaluable asset to the Williams Empire. Billy trusted James, like he had trusted no on else before. Having no children that he claimed, James was like the only son Billy never had. Business soared and he and James banked a lot of dough.

Business expanded across Manhattan, into the Bronx, Queens, and even New Jersey. Soon, Billy bought a house on Long Island, and James graduated from high school and earned a scholarship to Rutgers University in New Jersey. Mimi moved to Jersey to be with James. During the week, he went to class and studied. Every weekend he went to New York and ran the Williams Empire, and oh yeah, went to attend Sunday service with his "proud parents." Once in a while he would have to leave school midweek to handle a financial crisis. To compensate for his unexcused absences, he would pay off an instructor who would allow him to take a make-up exam, or he would simply charm the female professors into fudging his grades. Due to his resourcefulness and boyish charm, James maintained a 3.7 average, while earning an income in excess of half a million dollars annually, tax-free.

Unfortunately, while James was away in school, Billy D. developed a wicked cocaine habit, and was not as sharp as he used to be. James found himself having to handle an increasingly amount of the business. Billy D. was beginning to get sloppy, and was getting in the way of their profits. Over the years, James was becoming more and more greedy, and decided that Billy had to go.

James and Mimi had agreed to spend the Thanksgiving holiday at Billy's home on Long Island. James had an exam on Wednesday morning, so he suggested that Mimi go on up to New York ahead of him. Mimi arrived in Long Island on Tuesday, and began the seduction routine that she and James had concocted. Mimi began her trap by feeding Billy cognac and cocaine. She preyed on his sympathy by feeding him stories of how "cruel" James was to her in New Jersey, and of how she would rather be with Billy D. Mimi and Billy D. fucked, off and on, for the entire night; after all, Billy D. was an "old fuck" that needed time to recuperate between sessions. By two a.m., he was still alive and she was getting bored. While he did more blow, she excused herself and went into his bedroom. She returned to the living room with a .22 caliber pistol, blew Billy D's brains out, snorted some coke and then went to sleep. Mimi loathed having to fuck old men.

The next day when James arrived, he found Mimi, half dead from the combination of the night's conquest and the unbelievable amount of drug use, and Billy D, his mentor dead. James was getting bored with Mimi and her expensive habit, so he finished Mimi off by shooting her in the head. You could never trust women to keep their mouths closed. James was the King. The King of New York!

CHAPTER 22
New York, 1968

Because nobody really knew who he was on the streets, James changed his name to *Lord Bless*, a title that was sort of a play on words. James felt that he was blessed to have become so successful in the drug business. He also saw himself as a drug lord and his last name was Bledsoe. Corny, huh?

Lord Bless transferred to NYU, to be closer to his business and to sustain his drug empire. Being in the city, he was able to expand further and service clientele who lived in all five boroughs. He even continued to increase his grades to a 3.8 grade-point average and, ironically, considered going to law school. Lord Bless did not have to deal with the same type of problems that Billy had to deal with, because James had situated the business among a higher level of clientele and communicated primarily with celebrities, corporate officers, captains of industry, dignitaries, and the like.

Paradoxically, his father's church also generated a great deal of business for Lord Bless. There were many musicians, movie stars, and politicians that were involved in the civil rights movement that also supported his business. They needed a drug connection that they could trust and Lord Bless was their man.

Lord Bless was also clever in that he did not have a lot of people working for him. For example, he only employed girls who had a 3.5 grade-point average or better and attended college full-time on scholarship. He knew that he could trust these females because they had so much to lose. He also only hired women because he knew male drug dealers were always trying to impress girls and usually ran their mouths. His employees' only interest was to generate income to pay college expenses and be lucky enough to fuck him every now and again. That did not happen too frequently, though, because one thing Billy D. did teach him was to *never shit where you eat*. James' mentor also taught him to never hire anyone who had "a habit." If Billy D. even *suspected* his dealers of doing drugs, they were immediately fired. Similarly, Lord Bless ran the same tight ship.

Lord Bless continued to attend the First Baptist Church of the Rock, where he was the most eligible bachelor in the congregation. James wore the finest suits and had the sharpest haircuts, and looked like he was going to be the first Black man to grace the cover of *Gentlemen's Quarterly* magazine. He was handsome, intelligent, and debonair. His father was so proud, that he didn't see all of the riches that his son was so flagrantly displaying. James had developed into a full grown man, but in the eyes of the congregation, he was still the precocious little boy that they fell in love with when he was born. Since Billy D. had done such a good job of keeping James' involvement in "the business," none of the church members suspected that he had taken over Billy D.'s enterprise, not even the ones who unknowingly patronized him. Lord Bless had made it. He did feel empty because he could not find a woman that could hold his attention for more than a minute, although James did find show-business women interesting and fascinating. Unfortunately, as he later discovered, the singers and actresses could not *act* their way through their drug habits or self-absorbed lives. For James, drugs were such a turnoff.

James became smitten with the arts after he had attended a concert at Carnegie Hall that featured a former child prodigy from North Carolina, named Zelda Knight. Billy D. wanted to expose James to some of the "finer" things in life outside of the church, so he somehow was able to convince Ophelia to allow him to take James to Carnegie Hall. Ophelia had never been to such a fancy venue and was only happy that her baby James would be able to go. She didn't see the harm in it, especially since the Pastor was out of town, again, as usual.

Zelda Knight was the fourth act of the concert, and James, who was not a big fan of classical music, needed to get up and use the bathroom. As he trudged up the aisle to the bathroom, he turned to pick up the wallet that had fallen out of his jacket. As he rose to continue his journey to the restroom, he stopped in his tracks as he caught a glimpse of one of the most exquisite young women he had ever seen. Her angelic face and passionate hands floated over to a white baby-grand piano. Her long black braids swung from side to side as her fingers fluidly glided over the keys. He was overwhelmed by the combination of her beauty and talent, as he felt a tear slowly trickle down his cheek. James stood in the back of the theater, soaked up the atmosphere, and absorbed her profile as the stage light illuminated her loveliness. He felt the surge of every *crescendo* and *piano* of every movement she played, and his heart stirred as she played "Amazing Grace." He had never felt like this without having sex. Sure, he had fooled around with a few of the girls at church and Mimi, but none of them held candle to this girl. James walked out into the lobby and asked an usher to backstage. James followed the directions and found the lounge where the performers sat in between acts.

Zelda finished her set and timidly sat down on the orange-and-beige Napoleon love seat. As James gazed upon this girl, he realized just how young she was. He sat beside her and started to introduce himself when a matronly lady deliberately sat in between them. Being the polite young church boy that he was, James introduced himself to the matronly lady first. Charmed by the smile of the young man, Mrs. Ida Johnson eagerly held her hand out. As James reluctantly kissed her chubby hand, Mrs. Johnson introduced James to Miss Zelda Knight, and quickly told him that she was only fifteen.

Mrs. Johnson excused herself to use the ladies room; unfortunately, she had sneaked one too many shots of whiskey from her hip flask in her pocketbook and the whiskey seemed to go right through her. A ten-minute conversation was just enough time for him to learn that Zelda and Mrs. Johnson were staying at the Waldorf-Astoria Hotel and would be checking out at noon tomorrow. James asked if she could meet him in the lobby of the hotel at midnight; they had both figured that Mrs. Johnson would be in a drunken slumber by then. To ensure that she cooperated, he would have a bottle of Johnnie Walker Red accidentally sent to the room. Zelda was so mesmerized by the charisma that this golden boy possessed, she merely nodded her head. She probably would have robbed a bank if James asked her to.

When Mrs. Johnson returned, Zelda jumped up and suggested that they go back to the hotel because she was hungry and was ready to retire for the evening. Thankfully, Miss Ida agreed and when they got back to their room, they dined nearby at Blarney's Deli. While Ida feasted on three whiskey sours and pastrami on rye, Zelda devoured a hamburger, fries, and a chocolate milkshake.

Luckily, the hotel was two blocks away because Zee had to damn near carry Mrs. Johnson back to the room. Bless her soul, Mrs. Johnson was drunk and passed out on the bed, again. Mrs. Johnson was the "church mother" and made it her role to ensure that all of the church's children were properly cared for. Zelda's mom was always in the streets partying and too busy to care for such a precious and gifted young daughter. As a matter of fact, it was Mrs. Johnson who always saw to it that Zelda went to her piano lessons and frequently ended up paying for them. Ida Johnson had herself been abused as a young woman, and over time, had found solace and comfort in her flask. Her husband had been dead for ten years now, but she could not find the strength to kick the habit. Although she thought that it was her own personal little secret, because she was so beloved by the church, they overlooked the smell of alcohol on her breath, and affectionately allowed her to function within the church, despite her alcoholic ways.

After Mrs. Johnson passed out, Zelda lovingly changed her clothes and gently tucked her in. While Mrs. Johnson felt sorry for young Zelda's situation, Zelda was connected to Mrs. Johnson, because *she* felt sorry for Mrs. Johnson. The young girl smiled as she gazed upon the older with such affection and reverence.

Quietly, Zelda changed her clothes, slipping into a little black silk dress that her cousin Nita had purchased at Macy's three years ago while in New

York. Zelda had sneaked and packed it into her suitcase. According to Nita, with a simple string of pearls and black high-heeled pumps, a little black dress was always in style. Zelda looked in the mirror and turned off the lights so that the neon light outside the hotel window illuminated her silhouette. She felt like a full grown woman, as she tilted her head to the side, pleased with what she saw. She gingerly moved her hand across her pearls and slowly moved it across her breast down to her tiny waist. Her heart beat madly as she thought about James, though she hardly knew him. She questioned her decision to meet with such a striking, big city stranger. Unfortunately for Zelda, her decision to meet James, a man whom she didn't really know from Adam, would not be a good one, although sometimes wonderful outcomes were derived through pain and misery.

She took the hotel key, hid it in her bra, and placed a ten-dollar bill in her shoe. She blew Miss Ida a kiss, gently closed the door, and walked to the elevator. The lobby of the Waldorf was so bright, elegant, and ornate, and represented the opulence and decadence that was New York City. Giddy with anticipation, Zelda hopped onto an overstuffed, leather, wing-backed chair and waited patiently for James to arrive.

Minutes later, James walked into the hotel like he owned the joint. He had changed into a dark linen suit, an oxford shirt, and Italian leather loafers. James was, in a word, sophisticated. He touched her arm and led her to the reception desk, and just as he was about to send a bottle of Johnnie to room 204, Zelda informed him that Ida was fast asleep.

As she confidently held his arm, they walked outside the hotel and waited for his car to be brought around to the valet. She was instantly impressed by how he beat the valet to the passenger side door and held it open for her. She giggled as she slid into this beautiful car, that up until now, she had only seen in movies. She had never seen a Negro, much less a young Negro, behind the wheel of such a grand and shiny new car. Neither of them uttered a word as he drove into the moonlight and made their way toward Harlem.

As his newest employee, Billy D. often let James borrow his car and use one of his luxurious flats in Harlem to "unwind and relax." An hour later

James was inside of Zelda, and she was sweet, just like a dream. He held her in silence afterward. The two dressed as the sun was beginning to rise onto the picture-perfect horizon. James dropped Zelda off at the Waldorf at five a.m. Zelda had written her address and phone number in North Carolina on an old napkin, and pressed it into his hands as he kissed her on the cheek, and drove off.

Nine months later, I, Sandora Knight was born and my sixteen-year-old-mother, Zelda, was shunned by the community. When Zelda's mother figured out that her daughter was pregnant, she immediately threw her out onto the street. Mrs. Johnson took Zelda in, but was pressured by the women in the community to throw her out as well. Living with Mrs. Johnson was both a blessing and a curse for Zelda, who constantly had to listen to her drunken tirades about the devil and fornication.

After two long years of listening to long religious speeches from Mrs. Johnson and tired of all those dirty looks that the church folk were constantly giving her, Zelda packed up me and her bags, and hitchhiked to New York. She needed to get away. Zelda hated the fact that the very people who raised her could so easily turn their backs on her. Plus, I was getting to the age where Zelda thought that people's treatment of us might affect my self-esteem.

The longer she stayed in North Carolina, the more she thought about James. Why hadn't he returned any of her phone calls? In four years she had not talked to him once so he did not know that he had a beautiful daughter. She had to get in touch with him. She had to see him, to touch him. She just wanted to be with him. In one night, she had fallen in love. In one night, her whole life had changed. Even her best friend in the whole world, Carla, told her that she had been used, telling her that James had just wanted sex. Since James had gotten what he wanted from Zelda, he didn't need to see her again. In her heart of hearts, Zelda could not bring herself to believe that Carla might be right; she had to see James and find out for herself. However, if she did find him again, she wouldn't mention the baby, until she was sure that he loved her as much as she loved him.

Luckily, since her hometown of Lumberton, North Carolina was located right on Interstate 95, which connects the entire East Coast starting at Miami and going straight up to Canada. With me on her hip, Zelda hiked up her dress, and put her thumb out. About ten trucks stopped before she agreed to accept a ride. Her friend Carla, who was a little more worldly than Zelda, told her to never accept a ride from a white man, so she didn't. After two hours of waiting on the side of the road and dealing with irate white truck drivers, a nice older Black couple, Mr. and Mrs. Homer Jackson, pulled over. They told her that they were on their way to New York because their granddaughter was singing at Birdland. Zelda thought that they looked nice enough, especially after Mr. Jackson bounced me on his knee while Zelda put our bags in the trunk. She closed her eyes and thanked God for sending this nice couple our way. Zelda felt that this was the beginning of a new life for her as they drove her away from Lumberton and her old life.

Eleven hours later, we arrived in New York. The nice couple dropped Zee off in the heart of Manhattan at 42nd and Broadway. Zelda lied and told the couple that her uncle was going to be picking them up there and it was the only landmark that she could think of. Zelda could not imagine where to begin to look for James. However, she knew that her first priority would be to secure a place for us to live. It was early Monday morning and Mom walked up and down Broadway and all the little side streets looking for a rooming house. She discovered that there were none that were available to accommodate a young Black girl and her baby. Finally, a little Jewish woman took her aside and told her that she may want to take the train to Harlem because it would be, "easier for a nigger to find a place to live."

Zee followed the bigot's instructions and hailed a cab that dropped her off "near" Harlem. After seeing five overpriced apartments, Zelda finally found a nice room for rent. Although the space was very small, it was warm and cozy with its pale yellow walls, bright flowered curtains, and a chenille bedspread to match—it was a very happy room. The landlord was an energetic and tender older lady who attended the First Baptist Church of the Rock. As good church women do, Mrs. Laura Thomas invited Zelda to attend church with her on Sunday. Zelda was grateful for her fortune and was anxious to thank God personally for allowing her to arrive safely and feel safe in such an immensely unsafe city.

On Sunday morning, Zelda got up early and dressed us in the finest outfits she had brought with her from Lumberton. Zelda, Mrs. Thomas and me arrived early and sat in the third-row pew. The choir came out and sang their opening hymn which resonated the message of forgiveness. It was during this rousing gospel message when Zelda noticed the handsome soloist approaching the microphone. Zelda fainted as James began to sing. Zelda awoke to find herself lying on a couch near the choir rehearsal room and James standing over her. Once again, James had saved the day.

Zelda could not believe her eyes and had a million questions to ask James. She fell in love with him all over again when James smiled and agreed to pick Zelda up on Saturday afternoon. James told her that they would spend the day together. Zelda was furious and excited because he didn't even seem ashamed that he hadn't picked up the phone to call her. However, she remained calm, because she needed to know how he felt about her. Zelda didn't understand that the fact that he never called her, should have told her exactly how he felt about her.

Because she was resourceful and hardworking, during her first week in Harlem, Zelda had already gotten a job as a maid during the day. At night she taught piano at the church, and arranged for Mrs. Thomas to watch me.

At noon on the nose, James pulled up to our house in his hot Mustang convertible, hopped out of the car, and opened the passenger door for Zelda. *He's such a gentleman and he's so handsome*, she thought. Unfortunately for Zelda, she didn't realize that she was about to be "the same fool twice." Again, she didn't realize that blessings didn't come to the impatient.

When they arrived at his home, or Billy D's old flat, all of the memories of four years ago came flooding back to her. Her mind was warm and fixed on the night of passion that they shared in this flat, and of how affectionate he was toward her. Zelda was so nervous that she began to fidget. James offered her something to calm her down. Since it sort of looked like the BC headache powder that she had so often used in Lumberton, she thought that James was offering her a fancier big-city version of it. She didn't understand why she had to inhale it through a small straw, and coughed as the white powder traveled into her nasal cavities. Immediately, Zelda felt herself feeling light-headed; she fainted and was out for about two hours straight.

James remembered being charmed by her innocence when he first met her, but he was by no means "in love" with Zelda. Hell, with Mimi around, he had already had a *real* woman. Why would he want to be bothered with this starry-eyed country bumpkin? He did think she was a beautiful and talented young lady, and he wanted to see if she was as good in bed as he remembered her being years ago. James figured that he would placate Zelda for a while; besides, he was getting bored with Mimi and her drug thing. So, he decided that would have sex with Zelda and offer her some money to tide her over. James knew that she would take more work than he felt Zelda would be worth, because he was *definitely* not interested in a relationship.

When Zelda came to, she found herself in a soft bed with gold satin sheets. Her head was pounding but she felt so snug in the bed of James Bledsoe. She lay back and realized in a panic that she was nude. She tried to remember what happened but she couldn't. She began to cry and she noticed blood on the sheets.

James came out of the shower and noticed the sheets.

"Damn, those cost me a hundred dollars."

"I...I...I...I'm sorry, James. What happened?"

"You couldn't keep your hands off me. You damn near raped me," James joked.

"You, you, you mean we had sex?"

"You mean you don't remember? Oooh, it was so good, Zee. I'm ready for round two, so how about it?"

Zelda was crying hysterically, and couldn't believe that she had made the mistake of having sex with James too soon. How could she tell him about me now?

"What do you say, Zee? How about hopping back on Big Daddy?"

Suddenly, the room began to tilt and spin. Zee jumped out of bed and ran to the bathroom, put her head over the commode, and out came her guts.

"Damn, bitch, what's wrong with you? I definitely don't want none now; you need to take a shower, get your shit, so I can take you home."

Zelda reluctantly cleaned herself off, gathered her things, and slowly got dressed, fuming about James' treatment, like she were a common whore. He dropped her off at the rooming house, and didn't even utter a word, not even good-bye. To think she traveled all the way from North Carolina to be with him. The fairy tale ending that she had dreamed about was fading fast. She could not have been more disappointed or hurt.

On July 5, 1973, nine months after the encounter, Malcolm Knight was born to a single mother, child prodigy, who had won hundreds of contests and had performed at Lincoln Center at the age of fifteen. Zelda was a single mother, who could have been anything that she wanted to be. However, because she chose to choose her own destiny, this single mother, was destined to be an unwed mother of two, who would become dependent on heroin to get her through her depression. Instead of being on track to establish a career that would have taken her around the world and living large, Zelda would die a drug-addicted junkie, in Section 8 housing at the hands of a homicidal drug flunky.

When James found out about her pregnancy, he made her promise to have an abortion, gave her $2,000, moved her out of the rooming house, and into a low-income housing development (the projects) in Brooklyn. He told her that he never wanted to see her again and that he would kill her if she tried to set foot in his church again. Zelda was all alone in a strange city, young and dumb, with two children to raise.

Being the "golden boy" of the church that he was, it was easy for James to convince Mrs. Thomas to stay away from Zee. James lied and told Mrs. Thomas that Zelda was obsessed with him, and that she was threatening to go to his father and claim to be pregnant if he didn't marry her. Mrs. Thomas didn't want to have a liar living under her roof, but needed the extra income to help make ends meet. So, in an act of "kindness," James promised to pay her entire mortgage for a whole year to help ease her conscience, and Mrs. Thomas was all to willing to oblige. *How could that nice young girl try and trap the Pastor's son? Something had to be wrong with her to bring that poor, sweet baby so far from home*, she thought.

Mrs. Thomas never returned Zelda's phone calls, and always pulled the drapes when she saw her come down the street. Meanwhile, Zelda gave birth to Malcolm, and again kept this secret from James. Soon after being evicted from Mrs. Thomas' home, Zelda lost her job as a maid because she could not afford the expenses of transportation to and from work in Harlem.

With two small children to care for, Zee tried to make as happy a life as she could. She loved her children more than anything in the world and was a good mother. Zelda was positive that she could find a way out for her family. Her daily prayer was for the Lord to make a way and to help her give her children as much love as she could.

As we grew older, Momma started to supplement our meager income by selling marijuana. We were both growing like weeds and it seemed like every time she turned around, I needed a new coat, or Malcolm needed a new pair of shoes. She used to tell us that we would be tall like our father. Our mysterious father, who we did not know and who never acknowledged us as his children.

Slowly, our lives became more and more pitiful. In the beginning, Malcolm and I never realized just how poor we were. We never had any money, but we always had lots of love, which was all that we needed. Malcolm and I studied hard in school and got good grades.

After Momma got involved in selling drugs, I saw her slowly begin to use her own product. Mostly weed, although she would use cocaine, on rare occasions. When this man named Lord Bless came through, he would give her a little white packet, if she was good. She was more interested in drugs, than she was in sex, and it seemed like Lord Bless was the only one she liked to "give it up to." Even though they hooked up on the regular, he never knew that the kids that he disrespected her in front of were his own. It never even crossed his mind. The only thing that Lord Bless saw was that each time he saw Zelda, she looked worse and worse. The sight of Zelda and her situation was beginning to repulse Lord Bless, until he finally told Zelda that she should never call him or come to his home again. To ease his guilt, Lord Bless slid Zelda an envelope that contained $5,000. Rather than taking the money to get back on her feet, Zelda found out about some "project scheme" that could "double her money in no time." Like most "get rich quick" schemes, Zelda quickly lost her windfall. Although she had set aside a little money, instead of buying her children toys, clothes, or books, she invested in her imminent downfall, and chose heroin as the "business of the future."

Our lives spiraled downward fast, as Zelda consistently violated the first law of dealing dope: NEVER get high on your own supply. Unfortunately, Zee didn't just get high, she stayed high, which left me with not only the task of raising Malcolm, but also in providing food and paying rent. I even convinced Zee to join the local church. The congregation made several unsuccessful attempts to get Zee clean through a rehab facility in Upstate New York, but it was a lost cause.

Although her shit was whack as a mother, Zee would come in and out of consciousness and every once in awhile, would attend a parent/teacher conference or help me study for a test. But those times were few and far between.

Once a month, there were eviction notices, and Zee would break down and call the home of Lord Bless, who of course, ignored each call. Whenever she showed up at his house, James greeted her with a wave of his hand, and told her to leave the premises. Sometimes, Zee was so desperate; she'd stand outside for hours, banging on the door, begging for him to let her in.

One time, in an obvious act of cruelness, James came to the door with a towel wrapped around his waist and let Zelda in. This time, James waved her in and told her to sit on the couch. As she sat on a seventeenth-century French provincial sofa, she noticed that she had a full view of Lord Bless, who had left her on the couch in order to resume having sex with a leggy blonde with long hair and powder-blue eye shadow. Lord Bless had the girl's hands tied to his bedposts and had a scarf covering her mouth.

Zelda was too terrified to move as Lord Bless writhed with pleasure; he looked directly at Zee and smirked. Then he would take a taut leather strap and smack the blonde. An asshole to the max. The sadistic sex continued for an hour, until the blonde finally passed out and Lord Bless slammed the bedroom door shut.

While Lord Bless continued to conduct his sick sex show behind the closed door, Zee noticed a large brown duffel bag that was tucked away behind the curtains in the living room. After James closed the door, Zee grabbed the bag, ran to the bathroom, and shut the door. She snuck a peek, and to her surprise, the bag contained countless bundles of hundred-dollar bills. There could be as much as a million dollars! Plotting her escape, Zee flushed the toilet and turned the faucet on high, and while the water ran loudly, she took the bag and placed it outside the front door in the bushes. Her mind was racing and she thanked God that she was not high, and was able to rationally think things through. Zelda sat quietly for another half an hour while James continued to have his way with Blondie.

Suddenly, two big men in suits came into the flat with a stretcher. They knocked on the door to the bedroom and James let them in. Exasperated by Zelda's presence, he said, "You still here, bitch?!? You have five seconds to get your butt outta here and I never want to see your sorry ass again." Lord Bless stormed out of the bedroom, threw several hundred-dollar bills at her, and told Zee to fuck off.

As she ran out the door of Lord Bless' house in Long Island, Zee grabbed the brown bag and ran as fast as she could. Zelda ducked into the first restaurant she saw and called a car service that the owner recommended. While she waited, Zee ordered lunch, although she picked at her food because she was way too nervous to eat. Deep down she knew that she had just committed suicide. When Lord Bless found out that she had taken the duffel bag, and he would find out, he would surely kill her. An hour later, she was on her way to the Long Island Railroad and shivered as she arrived at Baldwin Station. While trying to shake off her nervousness, Zelda purchased a one-way ticket to Penn Station.

Walking toward the lockers, Zee passed a stationery store, where she purchased the pinkest shade of writing paper and a ballpoint pen. She cried as she wrote the heartfelt letter to her oldest child. *"My Last Will and Testament,"* she thought.

She walked and walked by rows and rows of lockers. What locker should she choose? Which locker would be safe? Should she put this money in the bank? Her head was reeling and she became disoriented. She finally came to the number 007, because she loved those secret agent movies. That was the one, she was sure of it. She quickly placed two quarters in the locker and opened the door. She threw the bag in but first took one of the bundles.

For the first time in years, Zee felt good. No, she felt great. She walked on air. On the way home, she purchased two coats and two pair of sneakers for her children, and a Bible for herself.

CHAPTER 23
Washington, D.C., 2006

Deena hiked her skirt up as she sashayed into Mr. Bledsoe's office. She was interviewing for Karen's old position and wanted to make a good impression. She did think it odd that he was doing the interviewing. Since when did a Chief Executive Officer interview for secretarial positions? Well, whatever. She was determined to get the position, whatever it took. Lord knows she needed the money. Her last boyfriend dumped her when his wife found out that he was seeing her. As a matter of fact, Deena had just barely missed getting the beat down of her life. Luckily, in the nick of time, she was able to sneak out of the garage, but later found out that she had left her wallet behind. At any rate, that stream of income had permanently been eliminated.

Deena stopped in the ladies room on the way to James' office. She was an attractive girl, but in a slutty kind of way. She had that light-skinned, long-hair thing going, but most of the time she just looked washed out. She was a size six, but had size 40D implants, a gift from one of her boyfriends who thought that larger breasts would make him cum quicker. He had money to burn because he had just signed an $8 million NFL contract with the Washington Redskins. Well, this dude paid his frat brother, a plastic surgeon, to put these things in Deena, and she agreed. Now Deena always looked like she was bending over. They are way too big for her frame, but to let her tell it, they have increased her marketability by 100 percent.

She adjusted her tight, black Jones New York suit, so that the skirt fell right below the thigh. She had even practiced sitting down, so that she could show him the pussy, when necessary. Deena felt that underwear was overrated. She felt that wearing underwear kept all of the natural juices in, which is why so many women smelled bad. Consequently, she never wore them.

Deena also strategically opened too many buttons on her blouse, so that if she sat just so, Mr. Bledsoe would be able to get a full view of her breasts. Shit, her momma always said, "If you got it, go get it," and Deena had it. She took out her Gucci cologne and sprayed it lightly behind her ears, the crease of her elbow, and on her breasts. *Ready!*

Feeling pretty good about herself, Deena sashayed over to Phyllis and informed her that she was there for the 11 a.m. interview with Mr. Bledsoe. Phyllis sucked her teeth and buzzed James.

"Your eleven o'clock is here although I'm not sure if she is here for an interview or if there is a bachelor party in your office," said Phyllis.

"That will be all, Phyllis. Show Ms. Martin right in."

"Mr. Bledsoe says you may come in. You may want to button your shirt first," she replied.

Deena smiled and said "thank you" as sweetly as she could. She was used to women "hating on her." They were all just jealous, every last one of them. Deep down she knew that most women either wanted what she had, or wanted her. This old broad was mad because she probably hadn't gotten any since the seventies.

Deena strutted in like a drag queen with a newly approved charge card. She was out for the kill. She slid into the chair that was placed in front of Mr. Bledsoe's massive mahogany desk and crossed her legs. It was like something straight out of *Basic Instinct*.

"Thank you for allowing me to interview for the position," Deena said softly yet seductively.

"Your reputation precedes you, Ms. Martin," James said as he smoothed out his pants and his dick.

"I am very familiar with the duties of this position. I worked closely with Karen Anderson, and actually filled in for her that time she was out for a month."

"According to your application, Ms. Martin..."

"You can call me Deeeeenaaaaaa, Mr. Bledsoe," she said as she leaned closer to him.

"You can call me James, Deena."

Deena giggled just like a schoolgirl. Oh, she had this seduction thing down pat. She should have been a stripper because she sure had a flair for flaunting her femininity.

"Thank you, sir, I mean, James. I like that name. It's such a strong, masculine name."

"Er, a, Deena. The position will require you to attend meetings and take minutes at our seven major offices. Are you available for overnight travel?"

"James, I am available for anything you need." She deliberately opened her legs wide enough so that James could catch a glimpse. She crossed her legs back again and leaned in so he could get a view of the magic mountains.

James could barely contain himself. He got up and walked around his desk. He moved the picture of his wife back and sat on the desk directly in front of Deena.

"The position of senior administrative assistant is a very important one. You will be working very closely with upper management, especially me. It is therefore important that I feel that we can communicate effectively. There is a little test that I would like for you to take this evening so I can observe your communication skills first hand. Are you available at, let's say, around six p.m. this evening?"

"James, I am more than available. I am willing and able to show you my oral and anal communication skills. I suggest you take some vitamins and I hope you're not in a rush to get home." Deena was done being coy, she decided that she might as well get straight to the point...*pun intended.*

"Actually, I have all night because my wife is in Kenya. Please bring the appropriate materials. If everything goes as planned, you will have a decision by Monday."

"If everything goes as planned, I will have a decision by tonight. For each hour that it takes for you to make a decision, I expect that my salary will increase by $10,000. Do we have a deal, James?"

"Oh, we have a deal indeed, Deena. Meet me at the Mayflower Hotel at six p.m. in the suite seven-seven-six."

"Yes, sir. Oh, by the way, do you like schoolgirls?"

"I love schoolgirls. Just don't be tardy, young lady."

Deena stood up and firmly shook Mr. Bledsoe's hand. She turned around and shook her thang like she was JLo. She smirked and said loudly as she passed Phyllis, "I always get my man."

It was nearly 6:15 p.m. as Deena slid out of the Yellow Cab; she always kept her men waiting. As she walked past the Thomas Pink store and down the stairs through the sunken lobby, in a short blue skirt, a crisp white shirt, knee socks, and tweed jacket, Deena sauntered to the elevator, her two long braids swished back and forth. Two young men came to the elevator and started to flirt with her. Deena yawned at the game that these young boys, with their no-income-generating selves, were spitting "lame game." She had bigger fish to fry, and was about to land her Moby Dick! Or at least she hoped that he had a moby dick, he probably didn't, but it really didn't matter. She would fuck him until the cows came home. By the time she was finished with him, she would own BCI. James Bledsoe didn't know who he was about to be fucking with.

Softly, she knocked on the door that was left slightly ajar. She heard a voice say "enter" so she opened the door and entered.

"Hello, Mr. Bledsoe. I'm sorry I'm late. I have a note from my mommy," Deena said in her sexiest little girl voice.

"Don't worry about a note, young lady. Come here and let me decide what your punishment will be."

She really had him now. "Before you punish me, can you tell me if I have the job? Sir, pretty please, do I have the job, mister?"

"Well, you do if you promise to be a good girl and meet me here every Monday night after school. Do you promise?"

"Yes, I promise to be a real good girl and meet you every Monday night at six sharp."

"Well then, you definitely have a job, young lady."

"What is my salary, sir?"

"Forty thousand dollars."

"I'm sorry; I cannot take the position for that amount of money, sir."

"Fifty thousand dollars," James said. Deena just shook her head.

"Seventy thousand," James begged. Deena just shook her head and began walking toward the door.

"One hundred thousand and that's my final offer," James said emphatically.

Deena ran over to him and threw her hands around his neck and gave him a big hug. "Thank you, mister. Thanks a lot!"

"Now come over here and give Big Daddy some pussy."

In her most professional "grown-up" voice, Deena matter-of-factly replied, "You get some pussy after you have a contract drawn up. I'll meet you here tomorrow and sign it. Then you can have all the pussy you want."

Deena swished down the hall to the elevator. She thought about the events of the evening and thought to herself, *Damn, you're a bad bitch!*

CHAPTER 24
Washington, D.C. 2006

James was feeling real good about himself lately. He had hit the jackpot with Deena. He didn't know why he had wasted all those years with Karen when Deena was the superstar. Deena had sold herself short. He would have given her $200,000 a year for all that she was giving him. She was insatiable. He couldn't get enough. He wanted her noon and night. She was an animal, she was *his* animal.

✗ ✗ ✗

James was getting on her nerves. She should have asked for $200,000 for all the aggravation he was putting her through. On top of everything, he could only go for a few minutes, and sometimes he came before he even put it in. He was calling her all hours of the night wanting to hook up. It was hard for her to get her *real* mack on, because he was always sneaking up behind her at work. She even thought that he had a spy following her to make sure she wasn't getting with anyone else. Imagine trying to play her like that. He had a lot of nerve because he was married, and his wife was fine. What the hell was wrong with her? She could have anyone in the world with the kind of credentials she was pushing. He was paid, though, and he just struck that Japanese deal. He was listed in the year's *Forbes*. Yeah, sometimes she forgot about the bigger picture.

Deena looked at her cell phone, and sucked her teeth, another text message. *Damn, it's him again. I wish he would leave me alone.* She walked to the nearest pay phone because her cell was about to die. She made a mental note to ask him to get her another cell phone, so she would never have to use a phone that the general public used. Besides, pay phones were getting harder and harder to find these days.

"Hey baby, you rang?" she purred.

"What are you doing now?" he asked.

"Shopping. Why?"

"Well, I was hoping that we could meet, say, in an hour?"

"James, I'm busy. Can we hook up tomorrow?"

"I need to see you now, babe. I'll send a car over to pick you up."

"Well, I was going to braid my girlfriend's hair, because I need a couple of dollars."

"How much do you need?" he asked.

"Five hundred dollars."

"Done. Now where are you so I can tell the driver to come and get your sexy ass?"

"I'm at Mazza Gallerie at Neiman's."

"He'll be there in thirty minutes. I love you."

"Love you, too. Can't wait to see you."

In reality she would rather watch paint dry. All this love stuff was also starting to wear thin. He really needed to save all that talk for that wife of his.

Just then she saw a tall, brown gorgeous brother. She walked aimlessly, as if lost, and bumped into him. She excused herself and smiled. *Now that was a fine piece of meat, I really would love to grill him. Shit, I'd eat him raw like sushi, if I could.* His name was Abdul. *Abdul,* she thought. Now that was a name fitting of an African prince. He looked like royalty. He had on a pair of beige Antique Denim jeans, Puma sneakers, and a funky retro T-shirt that showed glimpses of his massive, hairy chest. Her panties got wet just looking at him. His hair was twisted like so many of the brothers were wearing now, and he looked to be about thirty-two, the perfect age. But damn, she had to go get grandpa off, what a fuckin' job.

Damn, I need to get with him, she thought. Deena checked her watch and realized that the BCI car would be pulling up soon, but took a risk and asked him for his number. *Guess he's checkin' for me, too! Although no real surprise there,* she thought. He gave her his card which had his cell phone number and e-mail address on it. On the back he listed his My Space address. He asked her if she would be calling any time soon. She batted her eyes innocently and answered his question with a coquettish grin, "What do you think?"

Perfect timing, the limo pulled up. As she slid into the limo, flashing him her favorite two "smiles," she looked through the shaded back window, and watched his fine ass fade into the background onto Wisconsin Avenue.

Stanley, the driver, offered her some weed. She jumped at the offer because she needed to get her head right for the upcoming festivities. The great thing about Stanley was that he had the thickest joints she had ever seen. The driver knew that Wisconsin and Connecticut avenues had too many lights and that Mr. Bledsoe was anxiously waiting for his passenger, so he slid down Military Road and through Rock Creek Park. By the time they drove down Massachusetts Avenue and around Dupont Circle to the Mayflower Hotel, Deena was feeling *real* good.

James was sitting at his desk, finishing up some last-minute work, when his cell phone rang. It was a number that he didn't recognize, so he picked it up quickly thinking it was Deena.

"Hello, lover," Karen cackled.

Damn, why did I pick up the phone? he thought.

"I am on my way to your office, James."

"Karen, I was just on my way out. I have a meeting."

Karen wasn't as stupid as she looked. She knew what kind of meeting he had.

"Well, can I see you after your meeting? Why don't I cook us a little dinner?"

"Karen, I really need to take a rain check. I gotta go, baby. *Ciao.*"

Ciao? Karen thought. *Since when did he start saying that? I bet he's seeing a white woman now.*

I got your meeting, she thought. She hopped into her Ford Taurus and drove west on K Street toward Connecticut Avenue. Karen knew that his favorite spot was the Mayflower, so she decided that she would beat him at his own game. If he was seeing a white woman, though, she would have to get a beat down just on GP.

Karen parked her car on Desales Street, across from the ABC office, and entered the Mayflower from the side entrance near the elevators. She put on her dark shades and big floppy hat, walked past the registration desk and peered through one of the doors next to the entrance to the Pink store. As the signature limo with the vanity tags, BLES1 pulled up, she waited for James to emerge, but to her surprise Deena got out and walked into the hotel.

"Isn't this a bitch," Karen yelled. "I'm the one that got Deena the job at BCI and she's gonna stab me in the back like that? I guess she doesn't realize who she's fucking with. It's time that I taught James and Deena a little lesson."

Five minutes later, another limo pulled up with vanity tags that read BLES2. This time James got out of the limo, and walked into the hotel.

Angered by what she had just witnessed, Karen headed to her car and took L Street and headed toward Sequoia down on the water so that she could grab a drink and calm her nerves. Water always relaxed her. One day she would own waterfront property. Still stunned by what, or rather *who*, she had just witnessed she sat at the bar an ordered a Cuba Libre. *It was one thing for a married man to cheat*, she thought. *It was quite another for a married man to cheat on his mistress, especially with her so-called best friend.*

"Bacardi and Diet Coke, please," Karen requested from the young, handsome bartender. For a split second her thoughts turned to the young buck behind the bar. Then she remembered what had just happened.

She asked the bartender for the Yellow Pages, and a minute later he returned with the phone book and her drink. Karen was so pissed, that she practically gulped the drink down in two swigs. After ordering her second round, she flipped through the large volume of businesses until she came to "P" for Private Investigators. She fingered through the names quickly; there were quite a few to choose from. It looked like the investigation business had grown at least tenfold in the last ten years—women checking on their men to see if they were cheating. Although the real question at hand in D.C. was, whether your man was cheating with another woman… or with another man. Damn! Welcome to the new millennium.

Karen stopped at an advertisement for William T. Buckley and Associates, Private Investigators. Their slogan was, "Before you make the biggest mistake of your life, call us." So it all boiled down to, William T. Buckley sounded like a reputable name, and his advertisement sounded like he could be trusted…as much as any man could be trusted.

Sure. Let's give him a shot, she thought.

Karen wrote the address and phone number down on a cocktail napkin, and ordered one more rum and Coke for the road. Like I said, girlfriend was pissed! She glanced at her watch. "Damn! Seven-thirty p.m." It was too late to contact Mr. Buckley's office now. Besides she realized that she had officially gotten her buzz on. No, she would wait until Monday, and would try to get through the weekend as best as she could.

On her way home she stopped at Good 'Ole Reliable Liquors on Fifteenth and Rhode Island. After the week she had, Karen needed to have a stash for the weekend, so she purchased a fifth of Absolut, cranberry juice, ginger ale, and three big bags of pork rinds. Like I mentioned before, she was still *pissed*! She had lost her job, her man, and her confidence all in one month.

Early Monday morning, Karen had such a bad headache, that she could barely move. She crawled over to the phone and carefully dialed Mr. William T. Buckley and Associates' phone number.

"Hello, William T. Buckley and Associates. May I help you?"

"Yes, may I speak with Mr. Buckley?"

"He isn't here. May I take a message?"

"Yes. I need to hire a private detective today. My tired-ass boyfriend is cheating on me with my best friend!"

"What?! I can't believe it! You must be kidding!"

"I wish I was. I am so hurt," Karen said, finally breaking down and crying.

"Girl, don't worry. If you can be here by ten-thirty a.m., I'll get you in with Buck. You need to kick that bitch's ass."

"Oh, believe me, I plan to do more than that. I'll see you in a minute. Thanks."

"You're more than welcome, girl. You know there is nothing worse than a cheating bitch. Women need to start sticking together. Then these men couldn't get away with this shit."

Blah, blah, blah! I didn't ask for a sermon, Karen thought.

She dragged herself to the shower and turned it on full blast. Thank God she had a weave. She could quickly hook that hair up. She had been crying all weekend and her face looked a wreck. As she stepped into the shower, she could feel her head exploding from the lethal combination of too much cheap liquor and pure fury.

He told her that he loved her. He had been lying all the time and she was too blind to see. All men say they love you when they are trying to get some, or get more. How could the player get played like that? She had been around the block a few times in her life. She couldn't believe that she had fallen for his lies. What Karen had to come to grips with was that she really was in love with James. It wasn't just the money. She had dreamed a million times of James coming in on his black stallion and rescuing her from a life of mediocrity. Karen threw on a pair of black slacks, a white turtleneck, black boots, and black sunglasses, a more conservative look than usual. She got into her Taurus and slid a CD into the player. Her favorite artist, Mariah Carey, began to sing so sweetly. *The Emancipation of Mimi, I need to be emancipated,* she thought.

Karen couldn't control the tears as they poured down her face and wouldn't stop. Karen thought that James would always be by her side. She had given him five years of her life, and had seen no other men during that time. James was always so jealous. She cried at the thought of all the wasted years. James wasn't always by her side, he was by Deena's, and they would both pay!

After I leave the PI's office, the first thing I am gonna do is cut this fake-ass weave off. I never liked it anyway. James was the one who liked to pull on it, Karen thought. Like her idol Patti preached, *New hair, new shoes. I'm gonna get, I gotta get a new attitude.*

It was the first time Karen had smiled in three days.

CHAPTER 25
Las Vegas, 2006

I sat in the seat and reclined as much as the first-class chair would allow. I was looking forward to relaxing in Vegas, plus Tanya and I had a lot to discuss. We had to solidify and coordinate our plans for James' demise. It wouldn't be long before BCI would be mine, and I wondered if it would be all that I thought it would be. I wondered if that was what God really wanted for me. I closed my eyes and tried to relax.

The first-class flight attendant tapped me on the shoulder, asked if I wanted to put in my order for dinner, and if I would like some champagne. I thought for a second, that champagne would be lovely right now, but I declined. I ordered whatever chicken dish they were serving, and got up to use the restroom.

I passed this white girl that looked to be about thirteen years old, who was wearing a "Girls Kick Ass" T-shirt, and was reading *Money* magazine. Now that really made my day! In the new millennium, young women have to have a kick-ass mentality. We have to go for ours, and if my actions are helping to foster that attitude, it's my pleasure. As I walked by, I winked and gave the young lady a thumbs-up gesture. She responded with a big smile.

The mist felt so good, as the hiss of the steam that enveloped the room soothed me. As the hot air filled my lungs, I inhaled deeply and exhaled. It felt as though my body was being purged of all of its sins. If I could only purge my soul. I had done so much good. Shit, I had a nation of young women sticking up for themselves. "Girls Kick Ass!" That was all me. So then why did I feel so bad? So drained? So empty?

Tanya walked in and interrupted my internal pity party. She felt her way around. The steam was so thick, you couldn't see two inches in front of you.

"Sandy?"

"Hey, babe. I'm right here."

"I'm sorry I'm late. My meetings ran over."

"That's *okay*. I've only been here about ten minutes. I do think I'm ready to move to the sauna, though."

"Boy, do I need this," Tanya said. "It feels so good. I'll catch you in five and then we can begin our discussion."

I wrapped my towel around my abdomen, so that my breasts were exposed. I knew that I was an exhibitionist at heart. I loved to walk around nude. *One day I'm going to try one of those nudist colonies*, I thought. I imagine that an environment like that would be totally liberating.

I had just finished a three-hour workout and felt great. You know, that good kind of pain. The kind of pain where you know you had really taken care of business. The next couple of weeks were going to be crazy. I had to be mentally and physically prepared. The School Yard Murderer was mine, I could feel it. He was drawing me toward him. I knew that the murderer was a man, a man with a deep-seated hatred for women and/or girls. Oh, that motherfucker's ass was mine and it would truly be my pleasure!

I walked out of the steam room and went into the sauna, laid my crisp, white Mandalay Bay towel out and allowed my body to enjoy its comfort. A few minutes later, Tanya joined me; luckily we were the only ones in the sauna at the time.

"*Okay*, what's up, girl?" Tanya asked. "Are we on schedule?"

"Yeah. Let me give you the four-one-one. Mike is due to graduate from NYU next week, and I was able to create a position for him at BCI as the Assistant to the CFO. We hired a Cuban photographer named Yan, who will obtain some illicit photographs of James and his many women. I feel that I'm at a loss, however, because I need to get something *more* on James than just his affairs. Shit, half of the shareholders are having sex with someone other than their spouses. We need to get something more low down and dirty on James. Something that, once the papers get wind of will blow it so out of proportion that James will have no choice but to resign. Do you have any ideas?"

Tanya paused for a moment. "Let me put some thought into it. I will try and do a little snooping and see what I can come up with. It shouldn't take too much because James' whole program is foul. By the way, Karen Anderson has been leaving messages for me at the hospital. Do you know what that is about?"

"Lord only knows. Girlfriend's got issues. I would leave that alone if I were you, Tanya."

"I don't know, Sandy. I am very curious to hear what she has to say."

"You know that she will tell you that she is sleeping with James and that he loves her and that she feels that you should gracefully step aside. She will then expect you to cry and beg her to stop seeing him. When you turn around and laugh in her face and tell her she can have him, won't *she* be surprised?!"

Tanya and I laughed for about five minutes, and then sat back in deep thought.

"The women in Africa can sure use more money; STOP is running on fumes. There is a little girl that was savagely raped that needs multiple surgeries and I don't know how we are going to pay for it."

"Relax. Before you know it, you will have more money than you can handle," I reassured her.

"Sandy, for a woman that is so together, how could I have made such a mistake and married a man like James?" she asked, as tears began to roll down her face.

In all of our planning and scheming, I had never stopped to think of how the plan would affect her. After all, James was her husband, and Tanya had, at one point, loved him deeply. For all I know, she could still be in love with him. No matter how beautiful or successful a woman is, she will always be vulnerable when it comes to love. How could I be so insensitive?

I put my arms around Tanya and gave her a big hug. I told her that she was the sharpest woman that I knew, and that one day she would fall in love with a wonderful man that would love her and only her. As I gave her my words of wisdom, I couldn't help but think that Tanya would love again, but I would never love at all.

CHAPTER 26
New York, 2006

I felt just like a mother watching her child on the proudest day of his life. It was a magnificent afternoon. Women held umbrellas up to sháde them against the effervescent rays of sun. I, on the other hand, the sun worshipper that I am, absorbed every ray that shined down on me. I looked over to see if I saw the procession starting but instead saw an overweight man sweating profusely. I handed him a handkerchief that I borrowed from Puma because the dude looked like he would pass out any minute. I became fixated as I watched the tiny little beads merge into a stream that careened down the man's jaw. My thoughts shifted and went to the School Yard Murderer; I wondered if he sweat like that when he stalked his victims. I wondered if he was obese like this disgusting man that I was presently watching. No, my instincts told me that the murder was extremely meticulous. He was probably in great shape and was good-looking. Why did he murder so many young Black girls?

I shook it off. I had to stop thinking about that butcher. I looked over at Puma who had fallen asleep and nudged him as "Pomp and Circumstance" began to play. Puma looked at me and smiled, we were both so proud. We had watched our boy grow and mature into an intelligent, dedicated, and loyal young man. He had overcome many obstacles and had worked very hard. Today, all of his hard work had finally paid off, and this was only the beginning. When he first came to the States, he spoke very little English. Puma and I had communicated with him in Spanish. However, we hired an English tutor for him and within nine months he was speaking English like a pro, and inside of two years, he had a better command of the language than most Americans. Since Mike knew that he wanted to eventually work within corporate America, he also mastered Japanese.

As the New York University graduation procession began, we anxiously awaited "our boy." We had all come such a long way professionally, emotionally, and spiritually.

I vividly remember the first day I saw Mike, dressed like a woman, with high heels and a sequined dress. I had heard that the son of Juan Perez had been thrown in the dungeon, but didn't believe it. Who would do such a thing to his own son? I remember that he looked at me with such hope with these deep, sad brown eyes. I was moved by Miguel's courage, and made a silent vow to God that I would always be there for him. That was nearly twenty years ago. At the time, I never would have never dreamed that the three of us would be still here, sitting together, still friends.

Mike's face beamed as he saw us in the crowd. He winked at me and I winked back. Although we were close in age, Mike was like the son I never had. I damn near raised him after he left Chile. I even thought about contacting his mother and inviting her to the graduation, but immediately decided against it. For all I knew, she was probably dead anyway.

The keynote speaker began her speech and talked about how the graduates were the crème of the crop. As graduates from one of the most prestigious universities in the most powerful city, she advised the young achievers to be socially responsible and about the importance of giving back and of volunteering their time.

Puma had fallen asleep again, this time he had started to snore, so I nudged him and woke him up. Puma and I had crazy bouts of insomnia, and consequently we were tired most of the day. It was probably our pasts catching up with us. There were periods where he wouldn't sleep for weeks at a time. Puma would find himself dreaming about cutting someone's head off in Vietnam, or finding a butchered child in Africa. He had seen so much death and destruction that it was surprising he could sleep at all. Presently, the only thought that kept me awake was the School Yard Murderer.

Puma got up and shot a series of pictures as Mike crossed the stage and received his Masters of Business Administration. With the proper credentials, Mike finally was ready to assume a high-level corporate position within BCI. Moving from limo driver to Assistant to the CFO would be questioned by many employees, but I made it happen. Folks would be tripping and swear that I was sleeping with Mike, but that's okay, let them think what they want. *Fuck 'em and let 'em eat beans!* For the past twelve months, I had been working with Mike, giving him the "ins and outs" of BCI. Mike had sat in on most of my meetings, and since he was the limo driver, no one ever questioned him quietly sitting in the corner. Even when I left the room, Mike was my eyes and ears. Everyone saw him as non-threatening, just a schmuck waiting to drive me somewhere. Little did these employees realize, but at some point they would have to answer to him. I had been grooming him for this position for years, and now it was time for him to take the reins.

As I watched Mike sitting on the stage, I knew how close we were to having our plan fully realized and tears of joy began to run down my face. My mother, God bless her soul, would be so proud. My dad, too, if only I knew who he was. The ceremony was over, and Mike headed straight to us. We embraced and hugged for about five minutes. Mike started to cry, and then I started to cry again, and then Puma, who I have never known to cry in the twenty-plus years that I have known him, grabbed the two of us and interrupted the crying game.

"Let's go to lunch, my treat," he said.

"Puma, I am not in the mood for McDonald's," I joked.

"I was thinking of the Russian Tea Room. This is a very special occasion. Miguel, we are both very proud of you. Considering all that we have been through, this is truly a miracle that you are not only alive, but are living the American Dream."

"Not quite the American Dream. I still need a blonde with a pair of implants and a set of kids, complete with a white picket fence."

"Very funny. You marry a blonde, and you're a dead man."

"Yes, Mother."

"I got your mother."

"Ooooooh, when can I see it?" Mike teased.

Lunch was spectacular. I have always enjoyed the ambiance of the Russian Tea Room. Even if it does connote old communism, there is something about its red walls, the grand ice sculptures, and antique furniture that screams power. Power was what I craved. Let me pose a question right now: Why do you think most businessmen who are legit millionaires and even billionaires continue to work twelve-hour days? Power. To possess genuine influence and command unwavering respect is what they crave most. The money is just a way of keeping score, a by-product of the power that they wield. The power is also what I yearned for. I was powerless as a child, so I craved power as an adult. Soon, as the CEO of a multinational conglomerate, I would have all the power I craved. Maybe then I would feel good about myself. Who was I kidding? I probably would never feel good about myself.

After lunch, the three of us took a cab to Mike's place. Puma had purchased a case of White Star Moët & Chandon Champagne, and I allowed myself to enjoy a glass in his honor. Mike was on his second bottle, and I was getting antsy. Puma had made his way over to me, and was giving me that *I want to get with you look*, that I had seen too many times. Twice a year, Puma would make a subtle pass. I figured that one day I would let him have a second go 'round, but tonight was not the night. My head was spinning from the glass of champagne. Shit, I was starting to go down. When I got with Puma, I wanted it to be perfect, no distractions. Puma was a great guy and he deserved the best; he deserved a lot better than me.

Mike had taken off his shirt and really began to relax. I thought about leaving so that he and Puma could go to a strip club or something. Lord knows that Puma could use a lap dance or two. I looked at Mike's pecs as he gulped down champagne straight from the bottle. He worked out twice a day to help relieve stress and, boy did it show. He could have almost any woman in the city. He was in love with me, though, and I knew it. I figured it was because I saved him in Chile. I glanced over at Puma again. *Damn, he looked good, almost good enough to eat.* I would love to make him cum right now. That would sure make his day. I smacked myself. One thing I did know, though, was that men always wanted what they could not have, and Puma knew that he could never have me, which would always make me intoxicating to him.

As I got up to go, Mike grabbed me, and informed me that I was spending the night, so much for my mother-figure relationship. It was a good thing that I was not drunk because if I were, there would definitely be some straight-up fuckin' going on! Luckily for me, the phone rang and I was literally saved by the bell. Mike went upstairs to his loft-bedroom and closed the door to answer it, and I took this as my cue to leave. Puma said that he would be going as well, so we gathered our things, and I called for the limo service on my cell. I wrote Mike a goodbye/congrats note, and sealed it with a kiss, a red imprint of my full lips on the envelope.

As Puma and I walked down three flights of stairs to the front door of the building, I told Puma that the limo would drop him off at his flat. Now that Mike would no longer be driving, I was in the process of interviewing new drivers/sidekicks. It was comforting to know that Puma would be with me, especially since it was so late at night. Puma Todd had always been there to comfort me and I suspect that he always will.

The limo arrived in fifteen minutes, driven by a chauffeur named Travis from Jamaica. He came to the front door of Mike's building and opened it for us to exit.

"After you, *mon*. May I say that you look radiant tonight, Ms. Knight."

"Thank you, Travis. Travis, this is Mr. Todd." Travis extended his hand to shake hands with Puma.

"Pleased to make your acquaintance, *mon*. Sit back and enjoy the ride. Everyting's *irie*," Travis quipped.

I liked this guy. There was something about him that made you feel safe. Maybe it was his six-feet-five-inch, 260-pound frame or it was his captivating smile. *Travis, I believe we'll become real good friends*, I thought. But I was probably guilty of talking shit, more than a little bit.

Travis started down Eighth Avenue and stuck in a Will Downing CD. *Why was he playing this slow shit?* I thought. Little did I know but Puma had slipped him a hundred bill to hook up the mood. Puma inched over to me and turned my face to his and kissed me sensuously on my lips. As his tongue began to explore my ear and my thighs started to throb, Puma began kissing my neck, making his way to my breasts and then stopped. As he ripped open my blouse, I grabbed his hands and tenderly sucked each one individually. I looked to the front of the limo and saw Travis grinning from ear to ear. I gingerly placed my tongue into Puma's mouth, and teased with mysterious sensuality, then voracious passion. I sucked his lips and bit his tongue. We were hot and heavy for several New York blocks, when I stopped myself and said, "Baby, I can't do this. The timing is all off."

"Just relax for a change and just let it happen," said Puma.

"I can't relax. There is just too much going on."

"There is always a lot going on. You are letting life pass you by. Work will always be there. The work will be there after you are dead and gone. You, of all people, know how precious life is. Why don't you allow yourself to enjoy it?"

"Puma, I can't allow myself the luxury of making love right now. I am in the middle of something that is out of my control. I can't really explain it to you, but just trust me, baby. One day soon, we'll make love again, and it will be beautiful. I care for you deeply and I want to be with you romantically. Now is not the time."

Puma kissed my hand and turned to face the window. I didn't deserve a man like him, and I prayed every day that he would meet someone who he could fall in love with.

CHAPTER 27

New York, 2006

He shut his office door and slipped in a Mozart CD, *Concerto eleven in F Minor*. As the composition commenced, his palms began to sweat. His subscription of *His Child* had just been delivered, hot off the press. His $10,000 annual fee entitled him to four *discreet* issues personally delivered by a young sexy Caucasian male. The fee also allowed him to participate in a child bazaar that was held annually in an Asian or Indian country. Last year he watched as many professional men had sex with boys and girls under the age of fourteen.

Wearing vintage Sassoon blue jeans and a black silk shirt, the twenty-something lithe, pale body sashayed down the hall. Roosevelt could barely contain himself as he sniffed the trail of Vincent's Tommy cologne wafting down the hall. He deliberately walked behind Vincent so that he could get a bird's-eye view of his tight ass. Roosevelt almost gathered the courage to invite the white boy into his office, but quickly decided against it. *What if he didn't like Black men?* he thought. Every year, he was finding it increasingly hard to find young, yet *refined* individuals who were attracted to Black men. No, he couldn't invite Vincent into his office; that would have been too risky. Roosevelt didn't want to draw any extra attention to himself, he was smarter than that. No one would suspect that a Rhodes Scholar, who wore $2,000 suits, and drove a $100,000 car, could torture and kill little girls.

↗ ↗ ↗

Roosevelt walked over to his wine cabinet and retrieved a bottle of Shiraz. He took his coffee mug that said *Boys Kick Ass, Too!* and poured himself a drink. The salesman at Calvert Woodley had convinced him to buy this $350 bottle from New Zealand. However, nothing was too rich for his palate because he deserved only the best. As he swished around the vino, he delicately sipped from it, threw his head back, and closed his eyes as he swallowed. The liquid slid easily down his throat, and the alcohol went to his brain. Roosevelt had already had three single malt scotches at lunch, so this drink of wine would only add to his current alcohol-induced buzz. He would finish the wine than peruse the under-aged nude bodies like any other child predator would do. Roosevelt could hardly wait for his annual child pornography jaunt, where he could enjoy his guilty pleasure in peace. On rare occasions, Roosevelt would give into his cravings and reduce himself to cruisin' the "common" child porn websites. However, today he would enjoy a delicacy that only two hundred and fifty other people in the country were privy to.

Startled by an unexpected knock at the door, Roosevelt threw the magazine in his desk, stood, and opened the door. His assistant, Joan Harding, handed him a memo that announced the new Assistant CFO, Miguel Perez, would be starting on Monday. *Who ever heard of hiring a limo driver as an Assistant CFO, even if he had an MBA*, he wondered. Roosevelt said a very polite "thank you" and dismissed Ms. Harding. God, how he hated her. She always wore cheap, off-the-rack, form-fitting garments and he frequently noticed how the young entry-level staff stared at her butt. He really hated how she always wore that bright red lipstick. Ms. Harding reminded him of everything he hated about his mother.

He read the memo again. "Miguel Perez." Why is it that *he* didn't have the final say in who *his* assistant would be? That damned Sandy. She would pick a Spic for an assistant, huh? Maybe this Miguel person would be good "eye candy" for his division.

That Sandy had a lot of nerve. He was sure that she was the one that had made the decision to hire Don Juan. Women loved Latin men, but he abhorred them because they were so *déclassé*. Always running around trying to fuck some woman, Spics always thought with their little heads and didn't have enough brains in their big ones. And all those damned babies! *Fuck it*, thought Roosevelt, he would have to make Mr. Perez' life a living hell and he would quit.

After Ms. Harding left the room, he was ready to set the mood again. He buzzed his assistant and let her know that he could not be disturbed, got up and locked the door, and pressed "resume" on the CD player. He sauntered over to his Italian leather couch imported from Milan, sat back, and unzipped his pants. He held the magazine in his left hand and his dick in his right. He stopped, only momentarily, to grab some hand lotion from his desk. The lotion made it much easier for his hand to glide up and down, as he stroked his sorry little dick with a vengeance. As the melody came to a climax, so did he. A picture of his mother popped into his head. She had caught him masturbating once, and locked him in a closet for two days, not giving him any food or water. She didn't even let him go to the bathroom. When she did let him out, he had to immediately clean his waste out of the closet before he could get something to eat. He shuddered at the memory.

He enjoyed afternoons like this. No meetings, no deadlines, no women. But he was becoming restless; it had been over two months since his last murder. He longed to touch a little girl's braids or maybe just to cut them off. Thankfully, the publicity about the *School Yard Murderer* had dissipated a bit, and with it a little bit of his "fifteen minutes of fame" was apparently over. His next victim would have to be able to inject some fuel into his fame flame. Who should the child be?

N N N

Cruising around Manhattan in his red Mercedes convertible always made Roosevelt feel superior, and he lived to feel superior. The clothes he wore, the car he drove, the food he ate, and the flat he lived in were all purposefully designed so that he could show the world how superior he was. Stopped at a red light, he watched as a woman crossed the street

with her son in tow. He looked to be about eight years old, and was wearing a Nike jogging suit and a pair of Air Jordans. He was a cute little fellow
and you could tell he was all boy, as he walked across the street and
bounced a basketball. His mother kept telling him to stop. Although she
was scolding her child, you could tell that she was proud of his athletic
ability. You could also see the love in her eyes as she held her son tightly
while crossing the intersection.

Roosevelt would have given his right arm for his mom to have looked
at him that way. He thought back to one day when they were crossing
Bourbon Street on a sweltering day in New Orleans. His mom held his
hand tightly, too, only he had on a little yellow taffeta dress and black patent
leather shoes. His ankle socks were the same sunflower yellow as his
dress. His long brown hair had been coiffed into two ponytails with crisp
yellow ribbons on each one. He was so cute. When they got to the corner of Bourbon and Canal streets, a white lady looked at him and told his
mother how pretty her "daughter" was. She smiled, just as proud as she
could be.

He envied that little boy, and quickly his envy turned to anger. He
wanted to kill that boy right now. Just take him from his ugly mother and
kill him. Why should he have the perfect life? What made him so special?

"I'm the special one," he said, as tears welled up in his eyes.

He continued driving and then veered onto the parkway. He felt like
he was mentally starting to unravel, as he drove for about an hour. That
damned shrink was no help at all, female shrinks were always inept. How
could she possibly think that she could help him? He got so mad during
the last session, that he took a letter opener and stabbed her in her heart.
That's what she gets for letting her secretary go home early, and since he
was an "unscheduled" appointment, no one even suspected him. Stupid
people! No one knew what had happened to the famous Black shrink that
was featured in all of the trendy magazines. His guess was that she was
too busy writing columns, and not paying attention to his needs. The
newspapers talked about the missing psychiatrist but the authorities had
never found her. He was too smart for them.

He downshifted after he crossed the Manhattan Bridge and passed Junior's

Cheesecake on Flatbush Avenue. After a few turns, he had maneuvered his Benz through Park Slope and into one of Brooklyn's many residential areas, and slowed down as he neared St. Mary's School for Girls. His heart started to race, as he thought of how he had never snatched one from a private school before. He almost started to hyperventilate at the thought of a well-mannered child, who he could truly wine and dine before he killed her. He parked the car and crept up to the chain link fence that dangled across the playground. There were hundreds of little girls running and jumping with their cute little blue and white uniforms, cornrows and pigtails swinging to and fro, neat little Stride Rite shoes, adorable little socks with St. Mary's written on the outside of the ankle. The playground looked like a potpourri of colors filled with little girls which could make for a stupendous treat. Vanilla, cocoa, cinnamon, chocolate, caramel-colored Black girls; blonde, red, brown-haired white girls; wavy, straight, nappy-haired Latinas; and slinky, silky, straight-haired Asian schoolgirls made him so dizzy that he had to sit on a bench near the perimeter of the playground. He leaned over as if to call Earl when *Little Ms. Kenya Knight* came and asked him if he was all right.

"Yes, I feel a lot better now that I have sat down."

"Would you like me to get you some water?"

"No, thank you. I love your hair style. Did your mommy do it?

"No, silly, my daddy did it. He does my hair every day."

"He does? Aren't you the lucky girl?" he said in a patronizing voice.

"I am. I have the best daddy in the whole world." The School Yard Murderer hated her instantly.

Kenya continued. "My mom leaves for work really early in the morning. She is the only woman lawyer at her job and she is trying to get a partnership and the men are mean. So she has to be the first one to work. My daddy has to do my hair because my mommy can't."

"Where does your mommy work?"

"She is a lawyer at Thomas, Gooding, and Jackson. She is a crim, scim, crimital lawyer so she has to take up for a lot of bad guys. She is always on the news. So is my dad."

"Really? What are their names?"

"Mr. and Mrs. Malcolm Knight."

Malcolm Knight, Malcolm Knight, where had he heard that name before?

"My daddy was just on TV because they interviewed about that guy that has been killing all the kids."

Malcolm Knight was the District Attorney for Brooklyn. He had seen Malcolm the other evening on the news and commented to himself about how handsome he was. If his memory served him correctly, Malcolm had attended Yale Law School.

Roosevelt's dick began to firm, as he hastily placed his hand on his lap.

"Mister, it was nice talking to you but I have to be going inside; recess is over."

"Nice talking to you, Miss. I didn't catch your name, sweetheart?"

"My name is Kenya Knight." She extended her hand and the killer shook it.

"It was a pleasure to make your acquaintance, sir. Have a nice day."

He rushed to his car and unzipped his pants, just in the nick of time, as he ejaculated into his linen handkerchief, rather than all over his Burberry suit.

He couldn't believe it; he had just met his next victim. She was smart *and* pretty, and he would have a *delightful* time with her. Kenya was intriguing, so he wouldn't kill her right away. He would spend some time with her, get to know her. He wanted to know what she was thinking, what she felt. Maybe they would go shopping. He would pretend to be an old college buddy of Malcolm's. She wouldn't realize what was happening until the second, maybe third, day. He couldn't wait!

He had a mountain of work, and needed to do research on Malcolm Knight, in order to prepare for the soiree. He needed to find out what year Malcolm graduated, what his undergraduate major was, who his siblings were. He also had to investigate what little Ms. Kenya liked so that he would surprise her with a basket of her favorite things. He would tie it up all nice and neat, with pink ribbons. They could play dress-up and would have tea. He would be her friend. *No*, he shuddered. They would not play dress-up; he had "dressed up" enough to last a lifetime.

CHAPTER 28
New York, 2006

I tossed and turned that night in the hotel. After the long spa treatment and massages I had in Vegas, I should've slept like a baby. Tanya and I had an excellent meeting, and were able to hash out all the details regarding James' demise. Although we both had a lot of work to do, the plan was about to come to fruition, and all of our hard work would be rewarded.

We decided that Tanya should speak with Karen, because she obviously was ready to spill her guts, and we could utilize this information if we needed to. For all we knew, Karen could become an ally. *The Godfather* always said, "Keep your friends close and your enemies closer." I had realized at a young age that if you are pretty, smart, or successful in any way, you are bound to have a lot of enemies.

I, on the other hand, needed to meet with Bird as soon as I arrived in New York. He had a Mafia associate that could go so low underground that he could get anything on anybody. I picked up my Gucci clutch purse and searched for my cell phone and could not find it. Panicking, I threw all of the contents of the bag out on the bed, and again, did not see my cell phone anywhere. I glanced at a batch of negatives that Bird had recently sent me, and held the proofs up to the light and thought abut the good work that Bird always did. The pictures captured James in a number of compromising positions with two hookers that were dressed in Catholic school uniforms. One depicted a young girl with her skirt hiked up with James paddling her butt. At the same time, the other girl was going down on him. The pictures were the essence of James, as he exploited the two young women.

Although I had been simultaneously concentrated on working out the kinks of the Japanese deal and getting the goods on James, I could not get the School Yard Murderer out of my mind. I had literally walked the streets of Brooklyn on Wednesday, going from school to school trying to catch anyone who may be lurking about. I realized that it was going to be hard to catch the predator because he had killed girls from all five boroughs in New York, and so far he hadn't left a single clue.

He was smart, I would give him that much, but I knew that sooner or later, he would make a mistake. Ironically, for some reason, I felt that there was some kind of connection between the murderer and myself. Even at work, I could almost feel his presence. Even during certain meetings, I could feel the hairs on my arm literally stand on end.

I thought about the killer all the time. I was sure that the murder was male. A woman, no matter how sadistic, would not be capable of killing so many children. Also the fact that only little girls were being murdered, suggested that the killer was male. In two years, he had butchered and tortured ten children. One of the girls was found in an apartment on the Lower East Side. She was the only little girl who had survived, but she would not speak. Luckily, Tanya performed the twelve hours of plastic surgery so that the girl wouldn't be scarred for life. Renee Porter could only stare into space, even when the police psychologist tried to find out what she could remember about her assailant. Six months after she had been brutalized by her attacker, she had not uttered a word.

For different reasons, Tanya and I both spent a lot of time by Renee's bedside. Tanya prayed every day that Renee would come out of her catatonic state, and resume a normal life. Tanya even brought in a post-traumatic specialist to work with Renee but to no avail. I sat by the young girl's bedside, hoping that she would be able to reveal a single detail about her attacker. I bought pads and paper, even crayons, hoping that she would jot down a clue that could help me nab the bastard, but poor Renee refused to communicate.

N N N

Roosevelt hopped out of his car to pick up his dry cleaning. He bounced in the store and left a $10 tip with a puzzled Mrs. Park. In the seven years that Roosevelt had been patronizing their establishment, he had never once smiled, let alone left a tip. But Roosevelt was feeling great today. He was going to see Ms. Kenya. It also helped that he had gotten lucky at Show Stoppers the previous night, and had enjoyed a lap dance with a beautiful waif of a girl. When the girl mentioned that for a few dollars more, she could make his dreams come true, he vomited all six Cosmos out of his system.

Kenya Knight was a feisty, ten-year-old fifth-grader who loved Nick Cannon and Bow Wow. She had posters of Raven Symone plastered all over her walls. Her parents insisted that she be well-rounded, so she attended ballet class and played basketball. Her favorite team was the New York Knicks, and she kept a picture of her standing with Patrick Ewing over her bed. Kenya was fascinated with science, and found the solar system electrifying. Once a month, she had her parents take her to the planetarium, and her favorite place in the world was her backyard on a clear night.

He had been watching Kenya for two weeks now. He noticed how very smart and perceptive she was. She definitely would be more difficult than the others were. Roosevelt always loved a good challenge, and he was sure up for this one. He eagerly anticipated the day when he could really get into the mind of a ten-year-old girl. Finally, he figured out how he could lure her away from the school; Roosevelt would surprise her with tickets to a Knicks game. He would pick Kenya up after school, and tell her that her dad would meet them at the game. He had spent a great deal of time researching the Knight family so he could drop names that would make Kenya feel at ease. She was a little lady, with impeccable taste, so he was sure that she would like him. He was, after all, a gentleman.

Today was dress-down Friday at BCI so, instead of wearing his customary Brooks Brothers suit, Roosevelt wore a pair of Versace slacks and a sweater designed by Hugo Boss, classic casual. Roosevelt developed his impeccable taste for clothing from one of his mother's many boyfriends, Big Sugar. Mr. Jason Toussaint was a ladies man who had caviar taste and an imaginary unlimited budget. Big Sugar was a tall, handsome redbone with sandy, wavy hair. All of the eligible women (and some who weren't so eligible) tried to catch him, but Annabelle was the one who nabbed him, although she probably should've thrown him back. Big Sugar always looked like a million bucks even if he only had a dollar in his pocket. Thanks to Anabelle, Big Sugar's suits were always pressed, his shoes were always shined, and his stomach was always full, even though half of the time he was going to visit some *other* woman. *Big Sugar* had *big swagger*, and he didn't care if he had to beat Annabelle to have his way, he had attitude and Roosevelt looked up to him.

The morning dragged as he had two important meetings. Casual Friday, and Ms. Harding was looking exceptionally whorish today, with tight blue jeans and a tight pink sweater, which was complemented by her usual bright red lipstick. She had literally stopped traffic while crossing the street to pick up his lunch.

И И И

At lunch, Roosevelt purchased a Knicks cap and sunglasses at the NBA store on Fifth Avenue. He also purchased posters of Patrick Ewing and Rebecca Lobo who played for the New York Liberty. He would buy her a pink taffeta dress and black patent leather shoes for dinner after the game. If the game ended too late in the evening, they would go to lunch the next day, his arrogance told him that Kenya would not catch on for a while. Maybe they could lunch at 21. The thought of two such beautiful people dining in such elegant surroundings made him weak in the knees. Roosevelt always dined at 21 when he was trying to impress a date or client. Using his corporate credit card, he reserved a suite online at the Sheraton on Fifty-Third and Seventh before leaving the office; that way, he would be able to "anonymously" spend quality time with Kenya. On Sunday, if she was a "good girl," he would let her live for an additional day, and move the party to an apartment he rented for BCI on the Lower East Side. He liked Kenya, so he probably would not torture her very long. He wanted to make sure that her death was as painless as possible. He shuddered at the thought of having to kill a creature so captivating and secretly wished that little girls didn't have such big mouths.

ᴎ ᴎ ᴎ

As he exited the BCI office, I noticed ol' Rosie had on a New York Knicks cap and a pair of dark sunglasses. Since when did *he* like sports and especially basketball? He would be more inclined to wear a *Cats*, or a *Miss Saigon* hat, anything but something sports related. It felt almost as if he were trying to blend in and look like a regular New Yorker, which was so unlike him; Roosevelt *never* tried to blend in. To the contrary, Roosevelt was a drama queen and a spotlight grabber who *always* tried to stand out. So, I decided to follow him for a while and see what ole boy was up to. He *had* been acting more weird than normal and for ol' Rosie, that was saying something. I could almost bet my life that he was up to no good. It was time to clean house entirely. James and Roosevelt both needed to go.

Roosevelt walked down the Avenue of the Americas to Broadway, leering at every young white boy that passed. *How pathetic*, I thought, as he continued down Broadway to Madison Square Garden. Roosevelt entered the renowned arena, skipped up the steps to the ticket counter, and asked the ticket agent for two tickets for tonight's game. Since the Knicks were playing the sorry-ass Boston Celtics, there were plenty of tickets. I wondered why he would want to see the Knicks play the Celtics. In the ten years that I knew Roosevelt, he had never talked about basketball or any organized sports for that matter. As a matter of fact, he would scwinch up his nose like something stank when the other men in the office discussed sports.

I stood at the cab stand in front of the Garden so that he could not see me. He went down Thirty-Fourth Street to Macy's, as I followed him to the little girl's department. He kept looking around suspiciously so I scurried over to the boy's department. Did Rosie have a daughter that he was trying to keep a secret? I would bet my life that Rosie had never had sex with a woman, but then again with all of this "down low" stuff, you never know. For all we knew, Roosevelt could've been married and have an entire family. Thank you, E. Lynn Harris, for telling us about brothers who like to swing the bat at both ends. I decided to head back to the office, because I had become bored with the whole Roosevelt thing. For all I knew, he could've been buying something for a niece or something.

When I arrived, I had a stack full of messages and twenty-five e-mails. Mike and I had been working very hard with the programming department to nail down specific shows. Before they signed on the dotted line, the Japanese affiliates wanted to have the full programming line-up for the first year on the air. This was difficult because BCI obviously could not yet sell any ads, so we were working on projected income. I was elated, however, that Mike had finally joined the executive team. I finally had a strong ally at the firm.

Because he was focused on the job at hand, Mike was a lot more efficient than his boss. He also had a better rapport with our clients, and I was having trouble communicating to Roosevelt that the clients preferred that Mike handle their business. Roosevelt was giving me the blues, and according to Joan Harding, her boss, whom she lovingly referred to as Liberace, was trying to sabotage three of Mike's accounts. So, I decided that I would have Bird do some investigation into Roosevelt's life as well. My life would be so much simpler if Mike was the CFO.

Roosevelt was feeling fine. He purchased a beautiful dress for Kenya, and was so keyed up about their weekend that he purchased a coat for her as well. He walked back to the office, grabbed some CD's, and checked his messages. He wanted to change into a pair of jeans but he remembered that he had left his suitcase in the car. He knew that jeans would make him more approachable, and make Kenya feel more comfortable. All kids loved jeans, and although today was casual Friday, he could never wear jeans to work. Jeans at work were so common, unprofessional, and undermined his authority. Certainly a man of his social status had to always be mindful of appearance.

He had rented a Range Rover for the weekend because he never drove his Mercedes when he snatched a kid. Folks always stared at him when he drove his bright red Benz, it was a real attention-getter, and satisfied the attention that he craved. However, this weekend, attention was the last thing he needed, except for Kenya's.

Although St. Mary's School for Girls was only about twenty minutes away, in New York traffic, it was more like forty-five. He had to hurry if he planned to grab Kenya during the afternoon recess.

Roosevelt was a loner. He had never had a meaningful relationship or a best friend. As a juvenile, he had killed his mother, but because he was a minor and there were extenuating circumstances, after he turned eighteen, his file was sealed. Roosevelt wouldn't know who his father was, even if he passed him on the street. And like most loners, Roosevelt wanted to be close to someone, anyone. Well, at least anyone with some semblance of class and style.

He knew that he had no real capacity to love, because his mother had ruined him and turned him into the asexual and confused man that he was. He would always be alone, and accepted the fact that he would never have children of his own. Once every few months Roosevelt did have a child. The relationship always started out great. The first day or so, they would have so much fun, and then they would start to ask for their mommy, and to doubt his sincerity. The whining would begin, and he *hated* a whining child. He would not have any choice but to shut them up. It wasn't his fault, if they just did as they were told, and accepted their fate, he would let them live. But inevitably, they would start screaming for Mommy and as much as he wanted not to believe it, he knew that Kenya would, too.

He parked the rented car across the street from the playground, took a deep breath, closed his eyes, and leaned his head back. He was ready. He spotted Kenya, waved, and got out of the car with the Macy's bags. Kenya ran over to the fence and stopped.

"Hey, mister. You're the guy with the pretty red car."

"Hello, Kenya. How are you today?"

"Fine. Whatcha got there in the shopping bag?"

"Wouldn't you like to know," Roosevelt teased.

"I like your hat. You know the New York Knicks are my favorite basketball team."

"Really? Well, I have three tickets to the game tonight. Your dad wanted me to pick you up, and he'll meet us at the game."

"Wow, see the game tonight? But I don't have anything to wear. I can't wear this outfit to see the Knicks."

"Well, I'll tell you what. We can go to Gap Kids and buy you a really cute outfit. How does that sound?"

"Cool. You're nice, mister. Wait one second, let me get my book bag."

"Don't worry about that. We have to hurry if you want to buy some new clothes. We also have to get a bite to eat. What are you in the mood for?"

"I love Thai food. Do you?"

Thai food, he thought. Most kids would have wanted McDonald's but this little lady wanted Thai food. He was really going to enjoy this weekend.

ϰ ϰ ϰ

Meanwhile, I was finishing some work and needed some financials. It was seven p.m. on a Friday, and everyone had left for the evening, so I let myself into Roosevelt's office to get the Burrell file. The file cabinet was locked, but of course that didn't stop me, it took me less than five minutes to get inside the cabinet. The files were neat and meticulous, so it was easy to find the file in question.

Curiosity got the best of me so I randomly perused the remaining files and came to one that had no heading. I took the file out and opened the folder. I almost threw up as I examined the pictures of naked young children in a variety of sexual positions, and quickly made copies of the file. I looked through the remainder of the files and the other drawers and found nothing but regular client files.

I went over to his desk. I rummaged through his top drawer and found the usual pens and office supplies. Under his desk, I found a metal box that was locked with a padlock. I ran to my office, opened my closet, and retrieved a bolt cutter and a pair of leather gloves. I went back to the pedophile's desk and cut off the lock, and found several copies of a magazine called *His Child*. I took a copy from the bottom of the pile and stuffed it into my jacket. There were DVDs as well, so I took one from the bottom of the pile and stuffed it into my pants, and put the box back in its place. I grabbed the broken lock, threw the items that had been retrieved into my Fendi business tote, and placed it under my desk. I ran to the elevator and took it down to the lobby.

I hurried down to the Rite Aid pharmacy, and purchased a lock that closely resembled the lock that I had just broken, and ran back to the BCI offices. I hopped on the first available elevator and went directly to Roosevelt's office. My heart was racing because I didn't know if Roosevelt would be coming back to his office to retrieve any of his documents or video tapes. I put the lock back on his box, took the key for the new lock, placed it under my shoe, and I rubbed the key with the thick heel of my black boots for about ten minutes. I then went into the hallway and found the largest plant available, stuffed the key in and out of the soil for a few minutes, and just let it sit.

After scuffing up the key for a bit, I washed my hands and I gathered my things from my office. I gathered some work that I could finish up at home, and called Travis to come for me in ten minutes. I recovered the key from the soil, and looked for the closest restroom. The men's room was closest, so I peeked my head in and looked around for a man, boldly walked up to the faucet, and let the water run. I held the key under the stream for what seemed like an eternity. I then held up the key and it had in fact lost some of its shine, and I was sure that Roosevelt wouldn't notice the difference.

I went back to Roosevelt's office and placed the new, less shiny key in his desk drawer. I then perused his office just to make sure that I had left it just as I had found it, closed the door and left.

Travis was waiting for me as I exited the BCI office building. He held the door and said, "Good evening, beautiful, I mean, Ms. Knight," and grinned a devilish smile. I looked at him, cocked my head to the side, and said, "You ain't so bad yourself. I would like to go to Washington, D.C. tonight, or do you have plans for tonight, Travis?"

"I'm all yours," he replied as he closed the door. Travis thought to himself, *One day she'll be mine.* No woman can resist the charms of Travis Jacque Tierney, III. He climbed behind the wheel and glanced in the mirror and smiled at the image that he saw.

CHAPTER 29
New Orleans, 1960

Annabelle Louise Guidry was born to a white woman named Ginger in a farmhouse in Baton Rouge, Louisiana, in 1924. Her father was a sharecropper who could pick more cotton than anyone else in the state, but he dreamed of moving up north to pursue a vaudeville career. He was the most handsome and eligible Black man in the county. Unfortunately however, the color of his skin limited the potential that Luther Guidry had. Luther was a pure ladies' man, tall, strapping, and handsome, with skin that was the hue of cherrywood. He was a charmer to most women, Black and white, in the three surrounding plantations; and men (both Black and white) hated Luther because he was such a pretty boy.

Like most men, Billy Guidry, the land owner, felt that no nigger should be treated more superior then any other nigger, no matter how hard they worked. The more Billy treated Luther like shit, the harder Luther worked at trying to fuck Billy's wife. Luther knew that it wouldn't take much, and like most women, she'd be begging to see him more and more. Ginger believed that she and Luther could marry, and move to a place like New York, where interracial couples were more commonplace.

It didn't take long before "Miss Ginger" became pregnant. And it wasn't much longer before the baby was born with Luther's beautiful caramel skin color. A week later, as she walked on her favorite path on the farm, Miss Ginger found Luther's naked body, minus his glorious penis, tied to an old oak tree. After six months of confining herself to her bed, Ginger eventually died of a broken heart, leaving baby Annabelle to fend for herself.

After her mother's death, Annabelle lived with Billy and his sixteen-year-old bride in the main house. Carrie Nell treated Annabelle like she was her own living baby doll that she could dress up, and have tea parties with. Although Annabelle was obviously not white, she was very light-skinned, and had green eyes. The Guidrys loved her like their own and tried to give her a life similar to that of their own children. Annabelle thought that she was white, and got into many fights with the Black children who worked the land, because they often alluded to the fact that she was Black. You know how Black folks always *know* when one of us is trying to pass.

By the time she was seven, she was considered to be one of the prettiest girls in the parish, wearing the finest dresses and dress shoes. Most of the other kids did not like her, because Annabelle was so sweet and prissy in one moment, and then would be mean and evil as a tomcat in heat in another.

One day while Annabelle and some of the neighboring Black children were skipping stones at the creek, one of the little Black girls named Ida Jo started singing:

Annabelle, Annabelle will not tell
Says she's white, says she's white
But her father was as dark as night

Annabelle glared at Ida Jo and, without saying a thing, and stomped back to the Guidry house. She was getting tired of these nigger girls always taunting her. She knew that Ida were just jealous that she was not white, like her. *One day, I'll fix her*, Annabelle thought.

After several days, Annabelle found Ida Jo and asked if she wanted to play hide and seek; they would have to go deep into the woods to play. Annabelle counted first and Ida Jo hid. Annabelle watched where she was going to hide, as Ida Jo ran off. She watched as Ida Jo hid in a ditch and covered herself with as many leaves as she could. Annabelle looked around, and yelled out for Ida Jo, as if she didn't know where she was. She calmly picked up a big rock that she had seen earlier in a clearing, walked over to the ditch, and stood there for a minute. Her knuckles turned white as she gripped the rock and stood over the ditch. Ida Jo was lying face down, covering her face as Annabelle raised the rock over her head and screamed,

"I am *white!*" and began to hit Ida Jo on the back of her head with the rock. Annabelle had hit her at least ten times and threw the rock into the ditch before she noticed a locket with a picture of Annabelle and Luther in it. Apparently, Luther was Ida Jo's uncle, and like they say, the genes don't lie. As Annabelle looked at the picture of her dad, she realized that she looked *just like her dad.* Thankfully, for Annabelle, no one would ever know, as she snatched the chain from around her cousin's neck, smoothed her hair, and skipped back to the house.

Late that night, Ida Jo's mother frantically banged on the Guidrys' back door, screaming that her baby was gone, and that she thought that some white men had got ahold of her. Feeling sorry for the woman, the Guidrys and Ida Jo's mother lit some kerosene lamps and went out looking for the little girl. Unfortunately, as the sun rose in the horizon, Ida Jo's body was finally found. Because Ida Jo was "just a little colored girl" no one ever knew, or cared, who had killed her.

Annabelle thought that everyone in the parish was talking about her behind her back, whispering, pointing fingers, laughing at her. Her father was Black and she cursed him every day because of it. So when she turned eighteen, Annabelle decided to "pass" and live as a white woman in a place where no one knew her. She changed her name to Anna because it had a more sophisticated ring to it. Anna was both repulsed by and attracted to colored men, but never allowed herself to get close to them. Although she was beautiful, she was often mistreated by her boyfriends and slowly grew to hate men, particularly after a series of unsuccessful affairs with married white men.

Anna took a job singing at the famous Hotel Monteleone in the heart of the French Quarter. One night, Anna met Mr. Johnny Huval, a thriving businessman with French noblemen lineage, after her final set. Johnny's aristocratic flair and elegant charm were exactly what Anna was looking for. As she sat very coquettishly at the bar, Johnny ordered a bourbon and another sherry for Anna. In her desperation, Anna told him she would do anything to be with Johnny, and that it didn't matter that he had a family.

So, for five years Johnny met Anna at a luxurious apartment that he kept for her. Anna shopped at the most exclusive stores on Canal Street, and dined at the finest restaurants in Jackson Square. Johnny came to the apartment every Tuesday, while his wife was at Bible study. His wife knew all about Anna but prayed that Johnny would eventually come to his senses. Anna had it made, and she was in love.

The pianist in the lounge, Red, was a handsome, mocha-colored man with brilliant hazel eyes, the kind that changed colors based on what he was wearing. He loved Anna and she liked him a lot, too, but would never allow herself to date a colored man. Like every other colored person in Orleans Parish, Red knew that Anna was passing. One night, after drinking too much between sets, Anna was too drunk to stand, so Red escorted her home. Since she was drunk, Red found the courage to tell Anna how much he loved her. In her drunken stupor, she helped Red unbutton his shirt and unzipped his trousers. Although she "loved" Johnny, she was not satisfied by their lovemaking. Red tenderly kissed Anna on the neck. He did not want to have sex with Anna while she was drunk. He wanted her to remember their first time. So, although he was rock hard, he kept trying to pull his pants back up. Anna, however, was overpowered with her desire and pushed the weakened Red to the floor. As he entered her, she felt a sensation that she had never experienced before, her first orgasm. Anna and Red made love all night, and Red left the apartment at about five a.m. just before the light of day, and before the residents could see that Red had just slept with a "white" woman.

The next evening when Anna came to perform, she simply smiled at Red, pretending like nothing had happened. Anna had hidden her shame down deep, as she woke up that morning with her head and heart pounding. She couldn't believe she'd had sex with a colored man. That Tuesday, Johnny came in like clockwork, and Anna barely made eye contact with him.

During the pregnancy and after the delivery, Johnny was excited. After four daughters, he finally had a son, Roosevelt. Johnny lavished Anna with lilacs and roses and started coming by on Tuesdays and Thursdays to help Anna with the baby. He even thought about marrying Anna. If Anna had spent even a few minutes in the Black community, she would have known that the dark hue around the baby's ears was an indication that her cute little pale newborn, would slowly became darker over time. Like clockwork, within weeks, Roosevelt's porcelain skin became a mocha coffee color. It didn't take long for Johnny to kick Anna and her colored baby out of the apartment and onto the streets of the Quarter.

Anna was forced to take her baby out of the lap of luxury, and move them both into a dark backroom in the Garden District. Angered by the loss of her lover Johnny, and the betrayal that Red had forced upon her, an embittered Anna slowly began to take her anger (at herself and her promiscuity) out on her innocent son Roosevelt. Anna blamed Roosevelt for driving Johnny away, and believed that all men were evil, and that they were only interested in using her.

Anna was embarrassed to be seen with a little Black boy, and began to dream of when she was a happy little girl growing up on the Bayou. Anna let Roosevelt's curly hair grow and soon it was shoulder length. She began to dress him in some of the dresses that she had kept from her childhood. At first it was an occasional thing she did when she was drunk and needed to feel better, but as her drinking fueled her psychosis, she began to dress Roosevelt as a little girl, more and more.

Roosevelt was very smart so he would study on his own.

As Roosevelt got older, his mother's drinking became increasingly worse and she became increasingly more violent. Anna mercilessly beat him with anything from a belt buckle to a spiked, high-heeled shoe. Roosevelt was always bruised, swollen, and had countless welts.

Whenever Roosevelt resisted being dressed as a girl, Anna locked him in the closet for hours on end. Once, because she had passed out from drinking too much, Roosevelt remembered crying and begging to be released for twelve hours. When she finally did let him out, Anna made him change into a blue-and-white sailor dress, with white bobby socks and black-and-white saddle shoes. She combed his hair into two ponytails and added two matching bows. Anna stood back and admired her daughter. *She looks adorable! My baby girl is as pretty as me!* she exclaimed to herself, and from that point on Roosevelt had become "Rosie."

CHAPTER 30
New York, 2006

Kenya and Roosevelt enjoyed the basketball game, as the Knicks crushed the Celtics. Kenya was seated approximately twenty feet from the Knicks bench and had a close view of Stephon Marbury and Steve Francis, her two favorite players. Since she didn't once ask where her father was, Roosevelt thought that it was a good sign.

After the game, Roosevelt took Kenya to the Stage Deli and ordered two chocolate sundaes. Kenya was having the time of her life. And as time was getting closer to midnight, Kenya was beginning to feel exhausted, as they walked to the New York Sheraton and checked into the suite. Kenya was asleep before her head hit the pillow, as she held onto her brand-new pink dress. "What a wonderful evening," Roosevelt said as he looked over his sleeping princess.

Roosevelt breathed heavily as he watched little Kenya, and groaned aloud. How would he be able to kill her? He was already becoming too attached. Roosevelt longed for a child of his own, that he could love, and who would love him back, unconditionally. For all that he had accomplished professionally and for all the wealth that he had accumulated, Roosevelt had never experienced real *love*. No one had ever loved him.

He opened the mini bar, retrieved a bottle of Hennessy, took a coffee mug and poured the contents from the tiny bottle into the cup. Suddenly, he saw a vision of his mother lying in a pool of blood. She deserved to die. She made him parade around town looking like a little girl for seven years. On his fourteenth birthday, Anna had purchased a rabbit coat and forced him to put it on so she could see if it fit. When Roosevelt refused, she went ballistic, and locked him in the closet. Some man that she had met on the street had invited Anna to Dallas for the weekend. On Sunday evening, she came home, drunk as a skunk. She opened the closet door, and Roosevelt had had all that any fourteen-year-old man child could take. So, after Anna finally fell asleep, Roosevelt took a shower, changed into boys clothing, and cut the pigtails out of his hair. He also took all of his "girl clothes," cut them to shreds, threw them into the fireplace, and lit them on fire. He sat in the overstuffed chair and looked over at his sorry, pitiful mother.

What had he done to deserve such an angry and resentful mother? He knew that she hated her blackness, but he didn't understand why she had to take it out on him. He would not allow her to victimize him anymore; he was becoming a man, and he wasn't going to take it. Without thinking, Roosevelt stood up, walked into the kitchen, grabbed a knife from the drawer, and plunged it into her back, over and over again, until his shirt was soaked with her blood.

Rosie wrote a letter to the police and confessed to Anna's murder, telling them that he was tired of her making him have sex with her boyfriends and dressing him like a girl, and signed the letter Rosie Guidry. He packed a small duffel bag and hitchhiked to New York. Annabelle's boyfriend of record, Big Sugar, had become concerned she hadn't shown up with dinner and his laundry, so after two days, he contacted the police. The police initiated a manhunt to search for Rosie Guidry, a fourteen-year-old "girl" with long brown hair.

Realizing that he'd had another flashback, Roosevelt blinked his eyes and gnashed his teeth at the thought of wearing girl's clothing, yet another reason why he abhorred drag queens. Roosevelt got up and went into the shower, feeling physically and mentally drained. Deep down, he wanted to stop killing, and wanted to find a nice young white mate, and adopt a few children. Roosevelt wanted, no, *craved* a normal life. After washing away his apparent sins, he got out of the shower, changed into green silk pajamas, and went to sleep.

N N N

Malcolm tried to console his hysterical wife. How could this have happened to the District Attorney of Manhattan's family? Was he the target? Was this a kidnapping? Yes, he was sure that the kidnapper wanted revenge against him. Detective Randy Wiggins, Chief of Homicide, vigorously questioned Martha Dixon, who was the Headmistress of St. Mary's. All of the major news station vans, Channel 9, Channel 4, Fox 5 and others were parked and manned outside waiting for information and updates.

Malcolm hung his head at the thought that he, and his job, may be responsible for the pain that his daughter may be experiencing. He knew firsthand what it was like to grow up with without a mother or father, so Malcolm's children meant *everything* to him. He would not let Kenya down. He would find this kidnapper and make sure he rotted in jail.

Unfortunately, Detective Wiggins wasn't able to get much information out of the Headmistress, who was upset, not because Kenya's life was in danger, but because of the bad publicity. This is what happens when you start letting Black children attend such a prestigious school. Kenya was such a free spirit, she always had a hard time following instructions. Well, this time her free spirit had gotten everyone in trouble. Mrs. Dixon only hoped that their school would be able to recover from this fiasco, and her main concern was that her position would not be compromised.

Randy Wiggins also questioned a few of Kenya's classmates. One little girl reported that she had seen Kenya talking to this white guy who had some kind of hat on. She did not remember what else the guy had on, but at least this was a start. He would bring the girl and her parents in for additional questioning.

Randy felt the presence of the School Yard Murderer. He had been working on the case with several detectives from the twenty-one to seventy-six, from Brooklyn to the Bronx. Malcolm Knight thought that he was the target, but Randy knew that the abductor was the child killer, which is why he could not afford to waste time. Every minute that the killer had Kenya was a minute that brought her closer to death.

Malcolm called me on my cell phone, as soon as he heard from the school. He was calm, but I could tell that he was worried. I was teaching a class at the Martial Arts Center. I slid my chaps over my martial arts uniform, eased into my Yamaha leather jacket, slicked my hair back and threw on a bandanna. My bike was parked right outside so I revved her up and was on my way. I rode so fast that I felt that I was flying. I made it to Brooklyn from the Bronx in less than an hour. Thankfully, I was in my "Sandy persona" but "Skyy" was in full effect. I could feel the presence of a monster, and I knew that he was trying to harm my baby. I could not let that happen. Some shit was about to go down. I was about to have a head-on collision with destiny. And y'all know that I was always ready for a fight.

On the way to Brooklyn, I called Bird and told him what had happened, and that I needed to get his contact on this case right away. While I wanted to be there to comfort Malcolm, I needed to get into my kick-ass mode. My niece's life was on the line. I hung up and called Mike. Kenya had been missing for about five hours. I knew that the killer would not kill her right away. He never did, because he wanted to have his fun first.

I told Mike to meet me at my spot, and that Bird would meet us there, too. I told Bird about the information that I had found under Roosevelt's desk, and wondered if there was any type of connection. I thought that Roosevelt was too soft to be involved in something so heinous. However, I still could not get those pictures of those boys out of my mind. When this was all over, I would tell James about the double life that his CFO was leading. Hopefully, that would be just the information to get Rosie's ass out of the company once and for all.

I hugged Malcolm and Karen, and talked to the lead detective. Later, I lied and said that I had been dating a Bronx detective that may be able to pull some strings. I promised that I would touch base after I talked to my "friend," hailed a cab and jetted to the crib. A half an hour later the three of us were together. The discussion began on who they thought the killer was. We all agreed that he was a male between the ages of thirty-five and fifty. I suggested that he was a white professional man, but Bird stated that usually serial killers killed within their own race. That would mean that he was a light-skinned Black man, since the little girl who was questioned thought he was white. Okay, we were getting somewhere. We decided that he probably worked in Manhattan because that is where the corporate action is. We knew from prior police reports that he would habitually dress the girls in elegant attire before he killed him. Therefore, we deduced that he was a sharp dresser himself and that image was everything to him.

What baffled the three of us, as well as the police, was that all the girls were not raped, yet they were tortured. We concluded that the killer had a loathing or hatred toward girls and/or women. We further resolved that the assassin could be bisexual. Jokingly, I asked Bird if there was some sort of data base available of bisexual executives who work in New York. He said that the aforementioned data could possibly encompass every male in New York.

Then it happened; Mike asked if there could possibly be a link between involvement in child pornography and the butchering of girls. Bird took it a step further and suggested that we look on the net at some of the sadistic pornographic sites. That sounded like a plan. Bird set up shop in my bedroom, logging into my WiFi connection. As he and Mike went to work, I decided that I would check in with Malcolm.

"Hey, sweetie, how you holdin' up?"

"As well as can be expected," said Malcolm. "Karen isn't doing too well though. She blames herself for leaving her in aftercare."

"That's not fair. Karen is a great mother."

"I know that but right now, she needs to blame someone, so who else best but to blame herself."

"Have the police received any additional information?"

"They brought one of the little girls from Kenya's class down to the station and from her description, the kidnapper had a New York Knicks cap on."

I almost choked. *New York Knicks. Damn, this is crazy. The killer might be right under our noses*, I thought. I didn't want to prematurely alarm Malcolm so I didn't let him in on my suspicions. I continued the conversation.

"Did the little girl say anything else?"

"She did say that she thought she saw Kenya talking to the same man last week, only he was driving a pretty red car."

As my stomach rolled over about ten times, I realized that there were too many coincidences now. I always knew that there was something strange about ole boy, but I never thought that he would have the balls to undertake something of this magnitude. Before I gave the police any information, I wanted to make sure that the killer was who I thought he was. I told Malcolm that my other cell was ringing and that I would call him right back. I also told him that I loved him and that we would find Kenya, so before I hung up, we said a short prayer together.

I went back into the bedroom to find out if they had made any headway. Unfortunately there were so many child pornographic sites. However, there was one that stood out. This site talked about a magazine subscription that included participation in an annual child fair where paying members had carte blanche and full exploitation of child sex slaves. I had Bird pull up the site.

While he worked on the assignment, I went to my Gucci business tote and retrieved the magazine that I had stolen from Roosevelt's desk. My heart was racing so I went into the kitchen and grabbed two beers for the guys and a bottle of Evian for me. As I entered my bedroom, my heart almost came out of my chest. The design on the website that Bird had pulled up matched the cover design of the magazine that I had stolen from Rosie. I threw the magazine on my desk, sat down cross-legged on my bed, and told them the whole story. Mike and Bird agreed that there were *way too many* coincidences for Roosevelt not to be somehow involved, let alone actually be the killer.

Bird decided that we should use a back-door route to find out what purchases Roosevelt may have made in the last couple of days. We needed hard evidence, and not a bunch of hunches.

I lay back on my bed because my head was starting to spin. Could Roosevelt be the killer? And if so, why Kenya? Was he trying to get back at the *Lady in Black?* I could feel the tears start to roll down my face, as I thought of me being the reason that my sweet little niece was in trouble. Mike noticed that I was starting to unravel and he came over and lay on the bed with me. He put his arm down and motioned for me to lie on it. I rolled over and into his toned body. I just let my emotions go and didn't care if my boys saw me lose it. They knew how much Kenya meant to me and they knew how much I had gone through in this past year.

"I got it!" said Bird.

Mike and I sprang up and dashed to the computer. Bird showed us that Roosevelt had used his American Express to purchase two tickets to the New York Knicks game, and that he also had bought some girls clothing at Macy's. Bird did another search to see if he had used any other credit cards in the last month. As it turned out, Mr. Guidry had a lot of activity on his Visa, MasterCard and Discover credit cards. Bird printed copies of each card's account and gave us each a copy to review. I saw nothing major other than drinks at a couple of nightclubs on his Visa. Mike noticed that he had used his MasterCard to make a few purchases at an Army-Navy store. It looked like he'd bought flashlights, a rope and a number of hunting knives, and I cringed at the thought of him using those materials on my Kenya.

While Bird was on the computer, Mike called Yan who had a contact in the CIA. It seemed that Guidry was on a list of suspected killers. There was the death of his mother's boyfriend, and her murder as well. His involvement in pornographic organizations had also raised some flags as well. Yan said that his contact would be faxing the information.

Bird hit the jackpot. Guidry had used a corporate Discover card to make a reservation for this weekend at the New York Sheraton on Seventh Avenue. Bird looked at me and smiled. I looked at him and said, "It's on."

CHAPTER 31
New York, 2006

Roosevelt had fallen asleep and woke up a few hours later. He got up from the couch and went into the bedroom to check on Kenya. She was sound asleep. Tomorrow they would have a lot of fun. He had the whole day mapped out. As long as Kenya followed the rules, she would live another day.

He went out into the living room of the suite, and turned on the TV. He channel-surfed for a while. It was 11 p.m. and there was nothing on but the news—and the news always depressed him. He turned to the hotel movie channel and decided that he would rent a movie. He glided through the cinema collections until he came to "Action/Adventure." There was no movie that tickled his fancy. He was always the drama type. He then utilized the remote and selected "Drama." Still nothing! He returned to "Action/Adventure" and chose *Gladiator*.

As he scrolled through the prompts that would eventually lead him to the movie, he noticed that the price was $13.95. He thought that was a bit high. Then he thought, *Well, I have charged a lot more on all three credit cards*. He suddenly remembered that he had charged the hotel suite to his credit card. He realized how easily the charge could be traced. He had never reserved a hotel room before when he had kidnapped children. He usually rented a room in a boarding house and used disguises and aliases. The excitement of being with Kenya had totally thrown him off. It was like he was trying too hard to impress her. He went into an instant state of panic. He may have made a fatal mistake. What should he do now?

Frantically, he packed his things and Kenya's. They had walked to the hotel from Madison Square Garden, so his car was parked at the office. He searched the room for a phone book. He examined the hotel section and found your typical Hilton, Hyatt, and Marriott. Roosevelt picked up the phone and started to dial the Hilton around the corner on Fifty-third and the Avenue of the Americas. Then he thought harder about it. If the police had traced him to the Sheraton, then the Hilton would be a second logical choice to look for him. So, he decided to "downgrade," to an Econo Lodge, Holiday Inn, Howard Johnson, Ramada, the Red Roof Inn. The Red Roof Inn; he shuddered. He knew that his best bet would be to pick a motel, because Kenya would not feel comfortable at the room he usually rented at the boarding house. Besides, that room was solely designed for the torture sessions, where he could not care how she felt at that point.

What to do, what to do. He picked up the phone and dialed the Holiday Inn. The customer service representative stated that there was availability in Newark, New Jersey. He could not be seen in Newark. Then again, he surely would not know a soul in Newark. Maybe this would work. He decided against making a reservation over the phone and thought it smarter to take a cab and pay cash.

He thought about what he would tell Kenya. He would figure that out later. Kenya was asleep and would remain that way for a while. To ensure that she would stay asleep, he took a miniature of rum and a Coke from the mini bar. He opened the Coke and poured some of it out. He then took the rum and poured the entire contents into the can. He shook Kenya to wake her up. He put her coat over her brand-new Barbie pajamas. She was sleepwalking. They caught the elevator to the lobby and he sat Kenya in an overstuffed chair and went out to hail a cab. Ordinarily he would never have hailed his own cab but he didn't want to draw any unnecessary attention to himself.

It took him a half an hour to successfully hail a cab. He was seething and could not believe that he had just endured such humiliation. He grabbed Kenya who, by this time, was wide awake.

"Where are we going?" she asked.

"It's a surprise."

"What time is it?"

"It's eight o'clock p.m. Don't you remember, we just left the basketball game?"

"We did? Oh. Why were we in the pretty hotel?"

"You sure are inquisitive. Are you thirsty?"

"Yes. May I have something to drink?"

"Here, drink this Coke. I brought it because you said Coke was your favorite drink."

"Thank you, Mister. By the way, you never told me your name," Kenya said as she took a long swig from the soda. "This tastes funny," she said.

"You just finished eating cotton candy. The mixture of the two is probably why it tastes weird." Roosevelt laughed.

"You're so nice, Mister." She took another swig. He offered her some M&M's. She ate the entire bag and then finished off the soda. She was fast asleep by the time the cab pulled up to the Holiday Inn. The cab driver carried in the bags while he carried her in. He delicately placed Kenya on a sofa, walked up to the desk and asked the clerk if there were any suites available. The young Black girl looked at him as if he were from Mars. She politely told Roosevelt that this was not the Ritz-Carlton. She said that there was a large room that had a microwave and a fridge available. He said that he would take it. He was much too weary to argue. She told him that it would cost $99 a night but she would need a credit card and some ID. He slipped her $150 in cash and she smiled. Two seconds later, he had the keys to room 208.

Roosevelt could not sleep. His head started to pound as he took in the full view of his surroundings. *The Holiday fucking Inn. What a dump*, he thought. He was starving so he looked around for the room service menu. He realized that he could not draw attention to himself. He went into the bathroom to take a shower so that he could make himself more presentable. The plan had been to have a late lunch at 21, then go to the Museum of Modern Art, and treat her to more Knicks memorabilia at the NBA store.

But now with the unfortunate turn of events, he would probably have to cut the weekend short because things were not going as planned. Maybe he should just kill her now. No, that would draw too much attention. The ghetto girl at the front desk would surely remember him and, as she put it, "The cute little girl that slept like an angel."

He would surprise Kenya with a potpourri of breakfast treats. He turned off the shower, wrapped a towel around his waist, and then opened the bathroom door. She startled him as she stood right at the door as he opened it.

"I'm sorry, Mister, but I have to go to the bathroom real bad."

Kenya ran in and closed the door. Roosevelt quickly dressed and put his socks and shoes on. He threw on his Knicks cap and sunglasses. He sat on the couch and waited for Kenya to come out of the bathroom. When she did, she looked at him as if she was about to throw up.

"What's up, honey? Are you sick?"

"Yeah, I think so. My tummy hurts."

"Well, do you want some aspirin or anything else, sweetie? A doll, a coloring book?"

"I would like to talk to my mommy. When are my parents coming to pick me up?"

Now she did it. *Why did she have to mention her mommy? Didn't she know that her mommy didn't love her? Mommies don't love their children. They just use their children. Why did she want her mommy? Wasn't I good enough? Didn't she like me?*

Roosevelt became furious with Kenya and snapped.

"We will meet your parents this afternoon after we have lunch. I was thinking about taking you to the Museum of Modern Art, and then to the NBA store. Patrick Ewing is supposed to be signing autographs there. Would you like to see him?"

"Yes, I would. Can my mommy come?"

"Maybe, I'll be right back. I'm going to get you some aspirin and some ginger ale. That should help your stomach, sweetheart," he said in the nicest voice that he could possibly muster and slammed out of the hotel room.

Kenya became frightened. Why did the nice man get so mad when she mentioned her mommy? Where was her mommy? Suddenly the room started to spin, and by the time that Kenya got up and ran to the bathroom, she threw up and instantly felt better.

She found the remote, turned on the TV, and lay on the couch. As she channel-surfed, she searched for the *Rocket Power* cartoon. She flipped through the stations and stopped when she saw a man on the television that resembled her father. Her heart stopped as she listened to the pretty lady newscaster talk about a little girl who had been kidnapped from her school, named Kenya Knight. They cut to St. Mary's and the camera closed in on her mother who was crying. Karen Knight pleaded to whoever had her baby girl to please return her safely. She talked about Kenya being a "straight-A" student, and told the audience that her daughter wanted to be a WNBA star and a Supreme Court Justice. Then the camera panned to Malcolm Knight who was speechless.

Kenya started to cry. The nice man had been lying to her. She had to find her mommy and let her know that she was fine. *He may try to hurt me*, she thought. She got up and frantically looked for her shoes. She looked for her coat and found some money, so she grabbed the bills, and placed them in her shoes. She thought about calling her father on his cell phone but thought that Mister might walk in soon. Kenya peeked out of the room to make sure the coast was clear. She didn't see a soul so she dashed out, and ran as fast as her little legs would carry her.

It was 4 a.m. and Roosevelt had found a twenty-four-hour drug store. He quickly purchased the items and began to wonder why did all of the children have to dismiss his presence? That's what his mother had done. No matter how nice he treated the girls, they always asked for their mom. He regretted having gotten angry with Kenya, because he really liked her. He would make it up to her. He bought her a potpourri of treats, more M&M's, Hostess cupcakes, Lay's potato chips and a big bottle of Coke. He also bought her a nail set so maybe they could play beauty parlor and a beautiful stuffed animal. *That would make her feel more comfortable*, he thought. I will make Kenya like me.

He started to feel good, but not great. This weekend would be wonderful; especially after she ate the goodies, she would forget all about her mommy. When she grew up, she would realize how fucked up mothers really were. He glanced at his Presidential Rolex and noticed he had been gone for forty-five minutes. He figured he had a little while longer, because Kenya was sick, she was probably in the bed. He walked over to the Path train station and picked up a schedule. There was a 5 a.m. train. Maybe they could get a real early start and see the sun rise from the top of the Empire State Building. Kenya would love that!

A few minutes later, Roosevelt slipped his plastic key into the sensored door. He slowly walked in, feeling that something wasn't right. He placed the bags of treats on the table.

"Kenya," he called. No answer. His stomach started doing flips. His brow began to twitch.

"Kenya? Where are you, honey?" he yelled as sweetly as he could. *She's probably in the bathroom. The little darling was probably still sick.* He threw the door open and pulled the shower curtain back. No Kenya.

"That bitch! Where the fuck is she?"

He looked under the bed, the couch and in the closet. Finally, a beaten man sunk into the shabby furniture and didn't know whether to laugh or cry. His life had been one big disappointment. Why should this weekend be any different?

CHAPTER 32
New York, 1977

Life was good. Malcolm had gone off to the fancy prep school, and I reluctantly had given him $1,000 that I took from the money Momma had left us. Malcolm didn't know about the stash, so I lied and told him that I had worked extra days. I took another $500 and bought him a bunch of uniforms so his shit would be laid. It was bad enough that he had to wear those tired uniforms. At least his would be tight.

Master Kwan began to give me a lot more responsibility, such as keeping the place clean and balancing the books. He knew that I had a knack for numbers and I had always gotten A's in math. There were additional duties that consisted of making daily runs to the bank so he never had a lot of cash or checks on hand. His business had increased after a string of Kung Fu movies like *Enter the Dragon* came out. It seemed like martial arts was becoming fashionable. Between Jim Kelly and Bruce Lee, kung fu and karate had become very chic. If you didn't take classes, you definitely walked around with numchuck in your pockets, and everybody in the 'hood was walking around in Chinese slippers and white tube socks.

Many parents would send their children to take classes for self-defense. For an hour they would just sit there waiting for their children. With that in mind, I initiated a deal where the parent could take classes for half-price, if their kids were enrolled. The promotion was a big hit. The parents that signed up ultimately spent more money on uniforms, shoes, and equipment for themselves than they did for their kids. Most also took the art very seriously.

Since most classes took place in the evening, I spent my days passing out flyers in schools and area businesses. The community was all too eager to embrace the weaponless system for self-defense. I persuaded Master Kwan that he should introduce the concept of kung fu and karate to the public school system. Marketing statistics that I found had convinced him that if he offered everyone who attended the demonstrations a trial membership for a month, at least thirty percent of those people would sign up. We also did demonstrations at ladies' organizations and churches. The promotions generated a sense of goodwill in the community as well as increased income.

Master Kwan was elated with the results of the various marketing promotions I'd implemented. He often referred to me as his little marketing genius. I must admit, I did feel that I had a certain flair for business. The most wonderful aspect of my life was that I hadn't had to have sex in six months. The bank account was getting fatter and my earning potential had increased without me lying on my back. Like I said, life was good.

Karate had also begun to occupy a great deal of my time and energy. While studying for my yellow belt, the objective was to be promoted to a green belt. In class, the teacher often made reference to my strength and discipline. The students knew of my desire to definitively kick ass. I would fight anybody. I just didn't care.

Master Kwan was amazed at the fearlessness evident in my demeanor. If he only knew how much I had been through in my sixteen years. Every moment that I wasn't balancing books or running off flyers, I was practicing my form. I had my forms down cold, and would easily get trophies as a result of my precision.

I had no life so martial arts became my world. Most of the students attending classes at the center were either in a vocational school or a university. Many of them had fulfilling jobs and careers. When class was over or the weekend came, they didn't feel like practicing. Many had friends, families, and lovers to spend time with. I had none of the above. I practiced karate day and night.

A number of male students asked me out and all of them got their feelings hurt. Rumors that I was a lesbian began to circulate. *Whatever*! There had been enough drama in my life to last me a lifetime. Moreover, a relationship was the last thing I needed now. My program demanded a certain level of focus, and sex would be a distraction that could keep me from the mission at hand.

Master Kwan was very worried about me. He thought it odd for a girl so pretty and young to be so focused and single-minded. He would try to hook me up with other girls my age, or in college, so I could go out socially. Refusal was the immediate reply, because there was an obvious level of distrust in my disposition. It was common knowledge that I felt that women could not be trusted. Zee had constantly confided in any number of female neighbors who would later "dis" her and talk about her behind her back. My continuous pledge to Zee was to never have a female friend.

There was, however, an older martial artist that simply caused me to feel weak in the knees. His name was Puma Todd. He was in his twenties, and was fine as shit. Puma stood about six feet two inches and had a huge Foster Sylvers' 'fro, and the most dazzling eyes I'd ever seen. Puma's voice was smooth as silk and his smile was simply intoxicating.

One night after all the students had gone home, he and Master Kwan were working on a routine for an upcoming demonstration. The movements were fierce and with his rapid, strong hands, he ripped off his shirt because he was soaked. Thick beads of sweat collected on his massive chest. He moved his thick juicy lips as he counted off the particular move for the routine. His hands moved through the air with the grace of a ballerina while his thighs bulged through his pants like a fullback.

He was in a word, perfect.

I would routinely catch him staring at me through the mirrors when we were doing our forms. Somehow he made me feel so feminine when he worked with me in sparring. He was training for his black belt, so he was way ahead of me. But he was never too busy to help me with my form or any other student for that matter.

As I mentioned earlier, most brothers were tryin' to holla, and most of them were angry when their advances were refused. Consequently, rumors ran rampant that I liked girls. The girls were mad because their boyfriends wanted me, and the guys were mad because they couldn't get with me, and everyone hated me because I was so proficient at Karate. *Player hatin'* in the seventies!

One night a brother named Donny was talking about how he saw me checking out some girl, when a blue belt named Russell interrupted and said, emphatically, that he had done me about a year ago at a bachelor party. Donny didn't believe him and bet Russell $20 that he was lying.

The news that there was a bet regarding my sexual proclivity traveled rapidly. Suddenly, everyone was acting cold toward me. Or shall I say, colder than usual. One night after class, Puma asked me out for coffee. The response was positive because he seemed like he was troubled, and may need a shoulder to cry on. Puma was one of the few people who had always been so nice to me. We walked to an all-night diner and ordered hamburgers. Puma explained to me that there were a few brothers that had been spreading the rumor that I was once a prostitute.

Either I needed to unload, or I simply trusted him, so I decided to tell Puma about the past sordid years of my life. Over fries and a hamburger, I told him everything in great detail. The truth about Zee, all about Malcolm, and how I had come to live with and work for Master Kwan. Puma was overwhelmed by the tragic tale, and I saw a single tear fall down his cheek. He couldn't believe I had lived to tell such an incredibly sad story.

Unfortunately, I had no tears left. My tired eyes didn't shed one tear. Not one.

As we strolled back to the center, I found out that Puma had a wonderful sense of humor. He made me laugh. It had been a long time since I had laughed. When we arrived at the center, he walked me upstairs to my apartment and I asked him in for a nightcap. Although I was too young to purchase liquor, the last tenants had left a refrigerator of beer. Puma told me that he didn't drink but he would still come in.

I was slightly embarrassed about the apartment's décor, or lack thereof. The furniture consisted of a television, a torn brown velvet sofa, a crate that served as a cocktail table, and a bear rug. The room was dark because there were no lamps. I quickly turned on the television and used its light to find my way around. I usually kept the matches in the kitchen so I stumbled in and found them. I took the matches and lit several candles around the room. I then went to the fridge and retrieved a pitcher of Kool-Aid. After pouring each of us a glass, I sat on the couch beside Puma. We watched *Good Times* and laughed our asses off.

Puma put his arm around me and I lay into him. He felt good. This felt good. I turned to ask him a question and he kissed me. His tongue fervently searched my mouth. He sucked my tongue and I sucked his. I took my hands and gently felt his beautiful face. I slid my fingers across his sexy thick lips. I kissed him this time and my heart began to race. I couldn't believe this was happening. I was excited and scared. I had never been in a position where I wanted the man that was touching me. I felt like a schoolgirl. My palms started swearing. I wanted Puma but I wasn't ready for what would happen afterward so I stopped him.

"What's wrong, baby?"

"I'm not ready," I answered.

"You're not ready for what? Don't you want me?" he asked.

"More than you know but I'm scared you'll hurt me. All men have hurt me."

"Look at me, Sandy."

I looked into his big brown eyes as the candles illuminated his face.

"I would never hurt you. I only want to protect you. Let me make you feel like a woman. I want to love you. Let me make *love* to you."

He slowly peeled off my clothes, one piece at a time. He turned me on my stomach and began to massage my back. I felt his tongue on my collarbone and it traced my entire body, starting from my neck and ending at my ankles. My pleasure was displayed by deep, successive moans. My throbbing body felt so incredibly weak with desire. My body was filled with anticipation and yearning.

He slowly turned me over and lifted my foot to his mouth. I closed my eyes, as I felt my foot in his mouth and my toes being slowly and seductively sucked. He moved to the other foot and then deliberately ventured up my thigh to my vagina. He attacked my pussy like a fat cat at a smorgasbord. Although I tried to play it cool, I squealed with delight and came twice. My body shuddered and my hands aggressively grabbed his torso and placed him inside of me. We amorously made love by candlelight and fell asleep in each other's arms.

Seven hours later the rays of the morning sun woke me. The memories of the previous evening's activities brought a smile to my lips. I instantly got up and threw on some jeans and a T-shirt. I grabbed my purse and headed for the A&P. Today's menu would consist of eggs, bacon, bread, grapefruit, and orange juice. A toothbrush was definitely necessary. The last stop produced a beautiful arrangement of posies, daisies, and carnations that would definitely brighten up the place.

When I returned, I discovered that Puma was in the shower. I found a dingy frying pan and started to cook the bacon. Puma got out of the shower and snuck up behind me. He snuggled me and hugged me from behind.

"That sure smells good. You didn't have to go to the trouble of cooking for me."

"It was no trouble at all. I never have any company and since Malcolm left, I rarely cook. I hope you like it."

"So far, I like *everything* you do," Puma replied.

He was such a flirt. "You're a man of many talents, too!" I said, trying to flirt back. I was obviously a bit rusty in that department.

We ate our breakfast and talked for about two hours. I had to be at the center at noon, so I started to end the date. It abruptly occurred to me that Puma might run into one of the students en route to the classroom downstairs. I panicked. The last thing I wanted was for anyone to know that I had hooked up with Puma. He decided that it would be best if he left via the fire escape. He leaned over, kissed me, and told me that he would see me later. I did not have a phone so we decided to rendezvous on Wednesday night after his class. I would be upstairs waiting for him.

For the next couple of days, the guys that I sparred with started fucking with me more than usual. In between sets, they would mumble words like, "whore," "tramp," and "skank" under their breath but loud enough for me to hear. I would hear giggles as I did my form. On Monday, as I entered the female dressing room, I heard someone telling the infamous bachelor party story. When I was in plain sight, everyone was silent. I grew very impatient with the situation and just wanted to kick everyone's ass.

During my sparring sessions, I would go buck wild, kicking as much ass as I could. They had to drag me off of one guy after he muttered, "How about a blow job?"

Depression started to kick in. Master Kwan got wind of the situation, and was at a loss for words. He didn't know if he should address the issue publicly or just hope it would blow over. On Wednesday, a group of guys were fired up after class. They decided that they wanted to teach me a lesson, so they snuck up to my apartment and knocked on the door. Puma, who had arrived earlier, hid in the closet. When I opened the door, Russell appeared and tried, in vain, to muscle his way in. Just then, five of the other guys appeared, forced their way in, and pinned me down. Before they could do any damage, Puma appeared and threatened to hurt them. The guys knew that Puma was bad, but he wasn't crazy enough to take on the five of them. They were right; Puma wasn't the only one who was crazy. So was I, but we destroyed them and kicked their asses. That was the last time I saw those trouble-makers. It was at that moment that there was an unwavering bond between Puma and me, that remained to this day.

CHAPTER 33
New Jersey, 2006

Kenya was terrified as she escaped from the back exit of the hotel and ran into the parking lot. She heard a noise so she ducked between a Ford Taurus and a Honda Accord. A stream of tears flowed down her flushed cheeks. She knew she had to be tough. Her daddy was always telling her that a girl had to be as tough as she was pretty. Her mother always said that whenever she was in trouble, she could count on the Lord. She was sure she was in trouble now, and didn't know how she would find her way back to Brooklyn. She got on her knees and bowed her head as she had done a million times before while bedside.

"Lord, please watch over me. I am lost and I hope that you will help my parents find me. Help me to be strong and smart so that I can make it home safely. Please forgive Mister for his sins because he knows not what he does. The television announcer called him an animal but I can see the good in Mister. Please put your arms around him, too! Amen."

И И И

He was lonely. He was always lonely. Everyone that had meant anything to him always eventually abandoned him. They always had to start whining for their mommies. He would not have to kill the children, if they would just be content with him. No one wanted to be with *just him*. He looked around the filthy room and found the stuffed animal he had bought Kenya. It was a pink fluffy bunny rabbit that said "Daddy's Bunny" on its white frilly dress. Kenya felt safe, and had fallen asleep with the fuzzy stuffed creature nestled in her arms, but she had abandoned *it*, too.

Roosevelt held the rabbit tightly to his chest, and he wondered if he should just turn himself in. He placed the rabbit gently on a chair and picked up the remote. He almost had a heart attack as he realized that the entire city was talking about him. His picture was emblazoned on every channel in the world, and was described as a "person of interest" in the School Yard Murders. They used nouns like *butcher*, *killer*, *assassin*, and *exterminator* to describe him, and adjectives like *crazy*, *insane*, *psychotic*, *deranged*, and *maniacal* to characterize his state of mind. He had to realize that he was indeed *mad*, and that *she* had made him that way. Instead of a nice, well-adjusted citizen, Annabelle Guidry had created a monster that was as twisted and sadistic, as he was urbane and intelligent. For thirty years he had lived a lie. He had been on a killing spree since he was fifteen years old, and now he was forty-five. Roosevelt was a walking dichotomy, an asexual pervert; a Rhodes Scholar, who was born on a farm; a Black man, who longed to be white. He, too, was an enigma.

ᴎ ᴎ ᴎ

The Sony digital clock read three a.m. Malcolm, Karen, and I had fallen asleep for a moment. The late-night hours had been spent at the Sheraton in Manhattan. After we discovered that the killer could be Roosevelt, I followed the hunch that he may have checked into the Sheraton. I wanted to go alone because I sensed that Roosevelt was waiting for me. The more I learned about Roosevelt, the more we were alike than different. I knew that now. However, no matter how tragic his life had been as a child, I also knew that I had to find him and stop him before he hurt Kenya.

As I changed into my Jenisa Washington black leather pantsuit and sunglasses, I also adjusted my attitude; *Skyy Knight* was in effect. I hopped on my bike because I needed to maneuver around the city quickly; a car in Manhattan can slow you down. Plus, even at three a.m., you can never find a parking space. As I sped from SoHo to the Upper West Side, I started to panic. What would I do if I lost my little Kenya? She and I had become so close in the past three years. She was the daughter I never had. But I had to leave Aunt Sandy behind, and let Skyy take over, as I changed gears and sped up.

That twisted son of a bitch is gonna pay dearly for this one, I vowed. Anger is an emotion that has always served me well. I used every bit of anger that I have ever felt in all of my thirty-something years to fuel this one. I knew that I would need every bit of it.

When I got to the Sheraton, I asked the clerk to give me Roosevelt Guidry's room. The clerk very politely told me that it was hotel policy to protect the privacy of their guests. I guess so many husbands had been busted that way, the entire industry had put safeguards in place. I handed the clerk a fifty-dollar bill, which motivated him to suggest that I try room 2306. I thanked him and slid over to the elevator bank. The elegant hotel was still buzzing with guests milling about the city that never sleeps.

I took the elevator to the twenty-third floor. I flirted with the non-English-speaking room service guy, and borrowed his key as I stopped to help him pick up a discarded tray in the hall. I think that he was also hoping to get some in the process. The language of S-E-X is universal.

To my surprise, as we entered the room, it was empty, although I could feel that Roosevelt and Kenya had been there. Roosevelt must've realized that he had charged the room on his credit card. I used a police-issued dusting kit that Bird had gotten from his contact, and dusted the room for prints. The young Latino, who had introduced himself as Julio, seemed to be extremely impressed and curious about what I was doing. I just wanted for him to sit there and look good. I had totally won him over, and he wouldn't leave now if his life depended on it.

I sat on the couch and turned on the television. I wanted to see what the news was reporting as far as the status of the case. There were no new updates. So, as I reached for the remote to turn off the television, I noticed a little pin under a chair and picked it up. It was the same "girl power" pin that I had given to Kenya last year.

Damn. What next?

N N N

Kenya didn't realize that if she had gone out of the front entrance, she would have been on a busy street and would have easily been able to call her parents. Instead, she left the parking lot through the back and ran into the woods. At least the thick trees would provide a hiding place until someone found her. Her head was spinning from the night before. She had already thrown up once that morning, and felt like she was about to throw up again. *Be strong*, she said to herself. *Just be strong. God will protect you*, and she believed that He would.

Kenya ran through the dense trees and heavy brush for what seemed like an hour. She decided to rest awhile on an old tree stump. It was dark and bitter cold. She was deathly afraid but she willed herself to be courageous, just like the lady in the movie *G.I. Jane*, and just like *Mulan*.

She still could not believe that Mister was a killer, as she snuggled inside of the new down coat Roosevelt had bought her the night before. He had been so nice to her and had such a pretty car. She wondered why he didn't drive his pretty car last night.

She looked around the terrain trying to gain some sense of direction, and had wandered through the dark trees for about half an hour and was hopelessly lost. The intense noises of the woodland creatures made her uneasy. The temperature had dropped significantly and she didn't have on the appropriate hat and gloves because she had rushed out of the hotel room so quickly. She realized that she had to get to a phone.

She thought for a second. Maybe she should go back to the hotel. Okay, she had a plan to sneak back to the hotel, and call her parents. Kenya looked in all four directions, and could not figure out which way the hotel was. She felt like Gretel, from her favorite nursery tales. Why had she not been smart enough to leave a trail of bread crumbs from the hotel? A tinge of sadness began to set in, but she fought it off. She was Daddy's little tough girl.

She got up again and randomly chose a direction to go in, walked until her legs were tired, and then took a little break. She tried to remain optimistic even though she knew she was as lost as she could be. Just then she spotted an orange color glistening in the distance. It looked like a fire of sorts. Then she heard a voice, no, it was two. She crouched down behind a huge willowy oak tree and listened intently. She ran toward the light and saw two little girls in the clearing wearing brown beanies and brown pants. They had orange sashes across their coats and lots of little pins and badges on them. She had seen girls that wore stuff like that at her school and recognized them as Brownies. As a matter of fact, she had asked her mom if she could be a Brownie. The two little girls were collecting sticks. In the distance she saw a series of green tents and an older lady giving instructions to a bunch of little girls wearing brown beanies. Kenya smiled, looked up to Heaven and said, "Thank You."

И И И

Methodically, Roosevelt packed his and Kenya's things, made the bed, straightened the room, and wiped down the room for fingerprints, something he had neglected to do at the other hotel. He had purchased a cowboy hat, a leather coat, and cowboy boots, and trashed the Knicks cap. He exited the rear of the hotel and threw away all of the items he had bought for Kenya. Roosevelt walked around to the front of the hotel and stared down the road that led to the highway. He wondered if the police would be staking out the train stations. He was sure that the New Jersey Transit police would be looking out for him, so he decided to hitchhike into Manhattan and determine what his next step would be.

He made his way over to the Jersey Turnpike and stuck his thumb out. He had pulled the collar of his coat up high to cover his face. The Rayban sunglasses and Stetson cowboy hat added to the disguise. The five o'clock shadow also had given him a whole new look. The old Roosevelt would have never gone without shaving. After fifteen minutes, no cars had passed or stopped. He wondered if he had made the right decision, to hitchhike. He was an open target and kept thinking that the police would be pulling up any second now to take his ass to the pokey. Finally, an old man pulled up in a 1982 dusty-brown, broken-down Chevy Chevette. Before he accepted the ride, Roosevelt thought for a second, that he could not ride into Manhattan in this car. After a quick reality check, it dawned on him that he was wearing Rayban sunglasses, and the time for pretense was over.

He leaned over into the car and said as politely as he could, "Hello, sir. I need a ride to the city. Are you going that way?"

"Why, yes, young man. I am going to the Port Authority to meet my granddaughter. I'm taking her ice skating at the Rockefeller Center and we figured we would get there before the crowd did. It is always real crowded during this time of year."

"Great." Roosevelt threw his bag in the back seat and hopped in the front seat.

The old man looked hard at Roosevelt as he got into the car.

"Have I met you before? You look so familiar."

"No, I don't believe so." Roosevelt knew that he would have to kill him, although he seemed like such a nice guy.

Well, you know what they say, Roosevelt thought. *Nice guys finish last.*

They rode about ten miles and pulled into a rest stop to go to the bathroom.

"That's what happens when you get old. You have to relieve yourself frequently," the old man said. They parked in the parking lot and went inside. Roosevelt told the old man that he was getting in line to get some coffee. The man responded by asking him to pick up a black coffee for him as well. "I like my coffee like my women, black, no cream and lots of sugar." He grinned.

"No problem," Roosevelt replied.

Roosevelt waited for him to go into the bathroom. Earlier, he had placed the knife in his coat pocket. Roosevelt and that knife were old friends, so close that he named her Annabelle; they had been through a lot together.

Roosevelt thought back to when he first got that knife. He had stolen it from one of his mother's boyfriends, Jason "Big Sugar" Toussaint. It saved his life when, after a night of drinking, Big Sugar tried to rape him as his mom slept.

Jason had been eyeing Rosie all night. That was not the first time one of his mother's boyfriends had come on to him. Anyway, that night Jason asked Rosie to come and sit on his lap. When Rosie refused, Jason took out his knife and told him to take off his clothes. Rosie knew that the drunk motherfucker was not going to take no for an answer. He went over to Big Sugar and sat down on his lap. Jason placed the knife down on the kitchen table. As he did, Rosie simultaneously picked it up and slit his throat.

Rosie dragged the dude out the back and put him in a large trash can. When they found his body, it was so badly decomposed that it could not be identified. The police never suspected that the sweet little "girl" who lived in apartment 203 could have been responsible.

Roosevelt took "Annabelle" out and placed her up the sleeve of his jacket. He snuck into the bathroom behind the old man and asked him for the keys to his car. Startled and surprised, the man asked why he wanted the keys. Roosevelt told him that he had left his wallet in the car. As the old man gave him the keys, Roosevelt put the keys in his pocket, took Annabelle out, and pierced the old man's aorta. He rinsed the knife off and placed it back in his pocket. He dashed out to the car, quickly got in, and sped off.

⚔ ⚔ ⚔

Kenya ran over to the girls of Brownie Troop 139. They took Kenya to the Scout Leader, Mrs. Janice King, who knew right away who Kenya was. All four major networks had plastered her picture on every broadcast. Malcolm Knight had made a plea to the kidnapper to turn himself in and he had promised that the system would go easy on him. Mrs. King hugged Kenya tightly and began to cry. She was one of those women who felt like all children were her children. When she first heard the story about the kidnapping, she had prayed that God would watch over little Kenya. So to have her wander into her camp site was like a miracle. She was glad that she had stuck to her plan and made the girls wake up so early although they all had complained. If they had still been asleep, Kenya would have never found them. *God is so good*, she thought.

Mrs. King used her cell phone to call the police. The ten girls of Brownie Troop 139 circled around Kenya like she was a celebrity. They asked her a million questions, which was good because that served as a distraction. For a while, Kenya forgot how cold and hungry she was. She forgot that she hadn't seen her mom and dad in over twenty-three hours. However, Kenya did realize that she was safe.

CHAPTER 34
New York, 2006

Julio and I sat in the hotel room deep in thought. I was trying to decide what my next move would be. He was trying to decide how he was going to get the panties. Even at three o'clock in the morning, the brother was trying to get his mack on.

The dusting kit did produce a few fingerprints. I sent Julio down to fax the prints to Bird so that he could trace them. I decided to help myself to the mini bar since Roosevelt was paying. I knew that the trace would take at least half an hour. I selected a bottle of Evian and a bag of peanuts, and took the liberty of retrieving a beer for Julio, who seemed like a Corona kind of guy. Julio came back in five minutes and proceeded to get on my nerves big time. I realized that I had to dismiss him for his purpose had been served. He was becoming worrisome. I finally thanked him for his trouble and told him that I would call him if I needed him.

At 4:30 a.m., my cell rang. Bird told me that the prints were a perfect match, and that they did indeed belong to Roosevelt Guidry.

Alrighty then. My job here was done.

I placed an anonymous call to the police and gave them all the details that I had. Mike went to the local twenty-four-hour Kinkos, and faxed them a copy of the prints Bird analyzed. I went downstairs and hopped on my bike. Where to? I decided to go to the office and see if I could get more information from Roosevelt's desk.

Riding my bike in the wee hours of the morning felt great. I was dead tired but that frigid air sure woke me up. The Yamaha was pushing ninety-five miles per hour and it felt like a jet flying through the New York sky. My intuition told me that I was closing in on him. For a second, I saw the face of one of his victims lying lifeless on the street clinging to her teddy bear. Roosevelt sure was a sick puppy and his ass was mine.

I parked the bike in the garage and walked to the elevator with my helmet on, because I wanted to remain anonymous. Believe it or not, some of our more ambitious employees worked around the clock. Working weekends was becoming the norm for many ambitious BCI staffers.

Luckily, today was not the day to worry about nosy employees. Five o'clock in the morning was just too early for most folks. The office was completely empty. The door to Roosevelt's office was ajar so I walked in. I sat at his computer and logged on. I was able to get into AOL without inputting a password. The "You've Got Mail" message sounded, so I logged into the mail center to see what messages the murderer had received. He had about ten from various pornographic websites advertising their wares, most very sexually explicit. A haunting message caught my attention so I hastily retrieved it. The eerie message detailed an event that was to commence in January in Bangkok, Thailand. The message was sent from HisChild.com. The name was familiar. My mind raced to try to piece together a correlation. I ran over to the file cabinet and pried it open. Just what I thought, there were several copies of *His Child* magazine secretly stashed away.

I printed as many messages as I could. As I retrieved the printed messages, I noticed that the file cabinet was still open. While walking over to the cabinet, I heard the elevator bell ring. Someone was coming onto the floor.

Who could it be at this hour, I wondered.

The restroom was next door so I lay on the floor and literally crawled through the bathroom door. I saw a cowboy hat was strutting through the office. I thought that it might be Roosevelt getting some items, but I knew my instincts had been proven wrong. Roosevelt would never wear a cowboy hat. Surprisingly, the hat went into Roosevelt's office after all.

How should I play it? I thought. It was clear that Liberace needed to be taught a lesson.

He emptied the contents of his backpack onto his desk. A notebook with Kenya's name scribbled all over it fell out and landed with a thud on his desk.

"Whatcha got there, cowboy? I asked.

Roosevelt looked like he had just seen a ghost.

"Who the hell are you and what are you doing in my office?"

"I wanted to get your autograph. Maybe you didn't know, but you're a celebrity now. Your picture has been plastered all over television. But you're a smart guy, you probably knew that folks would be looking for you. That's why you have that silly disguise on."

"I demand to know who you are."

"You are in no position to make any demands. Then again, you probably fantasize about scenes like this. Only I am nervous and you're about to torture me. Oh, I forgot, I'm too clever and too old, huh?"

"If you don't leave my office this minute, I will call the police."

"No need, I've already done that. Right now, though, I'm gonna kick your ass."

With that, I threw a swift kick that connected with his temple. His Raybans flew off and blood gushed from a large gash on his face. He put his hand to the wound and looked at the blood with rage in his eyes, whipped out Annabelle and lunged toward me. I grabbed his hand with one hand and used the other one to karate chop it. The force of my hand made the knife fall from his. With my hand still on his, I kneed him in the groin as hard as I could. He fell to the floor.

"Where's Kenya?" I asked.

"Who are you and what do you want?

SMACK! I hit that motherfucker on his face, right across his wound. I wiped the blood off on my pants and asked him again.

"Where's Kenya?"

"Oh, you mean the pretty little girl who likes the Knicks? Wouldn't you like to know?" He chuckled.

SMACK. I hit him in the head with my left fist.

Roosevelt tried to hit me but I ducked and my fist connected with his gut.

Not fully understanding what was happening, Roosevelt conceded and decided that fighting back was not a good plan.

"Who are you and what do you want?"

"I am your worst nightmare, a bitch with a beef. That's who I am. Now you asked me what I want. I want you dead, but I want you to suffer. I want you to feel some of the pain and terror those little girls you tortured felt before they died."

Roosevelt tried to get up again and stumbled and fell back down. The blood was gushing from his head and it made him lightheaded. I took the liberty of kicking him again, this time square in the chest. I always wanted to know how it felt to kick a man when he was down. I know, I'm such a smart ass!

"Look, you know nothing about me," Roosevelt whimpered. "I do know how it feels to live in pure hell, terrorized each day by my own flesh and blood. My whole life has been a nightmare."

"So you've decided to take your frustrations out on innocent children? My youth was a nightmare, too, but I made the decision to help others instead of inflicting more pain. You took the easy way out, and you justify it by masking your own demons with the fact that your childhood sucked. As Maximus told the Emperor, '*The time of honoring yourself will soon be at an end*,' baby. You won't be able to hurt anyone else again."

I pummeled him until he was nearly unconscious. It didn't require a lot of work because homeboy had such a low tolerance for pain. He was such a sissy. I took out some rope and hog-tied him. Done! Not quite.

I found his knife and taunted him by waving it in front of his face. His eyes began to bulge in terror as he was often the one doing the terrorizing. "No like?" I teased. "Want some?" I asked, "Do you, baby, do you want some pussy, I mean do you want some real, adult grown-assed Pussy?" I laughed.

I began to unzip his pants very slowly, deliberately, methodically. It was becoming difficult for me to breathe because it was so hot in the office. I fought the desire to take off my motorcycle helmet.

"I'm going to ask you one more time: where is Kenya, the last little girl you took? Is she still alive?"

He answered by spitting on my helmet. *Damn, he should not have done that,* I thought. I looked at the knife and slowly took the blade and leisurely traced the outline of his penis. I broke the skin just a bit, enough to get a blubbering whine out of him.

"She escaped, the little girl escaped. I don't know where she is. That's the truth."

"You wouldn't know the truth if it smacked you in the face. Why, Roosevelt? Why would you kill and maim innocent children?"

"My mother made me live as a little girl for most of my youth. She hated men, which meant she hated boys. I was a daily reminder of my father and she loathed my father. One night she locked me in the closet because I would not try on a dress she bought me. I had grown weary of the charade. When she released me after a weekend in the darkness, of peeing and defecating on myself, I killed her. She created this monster. She created this hatred that I feel toward women. The hatred is bigger than me. It comforts me. It keeps me going. Hatred is what has kept me alive all these years. So kill me if you must. You will finally end the suffering and the pain."

He closed his eyes in defeat. I almost felt sorry for him. I wrapped a bandanna that had fallen out of the knapsack around his mouth. I decided to spare his manhood; it had obviously been taken away already.

I ransacked his drawers and file cabinet and threw all of the pornographic material and the documents that I had printed earlier on the floor around him. A copy of his alleged murders, starting from the one he committed as a child to present, was taped to his torso. The number of murders that he had committed in his forty-five years totaled seventeen. The good news was that Kenya was alive. I had to find her.

CHAPTER 35
New York, 2006

I decided that I had to leave because the police would be there in any minute. I made my way to the staircase just as the elevator doors opened. I closed the staircase door, but not tightly. There was a sound of faint laughter coming from the hallway. I recognized one of the voices. Was that James? I peeked through the door and gasped. James and Deena were walking arm-in-arm toward his office.

So the two-timer was two-timing his mistress with her best friend. I thought I had seen everything. The two of them started making out in the hall right in front of the elevator. Wouldn't they be surprised when the police came rushing in to arrest Roosevelt. As badly as I wanted to see James busted, I had to leave so I wouldn't risk getting caught myself.

I ran down forty-four flights of stairs in twenty minutes. The adrenaline was pumping, as I hopped on my bike and rode out of the garage. The bike was floating on air. Girls Kick Ass! I took off my helmet and let the wind whip through my sleek do.

I was off to find Kenya.

↗ ↗ ↗

James and Deena were butt naked on the floor of the office suite. They were going at it so loudly, they didn't hear the muffled moans of Roosevelt. Deena was on top and James was screaming at the top of his lungs. He didn't care who heard them; he was in love and loved having sex with her.

He had begun to feel as much desire for her as he had for Tanya. Since Tanya had no time for him, he was more than willing to spend each spare moment he had with Deena.

Deena was pumping away when the elevator doors opened and ten police officers and FBI agents came flooding in. James jumped up and grabbed his pants. Deena boldly stood before the officers, one of whom openly stared at her loveliness. She licked her lips and James leered over at her. He took his shirt and slipped it on her and asked her to button it up.

"What is the meaning of this?" James yelled. He thought that the police were there to arrest him. If the police arrested everyone who was unfaithful to a spouse, there would not be enough jail space to house those people. James addressed a six-feet-four-inch dark brother wearing an FBI jacket and hat. He looked meaner than a junkyard dog. One thing James had learned over the years was if you conquered the leader, the rest would come tumbling down.

"What is the meaning of this?" he demanded. "Why are you here?"

"We are looking for Roosevelt Guidry. We got an anonymous call that he would be in his office. He has been accused of kidnapping Kenya Knight. He is also suspected of killing at least ten other little girls," the big brother said.

"Mr. Guidry is the School Yard Murderer?" Deena screamed. "His office is right over there," she said as she pointed toward his suite.

The ten officers paraded over to the office. The adulterous couple got dressed as quickly as they could. James could not believe that Roosevelt Guidry was the School Yard Murderer. He was a Rhodes Scholar, for goodness sake. There must be a mistake.

James ran to Guidry's office and stopped dead in his tracks. He had been hog-tied and there was pornography all over the place.

He stepped in the office and stood in the corner. The agents were cleaning out Roosevelt's desk and file cabinets. Big dark brother FBI was questioning him. One agent was on the computer pulling up all of Roosevelt's sleazy files. James could not believe what he was seeing. Roosevelt had always presented himself in such a superior manner. He was consistently demeaning to most of the employees and downright cruel to the women. How could he be so blind as to have hired a murderer? This debacle could certainly injure BCI's reputation. To top it off, he had been caught fucking a woman who was not his wife. James cringed and knew he had to do some serious damage control or this would be the beginning of the end.

He left Guidry's office and walked into his lavish executive suite. Manhattan was breathtaking this particular morning. The view from his office was spectacular. A lot of hard work, treachery, deceit, and murder had helped pay for this office. He wasn't going to let some sexual predator destroy everything he had worked so hard for.

He picked up the phone to call his Director of Public Relations, Douglas Brown, who answered on the first ring.

"I was wondering when you were going to call. Where have you been? I have been trying to reach you on your cell phone." James had taken Deena to Atlantic City and turned his cell phone off. He had been locked up in a hotel suite and had not turned on a television in twenty-four hours. Douglas Brown, however, had been on the case.

"This is a nightmare, James. Our Chief Financial Officer is a butcher."

"Correction, he is an accused butcher. Nothing has been proven yet."

"The television stations would not be airing this information if it was solely based on speculation. Just think of the legal ramifications. No, your boy is as good as guilty. I am going to put you on speaker. Jeff Clay, General Counsel, is here."

"Good day, James," Jeff said.

"No, it's not a good day. As a matter of fact, it is one of the worst days that I've had in a long time. And I have a feeling it's going to get a lot worse."

Douglas quickly jumped in. "Jeff and I have been going over this situation, trying to decide what type of damage control will be necessary. *The Enquirer*, *The Washington Post*, *The New York Times*, and even *Jet* magazine have already been calling. I am trying to hold them off because we haven't come up with a plan yet."

"My concern is our stock," James said. "When the market opens on

Monday, I'm sure this news will cause it to plummet. We need to put Mike in the forefront of all of this. The public has got to see him and have faith that he will not miss a beat within all of this turmoil."

"Well, I guess that's a start, but Mike doesn't have a lot of experience. A year ago, he was a chauffeur, for heaven's sake. The press will have a field day with him. This fiasco would turn BCI into a three-ring circus."

Jeff stepped in. "First of all, we must stop all of this doom and gloom. This, too, shall pass. We must start a scholarship fund to honor all of the families who have suffered at the hands of Roosevelt. James must make a public statement. You will put on your most distinguished suit and tell the world that while you abhor what Roosevelt has been accused of, BCI will in no way be affected. Doug, you will need to call all of the TV stations and newspapers and schedule a press conference for Sunday. Whatever you say on Sunday will affect the direction of the stock price on Monday."

James took a breath for the first time in about an hour. "Now you're talking! That's why you get paid the big bucks. I will go home right away and prepare a speech. Doug, call that speechwriter we used last month and tell her we need her in Maryland ASAP. We will hold the conference at the offices in Washington. Jeff, come to New York as soon as you can. There are ten police officers and FBI agents down here with Guidry. From the looks of things, the *Lady in Black* tied him up nice and neat."

"Are you kidding?! The *Lady in Black* was at your office?" Doug said, like a schoolboy.

"Yeah, she left her calling card: a rap sheet and pictures. She makes it so sweet for the police."

Jeff said, "I'm on my way down to the office now. Doug will handle the press. James, don't worry. We will get through this."

James felt better. He wondered if he should tell them about the incident with Deena. No, it was just too embarrassing. The Roosevelt thing would overshadow any of his infidelities. James sat in his chair and stared out the window of his huge office. He was still the king of the world. Nothing would ever change that.

He thought about his humble beginnings at the First Baptist Church of the Rock. His father had always said you get what you give. He wondered if that was true. He had done a lot of dirt and had mistreated a lot of people in his life. He got on his knees and bowed his head.

Lord, forgive me all of my transgressions, he prayed. *Help me get through this time of turmoil. Help BCI flourish and continue to grow. Please, Lord, help me be strong and stay away from those women. I am so weak, Lord. Forgive me, Lord. Please forgive me.*

James got up and went back to Guidry's office. Most of the officers had gone. The prisoner had been taken away. Deena was engaging some young officer with her tales of working at BCI. She was damn near sitting on his lap. *What a whore*, he thought. He walked over to her and grabbed her arm.

"We have to go," he said.

She looked at the officer and mouthed, "Call me." The officer responded with a smile.

James called for his car to be brought to the front of the building. They would roll back to D.C. and drop Deena off. He would explain the situation to Tanya and get ready for the press conference. Travis held the door and Deena and James got in. Travis grabbed Deena's butt on the sly.

That ass was good last week, he thought. He couldn't wait to get back to D.C. He would drop her off, drop James off, and then double back to her apartment. She would beg him to spend the night but that would never happen. He never spent the night. Women became too attached.

James called Tanya on her cell. She had been worried sick because Kenya was her girl's niece. She had stayed by the phone hoping for a call with good news. She had spoken to Sandy yesterday and she sounded upbeat. Sandy told Tanya that she didn't need anything. Tanya quickly picked up the phone.

"Sandy?"

"No, honey, it's me. I'm on my way to Maryland. I have so much to tell you. I'll see you in about four hours."

"Have you heard anything about Kenya? Is she all right?"

"The police have found her and she has been reunited with her family. She escaped from Guidry's clutches. She's a smart little girl."

"Oh, great. I'm sure she'll be fine. It seems like Roosevelt Guidry was the perpetrator. I never liked that guy."

"Well, Guidry might do a great deal of damage to the company," James said.

Tanya rolled her eyes. *All James ever thought about was the company,* Tanya thought. *He had twisted this whole situation into how it would affect him. I bet he hasn't even called Sandy.* "Selfish son of a bitch," Tanya said out loud.

James sensed some tension. He said his good-byes and hung up. Deena was staring at Travis through the rearview mirror, so James turned Deena 'round so that she was facing him.

"Darling, I'm sorry we had to cut our weekend short. I'm afraid that Guidry has caused quite a stir."

"Quite a stir?! That creepy motherfucker killed a bunch of little girls! I can't believe that I sat two inches from him in that meeting. I can't believe you hired a killer."

"He had flawless references and impeccable financial experience. It's not my fault that he chose to kill little girls in his spare time."

She hated his guts. He was so selfish. It was always abut him and his needs. He couldn't admit that he had made a mistake hiring Guidry. She started thinking about a night with Travis. He sure did curl her toes. He could go for hours. He would also pick her up and carry her around the apartment. They did it in the bathroom, the kitchen, the hallway. She ran her hand across her thigh. She got wet just thinking about him. Travis pulled the limo to Deena's place and Deena heard a noise.

"What? Oh, yes, James." Back to reality.

"I said that I wanted to come in for a minute."

She would rather read *War and Peace.*

"Honey, I'm tired. This experience has been overwhelming. I want to go to sleep. Give me a call after your press conference."

James reluctantly conceded. He just could not get enough of her. She was such a tart, but he still constantly wanted to be with her. Maybe he should divorce Tanya and marry Deena. She gave him the best sex he'd ever had. Maybe he would buy her a car. That would show her how much he loved her. He would call his business manager tomorrow.

She got out of the car. "'Bye, baby. Good luck tomorrow. I'll be dreaming of you," she said and blew him a kiss. Travis held the door open for Deena and whispered, "I want that pussy," in her ear as she passed him. She giggled and could not wait for him to come back.

James' phone rang. It was Karen. *Damn her. What does she want now?*

"Hello, Karen. I'm in the middle of a meeting. Can I call you back?"

"James, you've been putting me off now for the past three months. I told you that I need some money. I'm about to get kicked out of my apartment. If you don't want to give me the money, can you make me a loan?"

James acquiesced. "I put three hundred dollars in the mail."

"Three hundred dollars?! Is that all you can afford? Don't I deserve more than that? You're one of the wealthiest African American men in the United States. I was at your beck and call for over five years. Doesn't that count for anything?"

James sighed. He wondered how he would ever get rid of Karen. Maybe he should call one of his old contacts and have her dealt with. Permanently. After this Guidry disaster, he would have Karen taken care of.

"Do you want the money or don't you?"

"I'll take any bone you want to throw me. Thanks, James," Karen said in disbelief. This man was worth over $200,000,000 but he couldn't spare $1,000? That left her no choice. She would meet Tanya for lunch tomorrow. After she hung up with James, she dialed his home. Tanya picked up on the first ring.

"Hello. Bledsoe residence."

"Hello, is this Tanya Bledsoe?"

"Yes. To whom am I speaking?"

"My name is Karen Anderson. I have left several messages at your job. May I have a moment of your time?"

"Yes, but make it quick. I am expecting an important phone call."

"I have some information that you may find interesting. I would like to meet for lunch tomorrow."

"Why would I want to meet you?"

"Because I have been sleeping with your husband for five years. I have dates and times and pictures. I fell in love with him. He promised to marry me but has dumped me and is now sleeping with my best friend. While what I did was wrong, James has really mistreated me. I thought you might like this information."

"All right. I'll meet you at two p.m. at the Utopia on U Street."

"Great. I'll see you there. Oh, and Tanya?"

"Yes?"

"I'm sorry for all the pain I may have caused you. I was lonely and desperate. I thought I had hit the jackpot when James showed an interest in me. I realize now how wrong I was to sleep with someone else's husband. Please forgive me."

"Let's talk tomorrow. If God has forgiven you, so have I."

CHAPTER 36

Washington, D.C. 2006

BET, CNN, CNBC, CBS, NBC, Fox, MSNBC, C-SPAN, and even the E Channel had all sent representatives to attend the press conference. While the press waited, they dined on a lavish spread. There were about 200 people in attendance. Even Cathy Hughes, CEO of Radio One, had come to the conference herself. The rise and fall of a multimillion-dollar African American company was definitely of interest to her. Radio One was built with a lot of blood, sweat, and tears. She and James were also personal friends.

The speechwriter had flown in on the "red eye" from L.A. She basically wrote the speech on the flight, but spent all morning adding finishing touches. It was both moving and inspirational. James would weave a tale that started with slavery and depicted African Americans building this country but receiving none of the rewards. He would highlight how BCI employed hundreds of people and was responsible for sending countless African American children to college. He would also refer to its generous support of STOP, the international organization his wife heads that gives aid to oppressed women all over the world. The grand finale would be the announcement of a scholarship fund for all of the families of the murdered victims.

If handled properly, this publicity may even boost the value of BCI stock, James thought. "America provides the kind of opportunity no other country does. BCI is a true American company. A success story, about how a poor black kid was raised in Harlem but schooled at Harvard." He would skillfully turn all negative questions into positive remarks.

James was the master manipulator. The more he thought about it, the more he saw this as a blessing in disguise. James would use this press conference as a personal platform to display his greatness. After this, he could run for public office.

The press conference did go off without a hitch. Jim Vance of NBC started by asking the hard questions about BCI's future. He mentioned that some of the international press had been extremely critical of Bledsoe's poor judgment in hiring Guidry. James clearly walked on eggshells and managed to deflect the blame from him to society. Most of the other reporters were respectful and didn't dwell on Guidry too much. They bought the baseball, apple pie, and American flag speech. They all fell in love with James.

James had pulled it off, and he showed his appreciation to the speechwriter by treating her to a suite at the Ritz-Carlton. He obviously spent the night there as well. He told Tanya that he had to go back to New York so he could be near Wall Street when the stock market opened. Like she cared.

N N N

Tanya looked absolutely stunning in her crème crepe Marc Jacobs suit. The light color of the fabric was a direct contrast to her dark skin. Her coal-black, almond-shaped eyes sparkled brilliantly. Her professionally tapered haircut made her salt-and-pepper hair look so chic. She obviously took exquisite care of herself and looked damn good for her age. She was a class act.

She wondered what Miss Karen would look like. She fully expected some ghetto fabulous hoochie momma. She was surprised to see a short woman in a conservative black Yves St. Laurent suit and a sharp layered haircut. Karen had followed through on the promise she had made to herself to cut her hair. She had received so many compliments that she regretted ever wearing that horse hair. It's amazing how many black women still buy into the light-skinned, long hair thing.

Karen began by telling Tanya the whole sordid story of how they had met and a "relationship" developed. Near the end as she told her about how she was in Tanya's home when Tanya almost came up the steps, Karen looked into the beautiful woman's face and began to cry. Tanya comforted her as best as she could. She realized that this woman was not the enemy. She also realized that this woman was in love with her husband. Poor thing.

Tanya smiled and told Karen that she had a proposition of a lifetime for her. She continued and told her about the plot that she and I had hatched up and how they planned to bring James down. Tanya did not feel in her heart that Karen would risk divulging this information. She felt Karen was the perfect woman for the job. Karen's attitude began to brighten and the thought of an alliance with Tanya, such a glamorous and respected woman. She felt that her stock was beginning to rise.

Abruptly, Tanya's cell rang and she excused herself. Tanya stated that she had a medical emergency and unfortunately had to leave. They hugged for a while and then Tanya excused herself. She scribbled down her phone number on a napkin and asked Karen to call her if she had any questions. Tanya knew that she had just partnered with an ally that could help she and I accomplish their goal—destroying James.

✗ ✗ ✗

First thing Monday morning, Maria Bartiromo of CNBC was speculating about the direction that BCI stock would go. The talking heads had predicted that the stock would remain a viable choice for the aggressive investor. Jeff Clay had made a brief appearance on the CNBC Squawk Box, citing BCI's P/E ratios, betas, annual earnings projections, and the savvy management team. A communications analyst wasn't as optimistic. He expressed concerns about international rumors insisting that the savage murders committed by the CFO had completely shaken investor confidence. The contrarian further stated that there was little impetus for the stock to appreciate in the short-term.

Jeff Clay concluded the segment reinforcing that BCI was James Bledsoe, not Roosevelt Guidry, and that Mr. Bledsoe's reputation was beyond reproach.

The New York Stock Exchange bell rang and trading began. BCI opened at $64. Initially, trading for BCI was high and the price soared. By the afternoon, the trend reversed and the stock began to slide. A report had been leaked about James Bledsoe having once been involved in illegal activity. Although this information was not aired on television, the exposure had enough juice to send the stock into a tailspin. At the end of the day, the stock closed at $43.

James had tuned in to CNBC around noon, just in time to catch the beginning of the end. He had been involved in other activities that had prevented him from putting some sort of stops in place to try to prevent a run on the stock. He had also turned his cell phone off and could not be found.

BCI was in a frenzy and Sandy was enjoying every minute of it. Jeff and Doug had summoned Mike to formulate a plan of action. Mike, obviously distraught, had been in conference with me all day.

Stockholders from all over the world had begun calling for information regarding the viability of the stock. Mutual fund managers were threatening to dump large blocks of shares. The Japanese corporation that BCI had partnered with threatened to sue for breach of contract. It was a corporate nightmare and James was nowhere to be found.

Lena received a phone call from a colleague in L.A. who asked her if she was watching TV on the East Coast. At ten a.m. Pacific Coast time, 1 p.m. Eastern Standard Time, James finally called and spoke with me.

"What the hell is going on up there?!"

"Where the hell are you?! We've been trying to reach you all day! BCI is going to hell in a hand basket. James, you gotta do something!" Sandy smiled at the phone.

"What do you expect me to do in Washington? I pay you the big bucks to get us out of situations like this."

"James, this is bigger than me. You must somehow get on the air and make a statement. At this point it has nothing to do with Guidry. It's all about you now. A rumor has begun circulating that you were some big drug lord in Harlem. Is that true?"

"Of course, it's not true! I won't even dignify that statement with a response!"

"I'm sorry, sir. I am baffled as to how a rumor as preposterous as this could even get started. At any rate, it doesn't matter because it has already wreaked havoc on our stock. Somehow we will have to salvage the damage this disaster has caused. You need to get on the first plane out of National Airport so we can put our heads together and implement a survival plan."

"Where is the stock trading now?"

"Fifty-five dollars."

"I'm on my way. I should be at headquarters in three hours."

"Great. Don't worry, boss. We will survive."

"I hope so. Good-bye, Sandy."

"Good-bye and Godspeed."

CHAPTER 37
Mitchellville, MD 2006

I hung up the phone and picked up my cell to call Tanya. I didn't want anyone to be able to patch into our conversation. Tanya had taken the day off and was at home. She wanted to see firsthand how ugly rumors get started. She had used the information that Karen had given her and had put out a batch of negative press about James on the Internet. Tanya had released the intelligence at seven a.m. By ten a.m., the information had been reinvented and revamped. At approximately one p.m., the Associated Press had gotten wind of it. By four p.m., the stock had fallen twenty-one points, about thirty-three percent.

Last night, Tanya reviewed the contents of the package Karen had given her. The detective Karen had hired was very meticulous and had discovered a great deal of low-down and dirty activity. It was alleged that James had in fact been a drug lord in Harlem and had several people killed. He had been arrested but bought off the judges. He was basically untouchable in New York at that time. The police and judges on all benches were all on the take. His army of dealers was a close-knit community where no one ever snitched. The FBI had put him on their list of big boys to watch in the late seventies.

He managed to finish college at NYU while simultaneously running drug deals in all five of New York's boroughs. After he graduated from Harvard Law School, he decided to take a position as a business manager at a floundering radio station. Initially, he saw this as a mechanism to launder money. Eventually he began to enjoy the station and decided that he would enter the communications industry and turn "legit." He had saved enough money to buy the station outright and did so after a year of employment. He studied every inch of the business, training in every position from sales rep to disc jockey. After he had acquired all the knowledge he needed, he acquired the company. The owners were close to retirement and were only too eager to sell. James was able to negotiate a very reasonable price.

James utilized his contacts from Harvard to obtain legitimate lines of credit and quickly purchased two more radio stations and a TV station. Within five years, he was the Bill Gates of communications. Of course, the press ate up this rags-to-riches story. "Boy From Harlem Does Good." His dashing looks and charismatic personality didn't hurt, either. Within ten years, James had built a thriving corporation known as BCI and had become a multimillionaire. The rest, as they say, is history.

The thick package had included many photographs that captured James as early as eighteen years old. Tanya thought about how much she used to love him as she viewed the pictures of him in his prime. He was so handsome, not pretty, but handsome. Actually, James was still very handsome and had a pervasive air that was urbane and sophisticated. It was his arrogance that spoiled everything.

Tanya flipped through the pictures, staring at the different backgrounds of city life. She came upon a picture of James with a pretty, petite woman and two young children. She stared at the picture because they looked like a picture-perfect family. She wondered if that was a cousin and her children. As far as she knew, James had no children.

She looked through the rest of the stack but came back to that picture. She looked at the little girl. She looked to be about ten years old. The little boy looked like he was four. The little girl looked so familiar. She was puzzled because she had an eerie feeling. Her intuition told her that the picture she held was the key to a very important truth. She decided that she would hire her own investigator. Tanya was deep in thought while looking at the picture again when her cell phone rang.

"Hey, girl."

"Hey. I guess phase one of our little plan is working."

"Like a charm. I guarantee that the stock will be in the toilet by this afternoon," I said.

"Well, I hope it won't plummet to a point where it's worthless. Remember we need the company to be worth something when we take over. STOP needs an infusion of cash," Tanya said.

"Yeah, you're right. I just got off the phone with James and he is on his way to New York."

"He told me that he was spending the night in New York. I guess once a liar, always a liar."

"No comment."

"I have called Watts and Means Investigation Agency. They come highly recommended. They are rumored to have been hired by *The Washington Post* during the Watergate investigation. They cost an arm and a leg but I think they are worth it. There is a lot more than meets the eye and I think that Karen has merely hit the tip of the iceberg."

"I'm sure. Let me know if you need money for the detective."

"Right now, I'm cool. But you know that the whole investigations industry is a racket. They charge for any type of expense. Most of their clients are desperate and they know that."

"Mike and I have been on the phone with Yakura, Inc. all day trying to salvage the Japanese deal."

"How does it look?"

"It looks like we will have to go to Japan to work our magic. Mike and I make a hell of a team so don't worry. We will have them eating out of the palms of our hands," I boasted. I was feeling quite cocky.

"I have every confidence in your persuasive abilities."

"Mike is sharp as hell, too. Can you believe the luck we had with Guidry? We didn't even factor him into our initial equation."

"I know. I never liked him and knew he had to go. But who knew it would be so easy?"

"Yeah, what goes around comes around."

"Okay, enough with the clichés already. I have to get ready to go. Doug,

Mike, Jeff, and I are meeting at one-thirty p.m. We are preparing for the worse today. But somehow we must stop the stock's downward spiral. I'll give you a call a little later."

"*Ciao.*"

N N N

James had gotten himself together and was able to hop on a two p.m. shuttle. He had enjoyed his time with Lena. She was so young and vivacious. She was extremely smart and articulate for her twenty-eight years, and almost made him forget about Deena. Then he realized that no one could make him forget Deena. He picked up his cell and buzzed her. Deena told him that she was going to take Monday off. She told him that she was still in shock after the Roosevelt mess and needed some time to recuperate. What she really needed was some time alone with Travis. Travis was on call, but with everything happening in New York, he knew folks would be camping out at the BCI offices.

He was familiar with corporate situations such as this where the big brass would call for takeout around the clock. Those executive types live for events like this. It got their adrenaline pumping.

Deena quickly answered the phone. Travis had gone to the store and she was sure that he had forgotten something. That man was so good in bed. It was like he had an Energizer dick, it kept going and cuming and going and cuming. She couldn't get enough of him. She was becoming as obsessed with Travis as James had become with her.

Travis wasn't giving her any real play, though. Sure, he would come over once a month, but he would never spend the night. He would go home and then maybe come back in the morning. She was sweatin' him somethin' fierce as she could not control her desire to text and call him.

Travis knew Deena was playing him against his boss. He knew that the game he was playing was dangerous, but Travis had always walked on the wild side. He had left Jamaica two years ago when he got busted banging his boss's wife. Travis was a marketing manager for a large hotel resort in the Caribbean. He fled the country and decided to lay low before re-establishing himself within a corporate environment. He took the gig as a chauffeur because a woman he was doing owned a limo service. She needed an extra driver and he needed a gig. The work was easy enough and it sure paid well.

One night Sandy had to use a limo company after Mike had been promoted and she had not found a replacement. Sandy enjoyed Travis' charm so much she offered him a job driving for BCI. He jumped at the chance to work for the largest African American firm in the world. He thought he would get his foot in the door and resume his marketing career.

Deena picked up the phone and heard James' voice. He told her that he was on his way to New York and wanted to know if she could meet him. Deena inquired about his wife joining him during his time of need. He stressed that he needed her, not Tanya. Deena yawned and told him that she was still exhausted from their trip to Atlantic City. She quickly concluded the conversation and told James to call her later.

As Deena hung up, Travis was knocking on the door. He planned to see her one last time before he went back to New York. He was dumping her because I had tipped him off that James was hot and heavy with her. I explained that if he wanted a future at BCI, that type behavior would not be tolerated. He had already lost his career once for a piece of ass. Deena certainly was not worth losing it a second time. He had to admit the sex was good, but she was clocking him a little too hard anyway. Travis had great disdain for grown folks who lived at home. He felt that even if you had to rent a room, be independent.

Travis entered the house and sat in the living room. Deena's mom came out and rolled her eyes at him. Travis knew what was up. Mom wanted Deena to devote all her time to the rich guy, James. She felt that Deena was wasting her talents on a chauffeur. Travis chuckled as Mom acted superior to him as she walked around in Payless slippers and a K-Mart robe. The rollers in her hair really set the outfit off.

Deena came slithering down the stairs in a leopard bustier and a leopard robe to match. Travis wondered how she could prance around her

Mom like that, what a tramp. He had almost lost his desire to be with her. She led him downstairs to a dingy basement. She had her clothes off in two seconds flat, and she pushed him down on the couch and was on top of him before he knew it. One great thing about Deena was that she didn't waste any time. Deena was always ready, there was no need for foreplay. Travis picked her up and placed Deena on the bar. The wall behind the bar had a panel of mirrors. He angled himself in a position where he could watch himself while pleasuring Deena. Travis loved to see himself in action as he whipped his ten inches out and thrust it in. She loved it when he was rough. He, however, didn't care how she liked it, he was trying to get his. Deena had a lot of nerve and was definitely gonna get what was coming to her. Travis didn't want to be around when she did.

An hour later, he was on his way to New York; there were bigger fish to fry. Sandy had summoned him personally and he was always available for Sandy. She was smart and sexy and Travis liked her a lot. She had a lot on the ball. Something big was about to go down and he wanted in.

CHAPTER 38
Washington, D.C., 2006

Karen felt good about herself. It had been a rough three months. Trying to get over James had been an emotional roller coaster. She had been so stupid and had wasted so many years. The sad thing was that she knew that she was wrong but she was able to justify her actions. She also knew that James never loved her and was only using her. It took her being betrayed by both her lover and best friend to fully understand the significance of her own betrayal. She wondered why so many women were so vulnerable to obviously unavailable men. Thank God she had learned a valuable lesson while she was still relatively young. It was over now and she was looking forward to the future.

You know when it rains, it pours. Last week, she had received a second eviction notice from her luxury apartment in Alexandria, Virginia. Karen decided to vacate the premises before she got embarrassed. She took the $1,050 that she would normally pay for rent and put half of it down for a room that a Howard University professor was renting in upper northwest Washington, D.C. It was located on a quiet street in an older residential community. The professor was nice enough and said he could help her gain employment. She thought that he was a blessing because if she could land a position at Howard, she could go back to school and get her degree. She had not worked in three months and was beginning to realize just how much she actually had loved her job. She was always too busy trying to undermine Sandy and chasing after James to concentrate on her work. She was looking forward to obtaining a meaningful career and was in a mental place to take the steps to do so. Karen was anxiously anticipating the new opportunities that lay ahead for her.

Karen kicked back at her dismal basement efficiency feeling more than satisfied. Tanya had used the information she had given her to feed the investing public enough rope that would hang the illustrious Bledsoe Communications. She had called Karen that morning and told her that she and Sandy wanted to have a meeting with her tomorrow. They would meet at Tanya's and then conference call Sandy. Sandy was too inundated with the havoc BCI currently found itself in to get away to Maryland. Her curiosity was peaked at the thought of Tanya and Sandy wanting to meet with her.

Karen poured herself another shot of Bacardi and splashed a bit of Coke into the glass. Every station was running footage of Roosevelt being arrested. They showed him wearing a cowboy hat and jeans. She snickered as she thought that in all the years that she had known him, Roosevelt had never worn jeans. They also showed a picture of Sandy's beautiful niece. Apparently, she had escaped the clutches of the serial murderer. Kenya had been bright enough to wander into a troop of Brownies and the troop leader was able to contact the police. The press was calling Kenya a hero. A resurgence of young women started wearing their *Girls Kick Ass* T-shirts as the police credited the *Lady in Black* for the arrest of the first Black serial murderer in recorded history. Karen had purchased a *Girls Kick Ass* T-shirt that morning and was sporting it with skin-tight jeans. She looked and felt good and knew a man would eventually come into her life. *A single man!*

Those stations not airing Guidry footage were giving sound bites from the press conference that James had held yesterday. This story was a journalist's dream. It was an anecdote about a successful company that was essentially being run by criminals. White America especially loved it.

Another angle that the media was attacking was the serial murderer piece. Most of the serial killers to date have been white males, thirty to forty-eight, and mostly reclusive. I think that Black folks have taken pride in the fact that one thing that Blacks didn't do was arbitrarily kill folks. I guess we are breaking barriers in medicine, business, politics, golf, hockey, baseball, why not murder? The newscasters talked about how Roosevelt had been tortured as a kid, ergo his penchant for murder. When are people going to wake up and take responsibility for their own actions?

Just then a news break was announced. A spokesperson from Rikers Island confirmed that Roosevelt Guidry had hung himself while waiting to be arraigned. Guess he wasn't man enough to face the music.

Karen got up and took out a bottle of Bacardi she had chilling in the fridge. If there was anything to celebrate, the demise of a child-killing freak was one.

"One down, one to go," Karen said aloud as she watched the news detail the gruesome slayings that Guidry had perpetrated.

Karen was interrupted by the sound of the phone ringing. It was her best friend, better known as Judas.

"Hey girl, I hear you moved."

"Yeah, something like that. What do you want?"

"Sweetie, don't get your panties in a bunch, I just called to see if I could borrow your black dress for a black-tie event that I'm attending tonight." Karen could not believe this bitch was playing her like this.

"Look, Deena, my mouse trap just went off, I gotta go. I'll call you. Smooches." *Click.*

N N N

Tanya sat patiently in the lavish K Street offices of Watts & Means. The shiny marble floors and luxurious mahogany desks connoted success. The walls were colored a deep amber hue and decorated with numerous pictures of politicians taken with Mr. Watts and Mr. Means. Tanya was impressed with her surroundings and was pleased with the decision she made to contact this firm. A sexy brunette with big boobs and an equally big smile asked her to have a seat.

"Would like some coffee or tea?" she asked.

"No, thank you," said Tanya.

"Eviayan? Spresso?"

"Well, you just relax, little lady. Mr. Watts has been held up on an international conference call. He begs your indulgence and asks if he could have an extra ten minutes," she responded. Little Ms. Administrative Assistant had a smile as big as Texas and extended her sincere appreciation for my patience. Tanya liked this outfit already. Southern hospitality, at its best. Ten minutes to the letter, Mr. Watts came into the hallway. He was as charming as his administrative assistant. His robust build was a direct contrast to his snow white hair and a close-cropped beard to match. His bright yellow suspenders fit his vibrant personality. He vigorously shook Tanya's hand and led her into his majestic offices. He apologized profusely for taking additional time and insisted that she have a glass of Chardonnay. He flirted with, and complimented Tanya until she was grinning from ear to ear and for her, blushing did not come easy.

He became as serious as he was hospitable and broke it down to Tanya. Being a Southern gentleman, he wanted her to feel as comfortable as possible before he lowered the proverbial boom. He was direct and to the point. He told Tanya that her husband had held an executive position in the East Coast Drug Cartel. He stated that James had done very well for himself and was rewarded handsomely. The boys in Colombia appreciated James' class and intelligence, so he quickly was promoted through the ranks. A man named William D. Williams had initially brought him in. James quickly saw that Billy D., as they called him, was in the way so he put out a contract on his life. He explained that to achieve such success, James did complete a variety of murders personally and directed his soldiers to do the same. James was never convicted because of the monthly stipends he paid to a variety of judges, police officers and lawyers. Watts handed Tanya a list of people that James had allegedly murdered. James had killed many people. He also had a number of his drug lieutenants kill hundreds who got in the way of his business endeavors. It was rumored, but unsubstantiated, that he had the mother of his children killed because she had stolen a large sum of money from him.

He eventually parlayed his illegally acquired funds into a legitimate empire. Tanya nodded her head listening with great intensity.

He used the word "allegedly" because James was never convicted of any crimes. Mr. Watts further explained that James had two adult children living in the New York area and that their names were Sandora and Malcolm Knight. The mother of those two children was killed by a contract that was initiated by James and implemented by two thugs referred to as Six and LD.

Tanya very rarely drank. Once in awhile she would enjoy a glass of merlot. That afternoon, she had three martinis. She simply could not believe it. How could she tell Sandy?

CHAPTER 39
New York, 2006

James hopped off the shuttle at approximately 2:52 p.m. The ensemble of the day was Adidas sweatsuit with a Redskins cap and dark shades. The usual first-class ticket had been downgraded to two coach tickets for him and his bodyguard because he did not want to be recognized. His nerves were shot so he ordered three neat Grey Gooses within the fifty minutes that it took him to fly from Washington to New York. Upon his arrival it took about fifteen minutes for the two Black men to hail a cab from Kennedy Airport.

Welcome to New York.

As the cab pulled up to the BCI offices a barrage of reporters turned to see who was approaching. As soon as they spotted the Redskins cap, they turned and looked for the next glimmer of the infamous CEO to arrive. The reporters had been camped out overnight and literally stalked each person who walked into the building, soliciting any comment they could obtain, be it fact or fiction. As he exited the cab, a young redheaded woman with a BET microphone recognized Mr. Bledsoe and nearly assaulted him as he departed the cab. He had made a good call bringing Duke Davis with him that afternoon. The three hundred-fifty pound mass of muscle was not going to allow anyone close to his client. The CEO smiled as he thought that he was still ahead of the game; he would always be ahead of the game. They could never keep a man of his magnitude down. He would come out of this on top. He pictured himself on this year's cover of *Time* being selected as the "Man of the Year."

James walked into the type of corporate chaos that nightmares were made of. He never imagined that things could have ever gone so awry. The Guidry issue was bad enough, but now his business was in the street. He used to be such a brawler, a street fighter. Now all he wanted to do was crawl in bed, preferably with a young woman. He fought all negative thoughts and focused on all that was good and pure about BCI. He had paid big bucks to a psychiatric pimp who was always expounding positive energy. This shit had better worked today. *I need all the positive energy I can get*, he thought.

Sandy, Doug, Jeff, and Mike had been held up in the conference room for the past five hours. The local Thai restaurant had just delivered an array of noodles, chicken, rice, and veggies. The cans of Coke were flowing as they continuously gulped those down to calm their nerves. Of course, this was all an act for Sandy and Mike. Everything was going as planned. She figured by this time next month, she would be the next CEO of BCI, Happy New Year!

The king entered the room and started to throw around orders. He demanded to know the status of the current trading price. The stock was down to $49. News was being disseminated from all venues and none of it was good. Guidry killing himself was just confirmation of his guilt. The whole ball of wax was quickly unraveling right before his eyes.

"Guidry has killed himself?" James was startled.

"The news came over the wire about ten minutes ago. It doesn't look good, boss. Most of our institutional investors have been threatening to dump the stock. They have been swamped with calls from their mutual fund holders demanding they divest from a company that could employ and promote a child pornographer and murderer. BCI is holding on by a thread, James. We need a miracle," Jeff said.

I was called away for a conference call. Lyle Turner, the Chairman of the Board, had called an emergency meeting yesterday in light of the weekend's events and the press conference that James held. The board had met at noon and decided that the annual stockholders meeting must be rescheduled immediately. Investors needed to hear from upper management as soon as possible, if they wanted to prevent a total run on the stock. The annual stockholders meetings were usually held in June of each year at a variety of tropical locations. It would truly be a new experience to hold the meeting in New York in December, but it had to be done. Lyle had given one the specific directives to schedule the stockholders meeting for next Friday, December 8, 2006.

I returned to the conference room and disseminated the newly acquired edict. James was enraged by the command that Lyle Turner had the nerve to give. Lyle was a little nobody who he had allowed to be the Chairman of the Board. Who the hell was he to tell him what to do?

"We will not reschedule the annual meeting at the whim of some dentist in East Orange. That would be corporate suicide. We need to wait for this to die down. Today, everyone is screaming bloody murder, but by next week folks would have forgotten all about Guidry."

"James, Guidry is one thing that was out of our control. But we have to face the facts that there are very destructive rumors circulating about you. You know as well as I do that we have always stressed to the public that you are BCI. We have to find a way to nip those rumors in the bud and expose the liars for who they are," Jeff said.

James thought to himself, *What if they could not quelch those lies because they are not lies? Somehow, someone had discovered the truth. How could they have found out about Lord Bless? What if the public found out he had committed murder as well? BCI would be dead in the water. There has to be a way out of this mess. Damn that Roosevelt Guidry! This is all his fault.*

I brought the conversation back to the matter at hand. The annual stockholders meeting needed to be rescheduled. James was adamantly against it. I decided to have another conference call with everyone present, including Lyle. The Board of Directors had demanded a change in the meeting and they had to be accommodated. Jeff and Doug both agreed. Mike had no comment; he knew that I was running the show and wanted to give an impression of neutrality. The group had to be on point as a whole. They had to collectively make decisions on how to proceed.

Before I set up the call, they had to get Mike on a plane. He had to meet with Kim Yakura of Yakura Industries. Their representatives had been calling all day, threatening to pull the plug on the multimillion-dollar deal. If that deal didn't go through, BCI was done. The Japanese pulling out now would send a message to the world that the public's confidence had been completely shaken.

James was opposed to Mike handling such a Herculean task and wanted to handle the Yakuras himself.

"What you fail to realize is that I built this company. No offense, Mike, but you just do not have enough experience. This is a very delicate situation and I am the only one with the business acumen and public relations savvy to pull this deal off."

"James, Jeff will go with Mike," I said. Doug's new public relations assistant, Carmen Jones Cook, will fly out tomorrow. She is packed and ready to go. Mike will handle the financial piece, Jeff will handle the legal piece, and Carmen will have them eating out of her hands. I have seen her work. She's smart, sexy, and can work her thing."

James could not accept the fact that I was trying to take over. After this whole mess had been cleaned up, he would have to get rid of me. He felt that I was getting too big for my britches. The thought of my britches caused him to lean over and look at my ass.

She sure was fine and that ass is perfect. That is the problem with fine women, they think they can go around conducting themselves any way they please. Don't let a woman be fine and have brains; then she's just trying to run shit, James thought.

I continued, "The limo is outside ready to take Mike and Jeff to the airport. Are there any reservations with them taking off now?"

Everyone looked at James and he shook his head no.

"Great. Good luck in Japan, guys. Keep us posted every step of the way." Mike and Jeff got up and left.

I was on a roll. "My assistant should have the entire Board of Directors on a conference call within ten minutes. The three of us must placate the board. They need answers and the only way to give them those answers is in the form of a mass meeting for the stockholders. Our office can be ready in a week. Can you conceivably pull all the information that we will need together in a week, Doug?"

"Definitely. It will require some work, but we can do it. The company will have to pull together for the greater good. James, I know you are against the meeting, but how can we not reschedule it?"

"For years, the stockholders meeting has been in June. How dare the board even suggest that we change it! We are all making a mountain out of a molehill. Please believe me when I say that this will all blow over," James said.

The conversation went back and forth for the next ten minutes. The three executives spoke with the entire board for about an hour. By the end of the conversation, the market had closed and BCI's stock had lost a significant amount of its value. James finally conceded and agreed to have the meeting next week.

Meanwhile, I had instructed Travis to tag along with Mike and the crew on their trip to Japan. Travis had a sense of street savvy mixed with a head for business. I had discovered that he was quite the little business tycoon. He was responsible for most of the successful land acquisitions for the Triangle Corporation in Jamaica. In the capacity of a chauffeur, Travis could be privy to many conversations. People would freely talk in front of him because, after all, he was only a hired hand.

However, I had a positive gut feeling about Travis. If he did a good job in Japan, who knows how I would reward him? My thoughts turned to a magnificent vision of Travis' massive body pounding on mine. I quickly snapped myself out of it. I moved both hands to the top of my head and began to beat my horns down.

James rang his assistant and had her make a reservation for a suite at the Marriott Marquis. Ms. Dillinger promptly phoned me and gave me the information. James was feeling down and he needed to get away from it all. He had left word for me that his cell would be on and that he would not leave his suite. I told him to go ahead and I would hold down the fort. Doug and I had a lot of details to flesh out.

James slithered through the ornate foyer of the luxury hotel. Meanwhile,

Yan was upstairs feverishly installing bugging devices. James started to sit at the lobby bar, but decided against it. What he needed was a hot shower, some Goose and some pussy. He took the shower and then sat in an unbelievably relaxing, hot Jacuzzi, and sipped his Grey Goose. His sense of confidence was coming back. He was James "Fucking" Bledsoe, Captain of Industry. He would not be defeated.

After he had dried his body off, he threw on a silk robe that he had acquired on his first trip to the Orient. As he closed his robe, he peered into the enormous mirror that was situated over the chest of drawers. He still had it with a forty-four-inch chest and a thirty-six-inch waist. He was six feet four inches of pure man. His salt-and-pepper beard comple-mented his golden brown skin. Truth be told, James was as fine now as he ever was. He picked up his cell and dialed Deena. He sure could use some of that snapping pussy tonight.

Deena saw his digits on her phone and debated on whether she should pick up. She just wasn't in the mood. She answered the phone anyway.

"What's up," she answered in the most patronizing tone she could muster.

"Hey baby, I miss you and I need you. Why don't you hop on the train and come on up. I have a suite at the Marriott Marquis. Isn't that your favorite hotel?"

"It's alright. I'm sorry, James, I am still under the weather. Guidry's sui-cide has really thrown me for a loop." Deena was really hoping that Travis would call.

"Come on, baby, I want to see you. I have had such a hard day. I want to feel your beautiful body beside me. We don't have to do nothing; I just want to be with you."

Deena rolled her eyes. She could not miss out on the opportunity to be with Travis tonight. She wanted him so bad, but she didn't want to blow her millionaire connection. "I'm sure that I will be feeling better tomor-row. I'll come up first thing in the morning, if you can smooth out my work situation."

"Well, you haven't been to work in about two months now, so one or two more days can't hurt. Besides, I run this show, in case you haven't noticed."

"That's why you are my Big Daddy. Think of me tonight, baby. Your kitty cat is coming to see you tomorrow. 'Bye, baby."

James smiled at the thought of his kitty cat butt naked on all fours. He couldn't wait until tomorrow. As excited as he was about tomorrow, tonight he would have to have his needs met. He called his boy Six and put an order in for a seven p.m. delivery. He and Six went way back. Six had become the biggest pimp in Manhattan. He had since cleaned up his act a bit and only serviced affluent politicians, celebrities, and businessmen.

At seven p.m. sharp his delivery arrived: three girls under the age of sixteen with their school uniforms and bookbags. The music was turned up so high they didn't hear the digital sound of Yan snapping pictures.

CHAPTER 40
New York, 2006

The flight to Japan was fourteen hours long. Mike, Jeff and Carmen went over every inch of information, anticipating any objection that Yakura would present. Travis hung on to every word. He didn't like the tone of the conversation. The three executives did a lot of whispering, like they had something to hide. Travis ordered a saki and laid his head back. *Sandy was on to something, he thought. This was going to be an interesting trip.*

✗ ✗ ✗

Karen rang the Bledsoe doorbell. The loud melodic sound reverberated about her eardrums. She was a little nervous about the meeting, because she didn't know what to expect. She wasn't used to coming in the front door and she sure wasn't used to leaving that way. Her suit was a little ruffled, so she smoothed it out. Her nerves were fried. What did Tanya want?

Tanya opened the door and invited Karen in. Karen noticed how spectacular she looked as her gold tunic glistened on her bronzed skin. Her beautiful gold understated jewelry complemented the outfit perfectly. Karen realized that she would love to have a friend like Tanya. Maybe one day.

The two ladies sat down and Tanya offered her a glass of Merlot. Karen had never tasted that type of wine so she declined the offer. Besides, she wanted to be fully alert for what was about to go down. Tanya got right down to the point. She patched into my office and started the conversation.

"Well, Sandy, Karen is here and we are eager to hear what is happening up there."

"Let me first say thank you for joining our team, Karen. The information that you have given us has proven to be invaluable. Everything is going exactly as we planned. However, we still have a lot of work to do. Karen, you have the hardest job of all. I need you to come to New York as soon as possible and make copies of every file in James' office. You must go through and organize the files, pulling any information that we can use as proof of the mismanagement of funds."

"Sure, Sandy, whatever you need. I have nothing but free time. The only thing is that I have absolutely no money. I am officially tapped out."

"Please understand, the work will be very tedious and the next week you will work harder than you have ever worked before. Karen, the least of your worries from here on out is money. If everything goes according to plan, you will have more money than you will know how to spend." That was the best news Karen had heard in a long time. The thought of earning a decent wage and making some new friends warmed her soul.

"What do you want me to do, Sandy?" Tanya asked.

"Tanya, I need you up here in New York as well. I reserved a suite for us at the Tribeca Grand Hotel. I hope you ladies don't mind bunking together, although we won't be getting much sleep anyway. We need to meet because I need the information that you have received from your contact in Washington. You will need to supervise our men to ensure that they have everything in place by Friday, which is six days away. In six days, ladies, each of our lives will change in a drastic way. Are you up for the challenge?"

"Yes," they both said.

Tanya thought about the talk that she would be having with me tonight. She still couldn't believe the news that Mr. Watts had given her. She wondered if after hearing the report if I would still want to go forward with the plan of mutiny. Only time would tell.

"Hey Sandy, how are you holding up? I know it's crazy up there," Tanya said.

"Crazy ain't the word. There are reporters everywhere and we are being flooded with phone calls from every little radio and television station imaginable. James has offered little assistance, which is just as well. He is held up at the Marriott on Broadway. The way he is acting these days, it's hard to believe that he even built a company of this magnitude from the ground up. He is not the James that we know and hate."

"I know," Karen and Tanya spoke in unison. They looked at each other and laughed.

"Okay, ladies, I gotta go. Ring me on my cell when you arrive and are settled. Good-bye."

Tanya ran upstairs to pack. She turned on the television for Karen and told her to relax and that she would be ready in an hour. The doctor called into the hospital and told them that she would be going on leave because her husband needed her. Her mind raced as she packed. The turn of events was frightening and almost inconceivable. In less than one week, her entire life would be different. The change in her life would certainly be welcomed, especially with her education and commitment to well-being. Tanya was physically and mentally exhausted and was hoping the fruits of her labor would ultimately allow her to enjoy a breather. Two large suitcases and one huge carry-on later, Dr. Bledsoe was ready to go.

She drove the Lexus SUV instead of calling a limo service. They hoped to be as inconspicuous as possible. Karen took less than a half-hour to prepare. Most of her clothing had been hoochie gear and was no longer appropriate. The selection of a pair of jeans, some sweaters, two suits, pajamas, and a pair of black slacks was all she took. She needed a whole new wardrobe to match her new attitude.

They were off!

И И И

When the BCI delegation arrived in Tokyo, Doug and Mike were drunk. Travis encouraged Mike and Doug to overindulge in the free-flowing alcoholic beverages. At one point, since they were bored, he challenged them to a drinking contest. Travis had to soldier and get them to their hotel. Luckily, the hotel wasn't too far from the airport. They had three adjoining rooms. Travis put the two in his room and immediately went to work while they slept it off. He figured that he had about two hours to install the bugging devices. He was able to bring a small listening device but wasn't quite sure how to use it. It took him approximately two hours to figure it out, but he did. He went back into his room and carried the men into each of their rooms. Sandy had alluded to the fact that she wanted him to keep his ears open and his mouth shut. He could read between the lines. He'd brought a little insurance with him so that he could definitively prove who was an ally and who was her nemesis. There was about an hour before the meeting, so he fell asleep.

The phone in room 304 rang. It was James.

"When is your meeting with Yakura scheduled?"

"In an hour, sir. They will meet us at our hotel. Are there any specific instructions?"

"The goal is to get Sandy out of the picture. Try and downplay her involvement in management and her accomplishments. As far as Guidry is concerned, emphatically tell them that Sandy hired Guidry. Subtly put the blame on Sandy for everything."

"It's done, sir."

"Glad you are on the team, or should I say *my* team. If there are any new developments, call me. *Ciao*."

ℵ ℵ ℵ

The ladies made it into New York and they were pumped. As a new bond had been formed, they traded war stories on the drive up and laughed all the way. Some of the lies that James had told were so outlandish that the only thing to do was laugh. They both knew that this was a week that would change their lives and they were ready to do battle.

I met them at the hotel and gave each of them their assignments. Most of Karen's work would be done at night after all of the staff was gone for the evening. A security firm had been retained so their safety would be assured during the late-night activities. Yan had taken at least a hundred pictures that needed to be organized for the PowerPoint presentation and slide show. Tanya suggested that Karen go into her bedroom and take a nap so that she would be fully refreshed before her shift began.

A tender moment between the determined allies commenced. We held each other as if we were sisters. We were each sad for the other for the losses we all endured. The upside was that we had each other and a long life ahead of us. Then Tanya began the sad story. She gave me a packet of information that Mr. Watts had given her.

"Honey, Mr. Watts told me that James is guilty of at least a dozen murders."

"I figured he was, the lying bastard," I said.

"There's more. Before he was CEO, he was a notorious drug kingpin. James was responsible for your mother's heroin addiction. She stole money from him so he put a contract on her life. He had some men named Six, who is now a pimp, and LD kill your mother because she stole approximately half a million dollars."

I began to cry. I thought about the bag that I had found in Penn Station over twenty years ago. Tanya held her breath, she couldn't stop now.

"Sandy, there is something else that I must tell you. It might change everything for us, but you have to know the truth…James is your father."

CHAPTER 41
New York, 2006

I ran out of the suite as fast as my legs could carry me. I caught a cab to my apartment in SoHo and fell out on my bed. How could that be! How could he be my father! We are nothing alike. He is a thief and a killer, a liar and a crook. I help people, but I have killed. I have tried to do what's right, but I have lied. My whole life has been based on vengeance, retribution, and punishment; his whole life has been based on greed, desire, and power. How are these adjectives any different? How am I any different? Lord, please tell me how am I any different? I am not. Who the hell am I kidding? I began to sob. I needed to talk to Puma. He was the only one who I had ever confided in. He was the only person who truly understood me. I had to see Puma.

My cell phone rang, but I ignored it. Then my land line in the apartment rang. "Fuck you!" I yelled at the phone. The calls had snapped me back into reality. Fuck the tears, I had shit to handle.

I changed into my black leather pants and black turtleneck. I tied a bandanna around my head and put a ski mask over it. My black down jacket would keep me warm. I searched for my Glock and tied two hunting knives around my ankles. Just call me Ramba. Those motherfuckers were going to pay.

I had overheard James talking about a guy named Six. I called Bird and told him that I needed the 4-1-1 on a sleaze named Six who worked midtown. After giving me the third degree, he told me to give him ten minutes. I phoned Tanya to let her know that I was fine. I told her that I loved her and that I appreciated the information. I packed a black Gaultier dress and slinky black pumps into a backpack. I also threw in some rope, duct tape, and a mask. A girl never knew what she would encounter and she had to always be prepared. I searched the apartment for the letter that I had received from Zee over twenty years ago. I used to keep the pink stationery on my person, close to my heart. However, the older I got, the more resentful I was of her and her lifestyle, so I tossed it. Now I looked for that letter like it was a lifeline. When I found it, I held it and cried. I received a call from Bird with an address.

"Lord, forgive me for I know not what I do."

I hopped on my bike and headed toward Times Square. The lights in Times Square are the brightest that I have ever seen. Even at two a.m., New York is wide awake with people who are ready for action. I rode past a twenty-story billboard advertising Jay-Z's new single. I chose not to wear a helmet because I did not care if I lived or died. Suddenly my ski mask flew off and the wind blew my hair like crazy up to the heavens. The harsh New York winter wind stung my face and made me cry. The cold tears bruised my face, which caused me to cry even harder.

I rolled up on a peepshow on Forty-Second and Sixth Avenue and parked my bike. The storefront was a seedy and sordid potpourri of sex and fantasy. For a mere quarter, you could have your dreams come true. New York, New York, so nice they named it twice.

New York was no different than the great Roman Empire; sodomy, debauchery, deceit, indulgence. James and Caesar were the Emperors, and we were all pawns in this sick and cruel game called life.

As I entered the front of the store, I spotted a disgusting-looking clerk. I asked him where I could get two girls for a client. Five one-hundred dollar bills were placed in his hand as an incentive. My eyes darted around the room to see if I saw a six-foot brother who called himself Six. Various scantily clad women walked past me and looked me up and down as if to ask if I was a dyke or competition. I decided to use the competition angle and try and find Six. A bathroom was close by so I used it to change into the sexy little number that I had the foresight to bring. The black dress clung to my body as if it were skin. Every man within eye shot eyed stared me down like I was for sale. I asked a few people where Six was and then decided to take matters into my own hands. Knowing that Six was holding down his on a Monday night, I crept upstairs to the executive suite and saw a beautiful brown man who stood six feet and change. A powerful aroma of incense hit me and served as a powerful aphrodisiac. Six looked at me and immediately stopped the conversation he was having with a short ugly fellow. They inquired as to who sent me and I told them James Bledsoe.

"What you want, sugar?" the short ugly one said, gold teeth just a shining.

"I want you and you."

"Can you handle us both?" LD said.

"A woman that fine can handle anything that she wants," Six said, as he licked his luscious lips.

"What are your names?"

"They call me Six, sugar, and they call my boy LD, which is short for Low Down. What's yours?"

"It doesn't matter. You still work for James?"

The two smiled and Six said, "Yeah, we still do a few things for him."

"Well, if I need to have someone taken care of, could you boys handle it?"

"It depends on what you mean by 'taken care of.' Is your boyfriend bothering you, Miss?"

"I don't need a boyfriend. But I do need someone taken care of. Are you boys still in that line of business? Because I know that you used to be. Do you remember someone named Zee?"

The two criminals looked at each other and finally LD said, "What's it to you?"

I handed LD a fifty-dollar bill. He shook his head as if to say it would cost more than that. I handed him a hundred dollars. It's all coming back to me now.

"Zee, yeah, I remember a dopehead bitch named Zee that had done the whole neighborhood. That ho was really strung out. Initially, she was James' special bitch. Then she got strung out. She had stole some money from him, so I killed her. Remember, Six, I gutted her in the street, right on Amsterdam Avenue."

"You got that all wrong," Six replied. "I strangled her, then you gutted her because you wuz tryin' to rock the 'hood. Remember, after that all the peeps gave you mad props and you started running more business than you could handle."

"Right, I owe it all to Zee. Yeah, I remember that night like it was yesterday."

I did everything I could to control myself. I had to play it cool.

"Enough shop talk. Let's have a little fun. Is it true that big guys have bigger dicks or do the short men?"

"Doesn't the saying go the bigger the package the smaller the gift?" LD laughed out loud. "Shit baby, who do you think has the bigger dick? I'm packing a solid twelve."

"Yeah, right, dog. That's why your momma just couldn't leave last night."

"Boys, let me see for myself who the biggest is. The winner can get some of this."

Both brothers pulled their pants down. I whipped out my knife and threw it right at Six. I had learned in karate that if you are attacked by a mob always take out the big one first. The knife hit Six right in the leg. He fell to the floor, agonized with pain. I moved over to a thug who was shaking in his boots. He quickly pulled up his pants, but before he had a chance to do so, I had the other knife at his throat.

"Look, motherfucker, that dopehead bitch that you gutted was my mother. I would kill you right now if I didn't need you." I told him about the meeting on Friday, and I told him that if he helped me, I would make it worth his while. I took out a little insurance policy and slid him $1,000. The balance of $5,000 would be remitted on the day that the services were rendered. As a look of lust came over his face, I suggested that he get his friend to the hospital. The bathroom that I had used earlier was vacant so my transformation began again. Five minutes later, I was on my bike and heading toward the Tribeca Grand Hotel. The night shift was about to begin.

As I walked into the suite, Tanya grabbed and hugged me.

"Where have you been?"

"I had to see a man about a little insurance. I had to purchase a policy that will ensure our success this week. Luckily the insurance salesman was a sucker for a woman in a black dress."

"You are always working it, ain't you, girl? I just got off the phone with my colleagues in Pakistan. Three girls between the ages of ten and twelve were victims of an acid dousing. STOP needs a quarter of a million dollars to safely pay their passage to the U.S. and set them up with the surgeries and psychiatric therapy that they will need to survive."

"What do you mean, an acid dousing?" Karen asked.

"Men in various parts of the world view women as chattel. If a woman is raped or falls in love with the wrong guy, or is even wrongfully accused of having sex before marriage, her family is dishonored. The men in that family will either kill or maim her as a type of revenge for the dishonor. It is a hideous and insane system where little girls are routinely tortured. That is only one aspect of what STOP is all about. That is why I am fighting so hard for James' money."

"It's funny, I always thought you spent his money, I mean *your* money, on clothes and hair and furs."

"No, baby, everything I do, all of the money I make, goes to STOP. Once we take control of BCI, I am going to establish a fund that channels a percentage of all profits directly to STOP. Our organization has been able to help over one hundred acid victims and over two hundred-fifty women who have suffered female castration. That number represents the tip of the iceberg. Karen, there is so much work to be done abroad and in this country. It is our responsibility to do what we can to effect change. There is so much more than shopping malls and vacations."

Karen hung her head in shame.

"I can't believe how wrong I was about you. Y'all must think that I am a basket case, but I am just overwhelmed by the two of you beautiful and successful women being so concerned about people other than your-selves. All my friends ever think about was how they could get a man to buy them stuff. I definitely have a lot to learn. Thank you, Sandy and Tanya, for the gift of forgiveness. I promise I won't let you down."

CHAPTER 42
New York, 2006

The week flew by. Karen worked day and night copying and organizing the documents that were obtained from James' files. We were tempted to hire a temp company to help organize the paperwork, but decided against it. The risk was too great. So, the three of us sifted through the information ourselves. There was also a great deal of information that Roosevelt had left that had to be reviewed. The suite at the Tribeca Grand was turned into BCI Central. Obviously Jeff and Doug knew nothing about what we were doing because the trust factor had not yet been established. It was still up in the air as to whether one or both of them were pledged to BCI or James. Only time would tell.

Travis had returned and had seventy-two hours of tape to sift through. He was introduced to Bird and they worked on transcribing the tapes together. For some reason, I trusted Travis. My gut never steered me wrong. I was still taking a gamble, but I had no choice. We had less than two days before the meeting and we had to have all of our ducks in a row.

Mike, Doug, and Jeff were putting together the necessary financials. The board wanted to see balance sheets, income statements, profit and loss spreadsheets, etc. Jeff had hired five temps from a legal temp company in an effort to bring closure to the Yakura deal. The meetings in Japan went well. However, the entire Yakura family planned on attending the meeting on Friday as well. The Guidry situation had given the Yakuras some leverage as far as the terms were concerned. In order for them to sign on the dotted line, they wanted an additional two percent on all sales, which was unconscionable. Jeff was doing the research necessary to prove that the original deal was done and they would not be entitled to the additional funds. The invitation to New York would be a public relations gesture to the Yakura family that would once and for all seal the deal.

CHAPTER 43
New York , 2006

James always used sex as a tool of comfort and I guess could be called a bona-fide sex addict. The young girls that came to his room were always instructed to compliment his physical appearance, his sexual virility, and his intellectual superiority. Every time James called Six, he recorded the location and time of all of his exploits, as well as the girls' ages into a log book. Yan was instructed to take the pictures of the girls before they went to meet James and during the act.

James was truly unraveling and was desperately out of control. His mind was not focused on the matters at hand. He had decided to let his team handle things. I would have thought if it were me that if my ass were in a sling, I would want to provide crazy oversight. But all James wanted to do was drink and fuck.

Apparently, everything was going according to our plan. I had frequent meetings with the team. Mike, Karen, Tanya and I had our strategy down pat. We would present the body a written presentation of why James should step down as CEO. Karen had been extremely successful in obtaining the documentation that was necessary to oust James. Karen had become a diligent solider in the war to claim BCI. I was proud of her and I told her so. Her self-esteem began to soar.

There was one little kink in our unit. Mike had become reclusive and did most of his work independent of the "Team" and that worried me. Mike and I had always been so close yet I felt as if our friendship had become tenuous. I asked him to join me for lunch on Thursday afternoon. We would laugh and joke like old times. I realized that he had been thrust in the middle of such a big mess, shortly after taking the position of a lifetime. He had gone from driving folks around all day to damn near running a multimillion dollar corporation. He was tired and overwhelmed. I knew that I had to take some time out with him. I further hoped that he was not scared that he would lose his job. I wanted to make it crystal clear that after Friday, he would be the Chief Financial Officer, the Man. I was proud of Mike, he had come so far. He had grown from a scared young child to a strong and confident man. I was glad to have been a part of his metamorphosis. Lunch tomorrow was going to be great.

И И И

"I have all the information that you need, sir. Where do you want to meet?"

"You will have to come to my hotel because I cannot leave. The lobby is swamped with reporters and I can't bear to walk through the horde of vultures."

"I can be there within the hour. I will give you all the information that you need to fire Sandy."

"Fire her; I may have her killed. I will not tolerate anyone fucking me over. I have had people killed for less."

"Well, boss, whatever you need from me, I will provide. Sandy trusts me implicitly so she willingly feeds me information."

"You have done a great job. I'll see you in an hour."

Bird could not believe it. That motherfucker was a turncoat of the biggest proportion. Travis had been right about him. That Travis was sharp. He sure did have his number.

Bird picked up the phone and called me. After I hung up the phone, I nearly passed out. How could he betray me like that, after all that we had been through? The old saying goes, "war is hell." I had just found that out firsthand. I was numb. I tried to figure out exactly how much more betrayal I could take.

The only bright side to this unbelievable dark cloud was Travis. I was pleased to know I was right about Travis. I would have to give Travis something special for all of his hard work.

N N N

Friday rolled around and I was feeling great. We had reserved the ballroom at the Waldorf Astoria, which could accommodate five-hundred people. Bird had secured the most expensive video and communications equipment available. A large part of our presentation would culminate in an exciting slide show that would be talked about for years to come. Karen had five-hundred packets of information that would be disseminated to all attendees. She had literally worked for ninety-six hours straight but looked like a gem this morning. Tanya was radiant as well and excited about a day that we had planned for over a year. Mike looked handsome too, but Travis was fine! After this day was over, I would definitely take a vacation, maybe to Jamaica; maybe Travis could be my tour guide.

It was 9 a.m., and the meeting was about to commence. Before I stepped to the podium, I closed my eyes and thought about the fact that I had dreamed about this day since I was fourteen years old. I would finally have avenged my mother's death. I said a prayer and asked God to help me say the right words that would enable me to accomplish my mission. I gracefully walked to the podium.

"Thank you for coming to our stockholders meeting. Today, we will try to answer any and all pertinent questions that you may have regarding the future of BCI. BCI is as strong as ever. We are a company that has the strength to survive any challenges that are put before us. We will survive the CFO situation which we will address later, and we will survive President Bush." The audience broke into a response of laughter. Her intention on breaking the ice had worked.

"Without further ado, let me introduce you to our new CFO, Miguel Perez."

Mike expertly presented the financials. He outlined our financial forecasts for the next five years. He answered approximately fifty questions with intelligence and humor. His piece went off without a hitch.

I then introduced Doug who spoke to the audience about the security and growth of our national sponsors. Five of the largest sponsors spoke about the future of BCI and how they planned to be a part of it. They looked to BCI for continued international expansion and how they felt confident that we could ride the wave of prosperity.

The morning session had gone better than expected. Lyle Turner was due to make a presentation after lunch. The coup would take place then. A bountiful spread was served to the entire assembly. An hour break was so designated. The moment of truth was near.

After lunch, Lyle walked to the mike and started his speech.

"While I have enjoyed hearing from the sponsors and feel confident that BCI's future is sound, there is a huge problem that must presently be addressed. I look to this assembly today to put the proper leadership in place. My confidence in our current CEO has been shattered and I need to hear from him now. James Bledsoe, can you please address the stockholders?"

James stood up to an exploding applause. He sauntered to the microphone and started. "I am somebody, I am somebody, I am the CEO of Bledsoe Communications. I was born a poor Black child in Harlem, I went to school at the illustrious Harvard University, and I am BCI. I have had successes matched by no other African American. I have been successful in bringing the Yakura family into our family. I have brought the company this far and I am looking forward to leading the company into the new millennium." Applause. He had the crowed eating out of his hand. "I will be making some personnel changes. It is unfortunate that Roosevelt Guidry was hired. Sandy Knight was responsible for his employment so unfortunately, I must let her go. I have also found a great deal of irregularities in her record keeping and suspect that there has also been some embezzlement. I will be appointing Ms. Deena James as her replacement." Deena walked out to the sound of *ohs* and *ahs*.

Suddenly, the lights went off and the projector came on. A montage of pictures flashed, showing James in various compromising positions. A bio of each of the girls was detailed for the crowd to see as well. Most of the girls were way under the appropriate age of consent and the crowd went wild. All of a sudden, LD and Six came out in full pimp regalia. They told the anxious crowd that they had been supplying James with underage prostitutes for twenty years. James and Deena were speechless. As the two businessmen walked away from the podium, Karen walked toward it. Deena got out of her chair as if to hit Karen, but James held her back. The group did not know what to expect, therefore a deadly silence overpowered the room.

"Good afternoon, I am a little nervous, so bear with me. If you look under your chairs, you will find a packet of information. After reviewing the documents, you will find that James has been using corporate funds to pay for his sexual indulgences. Over the last ten years he has had a variety of girlfriends on the payroll that did, in fact, not work. I was one of them. Ms. Deena James has been paid for the last two months, during which she has not reported to the office. She has further been promoted to a position of Vice President, when she does not even possess a GED. It would be in your best interest to vote James out as the CEO and select Ms. Sandy Knight as his successor. Sandy has single-handedly run BCI and she is the perfect choice." All in attendance looked under their chairs and began to review the packet. Audible moans and groans could be heard as the unthinkable came to pass.

Lyle quickly rushed to the podium to try to contain the pandemonium that had obviously erupted. "I think that we have seen and heard enough evidence. I move that we vote in Ms. Sandy Knight as our Chief Executive Officer. All in favor raise your hands." Almost immediately every hand in the room went up in unison. "All opposed." Silence. "It has been moved and properly seconded. By a unanimous vote, I would like to introduce you to our new CEO, Ms. Sandora Knight.

"It's time for some for new blood. Let's go into 2007 with a whole new face. Sandy, I congratulate you and wish you luck." The entire room rose to their feet to honor the first female African American CEO of a Fortune 500 company.

"Thank you, Lyle, and thank you, BCI shareholders, for your vote of confidence. I assure you that we will swiftly clean house and put in place the most qualified and competent staff available. I would like to introduce you to our new Chairman of the Board, Dr. Tanya Oluwande Bledsoe, Chief of Surgery at Howard University Hospital. Our new Chief Financial Officer will be Travis Tierney, III. Doug and Jeff Clay will stay in the respective capacities of Promotions Director and Chief Legal Counsel. Our Chief of Security will be Charles Parke. My Executive Assistant will be Ms. Karen Anderson. I will keep the lines of communication open with James during this time of transition. James, I thank you for your vision, you have accomplished a great deal during your career. But it's time for new blood, new ideas, a new attitude and a new commitment."

The crowd, including Mr. Yakura, rose to its feet. Bird was grinning in the back of the room. "You did it," he exclaimed and then wheeled his chair out of the room.

Mike came over to me and asked me if this meant that his career at BCI was over. I expressed that his treason had hurt me more deeply than he could fathom. I asked him how he could've betrayed me like he had. He told me that he loved me so bad that it hurt. He wanted to hurt me as much as I had hurt him. Mission accomplished.

James walked over to me. He started yelling at the top of his lungs. He said that he had given me my start and that I owed him. He also told me that I would never succeed and that he was BCI. The last thing he said was that all I was good for was sucking his dick, then he collapsed.

CHAPTER 44

New York, 2006

We sat in the waiting room of the Harlem Hospital awaiting a report from the doctor. Miraculously, James had had a massive heart attack yet survived. Presently, he was undergoing open-heart surgery and angioplasty to clear his arteries as well as three valves. Slight guilt had developed as I realized that the meeting had caused my father to almost lose his life. He had started feeling bad last night but did nothing about it.

The surgeon came out and told us the prognosis. She said that while James almost died, he was lucky. Most people that suffered that type of damage usually died, but James was a fighter, he wasn't going out like that. She stated that for some weird reason he had survived. The recuperation period would be a long one. He would need to change his diet and his lifestyle.

I asked if he could have visitors and she said maybe tomorrow. Tanya and I went back to the hotel. It had been a long day and all I wanted to do was chill out. Karen was there cleaning up and organizing the remainder of the documents. Her first day would be Monday and she was anxious to get started. Karen was surprised at the announcement of her new position at the meeting. She almost cried when I told her that she would be paid $75,000 a year.

There was a knock on the door and Karen got up to get it. Travis had bought two bottles of Piper champagne and champagne glasses. He expertly popped the corks and poured four glasses.

"Here's to America's first black female CEO. She is as sexy as she is intelligent. May her capable hands guide BCI into the year 2007. To Sandy, Salute." The four friends said salute in unison. It was truly a time for celebration. We had all worked hard and our hard work had finally paid off. Travis asked me if I would join him for dinner tonight. I asked him if I could have a rain check, because I had some business to handle. I did tell him I would call him when I got home tonight and perhaps he could come over. I knew that it was unprofessional to mix business with pleasure but my cobwebs were starting to show through my pants. I needed a little tune-up, some maintenance, if you know what I mean, and I knew Travis was the perfect man for the job.

I hugged everyone good night and told them that I would speak to them later. Tanya told me that she was going to the hospital. Although the lawyers had already drawn the divorce papers, she still wanted to be a part of his medical recovery. Tanya felt sorry that it had ended this way, with James in the hospital. She wasn't fully convinced that the whole embarrassment of the meeting hadn't caused the attack. James normally exercised, but his many years of overindulging in everything had taken a toll. Whatever it was that caused it, she had promised herself that she would not divorce him until he had fully recuperated. Her plans, however, were to buy a condo in Georgetown. I had almost forgotten.

"Tanya, on behalf of the Zelda Knight Foundation, I would like to present a check to STOP for one hundred-thousand dollars." I had finally received the paperwork designating the foundation as a 501(3c) non-profit corporation. This was the first official business of the non-profit foundation dedicated to assist all women in need. Tears of joy flowed and everyone was ecstatic; 2007 was going to be a great year!

I slipped *The Miseducation of Lauryn Hill* into the CD player. I was melancholy about the events that lay ahead. The feelings were bittersweet in that I had achieved all that I had set out to do. Yet my father lay in the hospital. My father. A combination of pure hatred and unconditional love circulated through my brain. How could I explain to Malcolm that his father was alive?

As I pulled up to the brownstone, Kenya was peering through the window.

Malcolm's house was located in the fashionable part of Brooklyn where a lot of young urban professional African Americans dwelled. The street was quiet. This evening, it was eerily quiet. Wouldn't she be surprised to learn that she had a grandfather? Before I could even get to the door, Kenya had opened it and ran out to the car.

"Hey, Auntie Sandy."

"Hey, yourself. You better get inside before you freeze to death. Is your father home?"

"Yes, he is in his office. Can we play Monopoly? You can be the car."

"Not right now, honey. I need to speak with your father."

"Okay. Daddy, Aunt Sandy is here."

Malcolm came out to meet me. We hugged and kissed and walked into his office. I began the horrible story and Malcolm listened intently. By the end of the story, Malcolm and I were both choked up. Kenya ran into the office and was puzzled by what she saw. She hopped in Malcolm's lap and called for her mother and her brother. She hugged Malcolm for dear life. She asked us what was wrong and Malcolm told her that he wanted to wait for the entire family to come into the office. When everyone was present, Malcolm and I told his family the sordid story together and by the end of it, we were all in tears. Finally, I pulled out the pink stationery that Mom had written her last words on and read it out loud. I pulled out a check of $200,000 and handed it to Kenya.

"This is what your grandmother left you and your brother for college. Make sure you don't spend it all in one place." The family was speechless. This was Zee's wish, this was why she'd died. I hoped that Zee was looking down from heaven; she would be so proud of Malcolm and his family. Abruptly, Malcolm asked me to join him in riding down to Harlem to see our father. We walked arm in arm out to the car and drove approximately forty minutes in silence.

At the hospital, I started shaking as we rode the elevator to the fifth floor. What would we say to the bastard that abandoned us and killed our mother? What could he possibly say to us? The noise of the life-saving machinery reverberated throughout the room. He slept peacefully as the machine incessantly monitored his heart rate. Hours passed and he continued to sleep. When he woke up, he looked puzzled as he saw Malcolm and me sitting in his room.

"What do you want? Haven't you done enough damage?"

"I'm sorry that you had the heart attack, but it wasn't my fault. You are here now, your heart gave out because you have lived an entire life of overindulgence and selfishness. If you want to live to see your sixtieth birthday, you are going to have to give your life a full overhaul. It's not about you and your needs anymore, James. Believe it or not, I realize now, that what happened today, probably saved your life and possibly your soul. God gave you a wake-up call; will you answer the phone?"

"Sandy, why should you care if I live or die? You are now the CEO. Shouldn't you be ordering new furniture or meeting with the new Board of Directors?"

"I'm doing exactly what I should be doing, spending time with my father."

"What are you talking about? Your father is dead." He sat up quickly and began clenching his fist.

"No he isn't. James, you are my father."

"I'm your what?" James' head fell back onto the pillow. He sighed heavily and shook his head.

"You are my father. Do you remember a certain little child prodigy named Zee that hailed from North Carolina? Do you also remember that she got strung out on drugs and the bastard that was responsible later had her killed—no, *assassinated* right before her children's eyes. James, I will never forget that night."

James' eyes began to well up.

"That's right, Dad. Those two innocent children that witnessed their mother's slow death on heroine and her brutal finish at the hands of two drug dealers were me and Malcolm. We lived a harsh, cruel life, experiencing unspeakable acts perpetrated against our mother and oftentimes me." Malcolm looked at me in shock.

"Malcolm, you were too young to really understand what was going on. I shielded you, protected you from everything. But while Mom was strung out and after she died, I had to do what I could to keep a roof over our heads and us fed and clothed. The irony was that meanwhile we had a father that was building a communications conglomerate at the same time that we were living hand to mouth."

James held his head down and began to sob heavily. He breathed in and out and cried uncontrollably. It was like he'd been holding in a lifetime of tears, a lifetime of pain. Deep down James did have a heart and did want to do good. He was God-fearing and often felt conflicted by his own decisions and actions. James, after all, did know the Lord and was raised by the Golden Rule: "Do Unto Others." Why did he choose such a life of murder and mayhem? Yes, he was successful. But at what cost?

James' cries subsided and he looked at me and Malcolm. "You know, Sandy, all these years I did think we had a special connection. I knew that your brilliance was not too far removed from my way of thinking. You always thought as I did and I knew that there was a reason for that. I am not surprised that you are my daughter and I must say that I am proud of you both. I do not deserve such accomplished children. Malcolm, I have seen you on television and have read about your legal career. Although at the time I was self-absorbed in my company fiasco, when I saw your daughter on TV after she escaped from that fiend's clutches, I felt a special admiration and connection to her as well. You should be proud of your little lady. I cannot wait to get to know my granddaughter, my grand-children, right, Malcolm?"

"Yes, I have a son and a daughter, Dad," Malcolm said uncomfortably.

"I have a lot of catching up to do, actually all around. I am sure that Tanya will divorce me, but I would like to make it all up to her if I ever could. She is a wonderful woman that I never deserved. Now that I will have a lot of free time," he smiled, "I would like to get involved in that STOP organization. Maybe I can help her raise money and awareness of the international atrocities that she speaks of. It seems that the day of reckoning is here. I must atone for my sins."

"It's funny how God creates situations to get our attention. I think nothing but good will come out of this whole mess. I have found a dad, something I have craved for my entire life. I must say that I have a lot of unresolved pain and anger toward you, but a part of me has this unconditional love for you as well."

"A good shrink can help us all get through this." Malcolm smiled. "All American families are dysfunctional. How do you think Oprah got so popular? I am shocked yet happy at these turns of events. No matter what your past is, which by the way is not that different from the Kennedys, you did manage to create quite an empire! I am proud of you and glad that you will start to change your life. You have many years left. Right now it is about your full recuperation. Dad, Sandy and I will be with you every step of the way. Right, Sandy?" Malcolm asked. I smiled. I ain't gonna lie, I still needed time to digest it all.

Malcolm and I decided to let Dad rest. Shit, I needed some rest too. It had been a long week. Really, it had been a long life. But now I felt that I had some closure, on my mom's death and really about my DESTINY. I knew that the *Lady in Black* had been created for a purpose. I had created an entire women's movement. I smiled to myself as I thought about all those young girls with their *Girls Kick Ass* T-shirts.

✗ ✗ ✗

Kenya looked in the mirror and smiled. She was enjoying all of the new found fame. Everywhere she went people would stop her; girls, boys, even grown women would ask her about how she got the courage to escape from such a dangerous situation. Sometimes she wondered herself, how she did it. At the time she just did what she had to do. It was all instinct. She thought about the *Lady in Black*. The whole country was talking about the *Lady in Black* and all of New York was talking about Kenya.

Slowly Kenya put on her black pants, her black turtleneck and placed on a pair of black Dior shades that she saw laying on her mom's dresser. She pulled her hair back into a ponytail and then just posed. "The *Lady in Black*," she said. "You better watch out!"

ABOUT THE AUTHOR

Janet Stevens Cook is a graduate of Howard University and is a member of Delta Sigma Theta Sorority, Inc. Enjoying an early career appearing in various magazines and several movies, this native New Yorker decided to eventually pursue her lifelong dream in the entertainment industry. In 2005, she founded Event Staff Inc. which creates, manages and staffs major events. Event Staff has been responsible for producing plays, developing marketing campaigns and is currently coordinating a national book tour. Janet resides in Mitchellville, MD and is married with two children. You may contact the author at January Entertainment Inc. at 202-437-7082, email at janetstevenscook@aol.com or visit www.myspace.com/blackskyy07

SNEAK PREVIEW!

EXCERPT FROM

EASTSIDE

A NOVEL

CALEB ALEXANDER

AVAILABLE FROM STREBOR BOOKS

CHAPTER ONE

Travon smacked his lips. "Man, you're stupid."

"Why?" Justin asked, shifting his gaze toward Travon. "Just because your brother got killed don't mean I will. Besides, it's for the hood."

Travon exhaled, and lowered his head. "I told my brother that he was stupid too, and now he's dead."

The boys continued around the side of the old red-brick school building toward the back. Staring at the ground, Justin haphazardly kicked at gravel spread along the ground beneath his feet.

"Yeah, Tre, but at least Too-Low went out like a soldier," he replied.

They were headed behind the middle school to a pair of old wooden green bleachers that sat across the well-worn football field. They could see the others standing just in front of the peeling bleachers waiting for them. Travon shifted his gaze from the waiting boys back to Justin. He started to speak, but Justin interrupted him.

"Tre, what's up with you?" Justin asked. "You ain't got no love for the hood? Your brother was down; he was a straight-up G. Don't you wanna be like that? Making everybody bar you and catch out when you step on the scene?"

Travon stared at Justin in silence. His silence seemed to only anger his friend more.

"I know that you're still trippin' over your brother getting killed, but he'd want you to ride for the hood!" Justin shouted. "He'd want you to be down!"

Travon halted in mid-step, and stared at Justin coldly. "How do you figure that?"

Like a precious family heirloom, Travon considered his brother, his brother's thoughts and wishes, as well as his memory, to be sacred. They were his and his alone.

Justin paused to formulate his reply, but one of the waiting boys shouted. "Y'all lil' niggaz hurry the fuck up! We ain't got all muthafuckin' day!"

Now filled with even more nervous anxiety, Travon and Justin quickly ended their conversation and hurriedly approached the waiting group. A tall, slender, shirtless boy stepped to the forefront. His torso was heavily illustrated with various tattoos and brandings, while his body was draped in gold jewelry, glimmering brilliantly in the bright South Texas sun.

"So, y'all lil' niggaz wanna get down, huh?" the shirtless boy asked.

Another boy anxiously stepped forward. "Say, Dejuan, let me put 'em on the hood!"

Dejuan, the first boy, folded his arms and nodded.

Travon walked his eyes across all of the boys present. There were six of them, all adorned with large expensive gold necklaces, watches, bracelets, and earrings, and all of them had gold caps covering their teeth. They were members of the notorious Wheatley Courts Gangsters, or WCGs for short. The WCGs were one of the most violent drug gangs in the State of Texas. Their ruthlessness and brutality was legendary.

Travon nervously examined the boys one by one. Those who were not shirtless were clad in burnt-orange University of Texas T-shirts. Burnt orange was the gang's colors, and the University of Texas symbol was their adopted motif. It stood for the location of their home, the Wheatley Courts. It was their municipality, their ruthless domain, their merciless world. It was a place where their will was law, and where all those who disobeyed were sentenced to death.

The Wheatley Courts was a low-income housing project where drugs and violence were the rule, and not the exception. It was also a place where many more than just a few of its occupants had made millions in their professions as street pharmacists. Perhaps worst of all, the Courts were home to the WCGs, a gang of ballers, and stone-cold murderers.

Travon shifted his gaze to his left; Justin had begun to remove his T-shirt. He looked back at the group of boys, to find that several of them were removing their shirts and jewelry as well. The festivities were about to begin.

"Let me whip these lil' niggaz onto the hood!" Tech Nine asked Dejuan again.

Without waiting for a response, Tech Nine walked away from the group and onto the football field, where he was quickly joined by Quentin, Lil C, and T-Stew. Once out on the field, the boys turned and waited for Justin.

Hesitantly, Justin made his way to where Tech Nine was waiting patiently and cracking his knuckles. Once Justin came within striking distance, Tech Nine swung wildly at him. The blow slammed into Justin's face.

"Muthafucka!" Justin shouted. He quickly charged Tech Nine and tackled him. Both boys hit the ground hard.

Lil C approached from the side and kicked Justin in his ribs. Justin cried out and rolled over onto his side. Justin tried to lift himself from off the ground, only to be met by a fist from Quentin. Justin grabbed his bloody nose.

"Wheatley Courts Gangstas, you punk-ass bitch!" Tech Nine shouted, as he charged Justin. "This is WCG, nigga!"

Lil C delivered a kick to Justin's back, just as Quentin swung at Justin again.

"Get that muthafucka!" Dejuan shouted from the sidelines.

Justin was able to roll away from Tech Nine's lunge, but had to take another blow from Quentin. He was able to make it to his feet just in time to receive another punch from Lil C. Although tired and out of breath, Justin was able to sustain the blow and remain standing.

"WCG for life!" Quentin shouted, advancing again.

Lil C swung at Justin again and missed. Justin, however, was unable to dodge a kick from Tech Nine. It landed directly in his groin.

Justin stumbled back, and Tech Nine kicked again, this time missing Justin and striking Lil C.

"My bad, man!" Tech Nine shouted. "I was trying to kick that little muthafucka!"

"Shit! Aw, fuck!" Lil C slowly descended to the ground while clutching his groin.

This brief intermission gave Justin time to recover and go on the offensive. He quickly dropped to one knee and punched Quentin in his groin, just as Quentin was about to swing at him.

"Aaaaaargh, shit! Punk muthafucka!" Quentin fell to the ground clutching his crotch.

Tech Nine maneuvered behind Justin, and threw a hard punch to the back of his head.

"Yeah, muthafucka, this is Wheatley Courts on mines!" Tech Nine shouted.

Justin rose, stumbled forward, and tripped over Quentin's leg. Tired, he hit the ground hard; this time, he could not find the energy to get back up. Tech Nine hurriedly approached and began kicking.

Justin, unable to move, curled into a ball and waited for the pain to be over.

"Punk muthafucka, fight back!" Tech Nine continued to kick brutally. He kicked Justin until he became tired, and retreated to where the others were standing.

Dejuan turned to Tech Nine. "Do you think that's enough?" he asked laughingly.

Tech Nine, sweating profusely, swallowed hard before answering. "I think he can get down. I think he's got enough nuts." He shifted his eyes to Travon. "You lucky I'm tired today, but tomorrow, I'm going to enjoy putting hands on you."

Travon's heart slowed to a semi-normal pace once he realized that they would not be jumping on him today. He quickly walked to where Justin was lying curled in a ball on the ground. Travon dropped down to his knees beside his friend.

"Justin, are you all right?" Travon asked.

No answer.

"Justin." Travon grabbed Justin's shoulder and shook it gently. "Justin."

"Yeah, I'm cool," Justin answered weakly.

"Leave him alone, he's all right!" shouted Lil C, who was slowly rising to his feet again.

Tech Nine shifted his eyes toward his friend. "Say, C, are you all right?"

"Yeah, muthafucka," Lil C answered. "Just watch where in the fuck you kicking next time."

Justin slowly uncurled, and pain shot through his body as he tried to brace himself to stand. Travon helped his friend off the ground.

"Yeah, you WCG now, baby!" T-Stew shouted.

Quentin, Tech Nine, T-Stew, and Dejuan quickly surrounded Justin.

"You WCG for life now, baby!" exclaimed Dejuan.

"Gimme some love, homie!" Tech Nine shouted.

"It's all about that WCG!" Justin declared weakly.

"Yeah!" T-Stew shouted. He extended his right arm into the air and made a *W* by crossing his two middle fingers. Doing the same with his left arm, he cupped his hand and formed the letter *C*.

"Wheatley Courts, baby!" Lil C shouted, as he and Justin embraced.

"Wheatley Courts!" T-Stew repeated, maneuvering into position for his embrace.

Dejuan swaggered away from the group, over to a pile of T-shirts lying on the ground. He lifted up a burnt-orange University of Texas T-shirt and examined it. On the front of the shirt rested a large white *T*. On the back of the shirt, printed in Old English script were the words *Wheatley Courts for Life*. Dejuan turned and walked back to where the boys were waiting, and Travon watched in fear, disbelief, and a slight bit of jealous envy as Justin was given Dejuan's very own Texas T-shirt to put on.

CHAPTER TWO

Weeks Later

Tonight, like every other night since his brother's death, Travon dreamt of him. Sweating profusely in the blistering South Texas heat, he tossed and turned as his last conversation with his brother was replayed inside his head.

"How do you like these Jordans, Tre?" Too-Low asked.

"They're pretty clean." Travon nodded. "Are you gonna let me sport 'em?"

Too-Low smiled at his younger brother. "I gotta stay on the cuts all night, 'cause tomorrow's the first. If I make enough ends, I'll take you to the mall and get you some."

"Cool!"

"So, how are your grades in school?" Too-Low asked.

"They're all right."

"All right? They need to be better than just all right." Too-Low leaned forward and jabbed his finger into Travon's chest. "You better not be fuckin' up in school!"

"I'm not." Travon frowned. "My grades are okay."

"I'll tell you what," Too-Low told him. "I'll spring for some fresh gear for school this fall, if you do well the rest of this year."

"Put me down, and I can buy my own shit," Travon replied.

Too-Low slapped Travon across the back of his head.

"Fuck!" Travon shot a venomous glance toward his bother. "What the hell was that for?"

Too-Low jabbed his finger into his younger brother's face. "Tre, if I catch you anywhere near this shit, I'ma put a foot in your ass! Do you hear me?"

"You're doing it, so why can't I?" Travon replied. "You won't even let me get down with the hood! That shit ain't fair, Too-Low!"

Too-Low kicked a crushed beer can that was lying on the ground near his foot, sending it tumbling noisily across the roughly paved street.

"Fuck this shit, Tre!" Too-Low shouted, once he had turned back toward his brother. "I'm doing this shit so you don't have to! And I already made it clear to everybody that I'll kill anybody who puts you on the hood, and everybody who was there watching!"

"Everybody else is down!" Travon protested.

"Tre, you better not ever join a gang, or pick up any kind of dope. Do you hear me?"

Travon shifted his eyes away from his brother, to a distant spot down the dark and empty street.

Too-Low grabbed Tre by his arm and shook him violently. "I said do you hear me?"

"Yeah, yeah, I hear you!" Travon yanked his arm away from his brother and again stared down the dark, trash-strewn street. All of his friends were joining, and it wasn't fair that he wasn't allowed to. All the girls in school were falling all over the guys who had joined. He would almost kill to be able to wear burnt orange to school.

"This shit is dangerous," Too-Low added. "The first chance I get, I'm getting us the hell outta these fuckin' courts!" When he saw the moisture welling in his younger brother's eyes, Too-Low decided that he had been a little too harsh. He decided to make up for it.

"Here." He reached beneath his burnt-orange University of Texas T-shirt and pulled out his nine-millimeter Beretta handgun. He handed the cold, steel, death black weapon to Travon. "Take this home and put it under my mattress. Go straight home with it, Tre. And don't be fuckin' 'round with it either."

Travon lifted the weapon into the air and examined it. After a few seconds, he turned back toward his brother. "You ain't gonna need this tonight?"

Too-Low shook his head. "No. Lil Anthony, Pop, and Tech Nine are on their way. We all gonna stay down tonight. I know that them fools is strapped, so I don't need to be. 'Sides, if one time runs up on us tonight, I ain't trying to catch a pistol case."

Travon slid the gun into his pants and pulled his shirt down over it. Too-Low reached into his pants pocket and pulled out a wad of rolled-up bills. He counted out fifteen hundred dollars and handed it to Travon.

"Tonight, when Momma goes to sleep, put four hundred dollars in her purse. Don't let her catch you. If she asks you in the morning where it came from, just tell her that you don't know. You can keep a hundred for yourself, so that leaves a thousand. Put the G under my mattress, along with the strap."

"All right, Too-Low, thanks!" Travon extended his fist and gave his brother some dap. "Good looking."

Too-Low roughly rubbed his hand over his brother's head, messing up his waves. Travon smiled, ducked away, and turned and headed for home. Of course on the way to his apartment, he would have to stop by Justin's and show off his brother's gun.

Once out of his brother's sight, Travon turned and made a beeline for Justin's apartment. He cut across the alley, then through the playground, taking the shortcut to his friend's apartment. He could faintly make out the sound of deep bass notes resonating from a stereo system. The notes grew progressively louder until finally a dark blue Hyundai came into view and passed by on the street just in front of him, silencing its stereo system. Travon watched from the shadows as the car slowed and turned the corner. Moments later he heard the sound of semi-automatic weapon fire crashing through the midnight silence, and quickly decided that he had better head for home.

Once safely inside his apartment, Travon did as his brother had instructed, and then retired to his bedroom. After awhile, he heard a knock at the front door, which was followed by his mother's screams.

Travon bolted up from his bed. His bare chest heaved up and down, his breathing was hard and labored. Travon wiped away the heavy beads of perspiration from his face, and then tried to focus his eyes. A slow glance around his balmy dark room quickly confirmed what he had suspected. He had, once again, suffered a nightmare.

Seven a.m.

"Tre! Tre!" his mother called out to him. "Travon! It's time to get up and get ready for school, boy!"

"Shit!" Travon swore under his breath and rubbed his eyes as he slowly pulled himself out of bed, then staggered to his bathroom. After washing his face, brushing his teeth, and taking a piss, he headed back into his bedroom. He had just begun to put his clothes on when his mother appeared at his door.

"Travon, I got breakfast waiting downstairs."

"Momma, what are you doing at home this morning?" Travon asked, rubbing the top of his head.

"I had to change jobs, baby. The company I was working for only want to do home health care now, so they need people with cars. I have to work in a nursing home for right now, at least until I can get us a car. And the only positions the nursing home had open were night ones, so I work at night now," she explained.

Travon stretched his arms and yawned. "Oh, I was just wondering what you were still doing home at this time, that's all."

His mother smiled. "You're not afraid to stay at home by yourself at night, are you?"

Travon frowned. "Naw, I ain't scared a nothing."

Elmira rolled her eyes toward the ceiling and crossed her arms. "All right, bad ass. You just better have your butt in the house by ten o'clock."

Travon dropped his shirt. "What?"

She uncrossed her arms. "You heard me."

"I can't even sit on the porch?" he asked.

Elmira stepped into the bedroom and caressed her son's chin. "Tre, you know what happened to your brother. So just bear with me for a little while, okay?"

Travon shifted his gaze to the floor and nodded. He could never forget what happened to his brother. He could never forget the night that his life changed forever.

"Okay," he said softly.

Elmira turned and started for the door. "Now come on downstairs and eat you some breakfast." Quickly, she whirled back toward her son. "Speaking of food, I haven't seen Justin in a few weeks. Where is he?"

"Well, he um, he got himself some new friends."

Elmira tilted her head to the side. "Tre, look at me, and don't lie to me. You and Justin were as thick as thieves, and now he don't even come around anymore?" She placed her hand upon her hip. "What happened?"

"Uh, nothing, Momma. We just don't kick it that much anymore."

"I was born at night, but not last night," Elmira replied. "Justin done joined that damn gang, ain't he?"

Travon's gaze fell away from his mother. "Well, I guess. I don't know, Momma."

"Tre, baby, just stay away from them and find you some new friends. Baby, just as soon as things get better, we'll get the hell outta this place. It's just gonna take some time."

Elmira lifted her hand and pointed out the window. "I don't want those people's welfare or food stamps. I have to do it without those things, so it will take us just a little bit longer to save. But we will get outta here, baby. One day, we will get the hell outta this place!"

With his gaze still focused on the floor, Travon nodded. "Yes, ma'am."